IMPOSSIBLE STORIES I

Zoran Živković

Impossible Stories I
Copyright © 2006 by Zoran Živković

Time Gifts Copyright © 1997 by Zoran Živković
Impossible Encounters Copyright © 2000 by Zoran Živković
Seven Touches of Music Copyright © 2001 by Zoran Živković
The Library Copyright © 2002 by Zoran Živković
Steps Through the Mist Copyright © 2003 by Zoran Živković

FG-RS0012L3
ISBN: 978-4-908793-06-6

Cover: Youchan Ito, Togoru Co., Ltd.

Neoclassic Fleurons font used with permission of
Paulo W–Intellecta Design

Cadmus Press
cadmusmedia.org

IMPOSSIBLE STORIES I

Zoran Živković

Translated from the Serbian
by

Alice Copple-Tošić

Cadmus Press
2016

Contents

Time Gifts	1
Impossible Encounters	87
Seven Touches of Music	159
The Library	259
Steps through the Mist	339
Contributors	419
About the author	420
About the artist	422

Time Gifts

Contents

1. The Astronomer
2. The Paleolinguist
3. The Watchmaker
4. The Artist

1. The Astronomer

He had to escape from the monastery.

He should not have been there at all; he had never wanted to become a monk. He'd said so to his father, but his father had been unrelenting, as usual, and his mother did not have the audacity to oppose him, even though she knew that her son's inclinations and talents lay elsewhere. The monks had treated him badly from the beginning. They had abused and humiliated him, forced him to do the dirtiest jobs, and when their nocturnal visits commenced he could stand it no longer.

He set off in flight, and a whole throng of pudgy, unruly brothers started after him, screaming hideously, torches and mantles raised, certain he could not get away. His legs became heavier and heavier as he attempted to reach the monastery gate, but it seemed to be deliberately withdrawing, becoming more distant at every step.

And then, when they had just about reached him, the monks suddenly stopped in their tracks. Their obscene shouts all at once turned into frightened screams of distress. They began to cross themselves feverishly, pointing to something in front of him, but all he could see there was the wide open gate and the clear night sky stretching beyond it. The gate no longer retreated before him, and once again he felt light and fast.

He was filled with tremendous relief when he reached the arched vault of the great gate. He knew they could no longer reach him, that he had gotten away. He stepped outside to meet the stars, but his foot did not alight on solid ground as it should have done. It landed on something soft and spongy, and he started to sink as though he'd stepped in quicksand. He flailed his arms but could find no support.

He realized what he had fallen into by the terrible stench. It was the deep pit at the bottom of the monastery walls; the cooks threw the unusable entrails of slaughtered animals into it every day through a small, decayed wooden door. The cruel priests often threatened the terrified boy that he, too, would end up there if he did not satisfy their aberrant desires. The pit certainly should not have been located at the entrance to the holy edifice, but this utmost sacrilege for some reason seemed neither strange nor unfitting.

He began to sink rapidly into the thick tangle of bloated intestines, and when they almost reached his shoulders he became terror-stricken. Just a few more moments and he would founder completely in this slimy morass. Unable to do anything else, he raised his desperate eyes, and there, illuminated by the reflection of the distant torches, he saw the silhouette of a naked, bony creature squatting on the edge of the pit, looking at him maliciously and snickering.

He did not discern the horns and tail, but even without these features he had no trouble understanding who it was; now that it was too late, he realized whom the terrified monks had seen. He froze instinctively at this pernicious stare, wishing suddenly to disappear as soon as possible under the slimy surface and hide there. All at once the blood and stench no longer made him nauseous; now they seemed precious, like the last refuge before the most terrible of all fates.

And truly, when he had plunged completely into that watery substance, it turned out that it was not, after all, the discarded entrails of pigs, sheep, and goats, as it had seemed to be, but was a mother's womb, comfortable and warm. He curled up in it, knees under his chin, as endless bliss filled his being. No one could touch him here; he was safe, protected.

The illusion of paradise was not allowed to last very long, however. Demonic eyes, like a sharp awl, quickly pierced through the layers of extraneous flesh and reached his tiny crouched being. He tried to withdraw before them, to retreat deeper into the womb, to the very bottom, but his persecutor did not give up. The thin membrane that surrounded his refuge burst the moment he leaned his back against it, having nowhere else to go, and he fell out—into reality.

And with him, out of his dream, came the eyes that persisted in their piercing stare.

He could not see them in the almost total darkness, but their immaterial touch was nearly palpable. Suddenly awake, he realized that someone else was with him in the cell. He had not heard him come in, even though the door squeaked terribly, since probably no one had thought to oil it in years. How strange for him to fall into such a deep sleep; the night before their execution, only the toughest criminals managed to do that. They were not burdened by their conscience or the thought of impending death, and he certainly was not one of them.

He raised his head a bit and looked around, confused. Although he felt he was not alone, his heart started racing when he really did see the shape of a large man sitting on the bare boards of the empty bed across from him. If not for the light from the weakly burning torch in the hall that slanted into the cell through a narrow slit in the iron-plated door, he would not have been able to see him at all. As it was, all he could make out clearly were the pale hands folded in his lap, while his head was completely in shadow, as though missing.

He asked himself in wonder who it could be. A

priest, most likely. They were the only ones allowed to visit prisoners before they were taken to be executed. Had the hour struck already? He quickly looked up at the high window with its rusty bars, but there was no sign of daybreak. The night was pitch black, moonless, so that the opening appeared only as a slightly paler rectangle of darkness against the interior of the cell.

He knew they would not take him to the stake before dawn, so he stared at the immobile figure uncertainly. Why had he come already? Would they be burning him earlier, perhaps, before the rabble gathered? But that made no sense. It was for this senseless multitude that they organized the public execution of heretics, to show in the most impressive manner what awaited those who dared come into conflict with the catechism. The sight of the condemned, his body tied or nailed to the stake, writhing in terrible agony while around him darted fiery tongues of flame, had a truly discouraging effect on even the boldest and most rebellious souls.

Or maybe this was a final effort to get him to renounce his discovery. That would be the best outcome for the Church, of course, but he did not have the slightest intention of helping it; on the contrary, had he come this far just to give up now? If that was what was going on, their efforts were in vain.

"You had a bad dream," said the unseen head.

The voice was unfamiliar. It was not someone he had already met during the investigation and trial. It sounded gentle, but this might easily be a trick. He was well acquainted with the hypocrisy of priests. His worst problems had been with those who seemed understanding and helpful and then suddenly showed their pitiless faces.

"Why do you think that?" asked the prisoner, stretching numbly on the dirty, worn blanket that was his only bedding.

"I watched you twitch restlessly in your sleep."

"You watched me in the total darkness?"

"Eyes get accustomed to the dark if they are in it long enough, and can see quite well there."

"There are eyes and eyes. Some get accustomed to it, others don't. I ended up here because I refused to get accustomed to the dark."

The fingers in the lap slowly interlaced, and the prisoner suddenly realized that they looked ghostly pale because he was wearing white gloves. They were part of the church dignitaries' vestments, which meant that the man in the cell with him was not an ordinary priest who had been sent to escort him to the stake. So, it was not time yet.

"Do you think that you will dispel the darkness with the brilliance of your fiery stake?" The tone was not cynical; it sounded more compassionate.

"I don't know. I couldn't think of any other way."

"It is also the most painful way. You have had the opportunity to witness death by burning at the stake, isn't that right?"

"Yes, of course. While I was at the monastery they took us several times to watch the execution of poor women accused of being witches. It is a compulsory part of the training of young monks, as you know. There is nothing like fear to inspire blind loyalty to the faith."

"Yes, fear is a powerful tool in the work of the Church. But you, it seems, have remained unaffected by its influence?"

The prisoner rubbed his stiff neck. He could still somehow put up with the swill they fed him, the stale air and the humidity that surrounded him, and the constant squealing and scratching of hungry rodents that he'd been told were liable to bite the ears and noses of heedless prisoners. But nothing had been so hard in this moldy prison as the fact that he did not have a pillow.

"What do you expect me to answer? That I'm not afraid of being burned? That I'm indifferent to the pain I'll soon be feeling at the stake? Only an imbecile would not be afraid."

"But you are not an imbecile. So why didn't you prevent such an end?"

"I had no choice."

"Of course you did. The only thing you were asked was publicly to renounce your conviction and to repent, which is the most reasonable request of the Court of the Inquisition when serious heretical sins are involved. If you had done that, you would have kept your title of royal astronomer and been allowed to continue teaching students."

"Who would attend the lectures of a royal astronomer who had renounced his discovery out of fear?"

"There is a question that comes before that. Why did you have to announce it in the first place? What did you want to achieve by that?"

"What should I have done—kept it a secret, all for myself?"

"You were aware that it goes counter to the teachings of the Church. You should have expected her to take measures to protect herself."

"Of course I expected that. But I was relying on her hands being rather tied."

"It doesn't look that way, judging by the sentence you were given."

"Oh, you know perfectly well that the stake is not what the Church wanted. It was a forced move after all attempts to talk me into cooperating failed."

"Based on your condition, I would not say that they tried all possible means. You do not look like someone who has been given the Inquisition's full treatment."

"Well, I'm not a witch. They didn't have to force me to agree to some meaningless accusation. I did not deny my guilt. That is why the whole investigation proceeded like some kind of friendly persuasion, even though, probably just to impress me, in the background stood the power of all the devices to mutilate, quarter, cut, break, and crush. But I was not even threatened with one of them, let alone put to any device. You do not torture someone who is valuable to you only as an ally. What good would it be if the royal astronomer were lame or blind?"

"Not even after the alliance has been irrevocably called off? The Inquisition can hardly boast of the virtues of forgiveness and compassion."

"That is why it is renowned for its patience and acumen. The sentence was passed, but I have not been burned yet. There is still time. Attempts to win me over to the Church's side will continue to the very end. In any case, that is why you are here, isn't it?"

There was an indistinct commotion from the end of the hall, followed by the sharp sound of a key unlocking a door and someone groaning painfully as he was thrown into a cell like a bag of potatoes. The Inquisition's investigators did their work primarily at night. The main interrogation room was in the basement; in spite of the thick walls, horrible screams could be heard periodically, weakening the last remains of will and resistance in the other prisoners awaiting their turn to be taken down there. As they moved off after closing the door with a bang, one of the guards muttered something to the other, making him laugh raucously. For a long time his burst of laughter echoed like thunder through the stone hallway.

"But you, of course, will not relent?" asked the voice from the darkness after the echo finally died out.

"Of course."

"What is the real reason for that?"

"What do you mean?"

"You certainly are not a simpleminded idealist who has gotten involved in all this because you don't understand how the world works, what forces set it in motion. On the contrary, everything you have done from the beginning seems to have been carefully planned. You have lit a fire that only you can put out. It takes great resourcefulness to turn the tables on such an experienced service as the Inquisition, to tie its hands, as you say. And it takes the courage of a fanatic that is always lacking in idealists at the crucial moment, the readiness to go all the way, no matter what the cost. You, naturally, shy away from the pain that awaits you at the stake, but you will go to your execution nonetheless just because that will harm the Church the most. What is it that she has done to you?"

The prisoner started to rise into a sitting position on the hard bed, feeling a stab of pain run all the way down his stiff back. As he did so, a scene from his dream suddenly rose to the surface of his memory. It was very vivid, although fixed, like some sort of ugly picture: the twisted faces of the monks lustfully reaching for his tiny, helpless body.

"Isn't it still early for my last confession?"

"I'm not here to listen to your confession."

"Oh, yes, I almost forgot. You are here to prevail upon me to change my mind. But if you truly believe what you just said, it must be clear to you that it's impossible."

"It is clear to me."

"Then why are you wasting your time?"

There was no immediate reply from the other side of the cell. A hand rose and reached for something that was lying unseen on the wooden bench. A moment later it returned to the flickering shaft of light from the torch in the hall. It was now holding a slender black cane with a carved white figure on the top.

"I have more than enough time." The voice seemed to become muffled, more distant.

"But I don't. My hours are numbered."

"That's right. Soon they will come to take you to the stake, but before that you will be given one last chance to accept the Church's offer. But, as we know, you will refuse. Although it makes no difference, really."

"It does make a difference. If I accept, everything I did will have been in vain."

"No, it won't. The damage was done the moment you announced your discovery, and it cannot be undone. The fluttering of the butterfly's wings should have been prevented before it initiated the storm. Even if the Church made a sincere ally out of you, it would only slow down the harmful repercussions."

"Do you really think that this is sufficient to make me change my mind? I expected you to come up with something more convincing."

"I have no intention of dissuading you. But that is the way things stand nonetheless. Heresy has been sown on fertile ground. Neither the stake nor repentance will turn your students away. They will start to spread forbidden knowledge, to add to it. Once set in motion, this course cannot be stopped, even though the Inquisition will take every measure to obstruct it. You have let the genie out of the bottle, and he can no longer return to it. The Church will finally realize this inexorability, but it will be too late then."

The prisoner strained to make out the hidden face in the impenetrable obscurity, but without success, even though his pupils were completely dilated.

"Isn't it unbecoming for a man of God to have so little faith in the future of the Church?"

"Why do you think I am a man of God?"

A shroud of silence suddenly descended on the cell. Several long moments passed before the prisoner realized what was wrong. He had spent many nights alone in this place, and he could always hear some sort of noise: moaning from one of the neighboring cells, the screech of rusty hinges, the murmur of the guards, muffled cries from the basement, the rustling of mice and rats, the creaking boards on which he lay, distant sounds of the outside world. Now all of that had mysteriously disappeared.

"Who are you?" he said, finally mustering the courage to break this tomblike silence. The darkness did not answer; suddenly, once again the prisoner felt the stab of the piercing eyes that had followed him out of his dream. "The Tempter?" The word was almost inaudible, so that he didn't know whether he said it or only thought it.

"Why should that bother you?" The voice remained just as gentle. "If I am the Tempter, then we are on the same side. We have the same opponent."

"Why . . . why are you here? What do you want from me?" He had a strong urge to cross himself but at the last moment thought it somehow inappropriate.

"I don't want anything from you. On the contrary, I have a gift for you. Sort of a token of our alliance. A trip."

"A trip?"

"Don't worry, you won't leave this cell, and you will get back on time, before they come for you."

"What kind of a trip will it be if I stay here?"

"The only one possible under the circumstances: through time."

The prisoner blinked. This was not really happening. He was still asleep. However, there was none of the awakening that necessarily followed such a realization. He brought his hand to his face and pinched his cheek hard. The pain was real. Only too real.

"I don't want . . . to go . . . anywhere."

"But you'll like it there. I'm quite sure. The future has pleasant surprises for you."

"The future?"

"Yes. Almost three hundred years from now."

"Why would I want to go . . . to the future?"

"Out of curiosity, above all. Aren't you interested in checking whether you really succeeded in outwitting the Church? Even though you certainly appear self-confident, there must still be a shadow of doubt in there. What if your sacrifice is in vain?"

"But you said it isn't. That my students . . ."

"A moment ago that did not sound convincing to you. In any case, can you believe in the word of the Tempter, even when you're on the same side as he is?"

"What would the future corroborate? What would I see there?" As he asked these questions, he felt completely foolish. He had let himself be drawn too easily into a crazy, impossible conversation. Where was the common sense he took such pride in? Had he gone out of his mind? He had heard that this sometimes happened to people waiting to be burned at the stake. Fear twisted their minds.

"A better question would be what you won't see. First of all, you won't see a monastery on the top of this hill. Its walls will still be there, but it will no longer contain dark, humid cells, corridors all sooty from torches, or a torture chamber in the basement."

"The monastery will fall into ruin?"

"No, it will be remodeled."

"What can you remodel a monastery into?"

The answer was preceded by a brief silence that seemed to indicate a certain hesitation, indecision. "I suppose that in the end you would recognize it without my help, although it will certainly look . . . strange. But I would do well to prepare you. You will not have much time, and the future can have a stunning effect. At the time of your visit, instead of a monastery this will be an astronomical observatory."

He knew that he should say something in return, that it was expected of him, but he could not utter a word. His vocal cords were vibrating, forming confused questions, but his throat had closed completely and no sound came out. He stared blankly ahead, his mouth a void.

In the infinite silence that reigned once more, a white-gloved hand set the cane between the knees, then disappeared in the folds of the black robe. The hand took a moment to find something there, then emerged with a round, flat object on its open palm. Golden reflections shone from its engraved curves. The dark figure's thumb moved along the edge of the object and the lid popped open.

The hand extended toward the prisoner, but he remained stock-still. It was not indecision; the spasm that had closed his throat had now spread to his entire body. He wanted to move, do something, anything, he couldn't stay there motionless forever, but his muscles refused completely to obey.

"Yes, before you leave, there is one more thing you should know. It will please you, I believe. The observatory will be named after you."

The movement with which he accepted the watch had nothing to do with his will. It seemed to him that someone else received the Tempter's gift, that he was just an observer who should in fact warn the incautious sinner not to do it, that it was insane. He wouldn't have listened, anyway, his soul was already lost, so it made no difference; actually, nothing could help him anymore.

The watch face radiated a bright whiteness. In the dark cell it was a lighthouse summoning sailors, the flame of a candle attracting buzzing insects, a star luring the glass eye of the telescope. And over it were two ornate hands at a right angle, forming a large letter L.

II

Staring at the shiny surface, he failed to notice the changes that had started to take place. Something sparkled in the cell, apparitions passed through it more transparent than ghosts, and the specter on the other bed instantly dissolved into nothingness.

His attention was attracted only by sudden daylight in the high barred window.

Isn't it still early? he asked himself, raising his eyes in bewilderment.

But the time of miracles had just begun. His eyelids barely had time to blink before it was dark in the window again. The astronomer in him opened his mouth to contend the obvious, but he was silenced by the stronger voice of the child who cares not at all whether something is possible or not, as long as it is fascinating.

Many short interchanges of light and darkness took place before the child had had enough of this monotonous kaleidoscope, finally letting the scientist think about solving the mystery. There was only one explanation, of course. To accept it, however, one had to accept the impossible almost as an act of faith.

Before him the days and nights were passing at accelerated speed, but he could not ask the questions dictated by his reason. He had lost that right the moment he took the watch. In any event, was the "how" important? If this was the way to travel to the future, so be it.

Finally the hypnotic flashes of blue-gray and black images in the stone window tired even the astronomer. He turned around—and at first it seemed that the dizzy rush through time had stopped. Nothing was moving, everything looked fixed, unchanging. And then he realized that it was only an illusion. There could be no rapid changes here: the monastery walls were built to withstand the centuries.

Nonetheless, there were a few things in the cell

made of less durable material. He stood transfixed as he watched the boards on the bed across from him gradually swell up from the perpetual humidity and then split and fall to the ground, where they slowly turned into a shapeless mass on the flagstones.

He jumped up from his bed when it struck him that the same fate had to affect the boards on which he was sitting. Sure enough, they also ended up as a pile of sawdust. He, however, had not felt a thing: if this possibility had not crossed his mind, he would have continued to sit calmly on nothing, in midair.

The wooden door was considerably thicker, but in the end it, too, succumbed to the effects of decay. First the steel bars fell off, then the hinges gave way, cracks appeared, then gaps and holes, until finally there was nothing to stop him from going into the corridor. The cell ceased to be a prison. But on the other side of the threshold, freedom was an impenetrable darkness, since no one lit torches to dispel it anymore.

Thoughts of freedom reminded him of the many prisoners who must have sojourned here in misery after him. During this rapid movement through time he could not see them, of course, although here and there he had the deceptive feeling that there was someone else with him. During the instants of darkness that were nights, a shape seemed to bulge on the bed across from him, but this illusion was too brief to make anything of it. In the flashes of lightning that were days, something would flicker in front of him periodically, a certain hint of movement, but it was as cryptic as a flash seen out of the corner of the eye.

The ceiling disappeared so suddenly that he did not have time to catch his breath. It was there one moment and then suddenly gone without a trace, as though a giant had taken a huge lid off the monastery. At the same time, all the partition walls were removed, leaving only the solid outer walls that no longer had any windows.

The rapidly changing days and nights were incomparably more exciting with the entire firmament spread over his head than before, when he had only had a tiny corner of sky. The entire universe seemed to be hurriedly whispering some secret message to him. . . .

But he was not given the time to figure it out. Just as mysteriously as the lid was lost, it returned a few moments later, although not the old one. He found himself inside an enormous closed space over which there rose a gigantic dome. Only cathedrals boast such roofs, he thought, but this was certainly not a cathedral; their domes did not have a wide slit cut through the center, let alone a large cylinder pointing upward through that opening.

He did not realize that the voyage was over because there was no slowing down; it happened all at once. He was looking at the empty opening in the vault over his head, but many heartbeats had to pass before he finally noticed that the alternating light and darkness had stopped. The night sky that settled in his eyes was sprinkled with the clusters of stars found in the thin air of mountain peaks.

A click in his hand jolted him out of the paralysis that had overcome him. The watch had completely slipped his mind, although it had been in his outstretched palm the entire time. Now it had closed, since its magic work was finished. He originally thought to put it in his pocket but then decided he should keep it in his hand; his first idea would have shown inadmissible disrespect.

He slowly and timidly began to turn around in the semidarkness of the large area. As wondrous things whose purpose he could not divine entered his field of vision, he remembered the Tempter's words; he had said that in the end he would see for himself that it was an astronomical observatory. The Tempter must have greatly overestimated him. There was nothing here he could recognize: no telescope, sextant, map of the stars, or brass model of the planetary system.

Instead, the circular wall was covered for the most part with unusual windows. They shone in a variety of colors, but it could not have been the light from outside because it was night. Some forms were moving on them, and he cautiously went up to one part of the wall to get a better look. They turned out to be yellow numbers that proceeded as far as the eye could see in horizontal rows against blue or red backgrounds, appearing at one end and disappearing at the other, although the device that was writing them was nowhere to be seen.

He would have stood there a long time staring at this sparkling display, whose meaning he had not even tried to penetrate, had it not been for the sound of quiet voices he suddenly heard behind him. He started in complete surprise. During his first moment of confusion, all he felt was the instinctive need to hide somewhere, but there was no time for that. When he turned around, just a few steps from him were two tall figures—a man and a woman—dressed in long white robes, heading his way, talking in hushed tones.

They had to see him; it was unavoidable since he was standing right there in front of them, paralyzed and bewildered. But they went straight past him, paying no attention to his conspicuous presence, as though he were completely invisible. He stood there for a long time, immobile, trying to get used to this impossibility, as his temples pounded fiercely.

The figures in white went up to one of the windows that was considerably larger than the others and was unlighted and started to touch some of the bumps that protruded under it. The window suddenly lit up, but it did not have the stream of numbers as on the others. It showed something that the prisoner could finally make sense of. The star field seemed far denser, brighter, and sharper, but basically did not differ from what he had seen through his small telescope.

But how could the picture in the window and the telescope be the same? What kind of window was that? The answer soon followed, but his readiness to believe took considerably more time. The two people continued to touch the bumps, and the scene slowly started to change. The change itself was clear to him, but he could not figure out how it was done. He would have achieved the same effect if he were slowly to raise his telescope: some stars would disappear under the lower edge, while others would appear above. But here the window did not move at all.

Then he heard something buzzing behind him. It was quite feeble, like the sound of a distant bee. He probably would not have turned around if he hadn't been compelled by the pins and needles at the back of his head—the tension of premonition. Something was going on behind his back, something big was moving.

The heavy, upright cylinder in the lower part of the slit in the dome slowly rose toward the highest point, although he could not see how it moved. It seemed to be doing so by itself, without the help of ropes and a winch.

He caught on to what was happening before the cylinder stopped at an angle of about seventy degrees. So, the Tempter had not overestimated him too much. In any case, it was only a matter of proportions here. Even though it was gigantic, the telescope had kept its original shape. What he could not understand was that the eyepiece had been moved. Instead of being in the only place it could be, at the bottom of the cylinder, it was on the wall like a big window that everyone could look at.

The picture on it stabilized just for a moment, and then a new change started. The stars began to flow over all the edges as though the telescope were rushing through the air at an unbelievable speed, although it was resting immobile. It penetrated more and more into the dark expanse, reaching for unattainable infinity.

The impression was intoxicating, delightful. And then, as if this were not enough, music echoed. The woman in white went for a moment to a smaller window and touched something. At the same moment, the crystal sounds of heavenly harmony reverberated from all sides. He could not see any musicians or instruments, he could not understand a thing, but he did not care. He was experiencing what one undergoes perhaps once in a lifetime: exaltation.

The two climaxes merged into one. One point in the middle of the picture started to get bigger, to expand. At first it was a star like the countless ones around it, then it was a circle, then a ring, and then finally it burst into a lacy flower that filled the entire window. The moment it opened its rosy, vaporous petals, the music streamed upward, greeting with an upsurge of joy the appearance of the yellow nucleus—the hidden eye of the Creator himself.

He was not filled with frustration when everything around him suddenly froze and became silent. He knew this would happen, that the watch cover had to open once again. The moment of the about-face was perfect. The epiphany had just taken place. Dared he hope for anything greater?

Return trips always seem shorter than departures. There were no more surprises and wonders to slow down time. Even though he felt awe as he watched the reverse sequence of what he had seen before—the disappearance of the dome, the return of the barred windows, the formation of doors and beds, the flickering of days and nights—his thoughts were elsewhere.

His confused thoughts that gradually formed a crucial question.

The end of the voyage came abruptly once again, just

as when he had arrived in the future. At first, while his eyes were still blinded by the flashes, he could not make out anyone on the other side of the cell. Icy fingers of horror tightened around his chest. What if he wasn't there anymore? If he had only been playing with him? That would be just like the Tempter. Then he never would know. . . .

"So?" came a gentle voice from the darkness.

He tried to muffle his sigh of relief, but such effort was futile in the murky silence of the night. "You said the observatory would be named after me, didn't you?" There was no time to beat around the bush; he had to get straight to the point.

"Yes."

"Why?"

"What do you mean?"

"Because of the discovery I made or because I was burned at the stake for not renouncing it?"

"For both one and the other, although considerably more for the act of sacrifice. You know, in the age you just visited, your discovery has only historical value. It has not been refuted, but it is secondary, insignificant, almost forgotten. As you have seen, things have advanced much farther. But your burning will not be forgotten."

From somewhere in the heart of the monastery came the sound of heavy footsteps. It was not just two guards. A larger group was walking through the corridors.

"Does that mean I have no choice?" asked the prisoner quickly. "If the observatory is named after me because I was burned at the stake, then it necessarily follows that there is no way I can avoid that fate. But I can still do it. I still have free will. They're coming. What if I say yes when they ask me to renounce my discovery? That would spare me from the stake but would change the future, wouldn't it? And the future cannot be changed; I saw it with my own eyes."

The steps ceased for a moment, and then in the distance echoed the harsh sound of a barred partition door being opened.

"That's right. You can't change what you saw. And you saw only that which is irrefutable, that which you cannot influence in any way. What you did not see, however, is whether the observatory is named after you."

The prisoner opened his mouth to say something, but no words emerged. His sight had returned in the meantime, so that now in the obscure light of dawn pouring in from the high window he could make out the contours of his visitor. His head was somehow elongated, as though he had something tall on top of it.

"No, I did not deceive you, if that's what you're thinking," he continued. "The observatory really will be named after you if you are burned at the stake. But if you are not, it will be named after someone else. One of your students, for example, who will be braver than you. There is no predetermination. Your free will determines what will happen. You will choose between a horrible death in flames and the penitent life of a royal astronomer under the wing of the Church, whose comfort will be disturbed only by the scorn of a handful of students and perhaps a guilty conscience: between satisfying your own conceit and the wise insight that it actually makes no difference after whom the observatory is named. I do not envy you. It is not an easy choice."

The rumbling steps stopped in front of the cell door, and a key was thrust into the large lock.

"You know what I will decide," said the prisoner hurriedly in a soft voice. It was more a statement than a question.

"I know," answered the gentle voice.

The rusty hinges screeched sharply, and into the small cell came first a large turnkey with a torch raised high and after him two Inquisition interrogators in the purple robes of the high priesthood. The soldier who entered last was also holding a torch. There was no more room inside, so the three remaining soldiers had to wait in the corridor.

In the smoky light the prisoner squinted hard at the figure on the bed across from him. The strange object on his head was some sort of cylindrical hat with a wide brim, and its slanted shadow completely hid the man's face.

He had not expected his visitor to stay there. Would he let the others see him? But no one paid any attention to him, as though he were not there, as though he were invisible. In other circumstances this would have confused the prisoner completely, but in the light of his recent experience he accepted it as quite natural.

"Lazar," said the first priest, addressing him in an official tone, "this is the last time you will be asked: do you renounce your heresy and penitently accept the teachings of our Holy Mother the Church?"

The prisoner did not take his eyes off the figure in black, but he had turned into a statue. He sat with head bowed, silent, just like an old man who had fallen asleep, with his white hands leaning on the top of his cane. He seemed indifferent, as if all this had nothing to do with him, as though he were not the least bit interested. The silence grew heavy with tension, with expectation.

And then at last, the royal astronomer turned slowly toward the inquisitors and gave his monosyllabic answer.

2. The Paleolinguist

THE KNOCK ECHOED LOUDLY in the hollow silence, making her start.

She had not heard the steps approaching the door to her office. She must have dozed off again. Her head bowed, chin upon her chest, her round, wire-rimmed reading glasses had slipped to the tip of her nose. The book remained open in front of her on the desk in the lamplight, but she was still drowsy and could not remember its title right away. These catnaps were becoming more and more frequent, causing her to feel very ill at ease. Not because someone might find her in that unseemly position. She was not afraid of that; almost no one visited her anymore, not even her students, let alone her colleagues. She was an embarrassment to herself.

The knock came again. Brief and somehow reserved, hesitant. Certainly not as loud as it had seemed the first time. She looked around in confusion, wondering what time of day it was. The only window in her office looked onto the skylight, but this name was quite inappropriate since the narrow shaft that went through the middle of the building from the roof to the basement was filled only with gloom even on the sunniest days.

There was a simpler way to find out the time, but it would take her at least a few minutes to discover her wristwatch in the disordered multitude of large and small items that covered her desk. And she could not let the visitor wait that long, whomever he or she might be. Visitors were rare and therefore precious.

"Come in," she said. And then, since she thought she had said it too softly, she repeated in a louder voice: "Come in."

She did not recognize the person who appeared at the door. The neon lighting in the hallway illuminated him from behind, but even if the light had shone from in front of him, she would not have been able to discover very much without her other glasses that were also buried somewhere on the desk. The only thing she could conclude with certainty about the hazy outline was that he was a tall man in a dark cloak.

She pondered for a moment but could think of no one she knew who fit that description. That, however, still did not mean anything. She had learned with increasing certainty during the passing years that memory was a very unreliable support, particularly where the recent past was concerned. The more distant past was considerably sharper, which was rather apropos in view of her profession. But it made no difference: everything would become clear when the visitor started to speak. She had a hard time remembering faces, but she never forgot a voice, ever. This was probably the only department in which senility had kindly spared her from its humiliating veil.

"It's not easy to find you. You're completely hidden here in the basement." She had not heard this voice before. It sounded deep and drawn out, almost melodic. It would be impossible not to remember it, even without her aptitude.

"Oh, it makes no difference. When no one is looking for you, then it's all the same where you are. But are you certain that you're in the right place?"

"This is the office for paleolinguistics, isn't it?" It was more a statement than a question.

"Yes. Or rather what's left of it. In happier times we even had a brass plate that said so, but ever since we moved here, no one has taken the trouble to put it up. Maybe they're waiting for me to do it."

Continuing to stand in the doorway, the visitor contemplated the gloom of the rather small room. Three walls were covered with metal shelves, and the books and journals on them were more stacked, even thrown, than placed in an orderly fashion. A narrow vitrine rising to the low ceiling with its hot water pipes was on part of the fourth wall next to the window. It was full of tiny broken statues, pieces of pottery, and the remains of simple stone implements. These objects were also displayed without any order, often one on top of another as though the vitrine were a storage cabinet. Under the window next to the desk on a backless wooden chair covered with newspapers was a hot plate with a black kettle. Several used tea bags were lying on the newspaper like tropical fish that had died of asphyxiation.

"This is exactly as I imagined it," said the man at last.

"You imagined *this*?" she asked, bewildered.

"Yes, your office. Where you work."

She squinted, trying to focus her eyes better. "Is that supposed to be a compliment or a reproach?"

"A compliment, of course. What else could it be? I am an admirer of yours."

At first she did not know how to respond. She slowly took off her reading glasses and put them on the desk. When she finally spoke, her voice was critical. "If this is some sort of joke, then I must say it is rather out of place."

"Why do you think it's a joke?"

"I do not have admirers. I have never had any."

"But your work certainly deserves them."

She got up out of her armchair, numb from sitting

so long, and started to rummage through the things on her desk in search of her other glasses. She hunted for several moments and when she couldn't find them, waved her hand in a gesture of angry dismissal, turned her blurry eyes toward the door and said in a voice that was more nervous than she intended, "Oh, come in, for heaven's sake. We can't talk while you're in the hallway."

He entered, closed the door behind him and then stopped, uncertain where he should sit. There was another armchair in front of the desk, but it held a load of tattered folders with a fairly large stone figure on the top; with the help of a considerable amount of imagination, it resembled a bulging female torso.

"Put that somewhere, on the floor, it makes no difference," she said, noticing that he did not know what to do.

He did it with utmost caution, as though holding some sort of relic in his hands. When he sat down, the springs on the armchair squeaked in protest.

Now he was closer to her and partially illuminated by the light from her table lamp, so that even without her other glasses she could make out certain details she had not noticed before. In his lap he laid his derby, his cane with its decorated top, and a pair of white gloves. She had never given much thought to how she dressed and did not pay attention to what other people wore, but she found this quite amazing. It was as though he had come out of a play set in olden times, she thought, smiling to herself.

The man just sat there without a word and looked at her. She soon began to fidget under his inquisitive stare. Unconsciously she started to fix her disheveled strands of gray hair as she thought over what to say to the stranger. Why had she asked him to come in? Admirer! As if she were so credulous or vain.

"So, you are interested in paleolinguistics?"

"Yes, very much so."

"Why?"

He did not answer right away. He started to draw his fingers slowly along the smooth edge of the derby in his hand. "An unusual question from someone who has devoted her entire life to that field," he said at last.

"Not at all unusual," she replied. "The very fact that I've squandered my whole life in paleolinguistics gives me the clear-cut right to ask you that."

"Do you think you have squandered your life?"

She stared at his blurry face, outside the lamplight. She could not guess his age. His voice was not a reliable indicator. Judging by it alone, the man could have been in his twenties or even his forties. For his sake, she hoped it was the former; it would be much easier for him to lose his illusions. If only she had been lucky enough to have some sense knocked into her at that age.

"Take a good look around you again. You are in a tiny basement room that was the janitor's storage before and will return to that function when I retire in several months. Since I am not able to take these things with me, the books and other artifacts will all be thrown away. Useless. And even if I took them, it would not make much difference. Everything would end up on the garbage heap after my death. There, that is the best measure of the success of a life devoted to paleolinguistics. So please listen to my advice: get interested in something else. Anything. Forget primeval language and the far-off past. Who is interested in that in the modern world? Don't ruin your future for no reason."

"The past and the future, yes," replied the visitor, lost in thought. He paused for a moment, and she thought a smile flickered on his face. But she could not be sure. "I think there are other measures that can be used to evaluate what you have achieved." He said it with determination, like a man who knows what he is talking about.

She looked at him inquisitively. "What, for example?"

"If it weren't for you, the department of paleolinguistics would never have been founded."

"Probably, but what has been the benefit of that? Do you know the greatest number of new students I have had all these years?"

He clearly did not understand this as a question and so did not reply. He did not even shrug his shoulders.

"Eight. And that was long ago; it's been almost a quarter of a century. The average has been three and a half students. And only two of them at most finish their studies. Sometimes not even one. But not because I was too strict. On the contrary, I was considered a very . . ." she stopped for a moment, looking for the right word, "helpful examiner, which gave me a bad reputation among my colleagues. The young people simply gave up, primarily because they were disappointed, even though I did all I could to stimulate their interest not only in the technical aspects of the origin of language but also in a considerably less tedious subject: early human communities. They are inseparable, in any case. But nothing seemed to work. I never understood what they actually expected when they decided to major in paleolinguistics. No one made them choose it."

"You cannot blame yourself for the students' poor response. You said yourself that we live in a time that is not particularly predisposed toward the past."

She squinted at him briefly, and then continued to follow her line of thinking, paying no attention to his comforting words.

"In the last four years, no one has signed up in my department. How can you keep your position as lecturer if you have no one to lecture to? Only if the administration is sympathetic toward you. They didn't have to do it. They probably wouldn't have if it weren't for my age. I stayed here just because the dean was considerate enough to support me, although it would have been natural to fire me. He knew that at my age I have nowhere to go. I knew that myself, so I swallowed my pride and let them put me in this cubbyhole. Don't look a gift horse in the mouth, particularly not when the gift is given out of pity. What else could I have done, anyway?"

She stopped talking, wondering why she was telling all this to a stranger. She was only putting them both in an awkward situation. But the matter concerned him, too. He had come there with an idealized notion of paleolinguistics, hadn't he? Would it be fair to let him leave without seeing its other side? Certainly not. In any case, she had not had the opportunity to talk to someone for a long time, to pour out her grievances. There were no more students, and her colleagues avoided her more-or-less openly.

"Now I'm on sabbatical. That was the last chance for me to reach retirement age in this position. I was given a leave of absence quite easily. It was actually a gift. I didn't even have to present any sort of research plan, as is customary. No project that I would work on. No one even asked. No one expects anything from me anymore."

"But you have done so much already. You wrote several fundamental works on paleolinguistics. Isn't that more than enough?"

Her blurry eyes started to wander over the multitude of objects covering the desk in front of her. Had she known she would have a visitor, she would have tidied up the office a bit. Actually, she had been reproaching herself for some time for the clutter surrounding her, but she could never make up her mind to do anything about it. There was no incentive. What was the purpose, since she would be leaving there in a few months?

But then, couldn't that be expanded to all of life itself? Why make any effort at all when everything was transient? She used to know the answer, it had seemed obvious and irrefutable, but with the passage of time it had become hazier and darker.

"Would you like some tea?"

He did not answer right away. He seemed to hesitate. "No, thank you," he said at last.

It was only then that she realized there was just one tea cup. Had the man accepted her offer, she would have had to do without tea, something that would not have been easy for her. She had become a complete addict. Several years ago, when the doctor had advised her to stop drinking coffee because of high blood pressure, she had switched to tea, primarily to appease her habit of constantly sipping something hot. When she reached seven cups a day, she realized she had overdone it, but it was too late by then.

"I would. Do you mind?"

"Not at all."

She hobbled over to the small, cracked ceramic sink that stood next to the window, picking up the kettle on her way. Although her vision was very poor without her glasses, she did not need them to make tea. She had gone through this sequence of simple motions so many times that she could have managed in total darkness.

"There is nothing truly fundamental in my works," she said in a hushed voice, after plugging in the hot plate and returning to her armchair. "It is all just an educated guess, at best."

For a few moments all that was heard was the sound of water leaking in thin streams from several spots on the cracked exterior of the kettle, evaporating when they hit the red-hot plate.

"What do you mean?" asked the visitor at length.

"Do you know the first thing I told my students? So they knew right from the start what they were involved in. Paleolinguistics is not an exact science. It cannot be, since, in the strictest sense of that term, the subject of study is missing. Primeval language has been dead for a very long time. We have no direct evidence of it. And even the indirect evidence is quite scanty. All we do is make more-or-less questionable reconstructions. We try to recompose a mosaic whose original appearance is unknown, and we are not even certain that we are using the right stones."

"But didn't you convincingly show that living languages and the dead ones that have been preserved both contain traces of primeval language? Which is natural, in any case. They all arose from it, didn't they?"

"Convincingly, yes. Perhaps. There is one person, however, whom I have never managed to convince of this completely. The only one I really care about."

"Who is that?"

"Myself, of course."

The kettle suddenly whistled. She got up slowly, unplugged the hot plate, took a small tea bag out of a half-empty yellow box on the desk; lifted the kettle's little lid, removing her hand quickly so the steam would not burn her, waited for the cloud rushing out to disperse, and dropped the tea bag into the boiling water.

"They say you shouldn't put the tea bag in right away. If the water is too hot, it kills the aroma of the tea. But I don't have the patience to wait."

"You are unfair to yourself. You must not doubt your whole life's work. Just think of the enormous effort you have made."

"What else can I do? Resort to self-delusion? Repeat to myself that it can't be all in vain since I made such a tremendous effort? But effort itself is by no means a guarantee of success. There is something, however, that is even worse than doubt. The hardest thing for me is that the doubt can never be removed: there is no way to know how close I came to primeval language. But there's no one to blame for that. I knew from the beginning that was the main shortcoming of the field I had chosen."

"Except if you were to go back into the past."

She smiled at him briefly. "Yes, except if I were to go back into the past. I know many people who would sell their soul to the devil without the slightest hesitation for such an opportunity. All kinds of historians. People like me, obsessed with long-ago times. But either the soul is not enough payment or the devil himself is not that powerful. Probably the latter. Unfortunately, there's no going back into the past."

"If there were, would you accept the devil's offer?"

She looked at him without speaking for a time and then got up to wash out her cup and pour the tea. When she returned to the desk, the newspaper that covered the chair with the hot plate had a new fish steaming in agony.

"I don't think the devil would choose me. What use would he have for such a poor, worn-out soul as mine?"

"Maybe he wouldn't even ask for your soul."

"Oh, don't be naive. The devil isn't generous. You don't get something for nothing from him."

"I agree. He always collects payment for his services. But there are other rewards in addition to the soul that he might find more attractive."

"What else could he expect from me in return?"

"The devil is a sadist above all. He enjoys people's suffering. If he helped you return to the past, he would be putting you in twofold torment."

She greedily took a sip of tea. She knew it was still hot, that it would burn the sensitive lining of her mouth, but the addict in her had run out of patience again. Conversation with this stranger had become rather pointless, even though he amused her in some odd way.

"Twofold?" she repeated inquiringly.

"Yes. Imagine that you go back in time and there, on the spot, you reliably establish how things were. What would you do with that knowledge?"

"Well, I don't know. Publish it, probably."

"But you are a scientist. Wouldn't you ruin your credibility by citing that your knowledge stems from a trip into the past arranged by the devil? They would proclaim you a charlatan at best. At worst you'd end up in an insane asylum."

Before she replied, she took another long sip of hot tea. The cup was already half empty.

"Then I wouldn't publish it. But the devil would still have no reason to rejoice. I told you that I only care about convincing one person. And for her sake it would not be necessary to publish anything. She would be convinced without it, by firsthand experience." She stopped a moment, smiling again. "Let me hear what other trap the devil has prepared for me."

"What is the fundamental assumption of your field, that is, all fields that study the past?" The visitor had not acquired her facetious tone. His voice was as serious as before, and she thought it quite pleasant. Dignified. Too bad she had not found her glasses. A man with such a voice simply had to have an agreeable face.

"The immutability of what has happened, if that is what you had in mind."

"That's right, the past cannot be changed. That fact would be jeopardized, however, if someone from the future appeared in the past. The devil's services would desecrate something that is older and must remain inviolable. What would be the use of learning firsthand about the past if it were no longer final?"

"Why do you think that a visitor from the future would destroy the past? If he were a scientist—and we're talking about that kind of time traveler, aren't we?—it would not be in his interest. On the contrary, he would have every reason to remain an inconspicuous observer."

"Yes, he would have every reason. But would that be enough? There would be enormous temptation to influence the course of events. Take, for example, a historian who goes back to some turning point in history. If he remains simply an observer, events will take their well-known course resulting in the death of a large number of innocent people. On the other hand, it could all be avoided by his involvement. In that case, which would prevail inside him: the dispassionate scientist or the man who realizes that if he does not take any measures, his conscience will be burdened with unbearable guilt? It would not be an easy choice, and this would give the devil great satisfaction."

She stared for a moment at the bottom of the empty cup in front of her before answering.

"Not every traveler to the past would necessarily come up against such a difficult choice. There are peaceful times, without turning points. For example, if I went back to the period I studied, I could be an impartial observer without any encumbrance because nothing would drive me to get involved in the course of events, to change the future. Historically speaking, it was a completely innocent age. I'm afraid the devil would not get his due."

"There is no innocent age." He said it softer than before, as though it were confidential, secret. "Have you heard of the butterfly effect?"

She had heard of it but could by no means remember what it was. Even if her memory had been in better shape, it would quite likely have slipped her mind. She had never fancied such innovations. Her science was classical, more elementary. To avoid answering, she got up to pour a new cup of tea, and he waited for her to return to the desk.

"A butterfly suddenly starts to fly, urged by who

knows what, quite unaware of the fact that this movement might start a chain of events whose far-off final link is a storm of continental proportions on the other side of the world. The flutter of tiny wings sets the chaos equation in motion, whose solution can be completely disproportionate to this infinitesimal movement. A tiny cause sometimes leads to enormous effects."

"Yes, I know about that," she replied, "only I don't see what that has to do with what we were talking about."

"Regardless of how firmly you are resolved not to change the past, what happens does not depend on you alone. Quite unintentionally, by your very presence, you might bring about the butterfly effect. Maybe even literally. Imagine that your sudden appearance there disturbs a butterfly that has been idly perched on a flower. Frightened, it suddenly takes flight, and several days later, far from there, someone dies in a storm who was not supposed to die at all, someone who is the starting point of an inverse pyramid of history. You might be convinced that this outcome is highly unlikely, but the devil, as an experienced gambler, would not hold back from accepting the wager. It would actually be a safe bet. Chaos is his kingdom, when it comes right down to it."

"But if this is how things stand, if the devil can't lose, what's stopping him from coming with his offer? He hasn't visited me, or anyone else in my field as far as I know. And it's among us he would find the most prominent victims."

She expected an answer from the other side of the desk, but none was forthcoming. As the silence in the gloomy basement room deepened, distant unintelligible sounds from the upper levels could be heard.

"So, we are back to where we started," she said, finally breaking the silence. "Going into the past is clearly not within the devil's power."

"Maybe it is," said the melodic voice in return, "but in such a way that it would not give him the reward he wants if he were to offer it to someone. That is why there is no offer."

Now it was her turn to remain silent. She peered in bewilderment at the foggy figure across from her.

"If there were neither the temptation nor the opportunity to change the past, then the returnee would feel none of the torment that would suffice the devil as payment."

"But is that possible? Doesn't it follow from your story about the butterfly that the very act of stepping into the past would inevitably change it?"

"Yes, it does follow, but only if one went physically into the past. And it does not have to be that way."

She raised her cup to her lips, but the tea was already lukewarm. This was not the way she liked it; it was tasteless. She found a bit of empty space on the desk and put the cup there.

"Then how would it be?"

"What do you do when you watch a documentary film?" said the visitor, answering her question with one of his own. "You go into the past without the opportunity of changing anything. Film editors do have a few tricks at their disposal, but that doesn't count: that would be falsifying the past and not truly changing it. The viewer of a documentary film is in the position of the ideal unbiased observer: he can in no way influence the past."

"Yes, but that is only true for more recent history. It really is possible to return to the past that way. At least partially. The filmed version enchants us with its images and sound, but reality is something richer. But let's put that aside. I must remind you that, unfortunately, no documentary films have been made about the age that interests me."

If he noticed the irony in her voice, it was not revealed by any change of tone. "Of course not. I was not even thinking of such a return to the past. It is, as you say, quite incomplete. But the comparison with films is rather convenient. Imagine such a film about the past that would act upon all your senses, not just sight and hearing. A film in which you would feel exactly the same way you do in reality, except that you could not take part in it, change it. You would have the role of an infinitely empowered viewer who sees, hears, and feels everything, yet remains invisible and inaudible, unobserved."

She blinked. "That sounds like a ghost to me."

The visitor gave a brief laugh, resonant and clear. "Yes, the viewer would be like a ghost, for all practical purposes."

"That's all very well, but there are no such films about the past. None have been made."

She thought there would be some comment from the dusty armchair, but silence greeted her once again. She closed her eyes for a moment and rubbed the bridge of her nose with thumb and forefinger, thinking that it was time to bring the conversation to a close. What else was there to say? They had reached the topic of ghosts, hadn't they? Even though she was happy that someone had visited her, she was now feeling tired. A person should not be overly indulgent toward admirers.

"I wonder what time it is. My watch is lost somewhere in this mess on the desk. I can't wear it on my wrist all the time—it chafes—and then I can never remember where I put it."

She assumed that he would look at his left wrist, but he reached under his cloak and took out a pocket watch. A dull golden reflection danced about it, and she thought how strange it was. She could not remember the last time she had seen a watch like that. Had they come back into fashion? She knew nothing about fashion, but then how could she since she never went anywhere, never saw anyone, and passed the entire day between these four basement walls?

He handed her the watch. She took it impassively, simply because he had offered it. It was only when she had it in her hand that she wondered why he had not simply told her the time instead of letting her find out for herself.

She brought the object close to her eyes, so she could see without her glasses, but did not open the lid right away because her attention was attracted to the engraving on its bulging surface. An ornate letter E, with a series of decorative loops at its ends, just like the initial from some old-fashioned manuscript. Quite unusual, was the thought that flashed through her mind. E as in Eva. Like it was meant for me.

And then she moved the little catch and the lid jumped up.

II

THERE WERE NO HANDS. There was no face. Just a bright circle that contained some kind of image. The image was not quite steady but trembled as though alive. Confused, she brought the watch a little closer to get a better look, but when she wanted to stop, it kept on coming closer all by itself, without her influence. The casing started to get bigger, like a round fissure in reality that quickly expanded before her, its brilliance crowding out the gloom of the basement room, until it had pushed it all the way over the edge of the world.

She was blinded at first. Her pupils were accustomed to the poor light in the office and needed some time to adjust to the bright midday sun. But the rest of her senses immediately began to absorb the rich impressions of her new surroundings. She was struck by the unknown smells of wild vegetation, dense and abundant, prickling and stinging her nostrils as though someone had thrown a handful of pollen into her face. Her ears were filled with the undulating sound of tall, brittle blades of grass and the buzzing and humming of a multitude of insects engrossed in their ritual dances. The breeze reached her skin in uneven gusts, stroking her face and hands with the softest touch.

She knew what she would see even before her eyesight returned, but there was still no lack of surprise. She was in the middle of a field that stretched all around in gentle folds as far as the eye could see, but what her senses of smell, hearing, and touch could not tell her was that countless butterflies covered the expanse around her like some flickering, brightly colored rug. They were flying low over the ground cover or resting on it, completely devoted to their harmless business which, as she had recently learned, could result in unforeseeable disaster.

She froze at that thought. What if her appearance upset them? What if they suddenly started to fly, thereby disturbing something that should not be disturbed? She stopped breathing when a butterfly left a purple flower with large petals and zigzagged toward her, lazily fluttering its spotted wings. When it approached her face she instinctively closed her eyes, helplessly expecting it to fly into her at any moment. But no crash occurred. When she opened her eyes, the butterfly was gone. She first thought that it must have turned at the last instant. The other possibility was so unbelievable that she simply refused to accept it.

But soon afterward, when a somewhat stronger gust of wind raised an excited cloud of butterflies, she nonetheless had to accept the impossible. They flew through her as though she were not there, as though she were made of some airy substance, transparent, unreal, nonexistent.

At first she just stood there motionless, utterly confused, and watched the cloud stream through her body. She felt this rising tide like a weak sting, like light goose pimples flowing on the surface of her skin. The cloud had already thinned out when she finally emerged from her paralysis and extended her hand toward the last butterflies. She could touch them in flight. The touch was irrefutable, although one-sided: the tiny wings yielded unfeelingly to her invisible fingers in their multicolored fluttering.

She remained undecided for a time after the last butterfly had gone. Serious, distressing questions were welling up from part of her consciousness, but she quickly smothered the tiresome voice that only spoiled the magic. What difference did it make that it was impossible when it seemed so dreamy, so intoxicating?

Nevertheless, one question had to be answered. What next? She could stay there some more—quite a lot more, actually—surrendering to the fragrances emanating from the ground, the salutary warmth pouring down from the firmament, the caressing wind that wakened inside her long-hidden joys. But not for an eternity. Even the Elysian Fields inevitably lose their charms.

She had no reason to go in any particular direction, so she simply moved straight ahead. She did so unconsciously, taking a step forward, but instead of her foot landing on the grass again as it should have done, it stayed in the air.

She did not realize right away that she was flying. At first she thought she'd lost her balance and would fall, but she never did. She remained in midair, unsupported, bewildered because she had always been afraid of heights, although she was barely at knee level. She wished in panic to go down, and the very next moment she was resting on the ground again.

Some time passed before she mustered the courage to move once more. She thought she must look like a child, trying to take its first awkward steps. This time there was no need to step forward. All she had to do was will it: she wanted to fly—and the same instant she was in the air again, infinitely light, incorporeal.

She first took a horizontal birdlike position, extending her arms like wings, but quickly realized that this was not necessary. Undignified, in fact. Owing to her years, it was much more becoming for her to adopt the same position in the air as she did on the ground, so she straightened up with her arms crossed on her chest, as though perched on an invisible pedestal.

Fear faded and gave way to fascination. The experience of unhindered flight was thrilling, giddy. First she streaked high up until she reached the fluffy substance of a small cloud, and then, barely resisting the urge to scream with excitement, she started back down, enjoying the sight of the green carpet approaching at lightning speed. She stopped right above it effortlessly, without disturbing the swarm of buzzing insects quarreling over a cluster of red and yellow flowers.

When she soared to the bottom of the heavens again, she caught sight of something she had missed her first time up there. Her surprise was actually twofold, and she stopped suddenly in the middle of nothingness. When she saw a thin column of smoke rising on the distant horizon, it flashed through her mind that this should not be possible: she did not have her glasses with her. They had been left behind in the office, somewhere in the disorder on her desk. But it seemed that in this new form they were not necessary; she could see the spiraling signal of someone's fire clearly enough without them.

She hurried in that direction like an eagle that has spotted its prey, driven by impatience and foreboding. The suppressed questions started to surge to the surface once again. If she was truly where she suspected, although all this was beyond reason, of course, then she had lighted on her destination.

The tribe was small—she counted only twelve members. Next to the fire were two old women, an old man, and four children of different ages. The other five adults—how stunted they were!—were dispersed in a broad circle around this temporary habitat. They were engaged in what people of that early age spent most of their time doing: painstakingly collecting food—different berries, roots, shriveled fruit, small rodents.

She descended, not close to the fire, but a bit farther off. She could feel her heart thudding in her immaterial chest. The voices of the old people and children were muffled and indistinct, but that was what she wanted. She was not yet ready. When she was, she would go among them—a ghost who would know as soon as she heard their first words whether or not her former life had meaning.

She wondered what price she would have to pay for this unique privilege. It certainly could not be the assurance that she would not return from here. Even if she had that impossible watch, what was there to go back to? Lonely drudgery in a dark basement cubbyhole? The humiliation brought by neglect and old age? The implacable doubts that would follow her maliciously to the end? No, staying here would be a reward and not a punishment. So what would it be?

The answer came with the wind. The current of air brought to her insensate nostrils the hot smell of steam from the sooty earthen vessel in which water was boiling over the fire. The old women were cleaning some dried herbs, getting them ready for the pot, chatting idly, just as would be done in the countless centuries to follow.

Tea, of course!

An inaudible scream was wrenched from the addict. She felt neither hunger nor thirst, as was quite natural in this state. But the longing for a hot cup of tea that suddenly flooded her was something far beyond a physical need. The delusive impression that the familiar tonic was flowing through the inside of her mouth, the promise that her overpowering need would soon be satisfied, had the same effect as genuine agony.

As despair filled her, she thought that she would not have accepted had she known the price she must pay. But she had not actually been given the choice. All right, then, she concluded, getting hold of herself, there's no turning back. The price has been paid, even though unwillingly. All that was left was to take what was hers in return.

And she headed toward the fire to meet the voices of the primeval language that would tell her the simple truth.

3. The Watchmaker

THE CLOCKS STRUCK SIX p.m. simultaneously, just as they should in a reputable watchmaker's shop. The old man's trained ears had been carefully monitoring this sound, and they could not detect any divergence: not a single one of the four clocks adorning the walls of the rather small, ground-floor premises was either early or late. This was the only harmony that linked them, however, for what followed afterward was total discordance.

The grandfather clock, with its pendulum in a casing of worn mahogany and door of thick, etched glass, grumbled in a deep, solemn bass, like a mustachioed sergeant grenadier giving orders at a parade. The brass dwarf hit his worn hammer on the hanging bronze rod, creating a clear, sharp sound resembling the echo of distant bells. The call of the wooden cuckoo rushing out the round opening of the gaily colored alpine house had lost its original rapture long ago, becoming harsh and piercing. Finally, the chipped pair of ceramic dancers in ballroom attire nimbly started to turn on the small circular podium at the first bars of an old-fashioned waltz.

Although they began all at once, the sounds that struck the hour did not end at the same time. First the cuckoo went silent, suddenly, like a death rattle; it seemed almost as if someone with delicate nerves or no ear for its tired singing had ungraciously wrung its neck. The waltz and the ringing lasted about the same time, competing to the final note for futile advantage. The drawn-out tones of the grandfather clock filled the shop the longest; by virtue of its very size it was natural for it to have the last word.

When the final grumble of the grenadier's bass had died out, the old man reached adroitly for a small pocket on the left-hand side of his vest. He took out a gold-plated pocket watch with a thick chain, raised the lid—which had TO J. FROM M. engraved on the inside in large, ornate letters—and briefly nodded, satisfied that it was truly six o'clock. This was not an expression of distrust toward the other clocks which had just informed him of the same fact quite loudly and precisely. For more than a quarter of a century he had carried out this ritual every evening before he closed the shop and went home, as a sign of respect for a special memory. And a grief.

But he was not fated to spend that evening in the usual way: closing the door to the shop, taking the short walk along the usually empty street to the small, excessively neat attic apartment where no one waited for him, preparing a simple and for the most part tasteless meal that would probably satisfy only a bachelor or a single person, and going to bed. Sleep would rarely bring him refreshment or oblivion; it mainly gave him restless dreams that returned him to the past. He could not leave the past, not even in his dreams.

He had just put the heavy watch back into his vest pocket and was about to pull the little short chain with its silver ring to turn off the lamp with the green shade on his workbench behind the counter when the door opened suddenly, jangling the cluster of bells hanging above. Although mild compared to the discordant choir of the wall clocks, the unexpected sound of these signal bells made him start. He rarely had customers in his shop this late.

He looked up, but all he could make out in the

gloom was the silhouette of a tall man against the dull glow of the streetlight. The man was wearing a hat, probably a derby, and rather a long cloak, and in his right hand was a cane. He stopped next to the door without going up to the counter, as though hesitating for some reason.

The old man pushed his round, metal-framed work glasses halfway down his nose and asked, with an effort to sound obliging, "May I help you, sir?"

The man did not reply at once. He looked around the shop as though wanting to make sure that the two of them were alone. His eyes rested a bit longer on the grandfather clock; half of the pendulum's path was in shadow, and the circular base flickered in the other half as it reflected the muted light from outside.

The late visitor finally put his cane under his arm and stepped resolutely toward the counter, at the same time removing something from an inside pocket. When he reached him, the old man saw that he was wearing white leather gloves; he had long, slender fingers like a pianist's. His right fist was closed, and he placed it palm up on the felt-covered counter. Illuminated by the rim of light from the work lamp, its whiteness looked unnaturally bright compared to the green background and the darkness around them. The watchmaker suddenly had the impression that the man before him was a magician who was about to pull a sleight of hand.

The trick, however, did not take place, for when his hand opened, it contained quite an exemplary object: a pocket watch. The old man returned his glasses to the bridge of his nose and leaned over it to take a better look. Up until then, he had been convinced that all he needed was one look at a watch in order to recognize not only the brand but also the type and even the year it was made. He had spent almost four decades working exclusively with watches. He knew them inside out, one might say. Particularly pocket watches; he was a real expert where they were concerned. He knew each little spring, gear, screw, and nut. Every little hand and face.

But here he had a surprise in store. One look was not enough. He had certainly never seen this type before. The old man knit his brow in disbelief and leaned a bit closer. He was filled with the powerful urge to take the watch from the white palm, to finger it, open it, but manners prevented him doing so. He continued to look at it, putting his eager hands behind his back. He strove hard to find some detail he could recognize, but all his trained eye could ascertain was that the watch was exquisitely made. There was no doubt about that: it was the creation of a true master of his trade—an expert he had never heard of.

Shaking his head briefly, he straightened up and looked at the visitor inquiringly. The man's face was still in the darkness under the hat brim, so the watchmaker could not make it out. Suddenly he felt a mild prickling sensation at the base of his neck, the bristling of sparse white hairs. There was something unreal about the tall figure in front of him, something that filled him with agitation and unease.

This impression did not pass when the visitor finally spoke.

"I would like you to have a look at this watch," he said in a hoarse, dignified voice which did not need to be raised even when giving an order. A foreigner, concluded the watchmaker. Although he made an effort to pronounce the words properly, his accent gave him away as well as a certain drawl, although not one common in travelers from the north, who were the most frequent strangers in this area. It was impossible to say where he was from.

"Certainly, sir, certainly," he replied. "What is your complaint, sir? I mean, what is wrong with your watch? It is obviously quite expensive, although . . ."

He opened his mouth to admit that he had never seen one like it before, but he held back at the last moment, fearing this might stop the visitor from leaving his watch with him. He certainly had to have the chance to examine it in greater detail.

"I have no complaints," said the stranger, interrupting him. "The watch is fine. But all the same, I think it would be a good idea for you to have a look at it."

"Most certainly, sir. You are quite right. A bit of precaution would certainly do no harm. On the contrary, never enough caution. You were very wise to bring your watch to be looked at. Even the best watches need regular maintenance. People do not bear that in mind, actually, they are negligent for the most part, not only toward objects, unfortunately; many misfortunes would be avoided if precautionary measures were taken. . . ."

"There are no precautions that can thwart chance." The man said this in an even voice, as though saying something obvious, even banal. The watchmaker squinted toward the invisible face; although the statement sounded like a general principle, there was something in the stranger's tone that gave it the weight and credentials of personal experience.

"Yes, indeed. Of course. You understand things perfectly, sir. Chance, yes. Something you cannot influence regardless of how hard you try. For a watchmaker that is the effect of dust. I have yet to see a watch without dust, and countless numbers have gone through my hands in my many years of work. You can protect a watch however you want, even close it hermetically, but nothing helps. Dust will find a way inside, and one particle is enough—one single, solitary particle—to jeopardize the fine mechanism. You have no idea, sir, what a nightmare dust is for watchmakers."

"Yes, a particle of dust," repeated the visitor, drawing out his words, lost in thought. "The flutter of butterfly wings . . ."

The old man's eyes became suspicious. What was that supposed to mean? What "flutter" ? Maybe he wanted to say something else but expressed himself awkwardly in a foreign language—although he seemed to speak it well, at least fluently and correctly, if not without an accent. Or maybe he was some kind of crank, an eccentric? The old man was not prejudiced against foreigners and considered the stories that could be heard about their peculiarities, even abnormalities, to be exaggerated for the most part. But you never knew. There were quacks everywhere, in any case. Not even this neighborhood had been spared.

He had the impression that some sort of reply was expected from him, but did not know what to say. Really, "butterfly wings" . . . What could he say about them and still be nice, polite? He was saved from the awkward situation by a carriage that suddenly passed by in the street. The rapid thud of horses' hooves caused the plated wheels to produce a sharp rattle as they rolled over the cobblestones. The visitor seemed to flinch a bit at this noise, turning toward the entrance. But the carriage passed in a flash, and the fading echo of its passage was quickly absorbed by the heavy silence of the evening.

"Yes," said the watchmaker when the stranger turned his unseen face toward him once again, "you are completely right. There is no way to fight against chance."

"Oh, that's not what I said. I only said that you cannot thwart it, prevent it. But that does not mean that you cannot fight against it."

The old man involuntarily swallowed the lump in his throat. "Please forgive me, sir, but I'm afraid that I don't understand you very well," he replied timidly.

Before he answered, the visitor finally put the pocket watch on the felt-covered counter, as though for some reason he had concluded just at that instant that he could safely let the watchmaker take his valuable timepiece. When the white glove withdrew from the lamplight, the old man had the impression that a bright trace remained behind it for a few moments. With his free hand, the foreigner skillfully took the cane from under his arm, turned slowly on his heel and pointed at the clocks on the four walls with it.

"It is all a matter of time, you see," he said at last, after making a full circle and returning to face the watchmaker again. His voice took on that flat quality once more that spoke of reliable knowledge, his own experience.

The old man simply nodded, without a word, as though this statement explained everything. One had to be careful with eccentrics; it was not advisable to contradict them.

"What makes chance so powerful? The fact that you can't foresee it. If you knew exactly which particle of dust would ruin the watch mechanism, you could remove it in time. But you can't know that until the malfunction occurs, of course."

"Of course," repeated the watchmaker like an echo, with another nod.

"Cause and effect," continued the visitor. "The particle only becomes a cause when the effect takes place—the malfunction. Never beforehand. That is why alleged clairvoyance and similar illusionary sleights of hand have no meaning. The future cannot be foretold because then one would be able to change it. And if you changed it, then it would no longer be the predicted future. You cannot prophesy: this particle is the cause of the future malfunction—and then remove it, because then there would be no malfunction, and your prophecy would have no value, either. No, the consequences must happen in any case. And they do take place. You yourself said that you have never seen a watch without dust inside. And you undertook detailed precautionary measures, everything that was within your power, to prevent it."

"Oh, I did, I did, most assuredly. You can be certain of that, sir. I hope I am not being immodest when I say that this watch repair shop has an excellent reputation for industriousness. You will see this for yourself, sir, I hope. We leave nothing to chance here. . . ."

The old man stopped, biting his tongue; it was only after he had said this last sentence that he realized the expression he used might sound inappropriate, given the topic under discussion. But since the visitor did not react, he quickly continued.

"But, if you will forgive me my poor perception, sir, I cannot see how it is possible to fight against chance—your very words, sir—if the effects, the consequences, must take place?"

The foreigner did not answer at once. Led by some obscure impulse, he threw his cane a short distance into the air, then as it fell caught it adeptly near the upper end with his thumb and forefinger and started to swing the lower part as if it were a pendulum. It was only then that the old man noted in the gentle, milky gleam that the top of the cane was the stylized figure of an hourglass. Most likely made of ivory, he concluded. The man was without doubt quite wealthy. Perhaps only people like that could allow themselves the luxury of being eccentric.

"It's all a matter of time, as I said," he announced again at length, continuing to swing his wooden pendulum. "You truly cannot influence the cause *before* the effect, but there is another possibility—perhaps you can do so *after* the effect takes place."

The old man squinted again over the metal rim of his glasses. Watchmakers are like doctors, he thought, self-pityingly and comfortingly: they do not enjoy the privilege of choosing their clients. How would it look if a doctor refused to treat a patient simply because he had strange convictions? Should he now refuse to serve this obviously wealthy quack with a very unusual watch just because of his peculiar ideas? That would be quite against professional ethics, not to mention courtesy. And after all, there was the fee to think of.

"Oh," replied the old man briefly, trying not to sound too surprised.

"Yes," continued the visitor, "although extremely unusual, the idea is actually simple. Going into the past. Going upstream on the river of time, to put it picturesquely. If you returned to the past, you would be able to remove the cause and thereby the effect as well."

"Of course," agreed the watchmaker without hesitation. "Quite simple, as you said, sir. . . . Going back into the past and removing the cause. . . . Nothing easier, so to speak. No cause, no effect. You explained that quite well, sir, quite concisely. . . ."

The stranger did not reply for several moments, and the old man had the unpleasant impression that the unseen eyes were gazing at him in suspicion from under the hat brim. Did I say something I shouldn't have? he wondered. Maybe I shouldn't have said anything. A man doesn't know how to talk to such people.

"It is not quite as simple as you might think." The visitor's voice seemed to carry a touch of reproach. "Here's an example: imagine that you go back to the past and accidentally cause the death of one of your parents—before you were conceived. That would mean that you were never born and could therefore never go into the past and prevent your own conception. And if you were nonetheless born and then you went back to the past . . . and so on. *Reductio ad absurdum*. A paradox."

The old man stared fixedly at the dark figure before him, suddenly feeling sweat break on the palms of his hands. What was he talking about—causing the death of one of my parents? How could he think of something like that? Was that the sort of thing a gentleman talked to a stranger about, even if he was an eccentric? But what if this person before him was not some rich eccentric, but a madman who had escaped from a foreign asylum for the mentally ill, who would rob and maybe even kill someone? Where did he get those fancy clothes, expensive watch and ivory-tipped cane, anyway? Does he intend to attack me? What should I do? How were you supposed to act toward a dangerous lunatic, anyway? Humor him, flatter him? I must not let him know that I realize he is crazy. But they say that madmen can be very bright. . . . If only the ceiling light was on—damn the penny-pinching of the elderly!

"No, there is no solution to the paradox, at least not if you hold to the normal view of time—as a unique river. What has happened cannot be changed at all. The flow of time is like granite in which events are permanently chiseled. Both causes and effects. It is not a palimpsest that you can erase and write on again as many times as you want."

Another short pause ensued, and then the foreigner suddenly stopped the monotonous swinging of his cane. He held it in the hanging position for a moment, as though uncertain what to do with it next, and then with a sharp movement put it under his arm again. All that remained sticking out at the front was the figure of the hourglass—a milky spot before a dark background.

"But what if there were not just one time flow, one inscription in granite? If there were several flows—countless, actually? Imagine time not as a single river but as an enormous tree with countless branches, countless forks. Forks appear on those places where you change the past. One branch is the original flow in which a cause produced an effect; that is final—it must remain unchanged, chiseled—but from the other branch both the cause and the effect are removed."

The visitor stopped, as though wanting to check the impression his words had made. The old man was still staring at him fixedly, his mouth half open. In the sudden silence, the muted ticking of the wall clocks rose by several octaves.

"And you exist on both forks, in both versions, if we can put it that way. You have a sort of double—more than that, actually—whose course of life differs from yours in some respect. In an essential respect, perhaps. He could be spared the effects of an unpleasant, tragic accident, for example."

The visitor fell silent and the old man started to fidget, feeling that he should say something in reply. However, for several long moments he couldn't think of anything.

"Truly quite clever," he said at last, making an effort to keep his voice from trembling. "What an unusual notion! You have figured out something quite brilliant, sir. A tree and then a fork, and a double! Very picturesque, striking, no doubt about it. Something like that certainly would never have crossed my mind."

"Strange. And one would say that you have had both an opportunity and a motive to think about that."

"What are you thinking of, sir? I'm afraid I don't quite understand."

The visitor took the cane in his right hand again and described a rather large arc in front of him.

"Isn't this an opportunity? Look around yourself. You have spent your entire life in the midst of clocks. You are surrounded by chronometers. You are in the very center of time, I might say, in a very privileged position. I cannot believe that in all these past years you have never wondered about the nature of time, how it works, about the peculiarities linked to it. Who else if not you?"

"I am afraid you highly overestimate me, sir. I am just an ordinary watchmaker. Industrious, that is true, yes, and probably good, too, at least that is what they say, but nothing more than an artisan. For me, sir, and please don't hold it against me, time flows as it flows, and if a clock does not measure it as it should, I repair it. I can do that. And that is all. Clocks are here to measure time properly, aren't they?"

"Yes, that's true, but what about the motive?"

"Motive, sir?"

The stranger did not continue right away. The watchmaker could almost feel the piercing look of the eyes in the shadow.

"Nothing in your life has ever made you want to go back to the past and change something there? Remove some unforeseen cause that led to adverse effects? Cancel the consequences of some mischance that befell you or someone particularly close to you, someone dear? Has there ever been a man who has never had such a desire?"

Who is this? wondered the watchmaker in fear, feeling suddenly squeezed, as if in a trap. Behind him was a wall, and before him lurched a threatening figure, a voice from the darkness asking inadmissible, impossible questions. His hand unconsciously touched the watch in his vest pocket. This was not some eccentric or madman. Oh, no. Something else was going on here, something unreal, like a dream. Maybe I'm dreaming, he thought with hope. He did not wake up, however, as always happens when this question is asked in a dream.

"What would be the use even if I did want to, sir? It can't be done. I mean, all right, maybe time isn't, as you described, sir, a river, I don't contest that, but that . . . tree . . . with the forks in the branches . . . and the rest. The double . . . But how can a person ever get the chance to change anything? Go back to the past?"

There was no reply from the shadow. The seconds lapsed, long, silent, full of expectation. And then, instead of the stranger, the wall quartet suddenly resounded, breaking off the tense silence and prompting the old man for the first time in his life to jump at the harmonious announcement of the full hour; the very next moment it was transformed into a discordant confusion of grumbling, chirping, chiming, and waltz music.

The visitor remained motionless until the last echo of the grenadier's bass died out and then with a rapid movement placed the top of his cane next to the pocket watch that lay on the illuminated felt counter.

"You will look at it, won't you?"

A deep sigh of relief escaped from the old man, as though a heavy load had been taken off his chest. His eager hands finally caught hold of the precious object; they started to turn it over and feel it, examining it as carefully as eyes could.

"Certainly, certainly. Rest assured, sir. Right away. It's not too late. If you would be so kind as to come by in the morning. As soon as I open. It will be ready. At your service, sir. At your service."

The foreigner abruptly turned on his heel, missing the watchmaker's humble bow. The sound of the cloak's stiff fabric merged with the ringing of the bells and the closing of the door. The tall shadow passed quickly in front of the store window and disappeared down the street.

The old man slowly sat down on the chair next to his workbench and put the pocket watch upon the rubber surface. He gazed at it for a few moments, turning it over curiously, and then reached to open the lid.

But he did not complete the movement, for he suddenly realized that in the excitement of the moment before, he had forgotten something: he had not given the customer a receipt for the watch. Inexcusable, he thought. That had never happened to him before. All right, he had been disoriented by the visitor's unusual appearance, by that strange story, but even so! An unpardonable oversight for a watchmaker who cares about his reputation. What would the foreigner think of him?

He grabbed the receipt book and a pen from the counter and rushed toward the door with stiff movements. Suddenly disturbed, the bells above the door protested sharply. Outside it was cool and windy, a November evening at the foot of a mountain which already carried a great cap of snow. Shivering for a moment, the watchmaker looked for the visitor down the row of streetlights. But no one was there. Perplexed, he turned and looked in the other direction. Just as empty.

He stayed in front of the shop a little longer, turning back and forth in disbelief, and then returned inside. Where had he gone? Had a carriage been waiting for him nearby? But no, he hadn't heard anything. Standing at the door a moment, the old man finally shrugged his shoulders. He would apologize to the foreigner for this oversight when he came in the morning. In any case, it would make no difference then. The most important thing was for him to take care of the watch.

He returned to his workbench, interlaced his fingers and cracked his knuckles like a pianist before a performance, and then drew up the squeaky stool. Before he pressed the clasp to open the lid, he briefly rubbed his fingertips with his thumbs.

His eyes first went to the inner side of the lid. It was an inadvertent, almost automatic act: that was what he always did with the other pocket watch that he kept with him always. There was an engraved inscription there as well that for some reason seemed familiar to him. TO J. FROM Z. was on the gold-plated concave circle, and several long moments had to pass before the old man realized what it was. The shape of the letters, of course! The same large, ornate letters as . . . But how was it possible?

And then there was no more time for ordinary amazement; on top of the wreath woven of twelve elongated Roman numerals the two black hands had started their crazy dance.

II

They seemed to have a will of their own, moving by themselves—but in the wrong direction. They started to turn backward, as though measuring the past, first slowly, so he could follow them, then faster and faster. The watchmaker instinctively withdrew his hands from the activated watch, but his eyes stayed riveted to its face.

He stared at the big hand as it accelerated and then finally disappeared, transforming into an excited circle; it looked like some sort of film had been placed over the face. The spinning of the small hand was perceptible somewhat longer, and then it, too, melted into an indistinct veil.

This tremendous spinning made the watch tremble on the rubber surface. It suddenly occurred to the old man that he could stop the magic if he closed the cover, but he did not have the courage to touch it. Holding tightly to the edge of the workbench, he felt that the accelerating vibrations of the watch were being transferred to his body: he, too, was shaking as though he had a fever.

And then the trembling stopped, for the watch had detached from the tabletop and started to float slightly above it. Although it was illuminated by the strong lamplight, no shadow lay beneath it, just as though it were transparent. A high, shrill whistle started to sound, almost at the upper threshold of audibility; there was something unsettling in that sound, and the old man wanted to put his hands over his ears but was unable to do so.

As though bewitched, he simply stared at the floating object before him that continued to rise slowly until it reached the height of the old man's eyes. It rested there a few moments, hesitating as though thinking what to do, and then started to spin around its vertical axis. Just as with the hands on the face, the spinning became faster and faster until there soon formed the illusion of a small ball before the watchmaker's bewildered, slack-jawed face.

As though cut with countless facets, the ball first brightly reflected the light from the lamp on the workbench and then began to radiate its own light as the shrill noise became louder and louder. To the old man's relief, the unbearable sound soon rose above the frequency audible to human ears, leaving behind a muffled, almost palpable silence.

In just a few moments, the dull grayness turned into a reddish glow, then into yellow heat, and finally there was a rapid sequence of shades of white, rushing to the inevitable climax, the act of release. The old man greeted this orgasm of light with wide open eyes, unable to lower his eyelids; in any case, what could thin, wrinkled skin do against the uncontained fierceness of a summer sun less than a foot from his head?

Although he was completely blinded by the explosive flash, he did not feel any pain or even discomfort. The only thing he felt was the strange sensation of being in the middle of an endless emptiness, impenetrable and silent; he made his way through it effortlessly since there was no base or support to hold him back. His body seemed to have lost all weight and along with it all sense of direction: up might be down, or somewhere to the side—he was not able to distinguish anything.

Is this death? he wondered. If it is, then it is very mild, even pleasant. Like a dream. This was not how he had imagined it. Actually, he had not imagined it at all. Who imagines what death looks like, anyway? He had the vague feeling that he should be afraid for some reason, but instead of fear or at least discomfiture, he was filled with childish curiosity. Where was he? Would he remain incorporeal like this forever? Did time exist here? Why couldn't he see or hear anything?

As if in answer to this last question, sounds started to come from a great distance. He did not recognize them at first; they were too muffled. At first they resembled the scraping sound of gravel being rolled by waves on the shore and then the drumming of rain on the leaves in a forest on a wet spring evening. Then something in their rhythm seemed not only recognizable but familiar: the monotonous, regular repetition, harmonious only in the introductory chord and then completely dissonant. . . .

There were seven strokes from the moment he started instinctively to count the hour sounding in four disparate registers. How many had he missed until he understood what it was? Three—or maybe more? There was only one way to find out, although he did not understand why it was important to ascertain this fact. He reached for his vest pocket, forgetting completely that he had become incorporeal. But the pocket was there, real and tangible, as were his vest and hand—everything was there except the watch that Mary had given him, that day . . . The watch had gone!

How was that possible? Why, a little while ago . . . He looked at his vest in panic, only realizing when he saw it that his sight had returned. He was no longer blinded or surrounded by impenetrable emptiness. He stared at his body for a few moments, filled with disbelief, and then slowly raised his eyes and looked around himself.

He did not notice what was wrong right away. Everything seemed to be normal: things were in their proper places—the workbench which he was still grasping convulsively with one hand, the counter covered with green felt, the old-fashioned clothes tree in the corner with his winter coat hanging from it, two armchairs with reddish upholstery and the round coffee table between them with its thin, curved legs, the large grandfather clock with its pendulum, the mirror on the opposite wall with the black wrought iron frame. . . .

Only after he had taken all of it in did he realize where the problem lay: he should not be able to see it all. The only light in the shop was from the small lamp with the green shade in front of him, and the lamplight barely reached the counter. Now, however, he could see everything as clear as daylight. . . .

Day!

Daylight flooded through the large shop window with WATCHMAKER written in an arch of dark-blue letters. It was bright and clear, light that in this region was seen only in late spring and during the short summer, certainly not in mid-November. But it was not early winter outside; when a little girl skipped past the shop soon afterward, the watchmaker was perplexed to see that she was wearing a checkered dress with short, ruffled sleeves.

He got up from his workbench, finally lifting his numb hand from its edge, and took slow, hesitating steps from the counter toward the entrance. When he was in the middle of the shop, out of the corner of his eye he noticed something moving to his right and turned slowly in that direction, encountering his own reflection in the long mirror.

He squinted and stared at his image, refusing to believe what he saw. It was he, without a doubt, but different, changed—rejuvenated. The person returning his look from the glass was not an old man, stooped, his forehead full of wrinkles, gray-haired and balding. He was a young man, barely thirty, standing straight, with smooth skin and thick, dark hair.

He started to touch his face gingerly, afraid that even the lightest pressure might deform it into its former deteriorated grimace like a wax mask. His fingers slid over his mouth, chin, cheeks, striving to feel the trickery, but there was no deception: his youthfulness was real—as real as everything else around him seemed to be.

He continued to look at the long-forgotten person in the mirror, while the confusion in him slowly withdrew before the mounting excitement, when suddenly, like a bolt of lightning, he had a sensation that he had experienced only a few times before, but never as strongly. The feeling of déjà vu was all-encompassing, overwhelming: he had stood on this same spot before, looking at himself in the mirror, and the bright summer day had been exactly the same.

Something caught in his throat when he realized what had to happen next. He had no doubt that it would actually happen as he quickly turned around to face the entrance. The bells above it started to fly loudly in all directions that same instant. Only she entered like that: like a whirlwind of blond curls, with her long, rustling dress, her smile so enchanting in its radiant cheerfulness. . . .

Mary!

He knew that she would not turn to look at his wide open eyes, would not notice the paralysis that had come over him, that she would not hear the thunderous drumming of his heart that so filled his ears he felt as though the whole shop were echoing. He knew that she would rush to one of the armchairs and unload the armful of colorful boxes she was carrying.

Her words reverberated in his head a moment before she uttered them, like a reversed echo that precedes the original sound.

"It's so terribly hot. It's even worse downtown. And crowded. You have no idea. It's as if the whole town were outdoors. You should have come with me. You sit inside too much. It's not good for you. You could have closed the shop today. There are a lot of people here, too. You should see how many carriages there are in the square. Goodness, I'm all sweaty. And I'm terribly thirsty."

She started to rummage impatiently through her rather large handbag made of flowery waterproof fabric; it was always full and now seemed truly inflated. A full minute went by before she finally found what she was looking for. The small box was wrapped in shiny green paper, and the turquoise ribbon had curled ends.

He did not have to open it to find out what was inside. Nevertheless, he did it as inquisitively as he had earlier because he was impelled by the inexorable pressure of déjà vu. Once he had lifted the cover of the pocket watch and looked at the engraved inscription, he smiled broadly and said the sentence he knew went at that place.

"It's beautiful. Thank you."

He did not have the courage to be more eloquent in his thanks this time, even though he wanted to with all his heart. The object he held in his hand meant more to him than a present from his fiancée: it was an infinitely precious keepsake from which he had never parted in the many years which followed. Even so, the fear prevailed that if he used any other words he would cause an irreparable disturbance and would lose this feeling of déjà vu that was guiding him.

Mary returned his smile and then went up to him, raised herself on tiptoes, and kissed him. It was a light, brief touch of the lips, on the very edge of decorum, considering the time and place, but it made him tremble nonetheless. She suddenly turned toward the door, feeling awkward, to see if anyone was about to enter, and then began to pick up the boxes from the armchair. They were full of the beautiful things she had chosen to look stunning at the upcoming ceremony.

"I'm going to take all of this and get changed. I'm all sweaty and sticky. It's so hot. You should put on something lighter, too. You'll boil. Let's go have lunch at the Golden Jug. What do you say? It's the coolest there right now, in the garden under the linden trees. All this shopping has made me hungry."

She smiled at him again, a special mixture of affection and apology, and then rustled in her whirlwind manner toward the door—to meet the inevitable. The sequence of events stood before him, completely clear, illuminated by the powerful beacon of déjà vu: the wild music of the horse bells briefly muffling the thudding that was rapidly approaching; her hurried departure onto the pavement in front of the shop as the empty carriage jumped wildly on the cobblestones; incautiously crossing the street at the very moment the confused horses without a driver, left too long in the sun and frightened by who knew what, could no longer be stopped; the horrible shock at realizing that there was no way of escape; someone's scream from the other side of the street that seemed to last an eternity; and then the multicolored boxes flying in all directions, opening up and spilling their insides: an elegant lemon-colored dress with an abundance of lace, a yellow hat with a large brim and a wide ribbon tied in a bow, shoes with large, shiny buckles, a pile of silk undergarments that certainly should not have been displayed like this—the senseless nakedness of death.

"Mary!"

He had to overcome the violent river to utter this word, to scrape off the previous deposit on the palimpsest with his nails, to seize hammer and chisel to write a new inscription on the virgin surface of the granite. The magic of déjà vu shattered at that moment—there was no room for this call; his role had been to remain silent, to follow her out merely with his eyes. Stepping out of the play in which he was unwillingly acting, he was suddenly alone, exposed to the winds of time without a guide to light his way, but also without the ominous inexorability of the predetermined.

She stopped at the door and turned. "Yes, Joseph?"

He didn't know what to say. He certainly could not start explaining, particularly since he himself barely understood. So he simply went up to her and hugged her, together with her armful of boxes. It was a hard, awkward squeeze, calculated above all to keep her there, not to let her leave. He knew that this could arouse her suspicions, since such public displays of intimacy were not at all characteristic of him, but he chose the lesser of the two consequences.

"Oh, Joseph, dear, someone might come," she said in a voice whose reproach was only feigned. "Be patient a little longer. . . ."

Somewhere at the top of the street, from the direction of the square, dull thudding could be heard. It approached rapidly, mixing with the clatter of bouncing wheels. The sound was similar to thunder heard backward—from the dying out to the explosion. Mary tried to wriggle out and turn toward the window, but Joseph's embrace held her tightly.

"What was that?" she asked, turning her head to the side.

"Nothing . . . a carriage, probably . . . in a hurry. . . ."

If there was an end to his sentence, it was lost in the deafening stampede, in the strike of lightning. Just like the shadow of a low cloud, the unbridled team whizzed past the watchmaker's shop in a whirlwind of hooves, wheels, manes, empty driver's seat, foaming muzzles, spinning axles, terrified eyes, reins dragging on the ground, sweaty crupper—and afterwards the thunder resumed its natural course again.

"Someone could get run over," said Mary, after Joseph's squeeze finally relaxed. Now he was standing almost penitently next to her, not knowing what to do with his hands that had held her like a vise a moment before.

"Carriage drivers have become so inconsiderate, even arrogant. You should see them down in the town. They tear around like madmen. And how they whip those poor animals. It's terrible."

"No one will get run over, Mary. Not anymore."

She looked at him suspiciously, confused by the changed tone of his voice. He had said it too seriously, as though pronouncing some kind of oath. Even so, as he uttered them, he was aware that they were merely empty words of comfort similar to those said to calm a child the first time he asks about death.

Of course, someone would get run over. The inscription chiseled in granite could not be erased. On another fork of the tree of time he was now running into the street and bending in a convulsion of pain over the unmoving body, while tufts of yellow fluttered all around. He could pretend that this no longer concerned him, that he was now safe on this branch where Mary was standing next to him, the very incarnation of the vibrancy of life, sweaty, laughing, thirsty. But although he did not understand it much, the realization that both courses were equally real was painfully clear to him.

The clarity with which he remembered the anguish he felt as he lifted her off the bloody pavement, heavy with lifelessness, the hopeless insensibility into which he then plunged for a long time afterward, the slow succession of months and years filled with the deceptive oblivion brought by tedious work, and the lonely, nightmare-filled nights in which the past relentlessly visited him, until that far-off November evening when the bells suddenly rang above the dark door to announce the arrival of the mysterious visitor—that clarity, that hard certainty of memory was the price he had to pay for this unique privilege that he had been given for who knew what reason: to return to a past time and undo the effects of cruel chance.

He knew that this price did not give him the right to be dissatisfied. On the contrary, the shadow over his restored happiness was a very thin, transparent veil. Nevertheless, in the years that followed, only Mary's intoxicating, infectious cheerfulness managed to dispel the mask of melancholy that periodically and for no apparent reason covered Joseph's face.

4. The Artist

He unlocked the door and entered the room.

If it were not for the bars on the window, it would have looked just like an artist's studio. The half-open window with the thick drapes and pleated curtains rose almost to the ceiling, letting in an abundance of light during the day. Painted white, the bars were not too conspicuous, but they could not be overlooked. They were not there to prevent anyone from escaping, for this was not a prison, but rather to prevent the final retreat that the mind of the room's occupant might seek from its own darkness.

The room was sparsely furnished. To the right of the window, at a slant, stood a rather large easel spotted with dried streaks of paint and placed on a covering of newspapers, yellowed from long exposure to the sun. Next to the wooden easel was a tall, thin chair with a low back and rungs for feet. Part of the lower half of the wall nearby was covered with mounted shelves that held a disarray of art supplies: mostly squeezed-out tubes of paint, half-empty little bottles of paint thinner, brushes of different sizes, dirty palettes, a bunch of used charcoal sticks and pencils, soiled flannel rags, large sketch pads, a pile of rolled-up canvases, and several cans with bright labels and no lids.

The only light source turned on in the room was a reflector light on a short support attached to the middle of the ceiling. The narrow beam illuminated the canvas on the easel, reflecting brightly off the fresh layer of paint. The edges of the beam that reached the uncovered floor glistened off the polished parquet.

He headed toward the other side of the room and sat on the end of a narrow bed with a brass frame, next to the door that led to the small bathroom. In addition to the bed, there was only a little white table with drawers: on it was a lamp with a yellow canvas shade, a vase with large-petaled purple flowers, and an old book with a black cover, pink-edged pages, and a wide ribbon as a bookmark.

His eyes went to the wall facing the window. He could not see well in the semidarkness, but it made no difference. He knew what was there: three paintings in simple gray frames, unevenly arranged. Three scenes of darkness disrupted in the middle by a beam of light: the flickering glow of a torch in the corridor in front of a cell, cone-shaped lamplight illuminating a jumble of old things on an office desk, the green glow of the felt on a watchmaker's counter. And outside the beam, distinct from the surrounding shadows like a concentration of the night, was a spectral figure without a face.

"Good evening, Doctor." She said it softly, with her back turned, sitting on the tall chair. All she had on was a short-sleeved nightgown; her fragile shape could be discerned through its thin, semitransparent fabric. The scene was not stable because the light material trembled and fluttered under the gusts of warm breeze from the window. Her bare feet with their small toes were resting on one of the rungs. The brush in her left hand was making rapid, short strokes about the canvas.

"Good evening, Magdalena. The nurse tells me that you are painting again?"

"Yes."

"Isn't it a bit late for that? Wouldn't it be better for you to go to bed and then get down to work tomorrow morning?"

"I can't. I have to finish the painting as soon as possible."

"You were never in a hurry before."

"Now I have to."

"What for?"

"He was here."

The doctor closed his eyes a moment and drew his fingertips across his forehead. "He came to visit you again?"

"Yes."

"Did he tell you a new story?"

"Yes. The last."

"The last?"

"There will not be any more."

"Oh? Why?"

She did not answer right away. In the silence that descended, distant sounds of the summer night were suddenly audible: the soft rustle of leaves in the tops of the tall trees surrounding the sanatorium, the idle chatter of crickets in the grass, the sharp call of a bird.

"He's leaving."

"Is that why you are in a hurry?"

"Yes. I want him to see how I have painted him. He promised he would come one more time just for that."

"You are going to paint him? He finally showed himself to you?"

"Yes."

"But he has always remained hidden before. You never once saw him during an earlier visit. That is why he has no face in your paintings. Why the change now?"

"He will still remain hidden."

"How can that be if you paint him?"

Before she replied, she dipped her brush in the paint on her palette, mixing colors for several long moments.

"I'll paint him, yes," she said at last, returning the brush to the canvas. "I'll even tell you all about him, if you wish. But of course, you won't believe me."

"Why do you think that?"

"Because you think I'm crazy." She said it evenly, as though stating the obvious. "My madness conceals him. Better than any darkness."

"You know that we do not use such words here."

"I know. You have other, milder expressions. But that does not change the essence of the matter. There are still bars on my window, and you keep the door locked."

"The bars are there for your own good."

"So I don't lean out too far by accident and fall?"

"Accidents do happen."

She put her head close to the canvas for a moment, engrossed in painting some detail. "So, then, you could believe me."

"I could listen to you and then judge."

"That's fair." She moved back from the easel, taking a look at the detail. "Tell me, what do you think—who is he?"

"How would I know that?"

"But you certainly have some idea," she said, searching again for the proper color on her palette. "I have told you about our meetings. You know his stories."

"Someone very powerful, obviously, since he can do whatever he wants with time."

She found the right color, and her bared left arm started to move quickly before the canvas once again. "The devil?"

For several moments he silently watched her fluttering figure before the painting she was working on.

"He would be a very unusual devil," he said at last. "A devil who does good deeds without any recompense."

"Do you think he did the right thing?"

"Didn't he? Three unhappy people received a unique time gift, as far as I understood."

"And now they are less unhappy?"

"Why, I suppose. They should be. Particularly since they were not asked for anything in return."

"He, too, thought he would make them happy. At first."

"He doesn't think so anymore?"

"No. That is why he is leaving. He discovered that it is truly the work of the devil to fool around with time, even when you have the best of intentions."

"Where did he go wrong?"

She put her palette and brush under the easel, threw back her head, and tried to shake back her long hair. But the curly, auburn locks were too tangled from long lack of combing.

"Do you remember the story about the astronomer?" Without turning around she pointed her thumb to the right, to one of the three paintings on the wall. "If it hadn't been for his nighttime visit before the execution, Lazar would have happily gone to the stake, convinced of how correct, even exalted his sacrifice would be."

"But it was a mistake. Visiting the future showed him that his sacrifice had no meaning."

"Do you think that people should be freed from their mistakes? Even when it ends up destroying their happiness?"

"Happiness based on illusion, deception?"

"And what happiness isn't?"

He did not know how to reply at first. He felt like a chess player whose opponent has made what seems like a quiet move, but one riddled with hidden traps.

"What is the meaning of happiness if it entails the loss of a life?" he asked at last, in a muffled voice.

"And what is the meaning of life without happiness? That is the impossible choice Lazar was forced to make. With the best of intentions. Everything would have been much simpler if he had not seen the future."

"Your visitor did not tell the story to the end. He did not tell you what the astronomer chose."

"He didn't because it made no difference." She stopped a moment. "What would you have chosen if you were in his place?"

A somewhat stronger gust of air from the window raised the hem of the nightgown, revealing slender calves. It brought into the room the abundant smell of grass and certain traces of ozone—the first sign of the storm that was on the way.

"And what about the professor of paleolinguistics?" he asked, avoiding any reply. He raised his eyes inadvertently to the second painting on the shadowy wall. "She has no cause for regret because chance was thwarted; on the contrary, she went back to paradise."

The artist did not reply at once. She leaned toward the shelf behind the easel, started rummaging around in the tubes, selected one and squeezed out a bit of the contents onto her palette. Then she took the flannel rag and wiped off the tips of her fingers.

"To a paradise she was denied, actually. Eva was only an observer in paradise, without the chance to take part in it."

"I didn't have the impression that she felt it was unpleasant being . . . a ghost. Many of those studying the past would be ready to give half their lives, even more, just to be in her position."

She began applying more paint to the canvas. Now she was working on the middle of the painting. "She would have given it all up just for one sip of heavenly tea."

"Perhaps, but that was the price she had to pay. There was no other way to find out if everything she had written was accurate."

"But imagine if it turned out that she was wrong. That primeval language was quite different from what she thought. It would be a twofold defeat: she would have squandered her past life, and before her would be a paradise that she could not enter."

"It didn't have to be that way. She might have been proved right."

"Would that be enough comfort for unattainable paradise?"

"But if she didn't return to the past, she would have been left in doubt until the end of her life. That way at least she found out where she stood."

"Isn't it actually uncertainty that makes life possible?" Another quiet move full of hidden menace.

"Your visitor didn't tell you the end of that story, either," he said after a slight hesitation.

"For the same reason as before. It makes no difference what Eva hears when she gets to the fire. The best thing for her would be never to have left her basement office."

A blue flash suddenly appeared in the upper part of the window, but no thunder was heard. The storm was still some way off. Only the choir of crickets seemed to accelerate its chattering tune.

"The third story differs from the first two in this regard," he said, again turning to the paintings on the wall. "There is no uncertainty in the end."

"No, there isn't, but it still is not a happy ending, as it should be."

"It isn't?"

She turned her head toward the window and stared at the darkness.

"It's really sultry," she said. "I can hardly wait for the rain. It's hard to paint in this heat. I'm all sweaty."

He closed his eyes again and started to make little circles on his temples with his fingers. That was where he first felt the change in weather. The dull throbbing there that was slowly spreading to the back of his head indicated that he would spend the night wrestling with a headache.

"It isn't," she continued. "Perhaps it would be if he did not have the memory of the other stream of time in which Mary died."

"But, actually, that was not the memory of something real. It was more the recollection of a bad dream."

"It lasted too long to be just a dream. More than a quarter of a century. Why was it necessary to let Joseph suffer so long? If it was possible to help him, and someone was willing, he should have been put on the other branch of time right after the accident. Only then could it all have looked like a bad dream. This way the scars were too deep and real."

"Why wasn't that done? Did you ask your visitor?"

"Yes, of course."

"And? What did he reply?"

She drew the back of her hand across her forehead. "He said he could not have done otherwise because then the story would not be as good. If he had offered his time gift earlier, the hero certainly would have had a better time of it, but then the story would be weaker. The same holds for the other two."

"Strange. I had no idea that the devil cared so much for literary effect."

She stopped with her brush in midair, not finishing the stroke. "He's no devil, of course. If he were the devil, he wouldn't care at all about what happens to his heroes. And he is abandoning his time stories just so he doesn't transgress against them anymore."

"Well, who is he, then, if he isn't the devil?"

A dull roar finally broke the tranquility of the summer evening. The storm was about to break. As if by some inaudible command, the crickets suddenly fell silent.

"Wasn't it clear from the very beginning? The one who tells stories. The storyteller. The writer."

"The writer?" he repeated obtusely.

"The writer, yes. The writer who accepts responsibility without which his divine omnipotence becomes just unrestrained diabolic self-will."

"Responsibility toward whom? The heroes of his stories? But they don't exist, they are not real people. There is no reason to burden your conscience because of them."

The thin, pleated curtain on the tall window suddenly billowed out like a white sail. Leaves rustled sharply in the nearby treetops, and the edges of the old newspapers under the easel started to flutter restlessly.

"Do you think so?" she asked briefly, turning her face toward the fresh air entering from outside.

He pinched the bridge of his nose firmly with his thumb and forefinger. The pain from his temples had moved there, becoming more piercing, burning. This conversation had to be terminated. They had reached a dead end, and it was already quite late. They would continue the next day, when he was rested.

"So the writer is leaving us," he said, getting up slowly from the end of the bed. "There will be no more of his mysterious visits." He headed for the door, and then stopped, remembering something. "By the way, did he tell you how he managed to enter your room and then leave it, in spite of the bars on the window and the locked door? Did he perhaps transfer the omnipotence he has in his stories to reality?"

As soon as he said this, he thought that the question had not been formulated very skillfully. The fatigue and headache were clearly having an effect. She might think he was making fun of her, which would not be at all good for their relationship. It had taken him a long time to get her to leave the cocoon of silence in which she had enclosed herself, to start telling him about the pictures she painted.

"The storyteller cannot transfer his omnipotence to reality," she replied. There was no trace of rancor in her voice. On the contrary, it had a note of joy in it, probably from the excitement of the approaching storm. That often happened among the patients. It was as if they were permeated with the electricity that filled the air. The nurses would have their hands full tonight.

"Then how?"

Outside, it started to rain. The drops were still scattered, but their heavy drumming indicated that they were large, stormy.

"Don't you get it?" she asked. "There is only one other possibility."

He stared fixedly at her back, over which the thin nightgown was now wrinkling like ripples on the surface of the water. "I don't get it. What possibility?"

"This is not reality. This is also one of his stories."

He stood immobile in the middle of the room. He knew he should say something, that it was expected of him, but he could by no means find the proper words. He was confused not by what she said but by how she said it. That flat voice again, as though it were stating the obvious.

"I said you wouldn't believe me."

He snapped out of his paralysis. "It's not easy to believe. Would you believe it if you were in my place?"

"Oh, I would, certainly. It's not hard for me. I'm crazy, right? But you aren't. In addition, you are a man of doubt and not belief. You'll still be suspicious even after you see the proof."

"Proof?"

She laid the palette and brush under the easel again, wiped her hands on the spotted flannel rag, and reached for something in her lap. A moment later she turned to face him in the tall chair and raised her hand in the air. A yellow gleam danced in the bright reflector beam.

"Where did you get that?" he asked, squinting at the pocket watch.

"From the writer, of course. It is his gift. There is a dedication engraved on the back. Here, take a look."

She held out her hand with the watch, but he did not take it right away. He stared at the golden object on her palm, feeling the hairs bristle on the back of his neck. Everything is really full of static electricity, he thought. As if in reply, everything in the room suddenly flashed a blinding blue. He knew what would follow, but the violent explosion that resounded just a fraction of a second later still made him start.

She did not even blink, as though completely deaf.

"It's only thunder, don't be afraid," she said gently. "Go ahead and take the watch."

He did it hesitantly, timidly. It was heavier than he expected, convex on the top and flat on the bottom. His fingers felt the engraving on the back, and he turned it over in his hand. The inscription was tiny and curling, calligraphic. Two names above the middle of the circle. Hers, his.

"So that is the name of the writer," he said. It was something between a statement and a question.

She did not reply. The silence that reigned was disturbed only by the downpour from the low clouds. Periodic flashes of lightning illuminated the curtain of water just outside the bars. The rain was falling straight down, so the parquet before the window was completely dry. The air in the room was saturated with humidity and some new, pungent smells.

He started to turn the watch in his hand, looking for the latch that would open the lid.

"Are you sure you want to open it?" she asked quietly.

He found the latch but did not touch it. "Shouldn't I?"

"No, if you're not ready for a time gift."

"What kind of time gift could I receive?"

"One with the power to alter your entire life."

He smiled. "Is there something like that for me? There is no execution awaiting me at dawn, neither am I plagued by doubt in my old age as to whether everything I have done has been mistaken, and I don't have the least dark spot in my past that should be removed."

"Oh, it exists for everyone. Even someone crazy like me. It is the final time gift."

"Final?"

"That's right. Tell me, what is the only thing you know for certain about your future?"

He thought for a moment, looking at her suspiciously. "That I will die, if that is what you are thinking of."

"Yes. But you don't know when it will be, tomorrow or many years from now, right? And it is this very ignorance that allows you to suppress the awareness of your own mortality which would otherwise become an unbearable burden. Not knowing when you will die—that is life's main stronghold."

The third quiet move. He had the strange impression that an invisible net of checkmate was woven around him and there was no escape. "And if I raised the lid I would find out?"

"You would find out."

The jets of rain were suddenly slanted by the wind. They started to soak the curtains and drapes and made puddles on the floor under the window, reaching all the way to the newspaper under the easel.

He glanced in that direction and then turned toward her again.

"How do you know?"

"Because I opened the watch."

"And you found out when you will die?"

"Yes."

He shook his head slowly. "There's something amiss there. Didn't you say that your . . . writer . . . stopped giving time gifts after the bad experiences he had with them in the first three stories? That he had accepted the responsibility that goes along with omnipotence, that his conscience did not allow him to inflict harm on his protagonists? If this is his story, too, as you claim, then he has behaved very badly toward you: you have received the cruelest of all time gifts."

"I received it because I asked for it myself. He fought against giving it to me for a long time."

"But why did you ask for it? Didn't you just say there is no sense in finding out when you will die?"

"My case is special. If he had already imagined me

crazy, then I had the right to know how much longer I will have to be like that. It was the least he could do for me, although he did not find it easy."

"What about me?" he asked, rubbing his forehead with his fingers. "I can raise the lid, too. What would be his justification for me if I, too, am a character in his story?"

"You can, yes, but even so you won't do it."

"Why not? What's stopping me?"

"The writer's omnipotence, of course. He won't let you do it."

A smile spread over her face. His thumb started slowly toward the latch of the pocket watch, but the movement was not completed. The knock that suddenly resounded was short, sharp. The tall nurse did not wait to be given permission to enter. She stopped by the door and said quickly, "Ah, you're still here, Doctor. They need you urgently in room forty-three."

He stood there without moving, holding the watch in his open palm. A gust of wind filled the wet curtains again and lifted the newspaper all the way to the easel legs.

"Why, everything is open here," muttered the nurse, rushing toward the window. "Magdalena, you'll catch cold; put something around your shoulders."

Continuing to smile, the artist slowly took the watch from the doctor's hand.

"Hurry, they're waiting for you," she said gently. "We'll see each other tomorrow. There is plenty of time. The story ends here for you, but we will talk about it for some time to come."

II

The nocturnal storm had long since passed, leaving behind dense humidity full of the smell of decay that would float over the wet soil until the sun rose in a short while. Flattened blades of grass started to straighten up slowly, throwing off the remaining drops of water, but here and there occasional dripping from the leaves bent them to the ground again.

The wind had stopped altogether, so that the deep silence just before dawn was disturbed only by short birdcalls. They sounded inquisitive and fearful, like the calls of lost shipwreck victims on the high seas. The spectral echo of these cries remained in the motionless air long after the original sound had died out.

In the vague light of dawn that filled the large window, the white bars no longer stood out against the curtain of darkness. The milky morning light also dulled the sharpness of the reflector beam illuminating the canvas, making it milder, paler. The contours of the few objects in the room seemed to lose their solidity in this new light.

She was still sitting in the tall chair in front of the easel, staring at the canvas before her. She had put a terry cloth bathrobe the color of a ripe lemon over her nightgown, which made her look even smaller because it was too big: the hem reached almost to the floor, hiding the rungs and her bare feet, and the sleeves hid her hands completely. The cuffs were stained with paint and seemed to merge with the palette and the brush held by her invisible fingers.

The enormous face of the pocket watch covered the entire canvas, almost reaching the edge at four points. The corner sections outside this surface were mere dark voids that would certainly have been left out if the frame had been circular. Although the thickness of the large watch could have been neglected as well, since it was not part of the area encompassed by the circle, it was still indicated: a barely noticeable reflection of light from some unseen source conjured the gentle curve on the edge.

Compared to the surrounding dark tones, the bright

central whiteness almost burned the eyes with its cold glow, sharply emphasizing each detail on it. The twelve numerals were long and thin but not regular. They looked unstable, as though a restless flow of water were passing over them, making them bend and twist. The rippling was more distinct in some places, bending parts of the numbers into senseless shapes or pushing them all the way over the edge of the face.

The four hands were of the same length. The pointed ends reached the perimeter, widening toward the center just like narrow, elongated fern leaves, with a small slit in the middle. The leaves ended in thin stems that met in one point, as though sprouting from the same bud. The opposite hands formed two segments at right angles to each other. The vertical pair linked the numbers twelve and six, the horizontal nine and three.

A semitransparent body was resting on these crossed hands, following their shape. Its arms were stretched over the horizontal hands, tightly attached to them. On the palms of each white glove bloomed a large red stain although there were no nails. The fingers were clenched like claws but did not reach the red blossom.

Red spots spread also on the dark leather shoes, but they looked less conspicuous there. The pain inflicted by the unseen nails was manifested in the unnatural angle of the legs, whose pierced feet were trying in vain to lighten the load of a body without support.

The long cloak was covered at the bottom by a layer of dried mud, depicting clashing brown smudges on the black background. The edges of the cloak were worn and shabby, the hem unsewn in places. The lining was a fiery color and was torn in one place as though it had gotten caught on a thorn bush.

In front of the torso was a dark cane with the top downwards. It floated vertically without any support, casting a slight shadow over the surrounding whiteness. The ivory hourglass at its end was cracked in the middle. It seemed as though all the golden sand had poured out of this crack, leaving just an empty shell that could no longer measure anything.

The tall hat was covered by a film of fine dust, subduing the black silky shine. The shape of the derby was ruined by several uneven dents. The wide brim no longer concealed the face because the light came from below, yet it still could not be seen. The emptiness of virgin canvas gaped in the place where it should have been.

She knew she had to finish the painting, that the time of the last story was running out. The missing face was there before her eyes, perfectly clear in its repentant agony, but the fingers in the sleeve refused to lift the brush.

She had imagined the scene quite differently. She had wanted to paint him doing what he always did during his earlier visits. He would appear soundlessly at the bathroom door, but she would sense his arrival even though she was sitting at the easel with her back turned. He would take the hairbrush with the broad handle of lacquered walnut from the shelf under the mirror in the bathroom. It had stiff sharp bristles, which was what her tangled hair required.

He would brush her hair patiently and at length, just as long as it took to tell a story. When he reached the end, her hair would be loose and smooth, and the disorderly curls would be turned into a graceful row of waves. After the very first brushing, she no longer allowed anyone else to brush her hair and did not do it herself, either. She would wash it regularly but would leave it uncombed between stories. The nurses did not try too hard to dissuade her, seeing in her stubborn insistence just one of the caprices of their special patients.

It would be a nice painting, perhaps the prettiest of all four. But this still could not be a love story. Or not just that. It came at the end, after the others, linking them into a whole, so that it had to talk about redemption much more than about love. She had realized that necessity but could not understand why redemption had to be ultimately so painful. As she was painting, she herself had felt the torment of the rusty nails piercing the tender tissue of her hands and feet. She had somehow managed to endure the nailing while it was impersonal. Now, however, the crucified person had finally to receive a face.

When she started to make short, rapid strokes on the only unpainted part of the canvas, her eyes glazed over and her lips drew together with a slight tremble. But her hand was sure. From the seemingly unconnected lines, the oval emptiness started to take the shape of the writer's face, distorted by the primordial sin of his art.

And at that moment she understood why the pain was necessary. Without it, he would only be an indifferent god who justified the harm he did with good intentions. If he justified it at all. The suffering he chose brought him redemption by making him identical to those he had transgressed against. Without this sacrifice it would not be possible to accept the final responsibility that goes with writing.

When she had painted the last stroke, she slowly leaned her head backward, and her long, auburn hair spilled down her back. As before, it was a movement of ultimate intimacy, of surrender. She closed her eyes in anticipation. Somewhere outside echoed a protracted, joyous chirp, and the paleness of dawn was edged in pink.

The brush sank into the hair on the crown of her head. The curly locks were too tangled, so the combing out inflicted pain at first, although her radiance disavowed it. The walnut-handled brush made its way slowly, with short strokes, going back a bit whenever the tangle of wild waves offered greater resistance. The lower it got through the agitated sea, the harder and slower was the progress, and at the very bottom the curls were almost matted.

When her hair was finally untangled, the arc of the sun had already pierced the porous green of the treetops. The brush was raised again and this time sank smoothly into luxuriant waves. It made its way easily, straightening out the last rough spots, taming the most obstinate curls. Even though the ends were no longer matted, it stopped there a moment, unwilling to leave the locks that now seemed to have absorbed it. But this moment of hesitation quickly passed. When it slipped out, the curled ends rebounded as though on hidden springs.

She remained immobile, her head thrown back. The slanted morning rays pierced her closed eyelids. The shadow of the bars on the window threw a network over the yellow bathrobe. Many twinklings of eternity went by before she finally spoke. And even then the words were almost inaudible, more a movement of the lips than an utterance.

"Good-bye, Z."

Impossible Encounters

Contents

1. The Window
2. The Cone
3. The Bookshop
4. The Train
5. The Confessional
6. The Atelier

1. The Window

I DIED IN MY sleep.

There wasn't anything special about my death. I hardly even noticed it. I dreamed I was walking down a long hallway closely lined with doors on both sides. The end of the corridor was invisible in the distance, and I was alone. On the wall next to each door hung a framed portrait, slightly larger than life, and lit from above by a lamp.

I looked at the paintings as I passed by them. What else could I do? Only the portraits disturbed the endless monotony of the corridor. There seemed to be male and female portraits in approximately equal numbers, but randomly distributed. The people were mostly of advanced age, and some were very old indeed, but here and there was a younger face, or even a child, though these were quite rare. The images were formal studio-portraits, and the people were all elaborately, even ceremonially dressed. They looked conscious of their own importance, and that of the occasion. Most of them were smiling, but some faces were simply not suited to smiling. They looked grimly serious.

I was not overly surprised when I finally saw my own portrait next to one of the doors. I hadn't actually expected it, but it didn't seem out of place. After all, if so many others had their portraits hanging there, why shouldn't I? Where else can one hope for a privileged position if not in one's own dream? The only thing that momentarily confused me was that I could not remember when the portrait had been painted. I must have posed for it, I supposed. But maybe that hadn't been necessary. It's hard to say. I don't pretend to understand much about portrait-painting.

Regardless of its origin, I liked the portrait. It did me full justice—more, it showed me in exceptionally good form. Although I was depicted at my current age, the painter had skillfully diminished some of the more unpleasant aspects of aging: he had slightly smoothed the wrinkles on my forehead and around my eyes, tightened my double chin, removed the yellowness and blotches from my cheeks, darkened some of the gray streaks in my hair. This was not to make me look younger. The years were still on the painting, but I bore them with greater elan. And most important of all, there was no sign of the debilitating disease that had taken such a heavy toll on my looks. No effort on the part of a photographer could ever have produced the same effect, however great his skill.

I stood in front of my portrait for a long time, gazing in satisfaction. But all things have their measure, even vanity. I couldn't stand there forever. Someone might pass by sooner or later and find me in this unbecoming position, which would certainly be embarrassing. But where could I go? Continue down the corridor? That did not seem promising; it appeared to extend endlessly before me, with no destination to make for.

Should I go back? That possibility hadn't crossed my mind before. I turned around and immediately understood I could not count on going back. Just a few steps behind me the hallway disappeared, turning into deep darkness, as though all the lamps above the paintings had turned off as soon as I passed them. Maybe the lights would go on again if I headed in that direction, but I had no desire to find out.

I turned to face forward again—and suffered a new

surprise. The same thing had happened to the corridor in front of me. It had turned into a dark tunnel that began at the edge of the small, conical beam of light illuminating my portrait from above. This sole remaining source of light covered the painting, the door beside it and myself in front of it—a tiny island of existence bounded by an opaque, black sea of nothingness.

I had lost the right to choose; there was only one path before me. The moment I touched the doorknob, I was overcome by the feeling that something important was about to happen, but I had no immediate inkling what it could be. It was only after I opened the door and entered the room that I realized I had died. It happened in the middle of raising and lowering my foot as I crossed the threshold. I was still alive when I started the step outside, and already dead when I finished it inside. I barely felt the transition itself. Something streamed through me, a wave resembling a light trembling or momentary shiver. It lasted a split second, then passed, leaving behind no other trace than the certainty of death.

I was not afraid. Fear of death has meaning before one dies, and not afterward. The only thing I felt was confusion. I naturally knew nothing about this state. How could I, after all? I had not even tried to picture it in my mind. That had always seemed a pointless exercise to me, and as the disease got the upper hand, such thoughts had come to fill me with revulsion—to be avoided as much as possible.

First of all, I wondered if I was still asleep. It is said that the deceased rest in eternal peace, but that is probably a metaphor, not meant be taken literally. In any case, the sight before me did not resemble in the least any that I had seen in my dreams. There was nothing unreal or strange. On the contrary. The room I entered was some sort of study, elegantly furnished to be sure, but otherwise not the least bit unusual. There was no one inside. Feeling a bit uncomfortable, I started to inspect it, without stepping away from the door, which I had closed behind me.

To my right stood a large, black, wooden desk. A lamp with an arching neck and green shade illuminated numerous objects, arranged in orderly fashion upon it: a wide, leather-bound desk-pad; a decorative brass inkwell with a heavy maple-wood blotter; a rosewood cube, drilled with holes to make a pen and pencil holder; a shallow lacquer paper tray; an ivory-handled magnifying glass; a double silver candlestick (without any candles); three identical little boxes covered in dark velour whose purpose I could not make out; a white flowerpot containing a flowerless plant with long, thin leaves; an engraved pipe stand with three pipes of different shapes.

Across from the desk, on the left-hand side, were two large brown leather armchairs with a small round coffee table between them. On the table was a lamp with a tasseled yellow shade, a book and an oval tray containing a lidded jug of water and two glasses placed upside down on round paper coasters. Behind the armchairs rose a bookshelf that covered the entire wall. The books in it were of uniform height and thickness, and their spines were bound in a limited range of somber tones. A vertical ladder rose along the edge of the bookshelf, its ends firmly anchored to guide-rails on the floor and ceiling.

The middle of the wall facing the door was covered by a large painting in a simple rectangular frame, positioned longside up, and brightly illuminated from below. It depicted an area of clear blue sky seen through a double window. The deep blue was portrayed so convincingly that for a moment I even took it for a real window.

The window was closed, but there was a certain tension in the otherwise tranquil scene that indicated it might open at any moment—through a draft, perhaps, or by someone going up to open it, someone who was still not visible, but whose presence was hinted at by a shadow that flickered just inside the frame. The only thing that disturbed the harmony of the straight lines and uniform shades was a colorful butterfly that had already tired of its efforts to fly outside, clearly unable to understand the existence of a completely invisible, but still impenetrable obstacle such as glass.

To the right of the picture, in the semidarkness, stood a grandfather clock in a tall mahogany case. The glass door was decorated with geometric designs in the corners, and a disproportionately small key protruded from the keyhole. At first I thought I saw only one hand pointing straight up, but when I took a better look I discerned the small hand hidden under the big one. I stared at them for some time, but when they failed to change position I lowered my eyes suspiciously; only then did I notice that the pendulum was resting in the middle, motionless.

To the left of the painting, hard by the bookshelf, was another door. It was the same color as the wall around it and could only be distinguished by its edges, which appeared somewhat darker. It had an unusual characteristic that I did not notice at first glance. There was a lock, but no doorknob. If the door could be opened, then it was only possible from the other side.

Just as I was looking at it, that happened, quite soundlessly. Part of the wall seemed simply to arch forward, and a figure appeared in the emptiness left behind. I stared at it fixedly. Had I not been dead, I am sure that my heart would have jumped, and pins and needles would have run up and down my spine.

The man who appeared in front of me seemed unassuming, almost like a clerk: in late middle age, not very tall, balding, with a thick, narrow mustache that covered only the line under his nose, small, round, wire-rimmed glasses, and a dark suit of classic cut that did not quite succeed in hiding his extra pounds. The smile that appeared on his round, ruddy face seemed guileless and unaffected.

He hastened brightly to greet me, his hand stretched out. I had no recourse but to accept it.

"Welcome! Welcome!"

I didn't know what to say in return, so I smiled too, although mine was somewhat forced. We stood there like that for some time, gripping each other's hands, eyeing each other curiously, like friends meeting after a long separation.

He was the first to break the silence. "Please, make yourself comfortable." He indicated one of the armchairs in front of the bookshelf, waited for me to sit down, and then sat down in the other, hitching up his trouser legs a bit. He was still smiling.

"I was expecting you earlier. You stayed a bit longer than planned."

His voice seemed to contain a touch of reproach, but that might have been my imagination. He looked at me in silence for several moments, perhaps expecting me to say something. As I remained silent, he waved his hand at last, dismissively.

"Well, it's all the same. Some are late, some are early. There are very few who arrive on time. They all come, however, sooner or later. How do you feel?"

I cleared my throat before answering uncertainly. "Fine, I think."

He nodded his head in satisfaction. "Nothing is bothering you, there is no discomfort?"

I paused briefly. "No, everything's all right."

The man's smile broadened. "I'm glad to hear that. You're just a bit confused, yes?"

"Yes," I admitted after a moment's hesitation, "a little."

"You mustn't reproach yourself for that. You're no exception in this regard. They're all confused when they arrive. It's quite normal. Would you like a glass of water?" He indicated the jug on the table between us.

"No, thank you," I replied. I had the ghostly impression that my throat was dry, but somehow it didn't seem appropriate to drink water in this new position. Maybe later, when I was used to it.

"People are really quite full of questions," continued the man. "They are dying of curiosity. I'm sure that you are, too."

There was no reason to pretend. "I hope that's normal, too."

"Of course, of course. You are certainly interested in where you have arrived, what awaits you here, and who I am, as well."

"Certainly," I agreed in a faltering voice.

"There is a little difficulty in this connection. I, naturally, can answer all these questions. And many others that you might like to ask. But if I do that, I will deprive you of the possibility of going back."

"Going back?"

"Yes. You can return. To life."

I stared fixedly at the stranger in the other armchair. His tiny eyes returned my glance good-naturedly through his round glasses.

"But I'm dead," I said finally, in a half-questioning voice.

"Yes, that's clear. Otherwise you wouldn't be here."

"Well, then, how . . ."

"I can't explain it to you. Unless you decide to stay."

Now my throat felt not only dry, but tight. I tried to swallow, without success. As I poured water from the jug into one of the glasses, my hand trembled a bit. I hoped this clumsiness had not been too conspicuous. The water was cold, but it tasted a little stale.

"Do you mean to say I'm the one who decides—whether I go back or stay?"

"You, of course. Who else?"

"I mean, it doesn't depend on my behavior in . . . my previous life? I might be someone really bad, for example."

The man gave a short laugh. "Yes, you might. But it

makes no difference. There is no punishment or reward here. This is not the Last Judgment."

"So, it's enough for me to decide to go back. Do I understand that correctly?"

"You understand correctly. You can even choose the shape in which you will return."

I put the glass back on the coaster. Small puddles of water that had spilled from the jug sparkled in the yellow light on the silver surface of the tray. Several drops had even fallen on the book nearby. Had it not been for that, I probably would not have paid attention to the illustration on the front cover. It was a reproduction of the painting of the window on the wall next to us, and above it was the title written in slender, yellow letters—*Impossible Encounters.* I was not familiar with the author's name.

"I wouldn't change my shape," I said. "I'm used to this one."

The smile disappeared from the man's lips. "I'm afraid that's the only thing that's impossible. Your old shape has been used up, it is no longer serviceable. You can't go back to it. And it would not be wise. Disease has completely destroyed you, isn't that so? But you can choose something completely new. The choice is almost unlimited."

"Be someone else?"

"You would not be someone else, because you would have no memory of your earlier life. It would be a new beginning for you."

"I would be born again?"

"Most assuredly. You would return to the world as a newborn child, as is fitting. To live a new life. With the characteristics that you want."

"You mean, I can choose what I'll look like, or how tall I'll be?"

"And much more than that. You could change the color of your skin, your sex . . ."

"Sex?"

The look of amazement that appeared on my face caused the stranger to smile once again. "That is one of the most frequent changes. In both directions. I think it's not so much dissatisfaction with one's original sex as much as curiosity about trying the opposite sex."

I shook my head. "Well, I'm not curious."

"I understand. Would you perhaps be interested in going back as something other than a human being? That is also possible."

I squinted my eyes in disbelief. "What do you mean?"

"There are other forms of life on earth besides humans. There are countless numbers, in fact. They are all at your disposal."

"What, for example?"

"Oh, anything. Of course, it all depends on the inclinations of the one going back. People usually choose an animal."

I paused slightly before answering. "Why would someone want to be an animal, and not a human, in his new life?"

"Well, it doesn't have to be at all as bad as you might think. The life of a pure-bred cat or thoroughbred horse, for example, could be much more comfortable and carefree than many human lives. And if you prefer excitement, there are few human experiences that can compare to what a lion, an eagle or a shark experiences every day."

I thought it over briefly. "I still don't think I want to be an animal."

"Whatever you want. There are other possibilities as well. You could be a plant."

"A plant?"

"Yes, that is not such a rare choice."

"But plants don't have any . . . any consciousness."

"That's true, but this drawback is compensated by

other advantages. A long life, for example. Almost every type of tree lives considerably longer than a man. Sequoias are highly valued in this regard. They are protected, which makes them additionally attractive. But even short-lived flowers have their admirers. People sometimes decide to go back as an orchid or a rose-blossom, even though they know they will only live one short season."

"But that's absurd. Getting the chance for a new life and wasting it on some flower . . ."

"They don't look at it like that. Beauty means everything to them. That is something we must accept. But there are some decisions that are truly hard to understand. Even for me. What would you say to going back as a salamander, a worm, as a sagebrush, a stinging-nettle or a spider?"

"A spider?" I repeated. My face twisted into a disgusted grimace.

"Yes, quite unpleasant, wouldn't you say?"

"I would not change at all," I rushed to say, shaking my head. "I would like to stay as similar as I could to myself in my previous life. If that's possible."

"Of course it is. The great majority choose just that. So this means you have decided to go back?"

I did not answer at once. A multitude of confusing questions swarmed inside me. Finally, one outweighed all the others. "If I returned, I would live out another lifetime, right?"

"Yes."

"And in the end I would die again?"

"That is inevitable, unfortunately."

"After that would I . . . come back here again?"

"No, you only come here once. After your second life all that remains is death. You are given no further choice."

He said this in an even voice, as though it were quite banal. I looked at him for a few moments without speaking.

"But what is this choice all about, anyway? On one side there is a new life. I understand that. But what's on the other side? What am I supposed to choose between?"

The stranger removed his glasses, took a large white handkerchief from the inside pocket of his jacket and started to wipe them. He did so patiently and with extreme care, and in the end lifted them against the table lamp to check them. Without them his face seemed somehow bare. He put them back on slowly, pressing them onto the bridge of his nose.

"They rarely get around to that question," he said at last. "Almost all of them immediately grab the chance to return. They're not interested in anything else."

"What do you say to the others?"

"Nothing specific. The most I can do is give them a hint. Anything more than that would endanger their return, if they decided to go back after all."

"A hint?"

"Yes," replied the man. "Please come with me."

He got up, waited for me to do the same, and then took me cordially by the arm and led me. At first I thought we were heading for the door through which he had entered, but we stopped in front of the large picture in the middle of the wall.

His voice dropped almost to a whisper. "Look at it carefully."

My eyes were filled with the sight of the blue heavens seen through the closed window. The moments passed by slowly. Nothing happened. When the change finally occurred, it first affected my sense of hearing and not my sight. Suddenly, as though from a great distance, I started to hear an even, steady drumming. I didn't recognize it at first. It was only when it grew louder in the surrounding silence that I realized it was the dull ticking of the clock. I did not need to turn my eyes towards the large mahogany case in the right-hand corner to know that the pendulum was no longer motionless.

As though in answer to this awakening sound, the picture came to life. The butterfly fluttered once, sluggishly, without hope of finally breaking out, and slid down a bit lower. The shadow moved because the hand outside the frame moved. The hand entered the frame and made for the middle of the window. It tried to beat its own shadow, but they reached the handle at the same time and turned it.

The moment the window opened, I was almost stunned by a rush of dizziness. The man's firm clasp on my arm was a welcome support without which I would have lost my balance and fallen. But the butterfly had no one to help it. The gust of wind easily whisked it off the smooth glass surface and sent it rushing into the blue infinity.

That very instant everything disappeared: the picture frame, the wall, the stranger, the entire study. I was in the middle of nothing and started to fall. I knew that I had to move my wings, that I was supposed to fly and not descend headlong, but I suddenly no longer knew how. Many flashes of an eternity filled with icy horror passed before I once again mastered this simple, instinctive skill. First my descent slowed down, then stopped, and when I finally started to climb on an ascending stream of air, I didn't have to move my wings at all. I just kept them spread out like two enormous, colorful twin sails in the middle of the vast open sea of air that surrounded me.

Fear turned into the rapture that always accompanies flying. I could have stayed there forever, surrendering to this tide of joy. Then, at an unspecified distance ahead of me, I caught sight of something wrinkled on the uniform fabric of blue. Something had started to thin the air, to dissolve it, something that appeared from underneath. It was bright, radiant, inviting. I flapped my wings energetically, wrenching myself away from the main airstream. The call that drew me, the radiance coming from the other side of the firmament, was irresistible: the flame of a candle attracting a moth in the dark.

But I was not allowed to reach the light. The airstream suddenly changed direction. I tried to resist it feverishly, realizing in despair that I was being borne away from where I longed to go. The strength of my wings, however, was nothing compared to that powerful pull. I rushed backwards faster and faster, filled with a painful feeling of futility and helplessness. The window slammed shut after me when I flew back in, and the same moment I was swallowed up in darkness.

The darkness was not completely empty; it was filled with the beating of a colossal heart. It was a regular, uniform sound, but somehow I knew it would soon stop. That happened all at once, without any premonitory slowing. Dropping to the lowest point, the pendulum did not continue on the other side; it stopped there, having nothing else to measure. In the silence it left behind, my sight slowly returned.

I was still standing in front of the picture, staring at it, although there was no longer anything moving in it. The butterfly was drooping in one of the corners again, and the shadow was patiently waiting for the unseen hand to move. Another hand slightly increased its pressure around my arm.

"This way. You'll feel more comfortable if you sit down again."

I wanted to tell him that everything was all right with me, but I staggered at the very first step and was grateful for the support he offered. When we were settled in the armchairs, he poured some more water from the jug into my glass. I wasn't thirsty, but I still took a long drink.

The man did not speak right away, just watched me with his customary grin. He was clearly giving me the chance to collect my wits. And I was grateful for that, too.

"An exceptional painting, wouldn't you agree?" he said at last.

"Yes," I agreed after a brief hesitation, a little hoarsely. "Exceptional."

We stopped talking once again. Just then a thought crossed my mind, one completely inappropriate to the decisive moment at hand. The other glass was still turned upside-down on the tray, unused. I wondered if it was there incidentally, just like the multitude of other objects in the room, or if the stranger sometimes drank a little water from it.

"So? Have you chosen?" There was no impatience in his voice, and I felt under no pressure. He could have asked me something quite trivial in the same tone.

"A butterfly," I replied softly. "I would like to be a butterfly, of course."

He looked at me wordlessly for several moments, and then gave a brief nod. "Of course." His smile grew broader. He motioned towards the door next to the painting. "After you."

I got up, a little unsteadily, and headed in that direction, but after a few steps I stopped, confused. The door had no handle on this side. How could I open it? I thought about turning around to ask the man. But that very instant I realized there was no need, for there was no longer any door in front of me.

2. The Cone

I DIDN'T COME OUT of the clouds until I was almost at the top of the Cone.

Although it was the middle of summer, Dark Mountain seemed buried in autumn. Down in the valley this was just an ordinary overcast day, probably muggy and humid, but here at an elevation of almost two thousand meters everything was clothed in a grayness that was less transparent than mist and somehow denser and more palpable. The sky literally touched the ground right here. The clouds were filled with minute drops, embryos of rain, that seemed to be moving in all directions, not just downward. If the temperature were to drop by just a few degrees, they would turn into crystals of snow. This actually happened now and then, though they always quickly reverted. During the summer on Dark Mountain you could go through all four seasons in one day.

In such weather it was not advisable to take long walks since you could easily lose your way. If they went out at all, people stayed close to the hotel, keeping to the asphalt paths where the lighting was on, even though it was just past noon. But I was not afraid of getting lost. I'd been coming to Dark Mountain for years, both summer and winter, and not a day would go by without a visit to the Cone. I was certain that I could find my way there even on a moonless night, though I'd never tried.

The Cone was a projection on the western slope,

about two and a half kilometers from the hotel. The view from its peak was almost as fascinating as the one from the topmost craggy crest of Dark Mountain, accessible only to fully equipped mountain climbers. Owing to the Cone's almost perfect shape, from which it derived its name, it seemed to be artificially planted there. As you approached, it didn't give the impression of being steep, but it was. The climb to the top thus required not only agility but considerable effort as well, even though the distance to be covered was less than one hundred and fifty meters.

These difficulties discouraged most of the hotel guests from visiting the Cone. On fine days they would walk to its foot, but only a rare few would decide to undertake the climb. In any case, the small, windy plateau at the top only had room for three or four people at most. When the weather was bad, like today's, I could count on having the Cone all to myself.

I came out of the cloud all of a sudden. I wasn't far from the top when it started to lighten. The grayness around me didn't thin or become more transparent, it just changed shade, turning a bright white. And then I suddenly rose above the foggy mass, squinting at the blinding radiance of the sun.

I stopped, still in cloud from the waist down, and waited for my eyes to adjust. Above me stretched the immeasurable, bright blue firmament, and as far as I could see below me was a motionless sea, its uniformity disturbed here and there by the islands of mountain peaks similar to the one I had just reached, forming a scattered archipelago in the sky. This panorama was worth all the trouble of the climb.

"Strange to find yourself above the clouds, isn't it?"

I started at the unexpected voice. I'd been so certain that I would be the only one at the top of the Cone that I hadn't even turned to look around, fixing my eyes on the horizon instead. The man was sitting on a rocky outcrop, his back turned to where I stood. It must have been the sound of my steps that told him I had joined him on the plateau. He was wearing a dark green jacket that blended in with the color of the surrounding grass and low bushes. His hair was gray and longish, partially covering his ears.

"It isn't usually crowded above the clouds," I replied, making little effort to hide my displeasure. I wasn't pleased at having to share the Cone with someone just then. I sat down on a patch of grass behind the stranger, feeling beforehand to see if it was wet. Among the thick tangle I found an empty can of soda pop carelessly left there. I picked it up and threw it into the depths below. I was aware that this was just as careless, but it seemed somehow more fitting for garbage to be found anywhere but here.

"No, it isn't. I liked it best when I could be alone here, too." He said this without any reproach in his voice, which made me feel awkward. In fact, he could consider me the intruder since he had reached the top of the Cone first. "But I won't bother you for long. I'll be leaving soon."

"You don't have to go because of me," I said obligingly. "There's room for both of us."

The man did not reply, so we fell silent, gazing into the distance. The warmth I started to feel wasn't just from the strenuous climb. It was considerably warmer here in the sun than down in the clouds. I did not unbutton my jacket, however, even though I could feel the sweat breaking out; the wind that never seemed to die down here at the top might blow through me.

"I haven't been on the Cone for a long time," said the man pensively, as though addressing someone invisible in front of him, rather than myself. "The last time I climbed up here I was your age."

I stared at his back in amazement. How could he

know my age when he hadn't turned around to look at me? Probably by my voice. I hadn't seen his face, either, but even without the gray hair I could easily tell by his hoarse, wheezing voice that he was well into his sixties.

"You've missed quite a bit," I said with a smile.

"I know. I'm trying to make up for it now. I'm visiting places that meant something to me in the past."

"Did you stay at Dark Mountain very often?"

"Yes, at least twice a year. I never did learn to ski, although I loved to take long walks."

"Me, too. I'm not the least bit bothered by not being able to ski. Walking is just as pleasant, and you need a lot less equipment."

The gray head nodded in front of me. "At first I went for walks in different directions. But after I discovered the Cone, I gave up all the other places. I started coming here every day, almost like a ritual. Over time it became a real obsession. The only thing that could stop me was a snowstorm."

Strange, I thought. It's as if the old man was describing my own experience. I never imagined I'd ever find such a kindred spirit. Most people think I'm an oddball because of my pilgrimages to the Cone. There was, however, one important difference.

"But it seems you got over your obsession. If I understood correctly, you stopped visiting the Cone. What prevented you from coming?"

The man did not reply at once. When he finally spoke again, his voice became softer, so that I had trouble making it out against the howling of the wind.

"I experienced something unusual here. Afterwards there was no sense in coming here any more."

I expected him to continue, but as the old man didn't elaborate, I had to curb my curiosity. For some reason he clearly did not want to talk about it, and good manners would not let me probe. We passed another few minutes in silence. I could feel the skin on my face start to prickle under the strong mountain sun. I should have brought some sun screen, although I hadn't actually expected the top of the Cone to be above the clouds.

"I like to return to places that mean something to me, too," I said at length, just to keep the conversation going. Although he had said he would be leaving soon, the old man continued to sit there, and it seemed silly not to talk while we shared this cramped space. "But it's never like it was the first time. The place might be the same, but the time is always different. That can't be helped, I'm afraid."

"Except if you return to some place at the original time," he said, his voice still low.

"In the past?" I asked with an inadvertent cry of disbelief.

The old man raised the collar of his jacket a little to protect himself from the strong wind that had just come up. Although quite blistering, the sun was deceptive. It would be easy to catch cold.

"Yes, in the past."

"Then it really would be just like the first time. Except it isn't possible. You can't go back into the past."

"Even so, if you were offered the chance to go back, which time in your life would you choose?"

My eyes began to skim over the endless landscape that surrounded me. Far to the east the sun had finally triumphed over the clouds and now wooded hills could be seen though the mist. By late afternoon it would clear up here, too, and Dark Mountain would return to summertime.

"I've never thought about that," I said. "I don't know, maybe some point in my childhood. I would probably like to see myself as a boy." I stopped for a moment, staring blankly at the gray shroud beneath me. "That would certainly be strange—to meet your own self."

The old man turned his head a bit towards me,

enough so that I could see his thick gray beard and sunglasses, but then he faced forward again.

"Why your childhood? Do you feel you were happier then than later in life?"

"It's hard to say," I replied after a brief hesitation. "Perhaps more innocent. There were happy moments later on, of course, but they lacked that early innocence. It seems to be more and more precious as time goes by. But what about you? Which time in your life would you go back to?"

The man shrugged his shoulders. "At my age childhood is already far away and faded. I think I would choose something closer, something I remember better. I was very happy when I came here to the Cone. Perhaps even innocent, in the sense in which you talk about your childhood, although it didn't seem like that at the time. In any case, I left innocence behind me forever on the Cone. I would be happy to meet myself again from that time."

I wiped the sweat off my brow with the back of my hand. "I bet the other one would be just as happy. Maybe even more so. It would be a very useful encounter for him. You could tell him first hand what awaits him in the future, what he should stay away from, what he should avoid."

"Oh, no, not at all," replied the man quickly, raising his voice a little. "I wouldn't tell him that at all."

"You wouldn't tell your own self what the future holds in store?"

"No."

"Why?"

"Because I would ruin my own life if I did. The encounter itself would be extremely risky. It would be best if he didn't realize who he'd met."

"I don't understand."

"If I told him what the future holds, I would be depriving him of the foundations that make life possible.

Everything would become preordained for him, inevitable. He would lose not only hope but fear. And how can you live without hope or fear?"

"But what if, for example, there was some great misfortune or suffering awaiting him, that could easily be avoided if he was forewarned? Would you allow that to happen?"

"Of course."

"Wouldn't that be cruelty towards your own self?"

"Perhaps. But there is actually no choice. You cannot prevent what has already happened, can you?"

I didn't know what to reply. I had the vague feeling that there was some sort of paradox involved, but I couldn't put my finger on it. No doubt it all hung from the unfeasibility of the initial assumption about returning to the past.

The old man stood up and so did I. He was approximately my height, perhaps a bit stooped owing to the weight of his years. He picked up something he had been sitting on, and as he brushed off the bits of grass I realized it was a book. Before he put it in his pocket, I managed to read the large title—*Impossible Encounters*—but not the name of the writer.

He stayed a few moments more, staring at the sea of clouds that had now gently started to stir and thin out. Then he turned towards me and we were face to face for the first time.

I couldn't really see much of his face. It was hidden by his beard and the large sunglasses. Only his forehead was uncovered—it was even higher than mine because the gray strands had receded quite a bit towards the crown of his head.

"It's time to leave," he said. It might have been my imagination, but his voice seemed to tremble slightly, just like mine on the rare occasions when I am excited. He extended his hand and I took it in mine—a slim, bony hand, just like mine will probably be when

I reach his age. "The Cone is all yours. Enjoy it while you can. One never knows what the future will bring."

"I'm glad we met," I said, more softly than I intended.

"I'm glad, too. Very glad."

He let go of my hand with some hesitation, almost unwillingly. Then he turned and headed down the steep slope, without looking back. He walked slowly, carefully. Like an old man. When he disappeared into the cloud, I felt a sudden lump in my throat.

I stayed on the Cone for a long time that day. Almost until dusk. By the middle of the afternoon everything below me had cleared up. I slowly absorbed the endless, luminous panorama surrounding me. I wanted to remember it well. I intended, of course, to come again next day, but the old man was right: I did not know what lay in store for me. What if something prevented me from coming? What if a long time, several decades, passed before I happened to climb the Cone again?

3. The Bookshop

The fog, as usual, set in swiftly.

Only a few minutes had passed since the last time I'd raised my eyes from the computer screen and looked out of the bookshop's large display window. In the early twilight I had been able to see buildings on the other side of the river quite clearly, speckled with the first evening lights. Now everything had suddenly disappeared in the thick greyness; not only the opposite bank but also the long row of horse chestnut trees extending along the quay on this side of the river, just a few steps away. Although this transformation had taken place almost every evening since the middle of autumn, it never ceased to fascinate me. One moment the world was there, real, visible, tangible; then, in what seemed like the twinkling of an eye it would magically dissolve in the humid breath of the river spirits.

I could have closed the bookshop and gone home. For days no one had entered the shop after the fog rose. In autumn the river reversed its genial summer personality. When the weather was warm, the promenade under the horse chestnut trees was thronged till late in the evening. Then I would often stay open until midnight and sometimes even later, until the last customer had finally finished leafing through what I hoped would shortly be his book. The customer has always come first in this bookshop. But now I remained in the shop not only because the shop hours posted on the door obliged me to. I did not have a computer at home, and it seemed somehow inappropriate for me to write science fiction in the old-fashioned way, pen to paper.

But tonight I was not to be allowed to return my attention to the screen. My eyes were still gazing, unfocused, at the wall of mist on the other side of the window, when a figure took shape in front of the entrance, seeming to materialize out of nowhere. Its sudden appearance, unannounced by any footsteps on the pavement—unless, lost in thought, I had simply not heard them—made me start. Fog is apt to produce such eerie surprises, and I disliked it almost as much for that as for taking away my customers.

The man who came in was small and slight, with a short, sparse beard and wire-rimmed glasses. Although he appeared youthful, his grizzled sideburns and the silver streaks in his beard, particularly on his double chin, strongly suggested that he had passed the half-century mark. I have a good memory for faces, so one glance was enough to tell me that I had never seen him here before.

It must have been rather cold outside, for no sooner had the visitor entered the heated air of the bookshop than moisture condensed on his glasses, fogging them up completely. He stood by the door without moving, seeming to stare fixedly at me through large, empty eyes of unearthly blankness.

I pressed two keys at the same time, saving the text. This was not really necessary, as I had made no changes since the previous save, but that is what I always do, automatically, whenever there is about to be a break in work.

"Good evening," I said. "The fog is really thick tonight."

The man took off his glasses. He rummaged for a while through his long, green coat until he found a crumpled white handkerchief in an inside pocket and started to wipe his glasses. His movements were brisk and impatient, and left patches of condensation by the edges of the frame when he put them back on.

"This is a science fiction bookshop." It was somewhere between a question and a statement. There was something strange about the way he drew out his vowels, as if he were a foreigner who had learned the language well, but still hadn't quite mastered the proper accent.

"That's right," I replied with a smile, "*Polaris.* At your service. If it weren't for this terrible fog you wouldn't have to ask. There's a large neon sign above the entrance, but what good is it now? I paid a ton of money for it, but they forgot to tell me that it's completely useless in the fog. It would probably be better to turn it off. Drives customers away more than it attracts them. Even when you're right under it, it just looks like a bright, shiny rebus."

Still standing by the door, the visitor began to look around the shop. He slowly skimmed the shelves full of books and magazines, appearing somewhat bewildered, as though he had entered some amazing place, and not an ordinary bookshop at all. That is to say, maybe not exactly ordinary, since science fiction bookshops are a bit unusual, but they don't generally induce such bewilderment.

"I'm looking for a . . . work of science fiction," said the man, after his eyes had finally reached the counter with the cash register and computer, next to the display window, where I was sitting. His voice sounded hesitant, as though he had trouble choosing his words.

"Then you've come to the right address," I replied cordially. "We offer a wide selection of science fiction—new editions and secondhand. We really pride ourselves on them. We've got some truly old books. Real rarities you won't find anywhere else. And should we happen to be temporarily out of what you want, we can get it very quickly. In two or three days at most."

The visitor finally moved away from the door and headed towards the counter. He stopped uncertainly when he got close to me, as though not knowing what to do with himself. I got a sudden whiff of a fresh, outdoorsy smell. It immediately brought to mind newly mown grass. The man must use a deodorant based on plant extracts.

"The work I'm looking for is in this bookshop," he said. His tone had lost its previous uncertainty and become self-confident. Even more than that: he said it in a voice that would brook no objection. "And it's not old at all. Quite the contrary, it's just been written."

"In that case," I replied, "it must be here." I got up from my chair and headed towards the shelf where I kept the latest editions. "Here you are."

Seven narrow rows contained some fifty books that had been published in the last several months. Science fiction was on the upswing again. This time last year those shelves had held barely fifteen volumes. I reached towards the middle shelf and pulled out a rather small book with a shiny cover.

"This is our most recent acquisition—*Impossible Encounters*. Might this be what you are looking for?"

The customer briefly examined the book in my hand, then shook his head. "No, that's not it."

"I suggest you have a look at the other books. These are all recent editions."

I left the visitor in front of the shelf and returned to the counter. People don't like you to hover round while they leaf through a book. It gives them an unpleasant feeling of being under surveillance.

My eyes dropped to the screen, with its tangle of words. The story I was writing was practically finished. All that was left was to read it once again and polish it up here and there. I would have had no trouble doing so in the solitude I'd expected until I closed the shop. Now that solitude had been interrupted, but I hoped the man would quickly find what he was looking for so that I could resume my concentration on the text. I could not, of course, work while he was there. Not knowing what else to do while I waited, I pushed the 'save' keys once more.

My fingers were still on the keyboard when the visitor came up to me again. At first I thought he'd found the book he wanted, but when I raised my eyes I saw that his hands were empty.

"It's not there," he said.

"You've already looked at everything?" I asked, unable to conceal a note of disbelief.

"Yes, there are only forty-eight books," he replied in an even tone. If he'd noticed the surprise in my voice, he did nothing to show it.

I gazed briefly at the man in front of me, and then at the shelf with new editions. "Why, yes," I said at last, "only forty-eight."

"Where else could I look?" he asked rather quickly.

"If it's a really new book, then that's the only place it could be. I don't keep them anywhere else. The other shelves contain older editions. Which book are you looking for? If you tell me the title, I can help you find it."

"Title?" The visitor squinted in dismay through his glasses, which were now dry. "I don't know the title."

"It doesn't matter," I hastened to assure him. This was by no means a rare occurrence. I encountered variously incomplete requests almost every day. "The writer's name will be enough. That will make it easy for us to find the book."

The man took his handkerchief out of his pocket once again and wiped the top of his forehead. He was clearly dressed too warmly for indoor temperatures, and beads of sweat had started to break out. I was assailed by another outdoor smell. Instead of mown grass it was some wildflower this time, but I couldn't determine which.

"I don't know the author's name." A look of unease crossed his face.

I sighed inwardly. Any chance of finishing work on my story that evening was receding. This was likely to take some time.

"Why don't you make yourself more comfortable," I suggested. "It's rather warm in here, and it may take us a while to find this work, with its unknown title and unknown author. You can leave your coat on the hook by the door."

The visitor shook his head briskly. "No, no. I can't take off my coat. I don't have much time. It's an urgent matter. I have to find the work as soon as possible. I can't go back without it. You don't understand. . . ."

He said this very quickly, in one breath, and then suddenly stopped, as though for some reason he couldn't or didn't want to continue. A pleading look came into his eyes.

"I do understand," I replied after a short pause. "You want to find a specific work of science fiction and you are in a hurry. I certainly want to help you, but you have made only very scanty data available to me. All that I know is that it is some new work and that you didn't find it on the shelf over there. If you could tell me something more about it, I might recognize it. I read a lot, almost everything that comes out. Particularly new things. Could you at least give me some idea of what the work is about?"

A smile played on the man's lips. "That I can do, yes. Certainly. It is about my world."

We stood there several moments looking at each other without speaking. I was smiling too.

"Your world?" I repeated, breaking the silence first.

"Yes, but you on Earth know nothing about it. Or rather, nothing was known until recently. Until the work I am searching for was written. Our star doesn't even have a name here, just a number, although it is relatively close, less than eleven and a half light years away. But it's a small star, much less conspicuous than those around it, so there's nothing strange in it being anonymous."

I slowly nodded my head to indicate understanding, as if he were telling me something quite commonplace. So that was it. One more of those. Yet he hadn't the look of one. Quite the contrary. But appearances can be deceptive, as had been proved often enough. Clothes alone do not the eccentric make.

All kinds of oddballs visit my bookshop. They seem to be irresistibly drawn to it, and they constitute an ineluctable hazard of my chosen genre. I am most often visited by those who have had first-hand experience with extraterrestrials, and for some reason feel this is the right place to bare their souls. At first I entered into discussions with them, explaining that I class science fiction as imaginative prose. Their real-life experiences had no place in this category, for the very reason that they were real. As a rule, however, this distinction was too fine for them.

Then, in my naiveté and inexperience I tried to talk them out of it. Why go to the inconvenience and expense of shooting across from the other side of the cosmos, only to subject some commonplace citizen in an isolated house to unusual lights or sounds? That was when I got into serious trouble. Not only did they turn a deaf ear to the reasons I cited, they resolutely interpreted my unwillingness to believe them as reliable confirmation that I, too, was part of the great conspiracy to hush up visits by extraterrestrials. That was the milder version. Several flying saucer fans accused me openly and rather peevishly of being an extraterrestrial myself.

There is no complete defense against such accusations. Indeed, how can anyone prove he is not an extraterrestrial to someone who can see antennae sprouting from his forehead? What arguments can ever shake the believer's blind conviction? But to me the primary difficulty stemmed from my profession. As the owner of a bookshop I could hardly draw distinctions among my customers based on their view of the world, so my hands were tied. Should I meet this type of person in some other context, I could solve the problem simply by raising my voice. A slightly sharper tone has a truly amazing effect on them. They fall silent at once and withdraw, often in embarrassment. But here, that would be out of the question. How would it look if a bookshop-owner yelled at those customers who just happened to take a somewhat unusual view of his ancestry?

And so I resorted to the last means still at my disposal. Whenever an eccentric like this one drops in, I listen to his story with utmost patience, regardless of how far-fetched it is, taking great care to speak as little as possible. My most frequent reaction is to nod or shake my head from time to time, as befits the situation, to demonstrate that I am carefully following the story. This technique has often proved useful. First of all, the whole affair is concluded far more quickly than if one were to start a discussion; second, after baring his soul almost every single visitor of this kind ends up buying a book.

Over time this proved adequate compensation for approximately a quarter hour of my attention. I could almost have made this part of my price list: "The purchase of a book gives the buyer the right to squander fifteen minutes of the owner's time in any way he sees fit". At first my conscience bothered me a bit, feeling this partook of prostitution; then my business sense over-rode such improvident moral purism.

Furthermore, over time I came to see myself as a psychiatrist—a rather poorly paid psychiatrist, it's true, but at least there was never a shortage of patients. Quite the contrary. There were so many of them I could no longer rely on memory alone, and had had to buy a notebook in which to write down what each one of them bought, so they would not accidentally buy the same book twice. This, to be sure, didn't bother them in the least, since most of the books were never read—occasionally I even found them discarded next to a nearby trashcan—but for me this was a matter of professional attitude towards my work. Every customer deserves the best possible treatment, and the handicapped get a bonus to boot.

But never before had I encountered a case like this. This was the first time that an extraterrestrial had visited my bookshop! Perhaps I should have been jealous. Up till that moment the role had been reserved for myself. Granted, the situation hadn't changed essentially. It was just a matter of nuances. My basic strategy remained the same: don't question anything and encourage the speaker to tell his story without holding back.

"Eleven and a half light years," I said. "Why, that's really not so small. You had to travel quite a distance! It must have taken you a long time."

The man shook his head. "No time at all. It's hard even to call it travelling."

"I see. Did you spend the flight in hibernation, then? Is that why it seemed so short?"

"No, hibernation wasn't necessary."

"Oh. Then that means you must have a very fast spaceship. Judging by how quickly you got here, it must travel considerably faster than the speed of light."

He looked at me the way a teacher looks at a student who has blurted out an absurdity. "No spaceship can travel faster than the speed of light."

"Of course it can't," I said, hastening to correct myself. "How silly of me. I forgot that for a minute. Then how did you get here so fast? Excuse me for not being able to figure it out for myself—space travel is not one of my strong points."

"In the only way possible. Using the fifth force."

It's not easy to carry on a conversation like this. One must keep a straight face, and there is great temptation to poke fun. It's even harder to suppress the laughter that is ready to bubble to the surface. But through long experience I have become very skilled in self-control.

"The fifth force?" I repeated, expressing the mild surprise I felt appropriate.

"That's what we call it. You know about it, too, but haven't yet recognized it as a force, so you use another name. Actually, it has several names. One of them, for example, is imagination."

This time I didn't have to feign surprise. "Imagination?"

"Yes. Imagination, fantasy, daydreams, whatever you like. The ability to conceive of something that does not seem to exist." He indicated the shelves around us with a broad, sweeping gesture. "All these are the fruit of imagination, aren't they?"

I could only confirm that they were.

"And you are convinced that they are pure fantasy. You feel that there's no way the worlds of science fiction could ever be real. Isn't that right?"

"Well . . . yes. . . ." I mumbled, finding myself in a spot. "I mean, for the most part. . . . Although sometimes, of course, there might be certain coincidences. . . . It's not out of the question. . . . But very rarely. . . ."

"Tell me," he said, putting a stop to my stammering, "how does a work of science fiction originate?"

I didn't reply at once. The conversation had taken a completely unexpected turn. Who would have thought that we'd wind up discussing the problem of literary creation? I have discussed many unusual subjects with the eccentrics who visit me, but never this.

"Well, I don't know exactly. My experience in this regard is quite limited. I have only written a few stories.

I suppose the writer cogitates, and then an idea flashes in his mind and . . ."

"An idea flashes, yes! Do you know what actually happens at that moment—when, as you say, an 'idea flashes', seemingly out of nowhere?"

Of course I didn't know, so I shrugged my shoulders.

"The fifth force is activated!"

The pause that followed was deliberate, a dramatic effect calculated to ensure that the revelation would make the strongest possible impression on me. To demonstrate enlightenment, I nodded sagely.

"Unlike the four fundamental forces that exist on the level of the very simple, the fifth force appears solely on the level of the very complex. It can take effect throughout the cosmos, but in only a single class of locale: in centers of awareness of sufficiently developed species. In your species this center is obviously the brain." The visitor tapped his head with his middle finger.

"Obviously," I readily agreed, tapping my head in fellowship.

"The fifth force is unrestricted by space or time: it acts instantly, by completely cancelling the distance between you, the emitter, and whatever point elsewhere in the cosmos towards which you have directed it. For instance, by activating the fifth force, you are able to see another world as clearly as if you were actually in it."

"I see." The most important thing in such conversations is to give the impression that you accept what you are being told easily and without skepticism. The more outlandish the matter, the more easily you should appear to go along with it.

"That is the idea that flashes. If you don't really know what's going on, that the fifth force has been activated, it will seem that you have made it all up, that nothing is real. But actually, nothing has been invented. The world that suddenly appears in your consciousness is no less real than your own, regardless of how unusual it may appear."

"Very interesting," I commented.

"All these books here are considered fanciful prose, while in my world they would be regarded as commonplace documents of unimpeachable authenticity. Your misconception will be rectified once you have mastered the fifth force, instead of using it in the wild, uncontrolled manner you have until now."

"If I've understood properly, then this would no longer be a bookshop but some sort of . . . archive?"

"Yes, a place where data about other worlds are collected, stored and made available. That is my field of work. I use the fifth force to investigate other worlds and catalogue them. That is how I came across the Earth."

"And so you decided to visit us?"

He shook his head abruptly. "No, no, you don't understand. It wasn't that simple. The fifth force does not transport matter to distant places. Only information. Whoever uses it does not move from his own world."

"But you've come here to Earth, right?"

"That happened because of the interference."

"Interference?"

"Yes. When two fifth force beams overlap."

"Aha, so that's it."

The visitor did not continue right away. He took out his handkerchief again and wiped his face. Several streaks of sweat were now streaming down his forehead, winding their way downwards to lose themselves in his beard. The vegetable smell emanating from him had become more powerful in the course of our conversation, almost intoxicating.

"When I directed my beam towards Earth, something highly unexpected happened. Another beam was heading outwards from here in the opposite direction at the same time. Someone had just flashed an idea about my world. A writer of science fiction, obviously, using the fifth force quite unskillfully, because if he knew the slightest thing about it he would never have let it happen. He would have known how dangerous it is when two beams interfere with each other."

"Dangerous?" I replied, properly aghast.

"Quite so. Two beams that interfere create a gap in the space-time continuum. If this gap is not quickly closed, it will start to suck in everything around it. First of all its two end points, Earth and my world in this case, then the planetary systems to which they belong, and then neighboring star systems. There is actually no end to its voracity. It's as though a black hole has opened up, eleven and a half light years long!"

I could only express appropriate horror. "Why, that's terrible! Horrible! Is there anything that can save us, or are we doomed to annihilation?"

"Yes, there is, if I am able to cancel the interference. It's still not too late for that. But time is running out."

"Then you must not hesitate," I said in haste. "How do you cancel the interference? What needs to be done?"

"I have to find the work about my world. Then go back with it and join it to my documentation about Earth. When these two fifth-force products are joined together, the interference will disappear and the gap will close."

"But how will you go back? Please don't reproach me, but I still don't understand how you got here." This was not exactly in the spirit of my strategy. I usually avoid unnecessary questions, if for no other reason than because they are quite likely to be answered, which needlessly prolongs the conversation. But I felt I owed it to this eccentric somehow. He had taken pains to invent an admirable story, not some tedious inanity like most of the others. Many science fiction writers would envy him for this.

"Through the gap, of course. It can be used as a shortcut until it slips out of control. The crossing is instantaneous. I traversed all those light years in just one move, ending up in front of your bookshop. It was like stepping through to the other side of a kind of mirror, which was a new and very unusual experience even for me. I never thought I would ever go through a fifth-force interference zone. It may not look that way to you, but I am really no adventurer. Although I spend most of my time investigating other worlds, this is the first time I have physically left my own. Actually, I think I am more of what you would call a bookworm."

A rather uncomfortable smile appeared on the man's lips, as though in apology. I returned his smile, feeling suddenly sympathetic towards him. In other circumstances, this could have been an interesting exchange of ideas between two fellow writers, even somewhat kindred souls. I really liked his story. Even the bit about the shortcut wasn't bad. Not exactly original, but convincing nonetheless. As far as I could see, there was only one weak spot in the whole thing. I could have ignored it, but the hairsplitting critic in me prevailed in the end.

"I had no idea," I said, "that there were humans on other worlds, too. Yet so you must be—at least, to judge by your appearance."

"Of course there aren't."

"Well, then, how . . . ?" I asked, indicating his body with my hand.

"Transformation," he replied succinctly, as though this explained everything.

"Ah, of course. I should have thought of it. Under the influence of the fifth force, indubitably."

"That's right. It makes it possible, while it is in interference, if you know how to manage it properly. But only for a short period. That is another reason why I am in a hurry. I won't be able to stay in this shape much longer. And I don't feel very happy in it. It's very uncomfortable and clumsy. I don't envy you this body one bit. It's extremely unsuited for movement, in particular."

"Surely there must have been some reason why you couldn't appear here in your own body?"

"Of course. I would die within moments. This is an extremely poisonous atmosphere for me, and the pressure is very high. Rarely have I come across such a dangerous environment, and I am acquainted with a very large number of worlds. But even if the conditions on Earth were perfect, I would still have to take human form. Because of you."

"Because of me?"

A smile played on the visitor's lips again. "Yes, because of you. How do you think you would have reacted if I had appeared in your bookshop in my natural form? Would you be conversing so casually with a ball?"

"A ball?" I repeated. A bell rang softly somewhere in the back of my mind.

"Yes, a ball, perfectly round and soft. What shape is more suitable than a ball in a world completely devoid of uneven spots and obstacles, and covered with dense vegetation? It's almost as if the entire planet were enveloped in a gigantic plant carpet. There is nothing lovelier than rolling on it."

I tried to swallow the lump in my throat, but my throat had suddenly tightened. I could feel my pulse start to pound dully in my ears.

"And what a captivating smell it has! That's what is actually the worst thing about Earth. I could somehow become accustomed to all the rest, but never this foul odor." He sniffed the heated air of the bookshop with disgust. "If you ever had the chance to smell the fragrances of my world, you would never be able to stand it here again."

I feverishly started to think. This wasn't really happening. It could not be happening! There must be some simple explanation. But none that crossed my mind made any sense.

"Smells," the visitor continued inexorably, "that emanate from the diversity of grasses that do not exist on any other of the multitude of worlds I have encountered to date. Lomus, rochum, mirrana, hoon, ameya, oolg, vorona . . ."

". . . pigeya, gorola, olam," I continued with a voice deadened almost to a whisper.

The visitor's face lit up. "So that means you recognize the work!" he cried.

I recognized it, of course. It was truly a new story. So new that it had not yet been published, and thus could not possibly be found on the shelf over there with the recently published works. It was a story that no one but its author should or could know about at this moment. A story that resided, saved several times too many, in the virtual space of my computer.

I nodded briefly, wordlessly.

"Please give it to me. Quickly! If I don't hurry it might be too late."

As I slipped a diskette into the computer with automatic movements and pressed the keys to copy it, questions teemed furiously in my head. But I knew I would not ask any of them. Not only because there was no time left for him to reply, but also because I was not really prepared for the answers.

The visitor took the diskette that I handed him, examined it carefully as though his eyes could see into its contents, then glanced at me and smiled again. He didn't say a word. I tried to smile, too, but it looked more like a grimace.

He turned around and headed hurriedly for the door. A moment later he was swallowed up by the thick wall of fog.

I stood there for a long time, motionless, staring at the impenetrable greyness that had engulfed him. And then my fingers hit the keyboard again. The tangle of letters disappeared from the screen in an instant, leaving behind a yellow void. The story that I had almost finished faded into nothingness. It left no trace behind it, just as the visitor had left no trace behind him. I could pretend to myself that I had never even written it, and that, as on so many other evenings, no one had entered the bookshop once the wispy spirits had made their sluggish ascent from the riverbed.

But I was deprived of this privilege to delude myself. The story had, in fact, been removed—just one erasure had destroyed all earlier saves—but the visitor had left a trace behind him after all. It was very faint, yet undeniable. I noticed it the first time I breathed in deeply through my nose. A tangle of delicate vegetable smells of unknown origin hovered faintly all around me. It might be impalpable to other people, but as long as I could smell it I knew I must restrain myself from writing science fiction.

4. The Train

Mr Pohotny, senior vice president of a bank prominent in the capital city, met God on a train. In a First Class compartment, of course. Mr. Pohotny did not take the train very often, but whenever he did he travelled First Class; it not only reflected and reinforced his social position, it also minimized the probability that he would find himself in unsuitable company. Having a mistrustful and suspicious nature, to which his profession was attuned, he took pains to avoid the company of strangers whenever possible. Indeed, before setting forth this time he had even—guided by some premonition, perhaps—briefly considered reserving all of the compartment's six seats, to ensure that no one would bother him; but his banker's common sense had triumphed over that notion. It would represent too heavy an outlay to obtain something that, with a little luck, he might get quite free.

Luck was with Mr. Pohotny for almost three quarters of the trip. Then, at a small station where fast trains did not normally stop, God climbed into the First Class car and headed straight for Mr. Pohotny's compartment. The senior vice president did not immediately recognize God, of course. Although he couldn't explain exactly why, he thought at first that the gentleman who opened the door to his compartment was a retired army officer, most likely a colonel. He was a short man with greying, though still abundant hair; a trim mustache; slightly florid cheeks. He was wearing a suit of classic cut that cleverly disguised his somewhat excessive girth.

God entered, and favored Mr. Pohotny with a cordial smile and a brief nod. He took his train ticket out of his left jacket pocket, examined it, sat in the seat next to the window across from Mr. Pohotny, and crossed his legs. Then he looked his fellow traveller over without a word, smiling all the while.

In other circumstances his bearing and demeanor would have greatly annoyed Mr. Pohotny. He would have regarded the man as impolite, even impudent, for it is most unseemly to stare at a complete stranger, and even more to smile broadly while so doing. When he had toyed with the idea of buying up the whole compartment, it was just this sort of unpleasantness he had had in mind. Antisocial behavior was all too common, even in First Class.

Yet for some reason this stranger's staring failed to irritate him—quite the reverse, one might say. He took it as a completely acceptable invitation to talk, thereby shortening the dreary trip. What harm could derive from two polished gentlemen of similar age striking up a conversation, given that Fate had thrown them briefly together? Were they to remain silent until they reached their destination, simply because they had not been formally introduced? Certainly not! One should not be a slave to rigid social conventions.

Mr Pohotny deliberately laid down the book he had been reading on the seat next to him—a leather-bound edition of *Impossible Encounters*—and returned his fellow traveller's smile. "I hope you don't mind the open window," he said.

"Not at all," God replied, "it's very sultry."

"It's often quite sultry during the summer," the senior vice president remarked. Having delivered this truism, he realized that it was hardly a gem of perspicacity. He felt awkward; he was inexperienced in small talk. "If you wish, we can raise it a little," he added obligingly.

"No, no," God said, "there's no need, it's quite all right as it is."

"It's better to travel in other seasons," Mr. Pohotny continued after a moment's reflection. "Then it's never sultry, and you don't have to open the window."

"Yes," God agreed, "if you are able to choose, it's better to avoid traveling in the heat."

"Although sometimes in winter they overheat the cars, and then the window has to be opened for a short time, to cool the compartment a bit."

"It's really much nicer when it isn't too hot."

"The worst time, actually, is during the spring and fall. Then it's hardest for the passengers to reach an agreement. Someone always wants to keep the window open a bit for the sake of fresh air, particularly during long trips, while others are bothered by the draft."

God sighed. "It's not easy to satisfy people."

There was nothing to add to or subtract from that conclusion, but it nonetheless put the senior vice president in a predicament. He wanted to continue the conversation, but they seemed to have exhausted the topic of opening the window. Nor did a single further conversational gambit spring to mind. Truly, what are the interests of retired colonels? He had never spent any time in their company, so he had no insight into their tastes. They must be interested in military matters. What else? Unfortunately, Mr. Pohotny lacked the slightest understanding of the arts of war.

God continued to stare at him, with his fixed little smile. The senior vice president had already started to fidget, when he suddenly saw a way out of this predicament. Of course! Now was the right time to make each other's acquaintance. That would certainly help to unburden their mutual reserve.

He bowed, perhaps somewhat more deeply than was

customary. "Let me introduce myself," he said, extending his hand towards the figure opposite. "Pohotny, banker, senior vice president."

God shook the extended hand, bowed in response, and replied succinctly, without the blemish of superfluous additions: "God."

If anything surprised the senior vice president, even briefly, it was the fact that he wasn't the least surprised to learn the identity of his travelling companion. All at once it seemed not only obvious but even quite natural that the heavy-set, grey-haired gentleman in the dark suit across from him should be God. Of course, who else? Where had he got the nonsensical idea that he was some sort of retired colonel? Quite inappropriate!

Despite the surprising composure with which he received this information, Mr. Pohotny remained somewhat embarrassed. He had even less to say to God than to a retired colonel. It was immediately clear, however, that small talk would be quite out of place; besides, he had already displayed his lack of skill at it. He also felt that banking was not the proper subject, either, however expert his approach. No, he had to find something more suitable.

"Am I dead?" he asked, a little taken aback, finally letting go of God's hand.

"Dead? No, why do you think you're dead?"

"Well, I thought people only met you after death. At least, that's what they say."

"They say all kinds of things. You shouldn't believe everything you hear. To begin with, I meet everyone once while they're alive."

"I didn't know that."

"Of course you didn't. No one knows anything about it."

The senior vice president nodded slowly. Then he took a handkerchief out of his pocket and wiped his forehead, keeping the handkerchief in his hand once he had finished. "There must be a reason for these meetings, I suppose?"

"Yes, there is."

"Does it have to do with what people do, how they behave? Whether they're honest or not?"

"No," God replied. "Such considerations have no bearing upon it."

Mr Pohotny tried to hide his sigh of relief, but was only partially successful. "Then might I know your reasons for meeting people?"

"Of course. To answer their questions."

"What questions?"

"Any they may have. They can ask anything."

"Anything?"

"Yes. You can ask me whatever you want. Absolutely no holds barred."

The senior vice president thought for a moment. "And what is expected in return?"

"Nothing."

"Nothing at all?"

"Nothing at all. I'm not the devil. Take this as, let's say, rectifying an injustice. As God, I am supposed to be just, am I not? People are deprived of many things, so this is my chance to make up for it a little. At absolutely no cost to you."

"So, that's it," Mr. Pohotny said. "Very generous of you. I admit, I haven't been excessively devout, so to speak, but in the future, rest assured, I . . ."

"Don't act rashly. Wait and see whether you like what you hear. It's not always the case, and piety has a tendency to evaporate. So, what would you like to ask me?"

The senior vice president stopped twisting the damp handkerchief in his hand. "This is all so sudden. If only I had time to think it over a little, to prepare for it! It's not easy to be called upon to ask God something like this, out of a clear blue sky."

"Surely, there must be something you would like to find out, something that intrigues you, even obsesses you? Don't hesitate for a moment! I will answer any question you ask."

"It's hard to decide. There are things that clearly interest me, but . . ."

"I must draw your attention to the fact that we don't have much time. Your station isn't very far away, and I will get off the train before you. I advise you to use this meeting to your very best advantage. There won't be another."

"Well, all right, here goes. As you see, I am on my way to evaluate the reliability of a company that has asked our bank for a loan. A huge loan, almost one-third of our capital. I carry a great responsibility. If I recommend approval of the loan and it falls through, it would be a serious blow for the bank, perhaps disastrous. In any case, it would be the end of my career. On the other hand, if I turn down the loan and the job succeeds with the help of some other bank, I will completely lose my reputation. It would therefore be of invaluable assistance to know how to act."

The smile disappeared from God's face. "Are you sure you want to ask that?"

"Yes," the senior vice president replied without hesitation. "It is a very serious matter. I have never had to make such an important decision before. My whole career is at stake, and quite possibly the future of the bank too."

"All right. As you wish. You might have asked me a more general, ultimate, even transcendent question, but if you're not interested in that . . ."

"Of course I am!" Mr. Pohotny objected, interrupting God. "I think about such things occasionally, indeed I do, but, you see, at this moment . . ."

"I see, I see," God broke him off, "you don't have to explain anything. Here is the answer to your question.

Your evaluation will be that you should approve the loan, and you will not be mistaken."

This time the senior vice president did not attempt to suppress his sigh of relief. He was even briefly tempted to cross himself, but it seemed somehow improper. "Thank you so much. I shall certainly become very devout, you can count on that."

"Perhaps, but not for long. Just a year and a half."

"What do you mean? Nothing will be able to divert me from my faith! I assure you that I shall remain devout to the end of my life."

"That's what I'm talking about. You have a year and a half of life."

Mr Pohotny squinted at his travelling companion. "But that's not possible," he said finally in a hushed voice. "I mean, I'm completely healthy, I go to the doctor regularly for a checkup, I lead an orderly life. . . ."

"People die of other things than illness. You, for instance, will commit suicide. You will shoot yourself. A single, large-caliber bullet into your right temple."

The senior vice president raised his handkerchief to his mouth and wiped the corners with trembling movements. "Why would I do that?"

"Because you will make a mistake that will lead to your bank's ruin. In the wake of your forthcoming triumph you will become over-confident, and in circumstances similar to these you will make the wrong decision. Suicide will be your only honorable way out."

Not knowing how to respond to this, Mr. Pohotny continued to stare dully at the figure on the seat across from him, his pulse beating in his ears. But then a thought flashed through his febrile mind, and he grabbed at it.

"But that can be avoided! You have warned me of the danger. What if I don't make any decision? What if I withdraw completely from the bank?"

"You won't be able to rely on my warning, I'm afraid," God replied. "Remember I told you that no one knows of my meetings with humans during their lives. Why do you think that is?"

The senior vice president shrugged. "Because it's a secret?"

"No. That wouldn't work. Someone would have discovered it by now. That's human nature. I had to provide something more reliable. No one remembers meeting me. You will also forget it completely as soon as I leave the train."

"Then, if you don't mind, what is the purpose of meeting with people? You offer them answers that they cannot remember?"

"That was the most that could be done. The choice was between leaving human beings in permanent ignorance, and giving them knowledge that is paid for by being immediately erased. Between nothing and something, I chose something. It seemed to be more just."

"It doesn't seem very just to me, to tell a man that he will soon die, and then deprive him of the chance to save himself! Don't be cross with me, but that is more what I would expect of the devil."

"On the contrary. The devil would happily deprive you of oblivion, because that would afford him the opportunity to revel in your agony. But even if you remembered this meeting, you would still not be able to extricate yourself. Nothing you could do would prevent the ineluctable unfolding of ordained events. Why, then, expose you to the unnecessary anguish that must derive from knowledge of your approaching death?"

From a distance came the protracted whistle of the locomotive, as the train began to slow down.

"I might have asked something else," Mr. Pohotny reflected softly.

"Yes, you might have. But now it's too late, unfortunately. This is my station coming up."

"It's not easy to find the right question to ask God."

"I know. But if it's any consolation, it is also hard to satisfy people, as we had already concluded." God stood up and offered his hand to the senior vice president. "Goodbye, Mr. Pohotny. It was a pleasure to meet you."

Mr Pohotny stood up and shook the proffered hand. "Goodbye," he replied, although it seemed to him that the word was not quite suited to the moment.

When the train started moving several minutes later, the senior vice president raised his eyes from the book which he continued to read and briefly looked out of the window, wondering why they had made an unscheduled stop at this small station. But it made no difference, since there would be no more stops until his destination. Now it was certain that he would be alone in the compartment to the end of his trip. Wisely had he decided not to buy up all the seats! A successful bank vice president must make the proper decision at all times. This was a good omen for the evaluation he must shortly make.

5. The Confessional

The deep, harsh coughing that came from the other compartment of the confessional sounded almost like a distant growl.

The priest started in confusion and raised his eyes towards the gap in the partition that separated his cubicle from the area where the faithful kneel to confess. Through the slanted wickerwork that served as a semitransparent screen, he detected the outlines of a heavy-set man. He hadn't heard him enter because he had been asleep. He had secreted himself in the confessional for that specific purpose, not because he was waiting for a penitent. Here, this failing of his was least noticeable. It would not do to have a visitor catch him asleep in the open part of the church.

His conscience did not bother him overly on account of this sin. He found partial justification in his advanced age, which enhanced the periodic temptation to sleep during the day, particularly in the middle of the afternoon when the church was very quiet. But the faithful were equally to blame. If there were more of them, if they had not thinned out so much, he would not have had time for this improper repose. When he'd come to this parish many years ago as a young priest, the situation had been completely different. At that time he would never have been left alone in the church for so long. But now a secular age held ruthless sway. Recently, there had even been days when not a single person crossed the church's threshold.

There was one more extenuating circumstance that mitigated the sin of sleeping in the confessional. Whenever he felt his eyelids close, he would not simply go through the thick, dark-red velvet curtain as if into a sleeping berth; rather he would go with the worthy intention of reading—although once he drew the curtain it was rather dark inside, at least for his eyesight which was already quite poor.

In the beginning he had taken the Bible with him as the most appropriate reading material for such a context. But since he never got beyond half a page before sleep engulfed him, that seemed some sort of sacrilege, so he came to substitute other, less holy works for the sacred text. That, to be sure, did not seem to be the solution most respectful to God and His house either, but since this reading was of equally brief duration, the offence was not very great. In any case, he had never been unduly strict in granting absolution to others, so why be harsh with himself?

Startled out of sleep, he forgot for a moment that there was an open book in his lap. When he twitched, it slipped and fell to the floor, landing with a dull thud. He quickly bent down, picked it up and tucked it under his mantle. There was no way the visitor in the other compartment could have seen it, of course, yet he suddenly felt like a boy who has been caught looking at indecent pictures. The book that had for quite some time been his companion whenever he withdrew to the confessional for his afternoon nap was not indecent in the slightest; at least, not to judge by the few early pages that he had managed to read. Even so, its title—*Impossible Encounters*—seemed rather inappropriate for the Lord's house.

"I hear you, my son," he said, after clearing his throat. He wondered if he knew the man. Only a few still confessed more or less regularly, and he could easily recognize each of them by voice.

"Did I come at an inconvenient time?" It was the deep, velvety voice of a man somewhere in his middle years. He had never heard it before.

"No time is inconvenient to visit the church. God's ear is constantly receptive to those who would speak to Him. When was the last time you confessed, my son?"

The answer from the other side of the window was not immediate, as though the visitor was intently searching through his memory. "A very long time ago," he said at last.

"That is not good," replied the priest with mild reproach in his voice. "The soul must not endure the weight of accumulated sins for very long. Confession brings release and forgiveness."

"There can be no forgiveness for my sins," said the visitor in an even, casual voice, as though stating a truism.

"Certainly there is. God has infinite mercy. There is no sin that will not be forgiven if one is sincerely penitent."

"Yes, there is. My sins will certainly never be forgiven. But it makes no difference. I'm not at all sorry for them."

"Do not speak like that, my son. Everyone cares whether their sins will be forgiven. Do you want your soul to end up in Hell?"

"Why not? It's not as bad as people think."

The priest turned his eyes towards the bulky figure in the neighboring compartment, even though he could still see nothing distinct through the dense wickerwork.

"It's not bad in Hell?" he repeated slowly, emphasizing each word. "It's terrible even to think something like that, let alone say it. Are you at all aware of what you have just said, my son?"

"Perfectly aware. I know from my own experience. I just came from there."

"Where did you come from?" the priest asked softly, after a short pause.

"From Hell."

The priest shook his head. Here was yet another deplorable offspring of the secular age. He had already met others like him in this place. It was not enough for them to be non-believers; they came to the church specifically to blaspheme. But he knew how to handle them. It was for just such lost souls that he should fight the hardest. That the man had come here at all showed that all was not completely hopeless.

"No man has ever returned from Hell," he said didactically, like a teacher pointing out a simple, obvious truth to a backward child. "The Tempter would never allow it."

"He wouldn't, I agree. But that doesn't apply to me."

"Oh? Why not, if you please?"

"Because I am not a man."

The shroud of afternoon silence suddenly settled on the confessional. So this is what it's all about, the priest thought gloomily. Before him was not just an ordinary, contumacious non-believer, but one of those poor wretches whose clumsy wrestling with matters of faith had upset their minds. He hadn't met one of that kind in a long time, and they usually identified with the Savior. As far as he could remember, this *soi-disant* Devil was a personal first for him. So he had to proceed carefully, without ill-mannered contradictions, yet with firmness. In the end he might succeed in bringing the man to his senses, though it was certainly not going to be easy.

"So, that's it," he replied with studied calm, as if this were an everyday encounter. "You are the Tempter himself, if I understand correctly. He is the only one who is allowed to leave Hell."

The head on the other side of the wickerwork gave a brief nod. "You understand correctly."

The priest brushed the tips of his fingers across his wrinkled brow and sighed. "Very nice, but there is one problem. The Tempter would never dare cross the threshold of God's house."

"You think not? That is only one of the many prejudices against me. It is here that I have always felt most comfortable."

"Strange. How is it, then, that no one has ever seen you? It would be hard for your manifestation to pass unnoticed."

"Manifestation? Oh, the tail, horns, hooves, goat's head and all the rest? That is all pure nonsense, of course. No one notices me because I look quite ordinary, unassuming. Like you, for example."

The priest squinted to sharpen his vision a little, but the figure on the other side of the window still presented only a vague, incomplete outline.

"If you look quite ordinary, how can you convince people that you are who you make yourself out to be? Couldn't just anyone appear and claim to be the Tempter?"

"They could, yes. That even happens from time to time. But it doesn't work for long. Sooner or later they have to offer proof to support their claim."

"And you can offer that proof?"

"Of course."

"That might be, for example, an infernal fire that suddenly breaks out in the middle of the church, with all manner of freaks and monsters streaming out of it? Or maybe the stone floor would split asunder, revealing a chasm that leads straight to your red-hot throne?"

The visitor did not reply at once, and the priest thought he might have gone too far. If he wanted to help the poor man, he shouldn't appear to be making fun of him.

"It would not be anything so unrefined, so primitive, of course," the deep voice retorted from the neighboring compartment. "There is no need for that. Such ideas about me serve only to arouse needless fears in the ignorant. There is much more subtle and convincing proof."

"Would you perhaps show me some?"

"With pleasure."

From somewhere on the opposite side of the church, near the entrance, came the soft tapping of footsteps. The priest's trained ear told him it must be a woman, probably young, heading towards one of the last rows of benches. She sat down and immediately started to pray.

When everything fell silent once again, the visitor continued, "Let me ask you the same question you asked me at the beginning. When was the last time you confessed?"

"Me? I confess every day. If I didn't, how could I have the right to hear the confessions of others?"

"You confess to yourself, I assume, since you are the only priest in this parish?"

"That's right. My conscience is my best confessor. I can't hide anything from it."

"Your conscience, yes. But there are two pitfalls with regard to your conscience. First of all, it can be very lenient, very indulgent. It doesn't bother you too much that, for example, you sleep in the confessional."

I must have been snoring, the priest thought. There's no other way he could have found that out. He came in and heard me snoring. I'll have to do something about that.

"Falling asleep in the confessional once is only an ordinary human weakness, and no heinous sin. I feel remorse, of course."

"Just once?"

The priest grimaced. Somehow, he had lost control of the conversation. Usually he was the one to ask such questions here.

"All right, it might have happened a few other times. But I do not claim to be a perfect saint."

"Although you might be able to make that claim, considering the second problem with your conscience."

"Second problem?"

"Yes. Your conscience can be rather forgetful. If something doesn't please it very much, if it has a hard time finding justification for something, it has a tendency to discard it, to pretend it never happened. A real confessor should never act like that, wouldn't you agree?"

"I'm afraid I don't quite understand," the priest admitted after a short hesitation.

"It might be clearer to you if I explain it by means of an example. What would your conscience do if you were oppressed by feelings of guilt for the loss of two lives? Would it constantly remind you of that, make your life unbearable, or would it prefer to push the whole thing under the rug?"

The priest felt something tighten in his throat. Who was this man? Why had he come here? What did he want from him?

"I don't know. I can't even imagine that. I am not haunted by feelings of guilt for the loss of two lives."

"That is obvious. Although you should be. A conscience that is inclined to forget can still grant you forgiveness, but that doesn't count for very much, I'm afraid. There is another, much more important forgiveness, and nothing is forgotten there. It remembers everything and takes everything into consideration. Every tiny little thing."

"What are you talking about, my son?"

"I think you know perfectly well what I'm talking about. Your conscience does not really forget, it merely represses things. But that works only until someone reminds you of what you have repressed. As I am doing right now."

"Reminding me of what?" Though the priest tried to keep his voice firm, it began to quiver.

"Of the girl who drowned after jumping off the bridge. Five months pregnant. After finding out that the father of her child, a young priest she had fallen in love with, would not keep his promise. That he would not renounce his vows for her."

The sound of footfalls came once again from the entrance to the church. The young woman had finished her short prayer and was now leaving. She walked with quick steps, hurrying somewhere.

The priest could find no words for a while, staring fixedly at the thick, dark pleats of the curtain in front of him. At first he wanted to protest, to deny this terrible accusation, to challenge the identity of the large figure in the neighboring compartment. But he did not. There would be no sense in that. The memory, suddenly freed from the deepest, darkest corner of his mind, washed over him as violently as the icy water into which the girl had plunged so long ago. Not only had he turned his back on her, he had been unable to attend the funeral. The church does not give shelter to suicides. They are not even given a place in the cemetery. He never found out where she was buried.

No one ever suspected that he was to blame for the girl's demise. They had taken great pains to keep their relationship secret, and she had left no letter of farewell in which she might have accused him, thus making his infidelity all the worse. He remained blameless in the world of men, but certainly not before his own self. After great torment, he had finally repressed the memory, yet he knew quite well it was only temporary, that a true settlement of accounts awaited. Now the time had come. The Tempter had come to claim his due. The priest had no right to expect mercy for what he had done. He did not actually even want mercy. There was only one place for his soul.

"So Hell isn't as bad as people think?" he said at last, in a barely audible voice.

"It isn't. But you won't have the chance to find out for yourself."

"What do you mean?" He was just about to add the usual "my son", but stopped himself at the last moment.

"Your soul will go to Heaven."

The priest raised bewildered eyes towards the window, even though by now he knew he would never see his interlocutor any better.

"How could such a terribly sinful soul as mine go to Heaven? That certainly cannot and must not happen!"

"But it will nonetheless. I will make sure of it."

"Why? I don't understand. . . ."

"What benefit would I get from your soul? Almost none. Hell is already packed with sinners like you. You might even say we're overcrowded. Whenever I take a new lost soul, I'm only doing God a favor. I relieve Him of what He doesn't like. I take a bad creation out of His sight, so He can maintain the illusion that everything He's done is flawless. Why should I do that? Why should I play into His hands? We are opponents, not allies, right? I should do everything I can to injure Him, to remind Him constantly that the world He has created is imperfect. And what better reminder than to surround Him with the worst of sinners?"

"But He will never allow that."

"He will. He will have no choice."

"God will have no choice?"

"Yes. He's not quite as almighty as people think. For example, He could never exile from Heaven a soul that knows nothing of its sins, regardless of how great they are. Sending such a pure soul to Hell would be infinitely unjust. And God is proud of His justice, right?"

"I am perfectly aware of my sin."

"Yes, but not for much longer. That is why I came here."

"Why?"

"To remove your memory of the sin you committed."

"I don't want to forget it."

"What was the repression you resorted to until now? Another form of oblivion, correct? But incomplete. Now I will give you perfect, complete oblivion. You will no longer remember anything that might burden you. Everything will be permanently erased. No one will be able to convince you that you have committed any sin whatsoever. When you stand before God, your soul will be the incarnation of purity. You haven't actually the slightest reason to complain. The gates of Heaven will be open to you. What else did you dare hope for that could be any sweeter? Although, to tell you the truth, I don't envy you much."

The priest quickly rose from his seat in the narrow compartment. He suddenly felt enclosed in an upright coffin.

"You must not do that! I must go to Hell! That would be terribly unjust. . . ."

"Probably. But I am sure you understand that such considerations carry no weight with me."

The priest reached for the curtain. He did not know what he wanted to do. It was an instinctive move, a feverish attempt to find refuge, to escape somehow from the trap into which he had fallen. But his hand never touched the velvet. It sagged next to his body, which collapsed back onto the chair. The drowsiness that suddenly engulfed him was not his usual afternoon slump, rather something very deep, something he had never felt before. It had to take over at once, he didn't even have the strength to open his book, let alone read a few lines. His eyes closed by themselves and his head drooped on his chest.

If he had any dreams, he could not remember them when he woke up. He remained sitting there a few moments, gathering his wits, and then pushed aside the curtain and left the confessional. There was no one in the church. He always felt refreshed after this short rest, but what now filled him was not just renewed vigor. The thought crossed his mind that this was the spiritual state in which it would be most suitable to stand before God: tranquil, at peace with the world, with an unblemished conscience. Like the righteous. He turned slowly toward the aisle between the rows of benches to greet the light pouring from the entrance.

6. The Atelier

When the front doorbell rang, the silence in my atelier seemed to implode, like a balloon that has suddenly lost all its air.

I turned away from the computer screen where I had been sitting for a long time, and looked at the door in bewilderment. Before I start to write, I always turn off both the telephone and the intercom. It is impossible to reach me then. If someone calls me on the phone, they will think I'm away from home, or don't want to answer, and if someone rings at the entrance to the building downstairs, I won't hear it at all and will thus be unable to let them in. But someone had obviously entered, someone whom I hadn't let in, and who was now standing in front of my door.

I got up irritably and headed for the front door of the atelier. I can't stand being interrupted while working. No one has the right to disturb me, particularly now that my time is running out. I couldn't imagine who it might be. It certainly could not be someone from the building dropping by for a visit, because I had not cultivated even the most attenuated friendship with any of my neighbors. The most I do is to exchange polite remarks on the rare occasions I meet someone in the hall or elevator. I don't even know the names of the people who live on my floor.

Maybe it was a door-to-door salesman who had somehow entered the building and was now peddling from apartment to apartment, offering something I certainly didn't need. I should have stayed at my desk, without giving myself away. Even the most persistent intruder would give up after a while, concluding that there was no one home. But since I had already gone to the door, I put my eye to the peephole and peered out. I realized just then that I had never done this before, simply because there had been no need to check out any visitor. I always knew who was ringing the bell.

In front of the door to my atelier stood a distinctly elderly gentleman. He was short and thin, wearing a hat and a dark coat, and a dark-red bow tie. I had never seen him before. He couldn't have been a door-to-door salesman, not only because of his advanced age, but also because he was not carrying any bag for whatever he might have been selling. All he was holding was a rather small book. He took off his hat and bowed to me, and I moved back from the peephole in embarrassment. I'd had no idea that you could tell from the outside when someone was looking through it.

There was no longer any sense in pretending I wasn't there. I had to open the door; but whatever happened, I was determined it should be brief. The gentleman had undoubtedly made a mistake. He had surely come to visit someone else in the building, and then turned up at my door by mistake, for it had no nameplate on it. I could not, however, be of much assistance in directing him to wherever he wanted to go.

"Hello," I said, opening the door halfway. "May I help you?"

The man did not reply at once. He just looked at me, smiling slightly. We stood like that in silence for a few moments.

"Don't you recognize me?" he said at last. He had a rough, elderly voice, but with an element of good cheer.

"I'm afraid not," I replied in surprise. "Should I?"

"I believe so. Who else, if not you?"

"Please don't hold it against me," I said after a short

hesitation, "but I don't seem to recall when we met. Would you please remind me? With whom do I have the honor?"

Holding his hat in his hand, the old man bowed again. "I cannot tell you my name, unfortunately, since you did not give me one. I am a character from one of your stories who remained nameless. But so it is with many of your characters, is it not?"

I sized up the stranger angrily. "I don't know what you want, sir, or why you came here," I said, raising my voice a little, "but I certainly don't have time for tasteless jokes. You have interrupted me in the middle of very important work. Such conduct is not tolerated in polite society. Please leave."

I started to close the door, but his next words halted me.

"Your work is important, but you're making heavy weather of it."

"Excuse me?" The door that was almost shut opened a crack.

"Your writing. You have written five stories, and would like one more, a final one. Without it your book will be incomplete. But you seem to have run out of inspiration. Not a single letter has appeared on your screen for days, and you can afford to fritter away no more time, isn't that so?"

"Who are you? What is the meaning of this?" I tried to sound sharp, even wrathful, but a quaver in my voice betrayed me.

"I am someone you might find useful. If, of course, you invite me in." He looked briefly from side to side. "It would not be quite proper to talk about it here, in front of the door."

I made no move, not knowing what to do. This whole business was completely insane. The old man standing in front of me clearly could not be who he claimed to be, but, on the other hand, he could not possibly have known what he had just said. No one knew that but me. The seconds moved ponderously, crushing me with their growing weight.

"Maybe this will dispel your doubts," my visitor said at last, handing me the book he was holding.

I took it hesitantly, thinking as I did that it was irrational. I should cut off this senseless encounter at once, simply close the door without further ado; maybe even slam it shut. You have to act firmly with oddballs, even those of polished demeanor and advanced years. But curiosity, plus a certain vague premonition, prevailed over rationality.

It was a paperback book, not very thick, with a shiny, plastic-laminated cover. I turned the front over and squinted at it. Under my name was the title in large letters: *Impossible Encounters.*

I raised my bewildered eyes to the elderly gentleman, who was still smiling. I realized that I was expected to say something, but nothing coherent crossed my mind. This book could not exist, if only because it had yet to be written. The last chapter was missing. The computer screen on which it was supposed to appear gaped behind me, completely white.

"Where did you get this?" I finally stammered.

"May I not come in?" the stranger persisted.

I hesitated for just a moment before opening the door almost fully and stepping back. The old man passed by me, then stopped in my small hall. At first I didn't understand why he had done this, then I realized what was expected of me.

"With your permission," I said and took his hat, then his long, heavy coat. I had to put the book under my arm briefly in order to hang them on the coat rack next to the front door. "After you," I said, indicating the atelier's main room.

Once inside, the visitor turned this way and that, looking around but saying nothing, just nodding his head. He was wearing a dark blue suit of old-fashioned cut with wide lapels. A handkerchief matching his bow tie peeped delicately from his upper jacket pocket. He waited for me to invite him to sit down, then chose the couch to the right of the door. I was momentarily uncertain as to where I myself should sit, and then I chose the armchair next to the desk, under the lamp with the large yellow shade, so that we faced each other.

"Where did you get this?" I asked, repeating the question that had not been answered.

"From you, of course."

"From me?"

"Yes, you left the book on the coffee table next to the jug and the two glasses. In the room that is entered from the hallway with portraits. Several drops fell on the cover as I was pouring water. Surely you remember?"

I shook my head slowly, more in disbelief than because I could not remember.

He indicated the book in my hand. "In the first story. The first chapter, in fact. 'The Window'."

I opened the book and started to leaf through it with stiff movements. It was truly there, on the seventh page: "1. THE WINDOW". I read the short introductory sentence and then looked at my visitor again.

"As you know," he continued, "I am not exceptional in this regard. The other characters were given the book, too. It appears in each of the stories, although not always the same edition. The Old Man is sitting on it at the top of the ascent, above the clouds. The Bookseller has it on the shelf among his recent acquisitions. The Banker is reading it on the train. And finally, the Priest carries it with him when he withdraws into the confessional for his afternoon nap. You did well to give it to us. If it weren't for the book, this encounter could not have taken place. Regardless which of us came here, you would never have let him inside unless he could present the book."

"But none of that is real. I mean . . ." I knew quite

well what I wanted to say, but for some reason I suddenly couldn't put it into words.

"But what is real? Didn't you write *Impossible Encounters* in order to show that there is no distinct boundary separating the real from the unreal? In any case, were we to stick unconditionally to the real, we would be unable to help you at all."

"Help me?"

"Yes. What did the doctor tell you—how much more time do you have? Two, at most three months, isn't that so?"

"How do you know?" My voice had dropped almost to a whisper.

"We know all about you, of course. That is quite natural. No one knows a writer as well as the characters from his own books. Just as you know us perfectly well, when it comes right down to it."

My head was spinning slowly. One part of my consciousness was still trying to make some sort of sense of all this, but in vain. I had canceled my entitlement to any acceptable sense the moment I got up from my desk and headed for the door to see who was there. And maybe even quite a bit earlier, in fact. Back when I wrote the first sentence of *Impossible Encounters.*

"How would you be able help me?" I asked, my voice still low. "If you know what the doctor told me, then it must be clear to you that there is no reprieve. Soon I will have to go back to the hospital, and this time I will never leave it."

"There is no reprieve, yes, but only in the medical sense. That is not what this is about, however."

"Then what is it about?"

"You will soon die physically, and that is inevitable, alas. But you might join us beforehand."

"Join you?"

"That's right."

"How can I do that?"

"It's quite simple. You want to add one more chapter to *Impossible Encounters*, isn't that so? Fine, write a story about yourself as a writer. Introduce yourself into it as a character."

"What would I gain by that? I mean, it would just be . . . let me put it this way, dead letters on paper. Unreal . . ." It was not until after that last word had trailed away into silence that I realized how gauche it sounded.

The elderly gentleman gave me a reproachful look from the couch. "Do I seem unreal?"

"Well, no, but . . ."

"You see, the fact is you don't really know absolutely everything about us. You undoubtedly think that we have no other existence outside of the limited work in which we appear. But that, of course, is untrue."

"Untrue?"

"Quite. We actually spend relatively little time in the roles of your characters. We are only there when someone reads a story about us. We are best regarded as actors who periodically appear onstage and act the same part in the same play, every time. When no one is reading us, when there is no play, we do not cease to exist, as you have incorrectly assumed." He stopped for a moment, and his smile widened. "We do not turn into dead letters on paper. Quite the contrary. That is when we retire to a large drawing room."

"Where?"

"To a large drawing room. It is very beautiful, as you will see for yourself quite soon. It is cool and quiet. There are lots of comfortable chairs, tables with bowls full of ripe fruit, a piano in the corner, an enormous library. There is also a broad terrace with two well grown potted palms from which a magnificent view stretches towards the sea. To sit there is very pleasant. The sun is always at twilight, so it's not too hot. The only drawback is that we can never go outside. We have to stay close by because you never know when a new play will start."

"What do you do, penned up inside there? Aren't you bored to death as you wait for the next . . . play?"

"Bored? Not in the least! We know very well how to fill up our free time. It would be much better to call it gracious leisure. Primarily, we carry on interesting, stimulating discussions. We all enjoy them, and I think you will like them, too. In addition, each of us has a talent that serves to entertain the others. My collocutor from 'The Window', for example, plays the piano. He often accompanies those who sing for us. The gentleman who fulfills the demanding role of God in 'The Train' has a truly magnificent voice, while the Tempter from 'The Confessional' is an exquisite painter. I'm sure you will be fascinated by his oils, particularly his still lifes. The older character from 'The Cone' is a most astute thinker, you might even say a philosopher, and we listen to his lectures with rapt attention and curiosity. And there is also a writer, who periodically reads his latest pages to us. Can you guess who that is?"

I shrugged my shoulders after thinking for a moment. "I'm sure I wouldn't know."

"The man who plays the alien in 'The Bookshop'. His style is rather similar to yours, which is not, perhaps, surprising. You will be able to exchange experiences with him. It will be exciting to listen to your discussions." The older gentleman paused again. "But you have deprived us in one sense," he said regretfully.

I looked at him, perplexed. "Which one?"

"There are too few female characters. It would be much nicer for all of us if there were a few more ladies. Couldn't at least one of the main characters have been female?"

"What do you mean—several more ladies? There isn't a single female character in *Impossible Encounters*. Although, of course, that is quite by accident. If I could have imagined all of this, I certainly would have introduced a woman. My other books are full of female characters."

"There is one woman, though. You forgot the girl who enters the church while the priest and the Tempter are talking in 'The Confessional'."

"But you can't see her. Only her footsteps are heard."

"What difference does that make? In any case, she is the only one who could make those feminine footsteps. You'll understand that when you see her. Let me tell you a secret. We are all in love with her. It is quite certain that you will be no exception."

"Maybe I can still fix things," I said hurriedly, in an apologetic voice. "The last story hasn't been written yet. I could introduce another woman into it."

"But it has already been written. It is here in the book you are holding. The final story, unfortunately, has no women in it."

I stared at my guest several moments, at a loss for words; disturbing questions tumbled through my head. And then I opened the book and started to leaf through it again.

But I did not reach the place I wanted. I was interrupted by the sharp voice of the visitor, who suddenly got up off the couch. "Don't do it! You must not look at the last story until you write it. If you read it in advance, it would be as if the story were writing itself. That would destroy an order of things that nothing should be allowed to endanger. Should that happen, you would never be able to join us. Please give me back my *Impossible Encounters*."

I did not comply at once. It was only with great restraint that I stopped when I was somewhere in the middle of the book. I was spurred by a violent impulse to take at least a peek at the first page of the last story, to see how it started. I was aware that this would have been cheating of some sort, although I might not have been able to explain what kind exactly. This was not, however, why I stopped. Ethical considerations were not enough to overcome the frustration that was devouring me inside, quite as destructively as the disease that would soon curtail my days. The constricting helplessness I felt derived from the knowledge that my time was inexorably running out, while the monitor on my desk remained hopelessly, undeniably empty: death would come faster than inspiration.

What had made me finally stand up and reluctantly hand the book back to the old man was the hope I suddenly felt. It was deeply irrational, earnest and desperate—but all I had left. The faint hope of the writer that what he has written will afford him refuge from the ultimate void.

"I can't do it," I said in a quavering voice. "I've been trying for so long, but nothing comes. Soon the pains will begin. . . ."

A smile returned to the visitor's face. "Of course you can. Believe me. Here is the proof, after all." He raised the little book he had taken from me. "I must go now. You need peace if you are to write. And I can't stay away from the drawing room for long. The plays are about to begin."

We headed towards the front door. I held his coat for him in the hall, then handed him his hat. He placed it on his head with a skilled movement, then extended his hand. Thin, bony as it was, his handshake was firm. And more than that. Friendly. Encouraging. "See you soon," the elderly gentleman said, with a brief bow.

I returned the bow, but said nothing. I closed the door behind my guest and stood there for a while in front of it, staring blankly into space. Then I turned and slowly headed for my desk. The large monitor was waiting with its white emptiness, as though mocking me.

I placed my fingers lightly on the keys, barely touching them. I did not start to type right away. All at once

I was no longer in a hurry. The story now stood before me, formed, final, whole. Almost palpable. All I had to do was write it. I wanted this moment to last as long as possible.

Finally, a dense, buzzing swarm of letters started to fly on the upper part of the screen, appearing, so it seemed, from out of nowhere:

When the front doorbell rang, the silence in my atelier seemed to implode, like a balloon that has suddenly lost all its air. . . .

Seven Touches of Music

Contents

1. The Whisper
2. The Fire
3. The Cat
4. The Waiting Room
5. The Puzzle
6. The Violinist
7. The Violin-Maker

1. The Whisper

It was a small class. And a special one.

There were only five youngsters, three girls and two boys, their ages ranging from six to eleven. Dr. Martin had his hands full with them, but in one respect at least they gave him no worries: he had no need to discipline them. Peace reigned unchallenged in the classroom. It was so quiet that at times Dr. Martin actually longed for a little commotion, some kind of unruly unrest. But all he received from his wards was silence.

They sat silently at their low desks, physically present but mentally absent, detached—worse than that: unattached. They were wrapped in an almost impenetrable autistic shell—certainly, one with no shortcut leading through it. Were there a path, to trace it would require endless patience, heroic kindness and attention on a grand scale—not that even these could guarantee success.

Although he liked to regard himself as a teacher, Dr. Martin was truly no such thing. He never taught his pupils anything; nor did he test them, or even talk to them. He did address them, of course, but he could never be certain that they took in any of his words. There was rarely any reaction; when there was, it was enigmatic.

Even so, something was emanating from those five closed, inaccessible worlds. It was hard to understand, but at least it existed. When Dr. Martin had first given the children blank sheets of paper and pencils, he had done so with no great expectations. It was simply part of the standard program. First he had shown them how to use the pencils, which took a wearisome time. Even more time and persistence had been required to persuade them to use them for spontaneous self-expression. The final result was certainly disproportionate to the effort it had cost, but this was true of every aspect of work with these children.

Ana, the oldest but also the smallest in the group, with a face dominated by extremely large eyes, was the first to master the skill of freestyle drawing on paper. She held the pencil in a white-knuckled grip, but her movements were quick, short and nimble. She filled sheet after sheet, but Dr. Martin never saw any of her productions. Should he approach her as she drew her densely cross-hatched lines, she would quickly turn the paper over to prevent him from looking at it. When she decided that a drawing was finished, she would start to tear it up. She did this with geometric precision, first in half, then in quarters, and so on until her desk was piled with tiny squares of grey confetti. These she would carefully sweep into the pocket of her smock, taking them with her at the end of class. Dr. Martin never learned what she did with them.

Sofia was a plump nine-year-old with a round, pimply face which she bent over the desktop because she was very near-sighted. She drew only on the edges of the paper, leaving the middle untouched. She filled this narrow frame with curving lines of surprising accuracy. There were snaking waves, spirals and open loops that never crossed or touched each other, creating a complicated tangle reminiscent of fingerprints. She would interrupt her work occasionally and stare for a long time at what she had drawn. In the end she would hand her work to Dr. Martin with a grimace in which he thought he recognized a shy smile.

Alex, a tall, thin ten-year-old with unruly hair and

glasses that were usually halfway down his nose, didn't draw anything. He scribbled haphazardly over the paper with broad, nervous movements until there was not the least bit of white left. Then he would turn the paper over and continue on the other side. The sides of his hands were constantly smudged with graphite, and he often broke his pencil. Once filled, the papers no longer interested him. He would push them away or crumple them up and throw them on the floor. He paid no attention when Dr. Martin came to retrieve them.

Maria was a dark-skinned, slightly cross-eyed girl of eight with a harelip. She always flinched when Dr. Martin gently addressed her, and never changed her piece of paper. From the beginning she had drawn the same complicated design in which a certain regularity could be discerned, although nothing was recognizable. She worked slowly, spending considerable time on details which she constantly embellished while adding new ones. Sometimes she would mutter, quietly and inarticulately, as if talking to someone in the drawing only she could see. During the two months that the drawing class had lasted, she had filled barely half of her first sheet of paper.

Philip, the youngest pupil in the class, had weak capillaries in his nose, so from time to time his nose would bleed spontaneously. If Dr. Martin was slow to notice this, a red spot would spread over the paper in front of the boy. Philip was not bothered by the blood and paid no attention to it; he was completely devoted to his unvarying work of drawing endless rows of little circles on both sides of the paper. His hand was unsteady so the rows were rarely horizontal, and the little circles would gradually get smaller or larger, often distorting into ovals. He would put the completed sheets on the side of his desk next to the blank sheets, paying no attention to Dr. Martin should he take any of them away.

The drawing program did not call for music, but did not preclude it either. Dr. Martin reached gratefully for the idea, once it occurred to him, as relief from the oppressive silence to which he never could acclimatize. There could surely be no harm in some quiet but tuneful composition. It might even have an invigorating effect on his pupils. One never knew—although, of course, one should never allow one's hopes to become too buoyant.

The choice was biased. Dr. Martin brought his favorite CD from home: Chopin's second piano concerto in F minor, opus 21. It had the effect of a sedative, although not in the least like those that rendered you numb and insensitive; rather it was calming, making one tranquil and receptive to those vibrations of reality that one might easily miss in an ordinary mood.

When he listened to Chopin alone at home, Dr. Martin always closed his eyes. That would have been inappropriate here in the classroom, but a twinge of disappointment got the better of him. He watched the children for a few moments after the concerto started, secretly hoping for some sort of sign that they were at least aware of the sound of the piano and orchestra, but there was none. The five youngsters sat there, engrossed in their usual drawing, as if their ears had been plugged with wax, as if completely untouched by the harmony that so enchanted their teacher. Dr. Martin had been plagued by doubts about his work before; there had been moments when it seemed fundamentally futile. But he had never before plumbed the depths of such despair. He closed his eyes to remove himself from the scene, if only for a moment.

The first movement, *maestoso*, was already well under way by the time the music at last suppressed the rising tide of bitterness within him. He realized that he was actually being unfair to his unfortunate wards. He had greatly overestimated them. Of course they were insensitive to Chopin, just as they were to many other, far less complex joys freely available in the world from which they had withdrawn. It could not be otherwise, as he should have known. He should not have expected miracles.

He opened his eyes and looked at the children in front of him. There was no change: the same bodily positions, the same movements of five pencils on paper. He put out his hand to turn off the stereo. He could have let the concerto play to the end, since it wasn't bothering anyone, but it suddenly seemed senseless for him to go on listening to it by himself. Yet his finger never reached the stop button; just then he noticed that there had been a change, after all. And he was to blame. Had he not closed his eyes, irrationally and improperly, for several minutes, he would have noticed Philip's nosebleed.

By the time his rapid strides brought him to the boy, almost one-third of the sheet, tirelessly filled with little circles, was stained with red. It was a distressing sight, though it represented no real danger. The bleeding could easily by stanched by inserting a piece pulled from a cotton-wool ball into Philip's left nostril, and Dr. Martin always kept a supply to hand with just that in mind. The young boy did not object. He obediently put his head back, as so many times before, and patiently awaited what came next.

After wiping Philip's mouth and chin with a tissue, and mopping up the remains of the gushing blood, Dr. Martin picked up the damp paper and wiped off the desktop with another cotton ball. Then he took a new sheet from the pile in the corner and put it in front of the boy. He was just about to crumple up the paper and throw it away when his eyes strayed briefly to what was written on it. The red film covered something which should not have been there at all.

Dr Martin had never even tried to teach his young pupil how to write numbers. It simply would not have been worth it. Even normal six-year-old boys have trouble with them, and it was out of the question for autistic children of that age. Nonetheless, here was a long row of numbers, covered by the blood from his nosebleed. There was no interruption to set them apart. The circles suddenly stopped and numbers appeared in their place. Three rows of numbers once again gave way to little circles, except that now they all looked like zeroes. The numbers were not written very skillfully either, but they were easy to recognize, even so.

Dr Martin looked in amazement at the boy, but he was once again absorbed in his endless drawing of round shapes, as if nothing unusual had happened. The doctor stood over the boy for a moment, holding the sheet of paper which was starting to curl from dampness. Then, guided by a sudden thought, he started to check on the other children.

But there was nothing unexpected there. Ana, as usual, turned over her paper when he got close, with a reproachful, sidelong glance. Sofia stopped her slow drawing of a thin, sinusoidal line along the very edge of the paper, raised her head and smiled at him, more with her eyes than her mouth. Alex was making broad sweeps on the paper, scribbling with his already blunt pencil, completely indifferent to Dr. Martin's scrutiny. Finally, Maria first flinched a little when he came up, and then shyly returned to the details of a design that vaguely resembled a bird with an oversized beak.

Returning to his desk, Dr. Martin reached for the stereo again, but once more changed his mind at the last moment and left it on, although he could not have said why. The *maestoso* ended and the second movement began: *larghetto*. He placed the sheet of paper he had brought in front of him on the desk and stared at it, while the music wrapped him in its spidery web.

A little later he took a blank piece of paper and copied over Philip's three rows of numbers, then put the original in a drawer. There were thirty-two of them, and they seemed to be strung together quite randomly—at least he could discern no pattern, but numbers had never been his strong suit. Maybe someone more skilled in mathematics could make some sense out of them, although he thought not. The very fact that the numbers existed was inexplicable enough. Anything more would be a true miracle.

As a sober man, Dr. Martin did not believe in miracles; nonetheless, after class ended that day he emailed a mathematician friend with the list of thirty-two digits from the bloodstained paper, asking whether they might mean something. He was certain of receiving a negative answer, but he still needed confirmation. As he waited, he felt like someone who, in spite of being completely healthy, is mildly anxious regarding the results of a recent medical checkup.

Two hours later he received a reply.

Dear Martin,

It didn't take me long to figure out this was a trick question. The problem has nothing to do with mathematics, of course. The series has no numerical pattern, but it has great meaning in physics—at least, the first nine digits have. If you put a decimal point two places before the first seven, then you get 0.00729735308, which is one of the fundamental values of nature, the fine-structure constant. I don't know about the digits after the eight. If they weren't given at random, to confuse me even more, then it must be God himself who whispered them to you because at this moment only He is able to measure after the eleventh significant figure.

You surprised me, I must admit. I had no idea you were interested in theoretical physics. Working with handicapped children must be boring you rigid, if you have to seek refuge in riddles like this. Try thinking up something harder next time!

Isaac

Dr Martin thanked his friend for his swift reply. He praised his quick intuition, and admitted contritely that he was, indeed, a bit bored. Of course the numbers after the eight were arbitrary. How could it be otherwise? He had certainly underestimated Isaac in thinking they could have fooled him.

Dr Martin's conscience caused him not a twinge for hiding the truth in this way. At present it was out of the question to reveal the true origin of the numbers. He would be obliged to offer some sort of explanation, which he was not prepared to do for a number of reasons, principally that Philip would be exposed to unnecessary unpleasantness thereby. The boy's well-being came first, and he would be unable to withstand a multitude of strangers wanting to examine him. He would only withdraw more deeply into himself, making the whole exercise pointless. If anyone was to get involved in the matter, there could be no one more suitable than Dr. Martin himself! There would be time for others later, should that prove necessary or desirable.

He first had to establish what had brought the boy to stop drawing little circles all of a sudden. If that impetus had come from the outside world, then it must have been the music. Nothing else had interrupted the daily routine in class.

Once again Dr. Martin brought the CD with Chopin's second piano concerto and played it at the same volume as before. This time he didn't close his eyes. He watched Philip carefully, but nothing happened. The uniform row of zeroes did not change into anything else. The same happened when Dr. Martin sat through the whole first movement with his eyes tightly closed, feeling rather idiotic as he did so. He had never been tolerant of actions based on superstition.

Then he considered trying a new composition. For all he knew, the piano concerto worked only once. This assumption did not sound very rational, but he had little choice other than to give it all up. Of course he could not do that! He brought his large collection of CDs into the classroom and started to play them one by one.

Nothing had any effect on Philip, but there were some unexpected influences on the other children. During Ravel's suite no. 1, 'Daphnis and Chloe', Ana started to tear her completed drawings into long, thin strips, instead of tiny squares. Bach's toccata and fugue in D minor brought tears to Sofia's near-sighted eyes, but also a sort of coughing that resembled a throaty laugh. During Mozart's symphony no. 40 in G minor, Alex picked up a pile of scribbled papers and put them neatly on the side of his desk. Finally, at the sound of Debussy's Nocturne, Maria failed to flinch when Dr. Martin came up to her.

All this could have been pure coincidence, of course; Dr. Martin had no time to check it out because his attention was completely focused on Philip. When he had exhausted his own collection of CDs, he briefly thought of borrowing or buying some others in order to continue the experiment, but thought better of it. He realized it was senseless, since he could go on like that forever. No, he should not have gone beyond Chopin. The second concerto was of utmost importance, but not just the concerto. There had been something else. But what? And then it dawned on him. The blood, of course! Philip's nose had bled!

This was something he could not precipitate. He had to be patient, but he knew from experience that he would not have to wait long. The boy's weak capillaries broke once every two weeks or so. He had to be ready the next time it happened. He continued his normal work, but often looked in the little boy's direction, waiting for the thin red stream to flow from one of his nostrils.

When this finally happened, he reacted at once. He pressed the button on the readied player, and the classroom was suddenly filled with resounding piano music. Then he went up to Philip, squatted down next to him and watched him fixedly. The flow of blood first went over the double curve of his lips and then made a winding cut across half his chin. The boy did not stop, even when red petals started to blossom about the paper in front of him. The irregular circles came steadily, one after another, not changing into digits, while a damp red veil spread over them.

It was only when blood had covered a good half of the paper that Dr. Martin finally snapped out of his trance. He leaned the boy's head back with trembling movements and applied a large, white cotton ball to his nostril. All this had been not only senseless, but extremely unkind to Philip. A doctor, of all people, should be the last person to show such cruelty towards the boy. As he wiped his face with a tissue, he felt his conscience prick him with an almost physical pain.

Dr Martin went back to his desk and turned off the stereo. The room sank into silence, but no one paid any attention. He should not have played the music, not only because it was superfluous here, but because it had brought nothing but trouble. There had been even less reason to make a second attempt to penetrate something that was clearly way beyond him. If it truly had been a whisper, as Isaac had said in jest, then it had certainly not been intended for his ears.

Moreover, Dr. Martin was just an ordinary specialist in autistic children. His main obligation in that capacity was to protect his wards. The best he could do for Philip at this moment was to forget the whole incident, to pretend that nothing had happened. This wouldn't be hard to do as there was only one trace of evidence, which would be easy to remove.

Dr Martin opened his desk drawer. He took out the sheet of paper whose wrinkled third had long since lost its bright red color and turned dark brown. With slow movements he tore it into very tiny pieces. They were not as uniform as Ana's confetti, but they too ended up in a pocket, soon to be discarded in a place where no one would ever find them.

2. The Fire

MRS. MARTHA WOKE SUDDENLY, jerking up on her elbows. But that did not immediately dispel the dream; it lingered a while, like a frightful echo. At least, the sound did. The image quickly dissolved from under her lowered eyelids into the darkness of the bedroom, but her ears were still filled with music. It was so powerful, it certainly should have wakened Constantine, even though he was a very sound sleeper. But her husband's large shape remained immobile. He was lying on his side with his back to her, like a dark landmass. She stared at him in bewilderment, slowly waking up, as the music started to fade, giving way to his deep, noisy breathing, on the edge of snoring.

She looked around, still confused, feeling her heart thud hollow in her breast. It must be quite early. The large rectangular window was filled with a mute, pre-dawn greyness. From somewhere outside came the barking of a dog, and another more distant bark came in reply. She turned to the bedside table. The large, bright yellow numbers on the alarm clock said 04:47. She squinted at them for several moments, then got up, searched around her bed for her slippers and headed for the bathroom, tottering a little.

She drained a large glassful of water. As she drank the last gulps she realized it was not what she wanted. She wasn't the least bit thirsty. As she lowered the glass to the washstand she caught her reflection in the mirror. She stared at her face in the striplights, filled with disbelief, as though looking at some stranger rather than herself. Finally she shook her head, turned off the light and went back to bed.

It was going to be hard to get back to sleep, which was a nuisance because she would feel sleepy and out of sorts all day long; but on balance she was glad, because she didn't feel at all like returning to that dream. The dream, however, was inescapable. Lying on her back with the covers pulled up to her chin, staring at the ceiling where pale stripes had started to appear, she tried to concentrate on something ordinary, something innocuous, that would calm her. But her thoughts would not obey her. Something seemed to be pulling them, taking them back to the dream.

She was standing in the middle of a vast, sandy wilderness. Low on the horizon, the sun wrapped the sand in a reddish veil. A gentle breeze was raising little whirlwinds that danced around her bare feet, tickling between her toes. She was wearing a loose, long-sleeved, calf-length white dress resembling Bedouin garb. She felt comfortable in it, though the fabric was rough.

Suddenly she heard the sound of waves, faint but quite recognizable. She turned inquisitively, but could not see the sea, as she had hoped. Instead, she caught sight of a lone hill behind her. It resembled the shell of a giant turtle that had dragged itself up to end its days in the desert. A huge stone building—a temple, perhaps?—stood on its flat top, like some sort of cubical hump, surrounded by a row of stumpy columns.

A procession was slowly making its way up the left curve of the hill towards the temple. Tall figures wearing robes similar to hers, but dark brown in color and with hoods raised, stood out sharply against the deep blue afternoon sky. Each of them carried an object she did not at once recognize. At first she thought they were a detachment of soldiers carrying strange weapons of various shapes and sizes, but when she looked more closely she saw that they were actually carrying musical instruments. The musicians were on their way to the temple, probably to give a concert there.

How wonderfully propitious! Constantine, unlike herself, was not an admirer of serious music, so they rarely went to concerts. Here was a chance to make up a little for what she had missed, since he, for some reason, was nowhere in sight. She rushed towards the hill, her feet sinking ankle deep now and then in the soft sand. When she reached the bottom of the hill, the last of the musicians were disappearing into the temple. The slope was not gentle, but she climbed effortlessly, feeling the smooth, warm stones under her feet.

On reaching the top a surprise awaited her. There was no door where she was sure she had seen the musicians entering the building. Instead there was a flat yellow wall of massive stone blocks, faded from long exposure to the sun. An inscription was written across the four columns spaced along the entire lateral façade, but she was unable to read it as she didn't know Greek.

Seeking the entrance, she rushed to the right along a cobbled path. She went all around the rectangular temple but could find no opening, except for a row of slits at the very top of the long sides of the building, probably serving to admit light. Certainly, only a bird could enter there. Returning to her starting point, she stopped in confusion, not knowing what to do. The concert might start at any moment and she was very keen not to miss it.

As if to confirm her apprehensions, music started to pour out of the temple. It came from high up, probably through the illumination holes. At first she was frustrated at having been unable to enter the building in time, but then, quite unexpectedly, another feeling displaced her exasperation. Her soul was filled with anxiety, although she didn't understand what was causing it. The sounds from inside grew steadily louder over several long moments before she realized that they were actually what was upsetting her.

There was something deranged about the sounds. She couldn't determine exactly what it was, but she was overcome by a strange certainty that something in addition to music was issuing from the instruments of those hooded figures who had magically passed into the doorless temple. Whatever it was, it was as intangible as the sounds, but by no means innocuous. Spurred by a dark premonition, she ran towards the long side of the building. One look at the illumination slits was enough to confirm her fears. Tongues of flame were darting from the narrow windows.

Panic seized her. The fire could not harm the thick stone walls, but something much more inflammable was inside the building, and it was now in danger. She did not wonder what it might be, nor how she knew of it—none of that mattered now, and she could think about it later. First she had to find a way to put out the blaze. She was the only one available to do it.

Yes, but how? She set her mind feverishly to work, biting her lower lip as she always did in times of great tension. She needed water. Where could she find water in the desert? And then she remembered the waves she had heard while down in the flatland. A quick survey of the terrain surrounding the hilltop was enough; there, indeed, was the sea, its blue surface dotted with crests of foamy white.

It wasn't far, just a short walk away, but for her needs the sea might as well have been infinitely distant. Even had the temple been built right on the shore, there was nothing she could do. How would she carry the water to extinguish the fire? All she had were her cupped hands.

As if mocking her helplessness, the music and the fire grew louder and stronger. Flames were now flickering wildly out of the openings at the top of the wall, forcing her to step back from the heat to the very edge of the hill's flat summit. The music had grown so loud she was forced to place her hands over her ears. It was of little avail. The ground around her soon began to shake, evidently from the force of the vibrations, at first slowly and then with greater and greater intensity, as if in the grip of an earthquake. She lost her balance for a moment and fell to her hands and knees, but managed to avoid plunging down the hillside.

She was filled with horror as she saw that even the stone temple could not resist the destructive impact of the music. Completely deafened, she watched mesmerized as the columns swayed and toppled into cylindrical segments. One of them started to roll towards her, but all she could do was stare at it, unable to move. It passed so close it almost grazed her, then continued down the steep slope, picking up speed as it went.

For a moment she hoped that it was all over; then the heavy stone roof collapsed into the interior of the building with a tremendous crash. Pandemonium ensued. She felt not the slightest compassion for the musicians, who were presumably crushed beneath. It served them right. It was all their fault. Without their demonic music none of this would have happened. But the music didn't stop. It could still be heard rising from the fiery ruins, even louder now when there was no roof to dampen the sound; the collapse had hindered the musicians not in the slightest.

The fire now reached high into the sky. She was overcome with deep despair when it became clear that there was no way to save the delicate, fragile thing somewhere inside. She still didn't know what it was, but nothing could survive such infernal conflagration. It had been lost, inexorably and forever, leaving behind an emptiness as gaping as the tomb. She had not been able to do a thing, and now it was too late.

It was also too late for her to get away. The wall, with its large stone blocks, started to swell like an inflatable balloon. Only a few more moments and it would yield before the unimaginable pressure from within. Suddenly she realized she had no shelter. There was not even time to flee headlong down the hillside. All she managed to do, as the sounds rushed inexorably toward their demented crescendo, was to raise her hands instinctively to her face and close her eyes tight. Darkness swallowed the terrifying sight, but nothing was able to banish the final explosion of music.

Mrs. Martha did manage to fall asleep again, but not until broad daylight. This time there were no dreams. She simply sank into a lake of black ink that absorbed her into its blind, deaf sanctuary. She could have stayed there a very long time, but Constantine didn't let her. He reached for her, gently shook her shoulder, and pulled her to the surface. She tried to resist, not wanting to emerge, but he was merciless.

Her dream remained behind, in the inky lake. She hadn't the slightest memory of it after waking up the second time that morning. When her husband asked why she had overslept, she answered with a shrug. It seemed odd to her, too. She was usually the first one out of bed. She was vaguely aware of some sort of anxiety, but even though she tried to discover its cause, it remained unfathomable.

At breakfast, when Constantine put slices of fresh toast on the table, she glanced with hostility at the striped surface. She liked toast, but for some reason didn't feel like any today. Her husband gave her an inquiring look, seeing her push the empty plate away, but said nothing. She drank a full cup of coffee, blowing at it even though it wasn't hot. She knew she would have trouble with it on an empty stomach, but still wasn't able to eat a thing.

When they left for work, Constantine turned on the car radio. He had been doing this regularly for a long time, although he wasn't very interested in music. It was the best way to alleviate the strained silence that would otherwise engulf them during the half-hour ride. After more than twenty years of living together they were running out of topics for conversation. This had bothered her at first, but later she had got used to it, and even come to like it. Better to talk when they had a genuine reason rather than by the dictates of convention. She, too, was not always in a mood to talk.

Now, however, her hand extended itself; first she turned the music down, despite the fact that it wasn't loud, then she turned it altogether off. She said nothing while doing so, and when she had done it she couldn't have said why. The radio was tuned to a station specializing in light instrumental music, one she had always enjoyed before. This morning it seemed somehow irritating, although she would not have been able to give the reason. Constantine turned his head briefly towards her. She endured his inquisitive look, thankful that he did not ask her anything. They continued driving in silence, the traffic around them growing denser as they approached the city center. When they got close to the library where Mrs. Martha worked, her attention was drawn to something she would probably not have noticed previously. Two fire trucks were trying without success to make their way through the multitude of cars inching forward in the morning rush-hour traffic. Their sirens were blaring and their blue lights flashed, but to little effect. The cars in front of them simply had nowhere to go to let them pass.

Mrs. Martha became suddenly anxious and started to breathe rapidly, as she always did in that state. The thought that the huge red vehicles might not get where they were needed in time filled her with unusual discomfort. She had no idea where the fire had broken out, but that did not seem to matter. Regardless of what was burning, the damage would be enormous. Fire left an utter wasteland behind it, and this might be threatening something truly unique, something that could never be recreated.

The fire trucks turned left at the first intersection and drove out of sight. Their sirens could still be heard for a while, until they were gradually drowned out by the surrounding noise. As though emerging from a daze, Mrs. Martha wondered confusedly why this was having such an effect on her. Fires happened every day in large cities such as this. It was inevitable—just as it was inevitable that many people ended their lives daily, people who were also unique and could never be recreated. But one should not allow oneself to be overly burdened with the irretrievable losses of every day; that would turn life into a real inferno.

Before she got out of the car in front of the library, Mrs. Martha kissed Constantine—just a light touch of the lips that seemed barely more intimate than a handshake. They didn't say anything to each other, there was no need. He would drive on as he did every morning to the insurance company where he had worked for almost a quarter of a century. At the end of the working day he would wait for her at this same spot. Then they would kiss again, without a word. The radio would already be on in the car, freeing both of them from the obligation to talk about the arid monotony of their daily working lives.

As soon as she turned on the computer in her office, as she did each morning, she realized that something was wrong. A picture appeared immediately on the screen. That should not have happened; it always took about half a minute for the system to boot up. During that time a rapid sequence of vertical text filled with sundry abbreviations, signs and numbers would pass across the screen. They moved far too fast for her to read and their meaning had never interested her; she understood very little about computers. She could find her way around the basic library program, and that was quite enough for her. She hadn't the slightest desire to learn in more detail how the thing worked.

Now it looked as if she had turned on a television set. The picture was not the computer's usual coarse representation, which she had never liked; it was a very high resolution picture of the outside of an ancient building. She stared at it in confusion. It seemed vaguely familiar, yet she could not recall where she had seen it before. Four large columns ran at regular intervals along the façade, and between the two at the center stood an imposing rectangular entrance, its double doors wide open.

Above the columns was some sort of inscription. She moved her head a bit closer to the screen to get a better look, but this was not necessary. As if in response to her wishes, the camera started to zoom in on the carved letters. The letters were in Greek, but still she managed to read them. For some reason this did not surprise her very much. It was certainly the lesser of the two wonders confronting her just then. The second had to do with the inscription itself. Although it was most certainly impossible, she could nonetheless clearly read: Great Library.

She stared in momentary disbelief at the letters. Then she came to her senses, realizing she should do something. She had to call someone—maybe the computer maintenance department. This was certainly some kind of breakdown. These machines went on the blink from time to time, although she had never heard of anything like this before. She reached for the telephone, but didn't finish because that same moment the camera came back to life. It glided down from the inscription, went to the open door and floated inside.

Not much could be seen at first. The only light came from a row of slits near the top of the long lateral walls, but this was not enough after the bright sunlight outside. When the picture quickly started to get lighter, Mrs. Martha thought her eyes were becoming accustomed to the gloom, although she knew it was only an illusion. The camera was adjusting to the weak light. Then it began to rotate, slowly revealing the interior.

There was only one large space, resembling a hall. Its central part contained a row of wooden tables surrounded by simple chairs without backs, stretching all the way to the far end. The tables were placed in such a way as to catch the rays of light slanting from the high openings. That was enough to read by without straining one's eyes during the day, particularly if it was sunny. There did not seem to be any artificial light. There were no oil lamps or candles. Nothing that would burn. The Great Library clearly could not be used at night.

All four walls were completely covered with deep shelves from floor to ceiling. Ladders were placed at frequent intervals. These were connected to the shelves, giving access to their upper reaches. There were things on the shelves that Mrs. Martha did not immediately recognize. Having expected books, she stared in bewilderment at the tube-shaped objects that formed a vast honeycomb on all sides.

And then it dawned on her. If the inscription above the entrance were to be believed, there could be no conventional books here. It was too early for bound books. Documents were written on papyrus when this building existed. On the screen in front of her stretched an enormous repository for scrolls. She had never been good at making rough calculations, but she could not be mistaken in this case. Along the walls were thousands and thousands of scrolls.

It was an impressive sight; the first thing that crossed Mrs. Martha's mind when she realized what she was looking at, however, was quite practical. As someone who was proud of her profession of librarian, she couldn't resist wondering how it was possible to find one's way about this multitude when there were not even spines to help distinguish one papyrus from another. How could someone quickly find the desired scroll among the countless others that looked identical?

As if following her thoughts once again, the camera moved up close to one section of a shelf. The screen was now filled with only some fifty scrolls. Suddenly they were covered by a porous network of letters. This time they were in the Roman alphabet so Mrs. Martha no longer had to count on a miracle in order to read them. It also did not take her long to realize what it was all about. After all, she had spent her whole life cataloguing books.

Authors' names were written in somewhat larger yellow letters and under them, in smaller blue letters, were the titles. It wasn't clear whether they referred to the works contained in the few scrolls currently visible in the background, but if this were true then the total contents of the papyrus rolls was significantly greater than she might have guessed. What an incredible treasure was to be found in the Great Library! Mrs.

Martha's breath grew shorter for the second time that morning.

The camera glided smoothly to the next section of the shelf. The catalogue disappeared, but a new one soon took its place. This time Mrs. Martha concentrated on the text. She combed through her memory but could not recall ever having encountered some of the names written on the screen. She tried from the inventory of works to figure out who the authors might be—literary writers, historiographers, natural scientists, mathematicians—but was not certain of anything.

And then she saw a name she recognized. Her own library had recently received a new edition of his tragedies which she herself had placed upon the shelves. She well remembered that only a small number of this author's works had been preserved, only seven or eight, and yet before her ran a much longer list. She counted thirty-six dramas. Owing to the small size of the letters she had to count by drawing her finger across the screen. When she passed over a title, its light blue color immediately darkened.

Led by a sudden thought, she raised her index finger to the screen again and placed it on one of the titles that did not seem familiar to her. The letters first changed shade, and then a moment later the catalogue page disappeared and one of the scrolls began to emerge from the shelf. When it was all the way out, the scroll unrolled, covering the screen completely. Before Mrs. Martha was the original text of a long-lost tragedy.

The instincts of an experienced librarian hushed her mounting excitement. She had to try to do something. That was uppermost in her mind. All the rest could wait for a more suitable moment—all the disturbing questions that were trying to pour out of wherever she had tucked them away for the time being. Yes, but how? What should she do to save this invaluable treasury that had somehow surfaced from the depths of oblivion? She thought it over with care, but all that came to her mind was to resort to the customary way of recording data on the computer. She didn't think it would work, but what else could she do?

The moment she touched the first key on the keyboard, the papyrus scroll rolled back up and returned to its place in the honeycomb. Mrs. Martha jerked her hand back as though scalded. She had made a mistake. There was no opportunity to try anything else because the camera suddenly moved back from the bookshelf and withdrew to the furthest end of the room, high up under the roof; now it showed the entire Great Library, with the brightly lit entrance at the other end.

Nothing moved for several moments, as though the screen held a photograph. And then the speakers, which had been silent until then, came to life. The music they started to emit was barely audible at first, as though coming from outside, from a distance, so she did not recognize it right away. When the volume began to increase, however, Mrs. Martha felt an icy shiver crawl up her spine. Streaming out of the inky lake where it had lain submerged, the forgotten dream slapped her violently in the face. She knew who she would see even before the procession of musicians reached the entrance. Lit from behind, the hooded figures began to slip inside like faceless ghosts, as if not touching the ground. When they left the bright rectangle at the door, they melted completely into the surrounding darkness. Their presence could only be discerned by the unceasing music. When the last musician entered the Great Library, the tall double doors closed soundlessly behind him, leaving no trace that they had existed.

For a while nothing moved again on the almost totally black screen. Coming from now invisible sources, the music rose ominously. Then bright spots started to speckle the deep shadows. Several moments passed before Mrs. Martha realized what was happening. Torches were being lit one by one, gradually illuminating the spacious interior. What these smoking, flickering lights revealed seemed impossible. The torches were floating in mid air, without any support; no one was holding them. There was no sign of the musicians, although the music still thundered.

Once all the torches were alight, they took up positions evenly distributed round the large building, forming a long rectangle along the walls. Mrs. Martha gripped the edge of the desk in front of her, as if afraid of losing her footing. She stared fixedly at the screen. She was perfectly aware of what was to come, but the powerlessness she had felt in her dream tied her hands in her waking state as well. Although she tried feverishly to think of a way of preventing the inevitable, nothing came to mind.

The torches stood motionless next to the shelves for a moment; then, as if at some inaudible command, commenced their demented feast. Like the flaming paintbrushes of a crazed, many-handed painter, they started to dip and sway over the papyrus background. The huge fresco was covered with flickering, flaming colors. Mrs. Martha bit almost through her lower lip, as though sharp pain could release her from this unwanted dream. But this time no awakening could save her.

She watched in despair as the fiery orgy gobbled up the scrolls one after the other, reducing their invaluable contents to nothingness. Accompanied by the deranged music, the fire quickly gained momentum and finally occupied the screen completely. The image of the raging fire was so convincing that Mrs. Martha thought she could feel its heat on her face. The burning smell that seemed to fill her nostrils was even more intense. And then she saw with horror that this was not just an illusion: somewhere from the back of the monitor rose a ribbon of grey smoke.

She almost jumped off her chair, knocking it over behind her. Her hands flew to her mouth, but not fast enough to suppress the cry that escaped. The smoke in front of her became thicker, then turned reddish, and finally mixed with the flames that started to stream upwards. Mrs. Martha should have known how to cope with such a situation, she had been trained and knew what she must do, but she was completely paralyzed. She stared dully at the fire as it engulfed the whole monitor. By some miracle, the picture was still there, so the two fires now seemed to merge into one, while music still poured out of the speakers.

When water suddenly gushed from above, Mrs. Martha did not even try to get out of the way. Smoke had activated the sprinkler system and water started to shower from innumerable little holes in the ceiling. She stood under this dense, piercing shower, her eyes still riveted to the screen, by now empty. The speakers were also silent. The room's power supply had automatically shut down the moment the sprinklers started to work. Like every modern library, this one was properly guarded against the greatest threat to books since time immemorial.

Mrs. Martha spent the next two and a half hours wrapped in a blanket in the ladies' room, waiting for her clothes to be dried and ironed. When she returned to her office everything had been wiped up and put in order. She did not have to explain anything. No one even asked her what had happened, since it was quite obvious. Monitors had caught fire before. It was just an unpleasant incident without too much damage. In any case, everything was insured. A new monitor was already waiting on her desk, but she did not turn her computer back on that day.

Late in the afternoon, when she got into the car and kissed Constantine, she was briefly tempted to tell him what had happened, but held back. She would only get mixed up trying to explain something that she herself did not understand. In addition, he was even less in a mood to talk on the way home from work than in the morning. The drained expression on his face clearly said as much. Finally, the radio was already turned on. Without exchanging a single word, they joined the dense flow of traffic.

3. The Cat

Mr. Oliver did not start visiting second-hand shops until after the death of his wife. Mrs. Katerina had often visited such places, particularly during her latter years, and would occasionally bring something home, usually an ornament of some kind. He had never accompanied her, although she had often invited him to come along. He had a certain aversion to old things, especially ones that had previously belonged to other people. This was not shared by Mrs. Katerina. She bought whatever she found pretty and not too expensive.

She had bought Oscar in much the same spirit. She had seen him at a pet shop, priced cheap as he was not pure bred. The snow-white kitten with chestnut eyes had enchanted Mrs. Katerina at first sight, though Mr. Oliver had greeted Oscar's arrival with reserve. He was certainly not a cat-lover, although he had nothing against them. He would have said he was simply indifferent to cats.

At first he tried to have as little contact as possible with Oscar, considering the attention his wife lavished on the cat quite enough—more than enough, indeed. Sometimes he felt that she treated Oscar more like a child than a cat. She took meticulous care of all his needs, kept him neat and fastidiously clean, even gave him his own room, though he spent very little time there. In addition, she talked to the cat a lot, mainly in baby talk, which had aroused some misgivings in Mr. Oliver, though of course he never remarked upon it.

Over time Mr. Oliver and the cat evolved a truce. If they were unable to establish a closer relationship, at least they learned to put up with each other. Mr. Oliver became used to the tomcat's presence in the house and was no longer bothered by his smell, his hair everywhere when he molted, his habit of sharpening his claws on the upholstery, the compulsion to tear frantically about the house that seized him without warning and for no apparent reason at least once a day, and the agitation that came over him should a queen pay a call anywhere nearby.

For his part, Oscar stopped eyeing or sniffing suspiciously at Mr. Oliver, as if at a shady stranger, and was happy to avoid any physical contact with him. Mrs. Katerina tried briefly to bring them closer together, then gave up, seeing the futility of her efforts. She was nonetheless very careful to divide her affection evenly between them so that neither felt deprived.

The relationship between Mr. Oliver and Oscar changed when Mrs. Katerina first took to her bed, and shortly thereafter went into hospital. Mr. Oliver had to take over the care of the tomcat. At first he had trouble coping and Oscar found it difficult to accept the change. But gradually Mr. Oliver acquired skill in the basic things—preparing food and cleaning up after the cat—and Oscar became less distrustful.

Even so, when Mr. Oliver brushed the cat, although he clearly enjoyed it, he did not purr in response, as he had with Mrs. Katerina. This perturbed Mr. Oliver a little. Trouble also arose when once a month he leashed the cat and took him for a walk in the park, to find the grass that helped his digestion. Mr. Oliver always felt uneasy doing that, sure that many amazed and even reproachful eyes were on him.

But all this was bearable. The only thing Mr. Oliver could not bring himself to do was talk to Oscar. Although he made several attempts, he felt foolish every time, as if he had been caught talking to himself, and fell silent after only a few words. It was even worse when he tried to babytalk the cat. It seemed hopelessly artificial and affected, as if Mr. Oliver were adopting a persona entirely unsuited to his age.

As if affected by the same diffidence, Oscar meowed less and less. That had been his way of informing Mrs. Katerina of his wishes, but he preferred to convey his needs to Mr. Oliver by scratching, often suffering when this was not noticed in time. The two of them were clearly condemned to mutual silence; their intimacy had reached a point beyond which neither could proceed.

When Mrs. Katerina died, the question of what would become of Oscar was never even raised. It was, of course, out of the question for Mr. Oliver to turn the cat out, even had he wished to do so. Unaccustomed to fending for himself, the cat would not survive very long in the street. Had he wanted to get rid of him, Mr. Oliver would have preferred to consign the cat to a society for the protection of animals, or possibly return him to the store from which he had been bought. But Mr. Oliver did not want this by any means. Without Oscar, he would be left completely alone in the large, empty apartment, and that thought filled him with horror. Perhaps he and the cat did not get along perfectly well, but now they needed each other. In any case, Katerina would never forgive him if he let Oscar go.

Mr. Oliver's guilty conscience pressured him into visiting second-hand shops. Now it was too late, he realized he should not have refused Katerina's invitations to join her. Had he gone, they would have shared many more pleasant moments together. How strange that one only began to value such things when they were beyond reach. He thought briefly of taking Oscar with him, at least occasionally—it seemed somehow fitting. Yet he refrained; animals were probably not allowed in such places, not even on a leash.

At first he shied away from actually entering junkshops. In his inexperience he imagined they must be like other stores, in which eager salespeople immediately accosted you. If that were to happen, he would find himself in an awkward situation, because he wasn't looking for anything in particular. Luckily, however, there was no such pressure. If he were addressed at all it would only be with a polite greeting, after which he would be left to poke around the vast jumble of small and large objects which crammed every available corner for as long as he liked.

His aversion towards old, second-hand things slowly started to fade. Picking at leisure through crowded shelves and glass showcases, he came to see the items on display through the eyes of his late wife: he saw the beauty in them. The age of an object had no effect on it, and his recent experience with death reminded him painfully that any ownership could endure but a short time.

Indeed, how could anyone own beauty? Who actually owned all those decorative little things that Mrs. Katerina had brought home from junkshops over all those years? He did, presumably—but certainly not for long. If they had had children, he might take another view of the situation, but without heirs he had no way of knowing what would happen to these objects after his death. It made no difference, nor should it. Soon afterwards, when he started to buy things he found pretty, he regarded none of them as his possessions. They would be with him only temporarily. All he had been given was a brief time in which to enjoy them.

He discovered beauty in the widest range of objects: the chipped ceramic figurine of a ballerina, a cracked badge of honor, an incomplete set of tunic buttons, a worn-out brass pipe-stand, a pocket watch with half the big hand missing, a snuffbox whose lid did not close properly, a rusted key which must once have opened an elaborate lock, a small set of lead soldiers with most of the paint chipped off, a wall barometer from which the mercury had leaked, a pile of sundry old coins, cutlery that might have been gilded at one time, a dented thimble inscribed with a Latin motto in cursive script, a bottle of lavender water, now dried out despite its ground-glass stopper, an empty monocle frame, a tea strainer with its handle bent slightly askew, an album partially filled with old, yellowed photographs of people no one would now recognize.

After bringing these things home, he would not immediately put them on the narrow black shelf with its many compartments, made to order for this special purpose. First, according to his wife's habit, he would give Oscar a chance to sniff them thoroughly in order to become acquainted with them; then he would spend long, patient hours at the kitchen table repairing, fixing, gluing, straightening, fastening, sewing, polishing and painting. In time he collected a wide assortment of tiny tools for such purposes and acquired skills he had never before possessed. When each item finally reached the shelf, it was in the best shape it could possibly be. Only once, during an especially tedious undertaking, did he wonder in amazement that the things Katerina had brought from second-hand shops had never needed any refurbishing.

Mr. Oliver came across the music box by accident. He tripped over it, literally, when approaching a glass showcase in the corner of a junkshop in a suburb he had never previously visited. It was on the floor, partially covered by the long velvet drapes that framed the display window. He bent down and picked it up, fearful that he might have damaged it inadvertently with his foot. As the sudden, dull sound disturbed the silence, the shopkeeper, who had been engrossed in his accounts, stared inquisitively over his small, round glasses at his only customer.

In other circumstances, Mr. Oliver would certainly not have bought the music box. It was too bulky to fit on the shelf in the living room. Worse, he concluded that he did not care for it when he took a closer look. He did not mind that it was quite worn and most likely didn't work; probably he could remedy such defects. But he didn't see the spark of beauty that was crucial to him.

He doubted he had caused any additional damage to the music box when he tripped over it, but the dealer kept looking at him suspiciously, so he had no way out. Disinclined and unprepared to haggle, he simply went up to the counter and asked the price. When he was told, the price clearly included the dealer's experienced appraisal of a customer who was in a bind, but he did not attempt to bargain—he never bargained. He paid the amount without a word and waited for the music box to be wrapped.

A small problem arose in this regard. The shopkeeper, whose expression had relaxed into a smile once the money was in the cash register, had trouble finding anything large enough to hold the music box. He finally disappeared behind the curtain that covered the entrance to the back of the store and brought out a large cardboard box originally intended for boots. He then saw his esteemed customer out with the bow and broad smile proper to the occasion.

When he got home, Mr. Oliver was still uncertain about what to do with the music box. He could put it away somewhere and forget it, but that made no sense. If he hadn't wanted it, the best thing would have been to chuck it into the first trashcan he came across after he left the junkshop. He was certainly not the type to cling tenaciously to old things when they were certain never to be used again. Since he had already brought it home, why not try to fix it up a little? Maybe it would grow on him with time.

He went into the kitchen where he did his repairs, took the music box out of its wrapping and placed it on the table. As Oscar always did when something new was brought home, he came at once to sniff it, jumping first onto the chair and thence to the table. Mrs. Katerina would not have allowed this, but Mr. Oliver had relaxed almost all her restrictions. Even when he wanted to prohibit Oscar from doing something, he usually hesitated because he didn't know how to go about it.

Mr. Oliver expected Oscar to go up to the musical device, but for some reason the cardboard box attracted him instead. He sniffed it carefully all over, then climbed inside, pulling himself under the half-open lid. When the tip of his tail disappeared the lid went down with him, so he was completely enclosed. This did not disturb Mr. Oliver. Oscar often found his way into various inaccessible places and always got out easily, without anyone's help. All he had to do here was rise a little and lift the lid with his head.

There was a bit of scratching and commotion inside and then everything went silent. Oscar was obviously hiding, something cats do when they think they're in a safe environment. He would come out when he got bored. Mr. Oliver returned to the music box. He looked it over carefully, then took a flannel rag and started to clean it. To judge by the thick layer of dust, no one had used it in a long time.

After cleaning the outside, Mr. Oliver grasped the white porcelain handle that wound the device. Quite a bit of effort was needed to turn it. From inside the box came the squeaking of gears and springs that had not been oiled recently. He had to turn the handle very slowly, so that nothing inside would get stuck or break. It took him quite a while, but he was in no hurry. Undoubtedly it would take considerable effort to make the music box work, and the question was whether he was equal to such a job. It was one thing to fix up simple objects on the outside, quite another to repair a complex device like this. After all, he was not a mechanical engineer.

He had just decided that nothing would happen when to his surprise the mechanism started to emit sounds. The music was stiff, scratchy and broken, but he could make out the basic melody. It sounded gay and enthusiastic, with a lively rhythm—a polka, perhaps. Mr. Oliver thought he had heard it somewhere before, but since he had no ear for and little understanding of music, he could not recognize it. But all this suddenly lost importance when the lid of the boot box at the other end of the table started to rise.

The head that appeared was not Oscar's. It seemed somehow smaller, more like that of a queen than a tomcat; in addition there was not a single white hair on it. Gray, brown and black colors competed discordantly for supremacy, and jade-green eyes stood out against this mainly dark background. The cat examined her surroundings inquisitively for several moments, showing no interest whatsoever in the fixed stare of Mr. Oliver, either accepting his presence as part of the furniture or not noticing him at all.

Then she slipped out from under the lid and onto the table. The cat looked about the kitchen briefly, stretched after being cramped in the box, and jumped first onto the chair and thence to the floor. Mr. Oliver watched her without moving as she headed towards the dining room. He had the impression that she brushed against his leg as she passed him, but he hadn't felt any touch, probably because of the confused state he was in. The cat moved lithely, like Oscar, although somehow in a softer and more feminine manner. With brisk steps she soon reached the door which stood ajar and disappeared into the next room.

Mr. Oliver hesitated several seconds before starting after her. He was beset by the desire to peer into the boot box to see what had happened to Oscar. He didn't do so; not only because it was not the most important thing at the moment but also because he shuddered at what he might see if he lifted the lid. Instead, he headed towards the dining room, pursued by lively sounds from the music box. He did not open the door all the way when he reached it, although he already had his hand on the doorknob. He stopped in front if it: from the other side came something that positively should not have been there—the murmur of voices.

He tried to identify them, but the piercing music behind his back interfered. Several people were talking at the same time, and the squeaky, clamorous voices of children and their noisy laughter rose above the rest. Mr. Oliver stared at the door in front of him, bewildered, not knowing what to do. The reasonable part of his mind told him to open the door and find out what was going on in the dining room. But another part, deeply hidden, feverishly held him back, insisting the contrary: that he close the door at once, by no means look inside, get away as soon as possible, even flee.

When he finally started to open the door, slowly and hesitantly, he did so only because he believed he would never forgive himself if he didn't do so. In addition, something in the indistinct voices from the dining room was calming, and even more than that: familiar. He could not determine exactly what it was, but what he felt was enough to convince him that nothing bad would happen.

In the dining room he found the oval table laid for lunch. Five chairs were occupied, with two adults and three children sitting and eating. It was a family meal, its atmosphere gay and relaxed, because there were no guests whose presence would require formal behavior. Not a single head turned towards the uninvited visitor standing in astonished confusion at the kitchen door. He stayed there, immobile, like an invisible ghost.

His eyes first stopped at Katerina. He had some pictures of her from when she was young, of course, but the only place she remained as lively as she looked now was in his memory, although he couldn't remember her hair like this. Next to her was the youngest of the three children, a little girl with freckles and long, dark, curly locks, wearing a stained bib. Her mother repeatedly lifted spoonfuls of soup from a bowl, saying each time that it wasn't hot as she blew unnecessarily at the thick, red liquid, while the little girl tried, through a babbling string of words, to postpone the inevitable as long as possible.

The boys sitting on either side of their father were twins, three or perhaps four years older than their sister. They wore identical clothes and had very short hair. The one on the right was recounting, with a lot of giggling, one of his and his brother's recent larks, trying to keep everyone's attention by raising his voice. He continued to eat all the while, so his father had to quieten him down and remind him not to talk with his mouth full. The other boy was eating in silence, waiting for the chance when no one was watching to drop a bit of food to the tortoiseshell cat standing by his chair.

Feeling a swarm of needles land on the back of his head, Mr. Oliver finally looked at the father. What struck him first was how different he looked with a mustache. At one time, soon after he married, he had started one, but Katerina hadn't been very pleased with it, so he had abandoned the idea. Now he concluded that it didn't look that bad on him. It lent a certain seriousness to the young face, as befitted the head of the family. The glasses also contributed to this effect, although Mr. Oliver found them less appealing. He was proud that his sight was still quite good, despite his advanced age.

When Katerina got up, took the soup tureen from the table and headed towards the kitchen, the old man standing at the door, captivated by the impossible sight before him, was startled out of his paralysis. He couldn't just remain there, blocking her way, but what should he do? Complicated questions, which he had suppressed until that moment, started to appear everywhere, finding no answers, as the young woman drew inexorably closer.

And then, as if things were not hopeless enough, behind Mr. Oliver's back came a sharp, metallic rattle followed by a high-pitched gasp. His nerves taut, he jerked round, but nothing was happening there. The music box had stopped playing, either because the spring had wound down or (more likely, given the squeaky wheeze that had just echoed) because some part of the neglected mechanism had finally collapsed.

Mr. Oliver quickly turned his head towards the dining room, almost expecting to collide with Katerina, but no one was coming towards him any longer. There was no mother carrying a soup tureen. There was no daughter who didn't like hot soup, no son who liked to talk while he ate, no second son who liked to sneak food to the cat. There was no young father with a mustache and glasses heading the table at the family meal. The large room gaped empty and quiet, just as it had for so many years.

Mr. Oliver remained standing at the door to the room, glazed eyes staring, until a new noise came from the kitchen. It was considerably softer, so this time he did not have to turn around so suddenly. Out of the boot box appeared first a whiskered muzzle, then a white head. Oscar stayed like that for a while, as if wondering whether to go back inside his nice hiding place or leave it. Finally the lid rose a bit further and he glided onto the table.

Even before Mr. Oliver reached Oscar, he had come to a decision. He would not be able to repair the music box after all. Better not even to try. It might well not be fixable, and even if it were, the repairs might cost more than the price of a new music box—and in any case, he had no desire to own one. He put it back in the cardboard box, put the box under his arm and left his apartment, followed by Oscar's inquisitive eyes.

When he appeared at the door to the junkshop carrying the box, the owner eyed him suspiciously, sensing trouble. He was just about to tell the customer, with a suitably implacable expression on his face, that items purchased in his store could not be returned (as was clearly stated in the framed sign on the wall) when Mr. Oliver interrupted him with a movement of his hand.

After the shopkeeper found that he was not expected to return the money he had been paid, only to take back the music box without any compensation, he wrinkled his brow briefly, wondering what traps might be lurking behind such a strange offer. Being able to find none, he finally agreed, trying to insinuate by his tone of voice that he was doing so unwillingly and as a special favor. His conviction that he had made a very good deal was only slightly dented when the customer left the shop, with the bow and the broad smile of one who has got by far the best of the bargain.

Immediately on returning home, Mr. Oliver recounted to Oscar his experiences with the second-hand dealer. The tomcat listened attentively, not interrupting him with superfluous meowing. That would begin to happen somewhat later, as he listened to other stories, restrained and shy at first, and then increasingly uninhibited, as the voice of the old man with whom he lived gradually softened, on its way to turning into baby talk.

4. The Waiting Room

Miss Adele did not like travelling.

She had not enjoyed it much even in her younger days, and as the years passed she found the occasional need to travel ever less agreeable. But she could not avoid this trip, though there was nothing in its favor. First of all it was winter, and one of the harshest to hit the region in a long time, with heavy snowfalls that completely disrupted the rail system. The schedules had become unreliable, as the snowdrifts not only slowed the trains down but often stranded them for hours in the middle of nowhere. Moreover, the general situation was gloomy and tense. Although everyone felt that war would not break out before spring, no one would have been very surprised should it come much sooner.

When Miss Adele received the news that her younger sister, Mrs. Teresa, had been taken ill, her first thought was that this was a threefold vexation. She was naturally upset at her sister's illness, which came as a complete surprise, but she found the two necessities resulting from this misfortune almost as irksome. She would certainly have to visit her sister. That, even if everything went well, meant an exhausting five-hour train journey, and in such bad weather the trip's duration might be open-ended. She could already see herself shivering in an unheated compartment, in who knows what kind of company, as the train stood hopelessly trapped in the middle of a gloomy, white wasteland. But even that would be preferable to the meeting that awaited her.

She had never forgiven Teresa for marrying that man and going off with him so far away, leaving her alone. Adele had disliked him at first sight. He was so full of himself, so negative, and cynical as only men know how to be. And then there were those watery eyes of his that looked derisively down at you, and his thick, red beard that smelled of tobacco smoke even when he wasn't smoking that horrible pipe. What had Teresa seen in him, anyway? He certainly made her suffer, poor thing, although she was too proud to admit it. Miss Adele had reminded her sister on each of her rare visits, usually made alone, that she could come back to the family home whenever she wanted. But Teresa had refused even to talk about it, sometimes quite rudely, despite the fact that her older sister had only wanted what was best for her, as always.

The telegram she had received from him was so worded as to inflict maximum worry through a dearth of information. He had done it on purpose, of course. "Teresa sick STOP Wants to see you STOP Jacob." Truly, what could she conclude from that? How serious was Teresa's condition? It must be quite serious, or she would never have asked her to come in such weather. And what disease had she caught, all of a sudden? Maybe it wasn't all of a sudden. It wouldn't have surprised her a bit if Teresa had been sick for a long time living with that man, but had hesitated to tell her sister about it. As soon as Adele had gauged his character, and it had not taken her long, hadn't she warned Teresa that she wasn't safe with him, that he might even be the death of her? But Teresa, with her lack of understanding and simple, open-hearted nature, had waved that dismissively away.

She tried to call her sister on the phone, something she did very rarely and unwillingly, always horrified at the thought that he might answer. She had no desire to hear his voice, let alone talk to him. Now, of course, she must steel herself to endure that unpleasantness—but the long-distance lines were down. Even when the weather was fine it was hard to make long-distance calls. The blizzard must have brought down the lines somewhere. It was a wonder that she had received the telegram.

So she had no choice but to head for the railway station and catch the afternoon train. She might have called information first to see if there were any delays, but in the turmoil that overcame her that never crossed her mind. She quickly packed some warm clothes in a small suitcase, then put a full hot water bottle on top of them as final protection in case the train got stuck in a snowdrift. She filled a thermos with tea and, after a moment's hesitation, added a little of the rum she used to make holiday cakes. She included a box of the cookies that she usually nibbled with her tea and, as a final afterthought, put in another box.

When she arrived at the station she learned that the train was indeed late, but no one knew by exactly how long; more specific information was expected in about half an hour. The man at the window where she bought her ticket gave her a compassionate look when he heard where she was going, and suggested she take a seat in the station restaurant or in the waiting room. Miss Adele had never sat by herself in a restaurant, so she headed for the waiting room.

The corridor that led to the waiting room was full of soldiers. They stood talking in small groups or sat dozing on grey, wooden footlockers or even on the cold floor, their rifles leaning against the wall. They looked exhausted and there were patches of fresh mud on their untidy uniforms. Most of them were smoking cigarettes; a thick, bluish cloud of smoke hung motionless in the gloomy corridor. Miss Adele felt ill at ease as she made her way through them, head bowed and hand held over her mouth and nose, although no one paid any attention to her.

The waiting room was not very full. Only a calamity of the sort that had befallen her could force people to travel in such cold. Miss Adele found a seat in the corner across from a family of three sitting to the right of the entrance. The man was tall and thin, sitting stiffly, already bald although he was barely into his thirties. He had taken off his coat and placed it neatly on the bench next to him beside a rather large travel bag, but he had kept his long, blue woolen scarf round his neck. His wife seemed disproportionately small compared to him. She was wearing a pretty little grey hat the same shade as her fur coat, which she had only unbuttoned, although the waiting room was heated by a tall tile stove. Her cheeks were ruddy and her forehead was lightly beaded with sweat. Between them sat a little girl about six years old. She had inherited her mother's height, so her short legs dangled, swinging restlessly, not touching the floor. Whenever she banged the heels of her high-topped shoes together her father would look at her reproachfully, but without saying a word. The little girl frequently raised her lips to her mother's ear to whisper something, and her mother would reply briefly in a low voice. From time to time she wiped her daughter's nose with a large, white handkerchief.

On the other side of the waiting room, across from the stove and next to one of the windows that gave onto the empty platforms, sat a stocky officer with a heavy mustache, curled upwards and waxed at the points. His heavy overcoat and sheepskin hat were hanging from a hook on a nearby wall, and a small puddle of melting snow spread around his boots. He was engrossed in a brochure, although the weak light from outside made reading rather difficult, so that he had to hold it close to his face. On the bench nearest the stove, leaning against a small hand organ, dozed an old man of very unsavory appearance. His unshaven face was gaunt and heavily wrinkled, and everything he wore seemed old and tattered. The rim of his hat was ragged, gloves that had once been white now showed fingertips in two or three places, while a crooked bow tie, a thin coat with two large, conspicuous patches and flat shoes that were certainly not suited to such snow completed his ensemble.

Miss Adele did not mind waiting very much; she was accustomed to it. She had spent most of her life waiting. In her younger days it had often made her restive, although she had been unable to say exactly what she was waiting for. In any case, whatever she was expecting had never happened, and she had long since reconciled herself to that. Now she was only saddened when she felt that all she really had left was to wait for her life to pass. Like the small woman, she did not take her coat off, though she unbuttoned it. She sat with her hands folded on the muff in her lap, staring blankly out of the window.

Although it was only mid-afternoon, it had already begun to grow dark. The wind had died down temporarily, allowing the big, fluffy snowflakes to fall straight down, as if in dreamy slow-motion, and so thickly that buildings on the other side of the platform were barely visible. The silence of the gloomy waiting room was broken infrequently: somewhere outside could be heard the distant, rhythmic banging of a hammer, and from the corridor echoed the muffled laughter of several soldiers. The little girl continued to bang her heels together from time to time despite her father's obvious displeasure. In the tile stove the large logs emitted occasional sharp crackles.

Miss Adele started out of her reverie when she heard the hand-organ. Staring out of the window, she had not noticed when the ragged old man woke and picked up his instrument. She had never liked music—it was always too loud for her. She had a radio at home, but even on those rare occasions when she listened to it, she always kept the sound low. She glanced angrily at the organ-grinder. Such people should be excluded from waiting rooms, she thought—or at least they should be ordered not to bother decent people with their noisy instruments. She turned, expecting so see similar views expressed on the faces of the other occupants, but all remained strangely indifferent, paying no attention to the musician.

Then Miss Adele experienced her first vision. She had just directed another angry look at the organ-grinder when, although she could still hear him playing, he disappeared—suddenly, and without warning, along with everything else that had been within her field of vision a moment before. Something else appeared instead. The waiting room was still there, but on the edges, like some sort of frame, as if a smaller picture had been placed over a larger one.

The smaller picture showed a room principally occupied by a large, brass bedstead. It looked familiar to Miss Adele, but in her initial confusion she was not able to place it, nor did she recognize the woman lying motionless in the bed, with the eyelids closed on her pale, drawn face, and hands crossed on her chest. She only realized what she was looking at when the taller of the two men sitting beside the bed raised his head and turned his watery eyes briefly in her direction. He then turned back towards the priest on the other chair, who was absorbed in reading a prayer aloud from his breviary, and said something to him that she could not hear.

Miss Adele gasped in pain and raised her hands to her mouth. Her muff slipped off her lap. Her whole body shook, and her head was spinning. Only after several long moments of great effort was she able to regain partial control of herself. This certainly cannot be true, she tried to convince herself. Teresa could not be dead, if only because Jacob, with his malicious, hateful nature, would not for a moment have hesitated to inform her, taking pleasure in the suffering that the news would cause. His telegram had only said her sister was sick. It didn't even say seriously—simply, sick.

This was only a silly apparition, she thought, although very convincing, and that terrible organ-grinder was to blame. He had completely addled her brain with his impudent and unexpected music. Really, how dared he? It was only then that she realized she could see him again. He was no longer concealed by a ghostly picture. He had stopped turning the handle of his dilapidated organ, and was watching her from the other end of the waiting room. Four other pairs of eyes were looking askance at her too.

Her gasp must have caught their attention. What must they think of her now? That she was a senile old woman living in some imaginary interior world? Or even that she was clinically insane? If they knew what had just appeared to her, their conjectures would be completely confirmed. Just look what an unseemly situation such a vagrant could bring upon a decent woman! It was because of unpleasant encounters such as this that she was so disinclined to travel, or even to go out among other people. Miss Adele bent down and picked her muff up off the floor. She shook it gently and returned it to her lap, then waited stoically for the inquisitive stares to turn away.

The silence that reigned once again did not last long. It was broken by the old man near the tile stove, though this time not with his music. He was overcome by an attack of dry, wheezy coughing that appeared to come from the very bottom of his lungs. It seemed as if he would never be able to stop; at times it even resembled a death rattle. Although she was sitting some distance away, Miss Adele nonetheless took out her lace-edged handkerchief to cover her mouth, just in case. The last thing she needed right now was to get sick, like her sister. When the organ-grinder finally caught his breath, he stood up slowly, straightened his untidy clothes, raised his bulky instrument and headed ponderously for the door. Miss Adele felt relieved when he left. She only hoped that he had gone for good.

It was already quite dark in the waiting room, but it was not clear who should turn on the light. This was finally resolved by the officer, since he could no longer read beside the window. He laid the open brochure on the bench and headed towards the switch by the door, his boots squeaking on the bare wooden floor and leaving a wet trace. The very moment light poured over the large room from two bare bulbs in the high ceiling, Miss Adele's ears were once again filled with the organ-grinder's music. She thought at first that he was playing for the soldiers in the corridor, even though the music was quite clear, as if he were still here in the waiting room. But she had no time to wonder at this curious fact for just then she experienced a second vision.

The officer was returning to his seat when he was suddenly concealed by the smaller picture. Miss Adele could still hear his sloshing footsteps on the floor, but now she saw him not in the waiting room, but in some dark, bomb-cratered landscape. He was advancing cautiously, crouched down, revolver in hand, leading a small squad of soldiers, making his way through dense fog or smoke. Noiseless flashes flared up suddenly on this greyness, forcing the soldiers to hit the ground. As they were getting up after the third explosion, the officer suddenly grabbed his neck with both hands. He stood there frozen for a moment or two, and then slowly sank to the ground. His hands fell along with his body, revealing blood pouring in torrents from a gaping wound in the middle of his throat. It soaked the upper part of his overcoat that a moment before had been hanging from a hook in the waiting room.

Miss Adele quickly covered her mouth with her handkerchief, smothering a cry of horror. Terrified by the appalling scene, she closed her eyes tightly. Her rapid heartbeat seemed to boom loud as a drum. She waited for her pulse to calm down a little before she dared to look again, shuddering, at what she feared to see. But when she opened her eyes, all that greeted her was the innocuous waiting room, now harshly lit. The officer was sitting calmly in his seat by the window, once again intent on his reading.

Although she was not in the least inclined to stare at people, and particularly not at people she didn't know, for some time she could not take her eyes off the officer's powerful neck. The vision was gone, but the image of blood pouring unquenchably from it was vivid in her memory. He must have been hit by a stray bullet or shrapnel fragment. The wound seemed serious, so he had certainly lost a lot of blood before anyone could help him. How awful! thought Miss Adele. He was still relatively young. It was extremely unfair to die like that. She had to warn him of what awaited him. Then maybe he could avoid such a fate.

But she didn't do anything. She sat in her seat and finally, with great effort, lowered her eyes to her hands in her lap. What could she tell him, anyway? That she had seen a vision? That she had seem him die in a cratered battlefield? That it was all because of that ragged organ-grinder's music? She would only get tangled up in her attempts to explain something to him that she herself did not understand. He would think her an old fool, bothering people with her prattle. And what if the vision were wrong, just like the one of Teresa on her deathbed? She would look ridiculous! It was all so unpleasant. What had she done to deserve this, in addition to all her other troubles?

Somewhere from the distance came the drawn-out whistle of a locomotive. Miss Adele turned hopeful eyes to the windows. The sooner the train arrived, the sooner her suffering here would end. She expected the public-address system, located conspicuously above the door of the waiting room, to announce the train's arrival in the station, but it remained silent. Several minutes later a seemingly endless string of cars began to pass slowly by one of the platforms, a black clattering stream sliding through the barely paler night. From its lack of lighted windows, Miss Adele concluded that it must be a freight train, not scheduled to stop at the station. But if this train had arrived, that meant the track was passable.

The little girl sitting between her parents whispered something to her mother again. She nodded, and the two of them got up and headed out of the waiting room, holding hands. Father continued to sit there stiffly, staring straight ahead, paying them no attention. The moment the door closed behind the mother and daughter, the organ-grinder announced a new vision. Once again, he played so loudly and clearly that Miss Adele suddenly looked in suspicion at the two men sitting there, seemingly deaf to this obtrusive music, before she returned her fearful attention to the ominous, smaller picture, unconsciously clutching her handkerchief.

The inside of the car was cramped, particularly the back seat where the little girl was sitting. She seemed somewhat older, by maybe two or three years. She was surrounded by piles of luggage and even had a small suitcase in her lap. Father was driving and he often turned his head to say something to Mother on the seat next to him. Although she couldn't hear him, Miss Adele concluded by his wife's demeanor that he must be reprimanding her. Her head was bowed, and she frequently raised her fingers to wipe away tears.

Everything happened very quickly: the lights of another car suddenly appeared around a curve, aimed straight at them; Mother opened her mouth in a silent cry, her eyes staring; Daughter instinctively lifted the suitcase to shield herself; Father wrenched the steering wheel to avoid the collision, but was unable to turn it back again in time. The car flew off the road and started to plunge down a steep hillside, rolling over and over. Seen from inside, the car seemed to be immobile while the whole world spun madly around it. And then there was a violent crash against a boulder at the bottom of the cliff and flames that suddenly engulfed the whole of the smaller picture.

This time Miss Adele did not even try to hold back her cry. She jumped up from her seat, holding her muff to prevent it falling to the floor again. The fiery image suddenly melted before her when she changed position, to be replaced by two bewildered faces. But now they made no difference—no more misgivings about inappropriate behavior could stop her.

What had happened to the officer was horrifying, but his death had at least been something one could expect, a professional risk run in the line of duty, while this was a true tragedy. An entire family—and the child in particular! She had only begun to live, so to speak. No, this could not be allowed. Even if she looked ridiculous and they thought she was a crazy old fool, the child must be saved. Adele had to tell Father about this fateful event. All at once she felt certain that it would take place, that all the visions she had seen would come to pass. This, of course, meant that the vision about Teresa must also be a true one, but right then the inexorability of that event seemed less important to her.

She walked over to the man with the blue scarf and got straight to the point. "You must drive carefully, sir. You mustn't argue with your wife. Because another car will appear and then . . ."

She did not have time to tell him what would happen. The loudspeaker suddenly crackled and a mechanical female voice announced the arrival of the long-awaited passenger train. The door to the waiting room opened at the same instant and Mother and Daughter returned. Behind them came the sounds of the soldiers' commotion in the corridor. The woman looked at her husband inquisitively as she came up to him, but he only shrugged. The officer rushed past them, trying to put on his overcoat with one hand while holding his sheepskin hat and brochure in the other.

Miss Adele knew that she had to go on, that what she had said was insufficient and confused. She could tell by his expression that he hadn't understood a thing and didn't believe her. But somehow she couldn't find the right words. A feeling of increasing helplessness came over her as the precious seconds passed, and with them the chance to do something. Instead she just stood there, mute and foolishly staring. Finally, Father ran out of patience. He picked up his coat and travel bag from the bench and led his wife and daughter towards the exit.

Miss Adele was left alone in the waiting room, feeling useless and discomfited. She had not succeeded in warning them, and had made a fool of herself by trying. If she tried to approach them again on the train, they would certainly refuse to listen to her. Yet she had to do something—she couldn't give up on a literal matter of life and death. But in her overwhelming panic she could think of nothing. She heard the rhythmic clacking of metal wheels outside, and soon the nearest platform was filled with a moving string of lighted windows. That snapped Miss Adele out of her paralysis. She would think of something later, now she had to hurry. Since the train was late it would certainly not stay in the station very long.

She picked up her suitcase and hurried toward the corridor. The soldiers were no longer scattered but had assembled into two columns, ready to move out, the officer to the fore, giving sharp orders. Just as Miss Adele was heading past the military formation toward the platform, the organ-grinder's music started to blare all around her. At first she thought the ragged old man had somehow reached the public-address system and was now seeking to cheer the entire station with his unbearable music through all the loudspeakers. It was so loud that she wished she had both hands free, so she could cover her ears. But that desire soon lost urgency in the face of another vision.

She could not see the context; there was nothing but a pile of bodies. They covered the entire smaller picture, in which nothing moved: these were the corpses of the young soldiers she now heard marching in the background. Death had visited them in countless horrific forms. Here the back of a head was blown off, there was a bloody hole instead of an eye; scattered intestines, a red crater across a chest, stumps where there used to be legs, torsos without heads, unrecognizable joints of human flesh . . . some battlefield's insane harvest of youth curtailed and beauty mutilated.

Miss Adele started to trip over her feet and lose her balance. The last of the marching soldiers turned towards her briefly but had no chance to offer help. Their commanding officer was in a hurry to see his detachment settled on the train to military glory. She was overcome by nausea. Her hand over her mouth, leaning against the wall, she staggered down the corridor and found herself in the station's main hall. She headed for the restroom, not the platform, but ran into two waves of arriving passengers heading for the exit. In other circumstances this would have embarrassed her exceedingly, but now she barely even noticed.

Miss Adele spent a long time leaning over the toilet bowl, until her stomach was completely empty. Although it had been very disagreeable, vomiting had brought her some relief. She splashed her pale face with icy water from the sink, then wiped it with her lace-edged handkerchief, neglecting to remove the drops that had been sprinkled on the upper part of her coat. When she finally returned to the station hall, it was empty. The train was long gone, bearing into the snowy night people about whom she knew what she would have given anything not to know.

When she went back to the window to get a refund on her ticket, the ticket-seller had no way of understanding the sudden sigh that escaped from her as she watched him work, nor the bewilderment that appeared in her eyes, as if they were looking at something terrible, and not these commonplace surroundings. He was even less able to hear the repetitious music of the organ-grinder ringing in her ears—unsurprisingly, since there was no organ-grinder nearby.

The taxi driver who picked her up from the station was equally confused. Looking at her for a moment in his rear-view mirror, he saw her hold her hands over her ears and shake her head, eyes tightly closed. He was used to passengers acting oddly at times, but they were usually young people, not serious-looking, elderly women. He thought of asking her if she needed help, but abandoned the idea. He was suddenly sure he could do nothing to help this lady.

Back home, Miss Adele found a new telegram on the mat below the front door. She locked it away unread with the previous telegram in the carved wooden box where she kept her photo album and old letters. There was no need to open it, since she knew what it said. Just as she knew she would not go to Teresa's funeral. Not because the trip would be too strenuous, nor because she could not tolerate Jacob, but because she would inevitably encounter people along the way. And that had already become a nightmare she could hardly endure.

She had not been one to go out much before, and now she scarcely left the house. This did not seem unusual to any of the neighbors, since she was known to be a woman of retiring character who was not on intimate terms with anyone. Her behavior had become rather strange, indeed, whenever she ran into anyone, but it is well known that old maids sometimes lose their marbles.

Miss Adele's final wait took its time. She would have found it easier to bear could she have seen the end, but the organ-grinder who played for everyone else refused to play for her. After pondering this at length, she could not tell whether he was being especially kind to her or whether this was his ultimate damnation.

5. The Puzzle

Mr. Adam only started to paint late in life, after his retirement. It happened quite unexpectedly. For the first sixty-five years of his life he had never shown any predisposition towards painting, for which he had neither talent nor interest. The arts in general attracted him very little.

The only exception might have been music, although he didn't really enjoy it. Sometimes he would find a radio station devoted mainly to music and leave it on low, just enough to dispel the silence that surrounded him during his long, dreary hours at work. It didn't matter what sort of music was being played; almost any would serve his purpose equally well, although he preferred instrumentals since singing distracted him. All he did at home was sleep, and often not even that, so there was little opportunity for anything else.

Retirement brought Mr. Adam an abundance of empty hours which he must fill. Experience gained at work had taught him that whenever he had to wait an indeterminate time for something, he had to impose obligations upon himself, and then discharge them doggedly, regardless of how unusual they might seem. This at least gave a semblance of meaning to everything. And one could not live without some meaning, however illusory.

He set himself one obligation for every day of the week. On Sunday he cooked, something he had never done before. He bought the biggest cookbook he could find in the bookstore and set himself to prepare every dish in it, in alphabetical order. The uncertainty of how far he dared hope to get at this tempo did not disturb him. He was aware that he would require extreme longevity to reach the end of the book, but that was of no importance to him.

He followed the instructions for each recipe to the letter, and the only trouble he encountered was when they were not specific enough, but allowed the cook to use his own judgment or taste. He did not like everything he cooked, but that did not bother him greatly. He ate his culinary creations down to the last spoonful, throwing nothing away. This was almost a matter of honor to him. Sometimes, when the recipe was intended for several people, he ate the same food the whole week through.

On Monday Mr. Adam rode his bicycle. This was also a new departure. He learned how to ride easily and quite rapidly, despite his advanced age. He was not deterred by bad weather, though he would dress accordingly. The only trouble he had was when the rain spattered his glasses, unpleasantly fogging his vision. He preferred to ride without glasses in a downpour, though that rendered his vision equally foggy.

He always took the same route, each time increasing the distance a little. He tried to conserve his energy so he had enough left to go back by bike. He was only forced to return by other means of transport on the few occasions when there was a sudden turn in the weather, or he was overcome by fatigue. His conscience always plagued him when he gave up like that.

Unlike cooking, cycling had its limits. The route he took never actually ended, since it connected to many others, but even if he were to ride the whole day without stopping, which was not very likely, at midnight he would be required to stop. Tuesday was not for bike riding, but imposed its own obligation.

While still employed, he had read very little except professional journals. Not because there was no opportunity—many of his colleagues read for pleasure to pass the time at work—but because it seemed to him a sign of insufficient dedication to the job. Of course, his work would not have suffered for it, particularly since computers had taken over the bulk of his responsibilities. Now he decided to make up at least partially for this lapse. He became a member of the town library and went there every Tuesday. He entered as soon as it opened and stayed until it closed, only taking a short break early in the afternoon to eat something.

His initial subject was science fiction. This was a natural choice, but Mr. Adam soon gave it up. What he read about first contact seemed unsophisticated for the most part, often to the point of inanity—pulled out of thin air, at best. The number of writers demonstrating any knowledge of the real state of things was quite small, though such knowledge was easy enough to obtain. Disappointed, he was briefly tempted to abandon reading entirely. But giving up in the face of adversity was not in his nature, and besides, he had paid his dues a year in advance. Finally, were he to stop going to the library he would have to think up a new obligation for Tuesday, and that prospect did not please him at all.

He found a solution to this problem, using the same means he had often resorted to at work. Whenever his search in one area drew a blank, he simply broadened his field of vision. Not knowing what else to choose, this time he broadened the field to the farthest limit, like suddenly taking the whole sky instead of one small sector. Instead of science fiction he chose literature in its entirety, but as this turned out to be far greater even than the cookbook, he had no idea at first where to begin.

The main catalogue was indexed by author, and he briefly considered adhering to that order. But then he thought again, and concluded that this would not be a satisfactory approach. He spent some time at the library computer, classifying titles by publication date, and finally obtained a list of books from the oldest to the most recent. The scale of this list did not discourage him at all—he had become accustomed to such challenges long ago. He started to read steadily, without rushing, as if all the time in the world lay before him.

On Wednesdays Mr. Adam went to the zoo. The middle of the week was the right time to visit, when there were far fewer visitors than at weekends. Moreover, if the weather was bad, he would often see no one in the vicinity for long periods. That suited him best. Ideally he would have liked to be completely alone at the zoo, but of course, he was never able to count on that.

Mr. Adam did not behave like the ordinary sort of visitor, who just wanders around enjoying himself. First he found out which animals were housed in the zoo, then he drew up a schedule of visits. Each animal was allotted a whole day. Few of the zoo's inhabitants were worthy of such dedication, but the systematic patience with which Mr. Adam approached everything did not allow him to act otherwise.

He would arrive in the morning at the chosen cage and sit in front of it. When there was no bench he brought a small folding chair from home. He would stay in that spot until nightfall, doing nothing but observe the animal carefully through the bars. He did not know exactly what to expect. Certainly nothing special. What he hoped for was at least a certain reaction to his presence, just an awareness that he was there, perhaps a glance that deliberately crossed his own. Anything short of complete disregard.

It was actually quite easy to attract the animals' attention by offering them food, but Mr. Adam never did. It would be a form of cheating, and he would brook no cheating. Therefore he took no food with him, not even for himself. When he left the zoo on a Wednesday evening, he was often faint with hunger.

On Thursdays Mr. Adam visited churches. Not being religious, he had never been to such places before, and was surprised to learn that the town held sixteen of them. Sometimes he had to walk the whole day in order to take them all in. He could have used public transport, of course, which would have sped things up considerably, but that would have run contrary to Mr. Adam's basic intention. His Monday bike ride was by no means sufficient to keep him in shape, and his need for additional exercise was the more acute after spending all Wednesday sitting still at the zoo. What could be more appropriate than a seriously long walk?

In order to avoid the tedium of repeating the same walk every time, Mr. Adam took a different route every Thursday. This was not done at random; he had worked out a precise plan. He approached it as a simple problem in combinatorial mathematics. There were far more ways of ordering the sixteen points than he imagined he would ever need. The itineraries greatly varied in length, because the algorithm he had chosen took no account of the distance between the churches. He bore up stoically under this inconsiderate mathematical dictate, consoling himself with the reflection that he found longer walks more enjoyable.

Mr. Adam could have visited points other than churches. In principle, the direction of his walks was immaterial to him, so he could not have explained why he had made churches his choice. Luckily, no one ever asked him, which saved him from embarrassment. On reaching a church he began by walking all the way round it, examining it inquisitively, as if seeing it for the first time. Then he would take a little rest, sitting in the churchyard if there was one, before continuing on his way.

In time he got to know the exteriors of all sixteen

churches quite well, and came to regard himself as a real expert in this field. He believed that he alone had noted some of the details. For example, there was always an even number of birds' nests under the eaves. Who knows why? He rarely felt any urge to examine the churches' interiors. He was only tempted to enter on two or three occasions, but he always refrained, and here again he was unable to say what it was that had dissuaded him.

Friday was his day to go to the movies. Mr. Adam would always watch four films in a row, from mid-afternoon to late in the evening. This was by any standard too much. After the second film his impressions were already becoming confused, and by the end of the fourth he would feel truly exhausted, as though he had been working at some strenuous task, rather than sitting in a comfortable seat the whole time. But this did not prompt him to decrease the number of films.

Mr. Adam was not the least bit selective regarding the repertoire. He did not have a favorite film genre, although he felt most relaxed watching romantic comedies. Action films left him rather indifferent, and although they were loud as a rule, he even managed to doze off to them, particularly if they were the last of that day's four. He found thrillers unconvincing, although not as much as most science fiction films. Those sometimes appeared outrageously idiotic; he could never understand why filmgoers got so excited about them. Overly erotic scenes embarrassed him, but fortunately that was not noticeable in the dark.

Although it might have appeared that Mr. Adam chose his films at random, this was not at all the case. He bought his tickets with great care, concentrating on films that were expected to sell out. Just before the lights dimmed, Mr. Adam would stand up for a moment and look all around. He would feel annoyed should he spot any empty seats. Those empty places would bother him until the end of the show. He only felt at ease in a full house. That alone could temporarily lighten the burden of solitude which, like some sinister inheritance, hung over from his former work.

Mr. Adam passed Saturday in the park. He needed to spend time outside in the fresh air after so many hours indoors the previous day. Late in the morning he would go to the large city park with its pond in the middle, and head for the bench where he always sat. On the rare occasions when someone was already sitting in the place he considered his own, on the far left-hand end of the bench next to the wrought iron armrest, Mr. Adam would wait unobtrusively to one side for the bench to come free. It did not bother him if the remainder of the bench was occupied, though he avoided entering into conversation with strangers.

On warm, sunny days he would stay there until dusk, doing nothing but idly watching what was happening around him: people strolling by, dogs chasing each other frantically on the grass, leaves rustling in the surrounding treetops, birds gliding silently through the blue sky, sudden ripples on the smooth surface of the pond. Until recently this idleness would have seemed an extremely foolish waste of time. Now, however, the tables were turned. He saw everything which had gone before as a waste of time. All his previous life. All the years, all the effort, all the hopes.

That was not how it had seemed, at any rate not in the beginning. Not in the least. It was a pioneering time of great excitement. Great expectations. And great naiveté. They thought that contact was only a matter of time. The cosmos was teeming with life, messages were streaming between worlds, all that was needed was to prick up our electronic ears to hear them. Without this optimistic certainty the money for the first projects would never have been found—investments that could pay off stupendously as soon as the inexhaustible wealth of knowledge started to pour in from the stars.

Mr. Adam had fond memories of those early days, despite later disappointments. There was something romantic in the anticipation that overcame him whenever he put on his earphones. He spent countless hours listening to the cacophony streaming from the skies, straining to recognize some sort of orderly system in it. Like all his colleagues, he secretly hoped that he would be the first to hear the signal.

But as time passed and nothing arrived except inarticulate noise, the true proportions of the task started to emerge. Since listening to the closest star systems produced no results, there was a shift to more distant ones, but each new step brought a substantial increase in their number. The initial enthusiasm foundered when it was established that more than one generation might be needed to complete the task. This led many people to leave the search for extraterrestrial life in favor of more promising areas, and financiers were less and less willing to continue investing in something so vague and unreliable.

Fortunately, at that point computers were introduced, with their numerous advantages over people: they are incomparably faster, more effective and dependable, and do not quickly lose heart in the face of failure. Even so, Mr. Adam did not look upon their use with total approval. Computers reduced people to commonplace assistants whose sole purpose was to serve them. What had begun as a noble project for the chosen few degenerated into a routine technical duty that almost anyone could perform—mere waiting, leached of any true excitement. The last remnants of romance vanished without a trace.

After several decades had passed, and the computers had meticulously checked many millions of sun systems but detected no sign of extraterrestrial intelligence, Mr. Adam felt a certain gloomy exultation. His feelings were paradoxical, because only under opposite circumstances, with contact made, would he be able to say that his life's work had meaning. On the other hand, contact achieved with the assistance of computers would to him be some sort of injustice, almost an anticlimax.

Despite the silence of the cosmos, the search programs were not discontinued. Although large, the number of investigated stars was trifling compared to the total number of suns in the galaxy. In principle, one of the giant radio telescopes could start receiving the long-awaited message from the very next spot in the sky. However, as his retirement approached, Mr. Adam became more and more skeptical in this regard.

It was not just the realization that the prospects of finding Others within his lifetime were negligible; he could somehow reconcile himself to that if he was sure they were on the right track. But the suspicion started to trouble him that the reason for failure lay not in the fact that only a tiny part of the sky had been investigated, rather in something much more fundamental. What if some of the basic assumptions upon which the entire project was founded were wrong?

Maybe there was no one out there after all. Maybe sentient beings were so unlikely that they had only appeared in one place. Everyone was convinced of the opposite, but this conviction had no solid basis. Behind it might lie an unwillingness to accept the terrifying fact of cosmic solitude. As the years passed, Mr. Adam started to feel anxious under the unbounded wasteland. The starry sky pressed heavily upon him at times. The strange need arose for some sort of shelter, for consolation.

Suppose extraterrestrials exist and are communicating, but we don't recognize it? What if they were doing it in some other way, and not the way we presumed?

Mr. Adam had never asked himself this question seriously. Whenever it stole quietly into his consciousness he would expel it hurriedly, with a sense of hostility and guilt, as any true believer rejects a heretical thought. All his sober, scientific being opposed it. Similar inconsistencies had prevented him from coming to like science fiction.

He still considered this the proper approach, despite all the unfulfilled hopes in the life that yawned behind him. And at the end of the day, what other means besides electromagnetic waves could be used to communicate between the stars? With regard to his past, the daily obligations he set himself helped put it out of his mind. Perhaps these obligations really were meaningless, but the problem of meaning no longer plagued him. He enjoyed everything he was doing now, even idling in the park each Saturday, and that pleasure was all that mattered. In any case, he was not just idly passing the time. He had recently started to paint.

Music had been the catalyst. Upon reaching the park one Saturday at the beginning of summer, he found that a bandstand had been erected near his bench. It had not been there seven days previously, nor had anything heralded its advent. This had irritated Mr. Adam no end. Although pretty, with its slender columns and domed roof, he considered it an unconscionable desecration of the environment. In addition, the bandstand largely blocked his view of the pond, and he seriously considered looking for another place to sit. But habit won out and he stayed on his bench, scornfully endeavoring to disregard the interloper.

This ceased to be possible when musicians climbed onto the bandstand at noon. They were formally dressed and the conductor even wore a tuxedo with a large white flower in his lapel. They sat on chairs placed in a circle and spent some time tuning their instruments. Mr. Adam found this dissonance an additional nuisance. It not only sounded awful but started to attract park visitors, and rather a large crowd soon formed. A crowd of people, however, was the last thing Mr. Adam wanted after his Friday spent in a packed movie theatre.

He would have to move after all. He couldn't stand this. But just as he started to rise the music began. He stopped halfway, transfixed, then slowly sat down again on the bench. All at once he was no longer surrounded by too many people, his bad mood disappeared, and nothing existed beyond the music. He stared fixedly at the bandstand, immobile, listening intently.

This paralysis did not last long. He came out of it suddenly and began feverishly rummaging through his jacket pockets. It seemed to take forever to find what he was after. He always carried a notebook and pen with him. Since retirement he had not written anything in it, but he carried it with him nonetheless. He opened it hurriedly and started to draw. He dared not miss a thing.

He drew short, brusque lines, just like a stenographer taking rapid dictation. The pages in the notebook were small, so he filled them quickly. He was afraid he would run out of pages before the music ended, but fortunately the notebook was thick enough. Even so, he made the last drawing on the brown cardboard covers. Had the music lasted a moment longer, there would not have been enough room. The very thought suddenly filled him with horror.

The listeners' echoing applause after the last chords had the effect of an alarm clock suddenly going off. Mr. Adam jerked like one waking from restless sleep; he turned this way and that in confusion for several moments as if trying to figure out where he was. He feared he would arouse the suspicion of those around him, but no one paid any attention to the old man on the end of the bench, engrossed in his writing. All eyes were turned toward the conductor who was bowing theatrically.

Mr. Adam stood up and walked away unobtrusively. There was no reason to stay there any longer. During his extensive walks between churches he had come to know the town quite well, so he knew exactly where to find a shop with painting supplies. There might have been one closer, but he would waste more time inquiring after and finding it than it took to reach the other. The salesman noted with a smile that he was clearly preparing a serious project, judging by the quantity of materials he had purchased. Mr. Adam returned the smile, mumbled something vague, then hurried home.

Unskilled at painting, he had trouble setting up the easel properly, but then got down to work. He opened the notebook and began carefully transferring onto the canvas what he had written, as if neatly copying over rough notes taken in a hurry. He worked slowly but with passion, unaware of the passage of time. When he had finished it was already quite dark.

He did not know what he had painted. Viewed from up close it looked just like random strokes of paint. He was convinced, however, that not a single stroke of the brush had been accidental, that everything was exactly as the music ordered, in spite of his inexperience. When he moved back from the painting a bit, he thought he could make out part of a larger shape, but he wasn't sure. It suddenly crossed his mind that before him was just one piece of some larger puzzle. He thought briefly about what to do with the canvas, and then he hung it unframed on one of the bare walls.

The next Saturday he went to the park well prepared. He no longer needed the notebook as intermediary. He sat at his usual place on the bench and set up the easel in front of him, holding paintbrush and palette. In different circumstances he would have abhorred the inquisitive peering of bystanders, although a painter at work was certainly not unusual in the park. Now, however, he paid no attention, concentrating exclusively on the impending concert.

This time he painted rapidly. It lasted just as long as the music. When the applause resounded, Mr. Adam, panting and sweaty, had just finished covering the last white space with paint. Before the crowd dispersed, several pairs of eyes glanced at the painting, perplexed, since it did not depict anything recognizable. A short, elderly woman dressed in a bright orange dress stopped by the bench for a moment. She took an enormous pair of glasses out of her handbag and examined first the painting and then the painter. "Very nice," she said with a smile. She put her glasses back in her handbag, nodded in brief approval and walked away.

As a man unaccustomed to compliments, Mr. Adam felt ill at ease. The woman's words were by no means unpleasant, quite the contrary, yet he was still glad she had not lingered. He would have been in the awkward situation of having to say something in reply. He waited a while for the elderly woman to move on, then collected his equipment and hurried home. He could have stayed in the park longer, his work was completed and the day was very fine, but curiosity got the better of him.

He put the new canvas next to the other one on the wall. He had no expectations and thus was not very disappointed when it turned out they had no points in common. For a moment, though, he thought he could make out some part of a greater whole in the second painting, too, but here again it was most likely just his imagination. In the absence of any recognizable form he thought he saw something that was not actually there. This was a trap he had learned to avoid back in the early period, before computers, while listening to the stars with his own ears. If you're expecting a horseman you have to be very careful not to mistake your heartbeat for the beat of a horse's hoofs.

The next fourteen Saturdays, all summer long, each time Mr. Adam returned from the park he had one more painting to place on the wall next to the others. In time his brisk, almost frenetic painting became something of an attraction at the park, and a good many music-lovers would stand around to watch him work. He paid no attention to them. At the end of the music and painting he would quickly glance through those gathered around him, but never once did he catch sight of the slight figure in orange.

When Mr. Adam reached the park on the first Saturday in September, carrying his painting materials as usual, a surprise awaited him. The bandstand had disappeared as unexpectedly as it had arrived. It had been removed very carefully, leaving no trace behind—not even trampled grass. He darted in bewilderment around the spot where the little structure had stood, overcome by completely opposite feelings from those which had assailed him in the beginning. Now he missed the bandstand, and the environment seemed somehow naked and incomplete without it. For a moment he considered inquiring as to why it was no longer there, maybe even lodging a complaint, but he did not know where this should be done and in the end dropped the idea.

He returned home in a dejected mood and sat in the armchair facing the wall covered with paintings. The canvases formed a large square: four paintings in each of four rows. He stayed there for seven full days, only leaving the armchair to take a quick bite or go to the bathroom. He even slept there in his clothes, but the brief, restless, erratic sleep did not refresh him. He changed the distribution of the paintings from time to time. During that long week filled with almost constant pouring rain, he tried just a tiny fraction of all possible combinations of the sixteen canvases.

On the evening of the following Saturday he got up

from the armchair, stretched, and went to the window. Rays from the low sun in the western sky were cutting a path through patchy clouds, just like gleaming swords. He stayed there a while looking absently at the flickering play of light. Then he went to the wall and took down the paintings. He couldn't carry them all at once and had to make two trips to the basement, where he left them.

When he came up from the basement the second time, he went into the kitchen, took the large cookbook down from the shelf, opened it at the bookmark and became immersed in reading the recipe that was next in line. The following day was Sunday, his cooking day.

6. The Violinist

THE PROFESSOR KNEW HE would not survive the night.

Dr Dean did not tell him that, of course. At least not to his face. But his body language confirmed the inevitable.

As usual, the doctor dropped by to see him at 23:10, after his shift was over. Before he entered the room, he spent a few minutes in the glass cubicle outside, talking quietly with the duty nurse, Mrs. Roszel. They talked in low voices, periodically looking through the glass at the sick man's bed. At one point Mrs. Roszel shook her bowed head and raised clenched fingers to her eyes, as if to wipe away tears.

When he appeared before the professor, Dr. Dean tried his best to appear relaxed and cheerful, but he was not a very good actor. He must have had to play the role of false optimist many times in his long career, but the small things still gave him away. He avoided looking the professor in the eye, finding various excuses to turn his glance aside. He checked his pulse, though they both knew it served no purpose. Then he tightened and smoothed the bedclothes with brusque, nervous movements, which was also unnecessary and in any case Mrs. Roszel's job, which she performed frequently and expertly.

Then he went to stand by the large window and stare out at the spring Princeton night. Gusts of rain beat against the pane, making ephemeral streaks that distorted the doctor's dimly reflected face. He sighed, and told his patient that he actually envied him. What he wouldn't give to be in his place! The professor was already in bed, but before the doctor lay a good half-hour's drive through this foul weather, to be followed by at least another hour filled with various obligations, all to be discharged before he could finally go to bed himself. But such was life. Some people were lucky and some were not.

He hesitated after saying this, because the conclusion was somehow inappropriate, given the circumstances. His intention had been to cheer the professor up and instill some hope, however unfounded, but it seemed he had inadvertently gone too far. It might have appeared cynical or even cruel to claim that someone whose hours were literally numbered was lucky. He turned from the window, and for the first time looked at his patient's haggard face.

The expression on it made the doctor feel foolish, for it told him that his acting had been as unsuitable as it was inept. He had seen that expression before, albeit rarely. The professor was not only conscious of what awaited him, but prepared for it. He did not expect any consolation, nor did he need it. This was no place for empty words.

The doctor went up to the bed and shook the old man's cold, slender hand. "Good night, Professor." It took considerable effort to keep his voice from trembling.

"Good-bye, Doctor."

Dr Dean gently patted the back of his patient's hand with his free one. He tried to smile, but only managed a grimace. Then he turned and, more hastily than he liked or had intended, left the patient's room. As he put on his raincoat and hat in the cubicle, he exchanged a few more words with Mrs. Roszel.

Ten minutes later the nurse went into the patient's

room to prepare him for the night. She began by giving him an oval blue pill. The Professor was given one every night before sleeping, and he would try to swallow it quickly with a little water because it tasted bitter. He took it as dutifully as ever, although he felt it was a pointless exercise. Not to have done so might have been awkward for Mrs. Roszel, and she took care of him not only conscientiously but with affection.

As she needlessly straightened his bedclothes, she murmured something about the rain that had been pouring ceaselessly since early afternoon. Then she went to the window and closed the curtains. The drumming of the heavy drops became suddenly muffled and distant. She went back to the bed and spent a few moments silently arranging the yellow wildflowers on his night table. It seemed as if she wanted to say something else, but was hesitating for some reason. When she left the room finally, still without saying it, the professor felt relieved. He did not feel like talking to Mrs. Roszel right then.

The nurse stopped at the entrance to her cubicle and turned off the strip light. "I'll be here if you need anything, Professor," she said softly. "Just call for me. Good night."

"Good night, Mrs. Roszel."

He looked at her through the glass, sitting at her small desk. Now the only source of light in both rooms was a lamp with a thick yellow shade. Its dull glow made the white ribbon which kept the nurse's hair off her forehead look like a golden aureole. She had lowered her head to read a book, without taking her usual last glance at her patient.

The pill soon began to take effect. He first felt the dull, unremitting pain in his stomach soften to barely noticeable discomfort, as if a large pillow had been placed over his abdomen. Then the familiar feeling of floating began. Suddenly the bed seemed to disappear and he was lying in empty space, completely weightless. He knew it was only an illusion, but that did nothing to lessen the intoxicating pleasure of the feeling. Not even tonight.

The floating would not last long. Before he fell asleep he would experience a brief feeling that his body had separated into an assembly of weakly connected spheres. Soundlessly, the fragile links between them would start to dissolve, and he would melt into nothingness, merging with the black infinity that surrounded him. His last conscious thought would be that this must be what dying was like. Courtesy of the blue pill, he had died every night since his arrival at the hospital.

Come morning he would wake in a bad mood. It bothered him that he was not afraid of dying. Death seemed somehow attractive; it was almost as if he wanted to die, and he felt that he should not feel like that. If for no other reason, he hoped he would not die before finding the answers to several questions that had plagued him throughout his adult life. It would be quite unjust if he were denied them—but perhaps the world was only orderly, and not just. Certainly, there was very little time left for justice to be done.

On this occasion, however, he did not break up into spheres. He was prevented by the sudden intrusion of music. It was barely audible but certainly present, though he could not determine the source; it seemed to come from all around him. Mrs. Roszel kept a small radio on her desk, but she would never play it this late. He looked in the nurse's direction. She was still engrossed in her book, apparently not hearing a thing.

A violin was weaving a slow, almost dreamy melody. He did not recognize it at once though he had played the violin since childhood, but something stirred in the depths of his memory, striving to reach the surface. For a despairing moment he thought it would fail; that the memory, like so many others, would stay bound forever below the thick webbing that enveloped his aged mind. Then the sound, as if wanting to help, grew a tiny bit louder—and a bolt of lightning flashed through the gap of sixty years, taking him back to that long-ago summer day in northern Italy.

The small town in which he found himself as he walked the back roads from Milan to Genoa seemed to be completely deserted, even here on the main square, but this did not surprise him. All small places give such an impression during the siesta hour between two and four o'clock in the afternoon, when the inhabitants retreat from the unbearable heat into the shuttered cool of their homes.

This did not bother him very much. The fewer local people he ran into, the fewer difficulties he would have. He was a shy fifteen-year-old, and he found the language difficult. Almost no one understood his native German, and he had only a very limited command of the melodious speech of this area, with its open, resonant vowels. So he took pains to enter into conversation with people only when necessary, shrinking from their presumed distaste for his accent that must sound to them like the screech of rusty gears.

The *piazza* was approximately square in shape, with a small fountain in the middle. The young man put his canvas rucksack on the ground and started to fill his cupped hands with water from the arching stream. He splashed his face with water, letting it drip, and then looked around, head raised, squinting at the white stone façades. His eyes, used to the monotonous greyness of northern lands, constantly ached from the bright colors of Italy. Everything around him was vibrating, twinkling, glimmering, bursting. He had the feeling of being trapped in a crystal that absorbed light from all sides, but did not let it out again.

The silence was suddenly broken by the sound of

a violin. It came from the top of a wide, three-story building that was separated from the church belfry by an extremely narrow, shaded street. The window in the garret was open, probably the only one unshuttered on the whole square, and in the room behind it someone had chosen to fill this stagnant, bright, deserted hour with music. It was not a student practicing, but an experienced violinist, a master whose fingers had total command of the instrument.

The chance listener next to the fountain stared, enchanted, at the high window. Even had he not been a skilled violinist himself, there was no way he could have remained unaffected. Cascades of pure harmony streamed down from above as if from heaven. They penetrated deep inside him, to the very center of his being, where they created resonant reflections. To devote his utmost concentration to listening, he closed his eyes.

He was trying to expel the omnipresent light to take best advantage of the sound, but without success. The light did not disappear under his lowered eyelids. Not only was it still there, it suppressed everything else with the power of its unabated radiance. And then, in a moment of revelation, he understood. The light was still there because that was what the music was all about. Could there be anything more fitting? What was invoked could not have been presented to him so comprehensively by any other means. He was inside the light, and its secrets started to peel away before him, finally displaying the wondrous simplicity of its essence.

He stayed there so long, motionless, listening to the light, that he lost track of time. Something very strange had happened to time. Its course seemed to decelerate, gradually at first, then exponentially, until it finally stopped, frozen in a timeless ray that rushed through strangely distorted space. Under the tremendous pressure of light, space started to undulate, turn and twist, until it was transformed into a vortex that carried him, powerfully and irresistibly, towards the black point deep within its center. The point became a circle, then a wide opening in the fabric of reality, then an immense pit of deepest night, sucking him into itself like a speck of dust.

When he came to his senses he was at first uncertain where he was. For a moment he thought he was still in the heart of darkness, but then he realized it was not total, for it was pierced by sunbeams that slanted like sparkling spears through narrow windows in a thick stone wall. The rays were multicolored because of the stained glass they had passed through. The music had ceased.

The young man realized he was lying on something cold and hard. He tried to get up, but a pair of hands appeared and gently but firmly pushed him back. A figure in a brown mantle bent over him; it was a priest, with greying hair and beard, wearing small, round, wire-rimmed glasses. He smiled at the young man and then began to speak. The young man could make out only a few words in the deluge of Italian: sun, fall, brought into the church.

He started to get up again, hastily explaining to the priest that he had to return to the square as soon as possible so as to hear the remainder of the music of light—it meant so much to him. Otherwise he was fine, there was no need to worry: he had experienced enlightenment, not sunstroke. The priest's only reply was an uncomprehending shrug, but this time there was no need for the priest's hands to stop him from getting up. He had not even reached a sitting position when his head started to swim. Overcome by exhaustion, he lay back down on the marble platform by the wall of the church on which they had laid him when they brought him in.

The priest reached for the wet cloth on the weary traveller's forehead and started to wipe it over his cheeks and neck. He was still talking, but the young man could make even less sense of it than before. He stopped listening, as despair filled his soul. If only he had stayed there a little longer! If only that vortex hadn't whisked him away so soon, he could have grasped the essence of light. As it was, he could only remember broken fragments, loose threads from the tapestry, pebbles detached from the mosaic. But at least he knew the mosaic existed and that it was flawless in its irreducible, self-evident necessity. Yet it seemed he had no right to hope ever to see it again, though he knew that he would devote the rest of his life to its tireless pursuit.

It was sunset when he left the church. He still felt a bit light-headed, but he had to be on his way. The *piazza* was now full of people, and the shutters on the windows stood wide. All but one. He spent some time before the entrance to the three-story building, whose highest window was now only a blind, mute eye, but in the end he did not seek out the musician in the garret. It was not his poor knowledge of Italian that prevented him, for he would have done the same thing if he could have spoken German. What could he say to the Violinist, in any language? Moreover, he suspected that He was no longer there at all.

There was no radiance this time. Here in the gloom of the hospital room, he no longer had to close his eyes to listen to the message of the music. The thrill he had experienced once, so long ago, was not here, nor would it have suited this period of his life or his present circumstances. All that he felt, aside from the intoxicating effect of the blue pill, was a moment of happiness coursing gently through him, stemming from the knowledge that there was justice in the world, after all.

The great mosaic appeared before him, woven from

vibrating threads of air. It was almost completely filled in. He knew perfectly well which pebbles were missing. He had not been allowed to find them himself, as he had the others, but that no longer mattered; he had long ago discarded vanity. All that mattered was to see them at last, during the short time that remained to him.

The violin began to build shapes out of sound that slotted perfectly into the empty spaces. Each part represented a distinct revelation: amazingly simple, magnificently complex, wondrously unbelievable, insanely unacceptable. Now he understood why he would never have been able to find some of the answers. He simply did not have the right questions.

When the grand architecture of tones was finally complete, he had to confront its most disturbing characteristic: the whole and its parts were not in harmony. When he focused on the whole, the parts became fuzzy—and vice versa. He could not concentrate his internal eye on both at the same time. Once everything inside him would have rebelled at this imperfection, but not any longer: it was his preconceptions that had been wrong, of course. The world did not have to be orderly, at least not in the way he had imagined it. The Violinist based his composition on completely different principles.

He did not realize at first that the music had stopped. It was only when the mosaic came apart, giving way to the dark space it had temporarily occupied, that he became aware of the silence. He lay there confused for several moments, staring in front of him. Something must surely follow, this seemed inevitable. Death, perhaps? Was there any moment more suitable to die? But nothing happened. The spheres were still tightly grouped together.

At the thought of death he was overcome with fear. That had never happened before, but now something had undermined his previous readiness to die. For a while he could not identify it, but then it dawned on him: if he were to die right then, he would take the knowledge he had just gained to his grave. It would be as if nothing had happened, as if he had not finally comprehended. He had longed for it primarily to satisfy his own curiosity, but now that seemed selfish. No, he must at all costs leave a record of what he had learned.

But how? What could he do, lying here on his deathbed? And how much time did he have left? Certainly not much. He felt a cold wave of panic creep down the back of his neck. He started to look feverishly about the dark room, perceiving the outlines of familiar objects. Nothing he saw seemed of any help, until the lighted figure of the nurse in her cubicle came into his field of vision. His heart began to beat faster. That was it! There was no other choice. She was his last hope.

"Mrs. Roszel," he called, his voice raised and impatient.

The nurse lifted her eyes from her book, then got up and hurried to her patient.

As he watched her approach, it crossed his mind that he didn't actually know how to tell her what he had to say. The best thing would be if he had a violin. Then he could play it all to her, transmitting what he had just heard with utmost fidelity. There would be nothing of the vagueness, ambiguity or imperfection that went with words. Everything would be crystal clear, even the most difficult aspects. But there was no violin, unfortunately. He had to rely on language.

He did not hesitate for a moment over which language to use. The gears might sound rusty, but they fit together most precisely, leaving the least room for idle motion, friction and resistance. He thought with a smile how strange it was that this language, which came nearest to music in terms of expressiveness, was farthest away in terms of sonority. In addition, it was the language he felt closest to. He would never have been able to express something as complex in a foreign language. Even in his mother tongue he would have considerable trouble.

There was no time to waste on an introduction so he went straight to the point as soon as Mrs. Roszel reached the head of the bed. He spoke quickly, concisely wherever possible, more extensively when that could not be avoided. He was full of sympathy for the expression of bewilderment and disbelief upon her face, and for her periodic helpless shrug of the shoulders. What he was revealing to her was the very foundation which upheld the universe. Fortunately, she did not need to try to understand what he was saying. It would be enough to remember his words, clear and coherent, so as to transmit them faithfully to those who were capable of comprehension. That, at least, would not be difficult.

He was describing the last part of the puzzle when he felt the links between the spheres finally loosen. He was not afraid that time would run out before he finished. There was justice in the world, was there not? The ways of the Violinist might be subtle, but He was certainly not malicious. What would be the sense in stopping him now, at the very end, after everything He had offered him? None, of course. The professor continued to speak softly to Mrs. Roszel, who was still listening carefully. The patient darkness waited for him to reach the end before engulfing him. He fell into it cheerfully, with a feeling of accomplishment. He had given the world his greatest legacy. Had he dared hope for anything greater?

7. The Violin-Maker

To THE POLICE INSPECTOR, it was an open-and-shut case. Mr. Tomasi, master violin-maker, had committed suicide by jumping from the window of the garret of the three-story building where he lived and ran his celebrated workshop. The tragic incident was reported by two eye-witnesses, a baker's roundsmen, delivering bread and rolls, who had been crossing the square early that morning. After hesitating a moment they had fearfully approached the place where the unfortunate man lay. He showed no signs of life, even though they could not see any external injuries.

Inspector Muratori quickly arrived at the scene of the incident and found out from the agitated young men, who had never seen death at first-hand before, that nothing had heralded the falling body. They had heard no sounds before the dull thud on the sidewalk, which had frightened the pigeons at the little fountain in the middle of the square like a sudden detonation. Most suicides who take their lives by jumping from a height make their intentions known by shouting once they have stepped into the abyss and it is too late to change anything. Only those who are firmly convinced that they are doing the right thing remain silent to the end.

One glance at the three-story building told Inspector Muratori where Mr. Tomasi had jumped from. The only open window was in the garret. Actually, he could have jumped off the roof, but there was no reason to choose such a steep, inaccessible place since the window was far more suitable and served his purpose equally well. Although one might not expect it of a suicide, the policeman knew that they did not, as a rule, make their last moments more difficult than necessary.

His examination of the inside of the house revealed nothing to conflict with the suicide hypothesis—on the contrary. When he climbed up to the garret that looked out onto the square, the inspector found the door locked from the inside. This was a precautionary measure typical of someone who did not want to be deterred from carrying out his intention. The door had to be forced, because there was no way to push the key out of the lock so as to open it with a skeleton key. The small room was sparsely furnished: a table and four chairs, a single bed, a washstand with a basin and pitcher in the corner, a large mirror. There was no rug on the floor, no curtains at the window, no pictures on the walls.

Mr. Umbertini, the tall, thin man in his late twenties who was the late master violin-maker's assistant and lived alone with him in the house, explained that the garret was used exclusively for the final testing of new instruments. Mr. Tomasi would go inside and play there alone for some time. Then he would come out, either with a smile on his face, which meant that he was satisfied with his work, or with a handful of firewood and broken strings; then it was best to stay away from him.

The inspector's efforts, with the help of the visibly distressed Mr. Umbertini, to find a farewell letter that his master might have left somewhere produced no results. This was not unusual. Those who did not really want to kill themselves, even though they actually did in the end, were the most frequent writers of such messages. Determined suicides did not find it necessary to interpret or justify their actions to the world, or to make their farewells.

By all appearances, Mr. Tomasi belonged to that category. Obviously the man had been firmly resolved to take this step, and had set about it without hesitation. It was a textbook case, clear and unambiguous. There was nothing more to investigate. The causes that had led the esteemed master violin-maker to commit suicide had not been established, but were of no interest to earthly justice. Let divine justice handle them, for it alone could know what had been on the suicide's mind.

Inspector Muratori ordered Mr. Umbertini to pack his things and leave the house so that it could be sealed pending probate. For a moment it seemed that the assistant wanted to make a comment or add something, about this or some other matter, but he held back. That was just as well. Everything had already been said, and the policeman could by no means help the poor man who was suddenly out on the street. But Inspector Muratori had seen far worse fates. This fellow would manage. A man who had learned the violin-maker's trade under maestro Tomasi need never be without an income. Such a recommendation would easily find him a job with another violin-maker, or he might even open his own shop.

The experienced policeman was rarely mistaken in his conclusions about people and their fates, but he was wrong this time. Mr. Umbertini neither looked for new employment nor tried to set up making violins on his own. With the savings he had been putting aside for years, he rented a small room in one of the narrow little streets off the square where he used to live. The rent was not high because the room was partially below street level and quite humid. This did not bother him unduly. In any event he only went there to sleep.

Mr. Umbertini spent most of his time in a tavern not far from the maestro's house. He had not frequented the place before, primarily because he hadn't been the least inclined to drink, but also because it had a bad reputation as a hangout for the *demi-monde*. Now neither reason mattered. He started to drink, first moderately, just enough to feel slightly intoxicated; then more and more. He hardly felt when he crossed the line and became addicted. The tavern only served cheap, low quality wines and spirits that made Mr. Umbertini's head ache for a long time after waking in his dirty basement bed, but that did not deter him from going there every day.

At first the other tavern regulars were suspicious of the new patron and avoided his company. With his genteel manners and appearance, he was not part of their world. But as time passed and he became more and more like them in his person and behavior, they slowly started to warm to him. He no longer drank alone; they began to join him until finally all the places at his table were occupied almost all the time. They were a motley collection, and just a few months ago he certainly could not have imagined himself among them: frowning mercenaries from a regiment camped near the town, rotten-toothed and withered prostitutes, pickpockets on their way back from forays to the outdoor markets, tattered beggars, blemished and maimed.

Although Mr. Umbertini had no desire to talk about the suicide, with these people or with anyone else, the topic could not be avoided once their relations with the former assistant to the celebrated violin-maker, by now a thoroughly unkempt drunk, became familiar enough to remove their inhibitions. Unlike the police, who found it unnecessary to delve into what had forced the maestro to suicide, this mystery had never stopped intriguing prying minds, even in such a hole as this. Mr. Umbertini was subjected to a variety of approaches, from flattery through cajolery to threats, to get him to explain what had happened, but he withstood all such pressures without uttering a word. However, he could not avoid listening to the conjectures expounded by his fellow-drinkers at the table in the tavern, through the dense, stale cigarette smoke and sharp smell of sour wine.

One of the mercenaries, a man with a black patch over his left eye and a face full of scars, claimed that he had heard from a reliable source that a legacy of madness in the family lay behind it all. Mr. Tomasi's paternal grandfather, a carpenter from a nearby village, had also taken his life, but in a far more painful way. When his mind had gone black he had shut himself in his workshop and started to stick every sharp tool he could find into his body. Not a single wound was fatal, but he died in prolonged agony, from blood loss, without uttering a single cry during that multiple, self-inflicted impalement. When his household forced their way into the workshop they beheld a horrible sight. The carpenter's body on the floor, arms outstretched like some horizontal crucifixion, resembled a hedgehog with thirty-three quills sticking out of it. His wife, who was five months pregnant, had a miscarriage and his only son, who was four at the time, was haunted his whole life by nightmares that caused him to wake up screaming.

Mr. Umbertini could easily have refuted this awful story, but he didn't. In the early days of his apprenticeship he had met the maestro's paternal grandfather. He had been a watch-mender here in town and had died in his sleep from heart failure at an advanced age. He had outlived his wife by several years, leaving seven children. The third of them, the first son after two daughters, was Mr. Tomasi's father, a cheerful and rather unruly man, certainly unburdened by dark stains from childhood, who died of suffocation on a fishbone, having been so incautious as to refill his mouth before he had finished laughing. Although not yet full grown, the younger of his two sons, Alberto, who had inherited his mother's fine ear for music, took over his father's workshop where musical instruments were made and repaired. Not long afterwards he narrowed his activities exclusively to making violins, and over time earned a reputation for his exceptional workmanship.

One of the prostitutes, whose original beauty could still be discerned despite her dilapidated state, though she was barely over thirty, had a completely different story. She had learned from someone completely trustworthy that the cause of Mr. Tomasi's suicide was unrequited love. A travelling circus had camped near the town the previous summer and given performances on the square. Three musicians accompanied most of the acts, among them a young Gypsy woman who played the violin. At first the master violin-maker had complained about the noisy disturbance every evening in front of his house, but when he saw and heard the girl he became more cordial.

He went to the window evening after evening and pretended to watch the events on the square, but never actually took his eyes off the young Gypsy. Finally, he went up to her at the end of a show, bringing the best instrument he had ever made. He invited her to his house and proposed that she play this violin for him alone during the coming night, promising to pay her generously in return. The girl whispered briefly to one of the other two musicians, and then accepted. When she left Mr. Tomasi's house the next morning she was carrying the precious instrument wrapped in brown felt.

The next evening the master violin-maker waited impatiently on the terrace for the customary circus performance, but no one appeared. In the meantime the travelling show had decamped and continued on its way. Mr. Tomasi hired a horse at daybreak and set out in frantic search of them. He went to many of the nearby towns without finding a trace of the entertainers.

The earth seemed to have swallowed them up. Completely crushed, he had finally been forced to abandon his search. He returned home, hoping that time would heal his wounds and that he would somehow forget the beautiful violinist, but he couldn't get over her. He fell into a deeper and deeper depression, slowly losing the will and ability to make any more instruments. Finally, sunk in total despair, he decided to end his suffering.

The late master violin-maker's assistant knew from the outset that this story hadn't a grain of truth, but he didn't say so, among other things so as not to ruin the woman's pleasurable excitement as she recounted her tale. There was, in fact, a sad tale of love in the violin-maker's life, but it dated from his much younger days, when he was still learning the skills of his trade. Love blossomed between him and a close cousin on his mother's side. Although forbidden and clandestine, it was tempestuous, as often happens at that age. Who knows how things might have ended had illness not intervened. The girl came down with galloping tuberculosis and died only a few weeks later. He never became attached to a single woman after that, although he did not renounce them. He tried to be as inconspicuous as possible when he slaked his urges, usually going to other towns for that purpose.

One of the pickpockets, a man with long, clever fingers, but a face that was the very incarnation of innocence, swore on his honor that he had first-hand knowledge about the real reason why Mr. Tomasi had killed himself. It was because of a huge gambling loss he had suffered. The violin-maker had been in the clutches of this obsession for some time, although no one knew anything about it, not even his assistant who lived under the same roof. A group of gamblers used to meet secretly at his house every Friday, going up to the garret from which he had finally jumped to his death. They would cover the window with the blanket from the bed so no one would suspect anything from outside, and then the game that had started by candlelight would often last till dawn.

As an honorable man, the violin-maker had been convinced that his companions were his equals in integrity. He had had not the slightest inkling that he had fallen into a network of shrewd and unscrupulous cheats. At first they bet small amounts, and he mostly won. Then Lady Luck suddenly turned her back on him. He started losing, not only his money but his common sense. He agreed to increase the bets in the futile hope that he would win back what he had lost, but he only sank deeper and deeper into debt. When his cash and valuables disappeared, he started to write IOUs. First he lost his large estate in the country, then his house in town. He still managed to hold up somehow, but when the cards took away the last of his expensive instruments, he realized he had hit rock bottom. In the end he caught on, realizing he had been the victim of a trick, but there was no turning back. Unable to live with the thought that his violins were in the hands of cunning thieves, he sentenced himself to the ultimate punishment.

It was pure invention, of course, but Mr. Umbertini still made no comment. Gambling organized every Friday, however discreetly, would never have escaped his attention. Moreover, Mr. Tomasi had never had a country estate to lose. Far more important than these details, however, was the fact that gambling was the last vice to which the maestro would have succumbed; without ever being touched by it personally, he had experienced the grievous consequences of this addiction.

The violin-maker's older brother, Roberto Tomasi, had been a regular attender at large casinos since he was a young man. He had left his share of their father's inheritance in them long ago, but for some time afterwards continued to gratify this irresistible vice thanks to his brother's generous support. Alberto had shown a strange compassion for Roberto's weakness, agreeing to pay his gambling debts, until one day he refused to give him the large amount he had come for. Thereupon Roberto had, in a fit of rage, seized a newly finished violin and smashed it against the wall. The two brothers never saw each other again after that, even though the older brother had sent many letters of apology and even gone to plead at his younger brother's door.

A crippled beggar, who claimed to be the illegitimate son of a duke, patiently listened to all three stories and announced self-confidently that none of them was true. The master violin-maker had not committed suicide at all, whatever people thought. He did not jump from the window, he was thrown out of it. There was a third eye-witness to this tragedy, as well as the two baker's men. He was a beggar who had left town in a hurry immediately after the fateful event, fearing what he had seen, and pausing only long enough to confide in his lame friend.

The beggar had spent the night on the square and was sleeping under some stairs, when he was awakened at daybreak by banging from somewhere above. He looked around drowsily, then realized that the noise was coming from the open window in the garret of the violin-maker's house. It seemed as if someone was trying to break something in there, but he could see nothing from below. Then everything quieted down and a brief silence reigned. Just as the two baker's boys arrived in the square from a side street, each carrying baskets full of freshly baked bread and rolls, the terrified maestro appeared at the window. He held tightly onto the frame, trying to resist whomever was pushing him from behind. It was a silent struggle, which was why the young men were completely unaware of it. They crossed the square, unsuspecting among the pigeons, chatting in low voices.

The unrelenting pressure on the maestro's back grew stronger and stronger until his resistance yielded. As if hurled by a huge hand, he flew out of the window and plunged helplessly towards the pavement, still without uttering a sound. Behind him, however, the window was not empty as it would have been had he jumped of his own free will. A terrifying figure appeared for just an instant, curdling the blood in the observer's veins as he lay hidden under the stairs. It disappeared at once, but that fleeting look was enough for the beggar to recognize it beyond all doubt. He remained hidden for quite some time, not daring to move. It was only after the police inspector had completed his investigation and the dead man's body was removed that the beggar mustered the courage to come out.

It should surprise no one, the lame beggar concluded didactically, that Mr. Tomasi finally fell victim to the Tempter. Anyone who pledges his soul to the Devil for the sake of some vain and evanescent acclaim must be assured that the Devil will get his due—sooner or later. The master violin-maker had no reason to complain; he had gloried for many years in his reputation as the unsurpassed creator of magnificent violins, although it was clear to everyone that such talent could not be natural.

That was when Mr. Umbertini was first tempted to contribute a comment of his own. Unlike the other stories, this one was at least partially credible. The story-teller himself had probably been the eye-witness on the square that morning, rather than this nameless friend who had so conveniently disappeared. Most likely he was reluctant to admit as much for fear of being questioned by the police, but he had given too many convincing details for one who was merely recounting another's experience. The supplementary elements which he had invented were understandable in the circumstances; without them his story would not have been exciting enough for the listeners in the tavern. On the other hand, although he could not have known, they were not completely unfounded. Nonetheless, the ex-assistant decided once again not to say anything, principally because of his unwillingness to enter into the inevitable discussion about this aspect of the maestro's accident, for the secret at its heart greatly surpassed his own understanding.

He might never have spoken of it at all, had his hand not been forced by an extraordinary chain of events. The vagabonds and good-for-nothings who kept him company in the tavern started to lose interest in the violin-maker's suicide as it became clear they would get nothing out of his former assistant. They also found the man himself less and less interesting, since he passed most of his time sunk in gloomy silence, concentrating on the bottle. They gradually started to drop away, leaving him alone finally at the table. At last only the large, bearded innkeeper sometimes exchanged a word or two with him.

One rainy day in late autumn, Mr. Umbertini arrived at the tavern early, while there were still no other guests. He sat at a small table with two chairs in the corner, close to the hearth, and the innkeeper, without asking and giving just a brief nod, brought him three bottles of red wine and a glass. He peered briefly at his customer's thin, unshaven face, inflamed eyes and red nose, but said nothing. The innkeeper couldn't care less about the appearance of those who frequented his establishment as long as they had money to pay for what they ordered. It was not his job to warn immoderate drunks that every new glass only shortened what little life they had left. He picked up the coins that Mr. Umbertini put on the table without a word and slipped them into the deep pocket under his stained apron, then went behind the bar.

Mr. Umbertini was already halfway through the second bottle when new guests started to appear in the tavern. They were certainly not those he was accustomed to seeing there. First a little boy came in. He could not have been more than six or seven years old, but he went up to the largest table, sat at the head of it, took out a piece of paper and pen from somewhere, bowed his head and started to write something in a tiny script. From time to time he took out a handkerchief and held it briefly to his nose. After him came a middle-aged woman holding a bunch of rolled-up scrolls under her arm. She sat next to the boy, unrolled a scroll and became engrossed in reading. The refined-looking, older man who soon joined them brought a snow-white cat with him. He stroked it gently in his lap, whispering in its ear. The older woman who next arrived stood at the entrance, looking in bewilderment first at the innkeeper and then at the master violin-maker's assistant as though she had seen ghosts. She sat down stiffly on one of the three unoccupied chairs and put her muff on the table in front of her without removing her hands. The man who came in after her was a painter. As soon as he joined the others he opened a large sketching block, took a stick of charcoal and began sketching in brisk, rough strokes. Finally, the last to arrive was a rather casually dressed man with disheveled gray hair. He rummaged through his pockets for a few moments, finally found a piece of chalk and without the least hesitation began to write on the uncovered wooden table, erasing something here and there with the leather-patched elbow of his jacket.

The sight of six such strangers at the big table was extremely unusual in this establishment. During all the months that Mr. Umbertini had spent in the tavern he had never seen anyone even slightly resembling them. But what seemed to him almost as unbelievable was the fact that the innkeeper paid them absolutely no attention. He, who took great pains that no guest ever be left even momentarily without a glass or plate on the table in front of him, who kept an eye on empty glasses in order to fill them at once, and never recoiled from showing the door to anyone who contemplated sitting inside for free, had not even approached these dignified guests, although they clearly promised a good tab. Instead, he went up to the assistant's table, waved at the other chair with the dirty rag he constantly wore over his arm, and sat down.

He came straight to the point. He maintained that he knew why Mr. Tomasi had killed himself—a most unexpected statement as he had never taken part in the conversations on the subject. He had seemed totally uninterested, just idly listening to the stories told by others. The master violin-maker, the innkeeper now asserted, had wanted to make a perfect violin. He had invested years of effort and everything indicated that he was on the right track. Unfortunately, no human hands, not even the most gifted, are able to reach perfection. Although appearing perfect in every way, the violin was nonetheless not divine, as he had hoped. When he realized this after testing it that morning, the violin-maker understood that there was only one way out of this defeat, and he took it.

This time Mr. Umbertini could hold back no longer. Had the innkeeper's story simply been wrong, he certainly would not have reacted, gliding over it as he had the others. But he had found one essential aspect of this story deeply offensive, and he alone could now stand up to defend the maestro's besmirched honor. That was a debt he owed his teacher, and it took precedence over the pledge the assistant had made to himself never to reveal what had happened in the garret.

The innkeeper had been right, although Mr. Umbertini could not even imagine how that simple and greedy seller of bad wine could have found out something which the maestro had kept secret even from his faithful pupil. For eighteen years, with endless devotion and patience, he had indeed been working on a perfect violin. It was only towards the end that the assistant finally understood what lay hidden behind the violin-maker's periodic retreats to the highest room in the house. He would stay locked inside for hours, although he had taken no instrument with him to test, and no one dared disturb him.

The innkeeper, however, was wrong when he said, with an edge of malice in his voice, that the master violin-maker had been unsuccessful in his efforts. Sneaking up to the garret on that fateful morning when the unique violin was given its final test, Mr. Umbertini heard the sound of divine harmony for the first and only time in his life. Even though the closed door dampened the music, the magic of that experience had been so powerful that he had felt compelled to stay close to the maestro's house instead of going somewhere else, where he might hope to enjoy a more useful and fulfilling life—despite his awareness that he would never again be given an opportunity to hear it.

Mr. Umbertini knew the question the innkeeper would ask next, just as he knew that he had no answer. If the maestro had truly created a perfect violin, what had happened to it? Or to its remains, if the crashing that the beggar on the square had heard meant that the maestro had broken it? (Although why would he do such a thing to his masterpiece?) When the inspector had forced the door, nothing was found inside: neither a whole instrument nor its wreckage. So the garret must have possessed a secret entrance, concluded the cunning innkeeper, which the assistant had used before the inspector's arrival in order to remove all traces.

This was a logical assumption that offered an explanation for both possibilities: that the violin had been perfect and that it hadn't been. Its only defect was that it was incorrect. There was no secret entrance to the highest room in the building. When he finally entered the garret with the inspector, the assistant encountered his second wonder of that morning. Although the instrument had to be there, and in one piece, it was not. And the fact that it should have been in one piece constituted the first wonder.

As Mr. Umbertini stood in front of the door, still dazzled by the music that had just ended, he suddenly heard something inside that terrified him. He was quite familiar with that sound. The crashing could mean only one thing: the master violin-maker was destroying his life's work! But why? Not knowing what else to do, the assistant quickly dropped to his knees and tried to peer in through the keyhole. Had there been no key in the lock, he could have seen more, but even this way he was able to catch at least partial sight of the maestro's crazed figure as he swung the violin, holding it by the neck. He hit it against whatever he came across: the table, chair back, bed-frame, walls.

Even though the full force of his unbridled rage went into it, the instrument was not so much as scratched. The violin steadfastly resisted all his attempts to shatter it, remaining untouched, as though he were merely swinging it through the air. When he threw it to the floor and started to jump on it, again without causing any damage, he finally collapsed, sat on the edge of the bed, thrust his head in his hands and stayed there unmoving for a while. And then he got up slowly, went to the large window, grabbed the frame, remained in that position a few moments, then let go of his hands and simply leaned forward. The dumbfounded assistant took his eye off the keyhole and slid to the floor next to the door. It was not until the inspector banged the knocker on the front door of the house that he was startled out of his paralysis.

The innkeeper shook his head. Of all the stories he had heard, he said, this one seemed the most far-fetched. Thank heavens Mr. Umbertini had not told it to the police, because that would surely have focused suspicion on himself. He personally still thought that the only true explanation lay in the secret entrance. As far as the noise was concerned, it didn't have to come from breaking the violin, rather its maker might have banged the furniture around him in frustration over his failure, as people do when they are infuriated.

In any case, the innkeeper concluded, after the master violin-maker jumped through the window, Mr. Umbertini had gone into the garret and stowed the instrument somewhere. He had waited for the situation to calm down, then sold it under the counter. The violin might not have been perfect according to Mr. Tomasi's criteria, but the seller certainly would have received a pretty sum for it that would enable him to lead a comfortable life. For example, he could amuse himself at the tavern day after day without having to work. But Mr. Umbertini had no need to worry. The innkeeper certainly would not turn him in. What benefit would that bring him? He would only be losing a regular customer who had never asked for credit.

Seeing there was nothing more to say, he returned to the bar. He started to wipe glasses idly, continuing to neglect the six visitors at the other table. They sat there briefly, involved in their preoccupations, and then, as though at an invisible signal, stood up and left the tavern together, offended no doubt at being so rudely ignored. Mr. Umbertini watched them leave, and then, as though remembering something, quickly got up and headed after them, leaving almost a bottle and a half of wine, paid for but not drunk. He was never seen in there again.

For a while stories were concocted in the tavern regarding his disappearance. It was heard on great authority that thieves had slaughtered him and thrown him into the river, that he had left for the New World to seek his fortune, that he had opened his own workshop in another town, and that he had come down with leprosy and was now living out the miserable remainder of his days in an asylum on some island. Only the sober innkeeper, who was not to be cheated, knew that they were all fabrications and that, as usual, the simplest explanation was the soundest: the late master violin-maker's assistant had fled, fearing that someone might denounce him to the police once he had spent all of his dishonestly acquired money.

The Library

Contents

1. Virtual Library
2. Home Library
3. Night Library
4. Infernal Library
5. Smallest Library
6. Noble Library

1. Virtual Library

EMAIL ISN'T PERFECT. ALTHOUGH Internet providers probably do their best to protect us from receiving unwanted messages, there seems to be no remedy against it. Whenever I open up the in-box on my screen, I almost always find at least one from an unknown sender. Usually there are several; the record was thirteen junk mail messages, sent over just a few hours, in between two sessions at the computer.

When that happened I really got irritated and changed my e-address, despite considerable inconvenience. I gave out my new address only to a small number of people, but to no avail. The pesky emails soon began arriving once again. I complained to my provider, who admitted in a roundabout way that they could do nothing to help. They advised me just to delete everything that didn't interest me, particularly since dangerous computer viruses often spread through junk mail.

The recommendation was unnecessary as I had already been deleting my junk mail, even though I was unaware of the viruses. At first, I'd read these messages in bewilderment, but once I realized what was going on, I deleted every e-message of unknown origin without delay. I didn't even give them a cursory reading, despite the fact that the senders took all kinds of pains to attract my attention. Bombastic, flickering headings with fancy, ostentatious illustrations advertised a variety of exceptional offers not to be missed at any cost.

One proposal, for example, would make me rich overnight if I invested money through a glamorous-sounding agency from some Pacific Rim country I had never heard of. Or, after a two-week correspondence course, I could become a preacher in any Christian church I wanted, authorized to carry out baptismal, wedding, and funeral rites. I also had the opportunity, regardless of my age, to turn back the clock twenty-five years using some new macrobiotic remedy. I was offered the unique opportunity, for a modest commission of forty-nine percent, finally to get hold of the money that had been awarded me by the court, if I had any such claims. I could also satisfy my assumed passion for gambling at any hour of the day or night, playing in some virtual casino guaranteed to be honest. Lastly, to top it all off, I was offered at a mere pittance, under the counter, two and a half million verified, active e-addresses to which I could send whatever I wanted as many times as I wanted.

Perhaps the email that started it all would have ended up in the recycle bin along with the others, if it had not been so brief that I inadvertently read it. Against a black background, devoid of decoration, the first line announced: VIRTUAL LIBRARY in large, yellow letters, while under it the slogan "We have everything!"—written in considerably smaller blue letters—did not exactly assume the aggressive tone typical of this type of message.

Of all the exaggeration I had come across on the Internet, this one took the biscuit. Really, "everything!" Such a claim would be absurd even for web sites from the largest world libraries. Whoever had come up with this scheme certainly had no notion just how many books have been published in the last five thousand years. No one has ever managed to put such a library together in one place, even discounting all those works that have disappeared into oblivion.

And then there was that word "virtual." Used in its truest sense, "virtual" should mean a library composed of electronic books. The Internet has several sites containing such e-editions and I visit them from time to time. But they offer slim pickings. Only several hundred titles are available, just a drop in the ocean compared to "everything" in the literal sense. Who would even dare to hope that this vast multitude could ever be transferred into computer form? And who would ever find it worth the effort?

Although I was convinced this must be a hoax, my curiosity stopped me from proceeding as usual. If it had involved anything other than books, I would have ignored the message without a second thought. But for a writer this was like waving a red flag in front of a bull. Instead of deleting the message, I positioned the cursor on the text. The arrow turned into a hand with a raised index finger and I found myself at the Virtual Library site.

The change was barely noticeable. The background stayed black, with two small additions appearing under the name of the site and the slogan. The first was the standard search field: a narrow white rectangular space in which to type the search text. This, however, could not be the title of a work or some other data, since the word "Author" appeared at the beginning. I shook my head. More sophisticated capabilities were to be expected from a library that prided itself on being the "ultimate." At the very bottom of the screen was a short e-address.

I typed in my own name. This was not out of vanity, although it might have appeared so. I chose myself because, obviously, I am most familiar with my own work. If the Virtual Library truly contained what it claimed in its slogan, then my three books should be no exception. I am certainly not a well-known or popular writer, but I still should be included in a library containing all authors. In such a place there should be no discrimination of any kind.

There were two possible outcomes. If the search did not produce the expected result, which was quite likely, then the whole thing was probably a practical joke. Someone had decided to have some fun at the expense of writers, or perhaps publishers, critics, librarians, bookshop owners, and the book world in general. Who knew what kind of trick might be played instead of a page listing my works. But I had no right to complain; no one had forced me to visit the site. A joke would serve me right for not minding my own business.

If, however, my books appeared in electronic form, then the situation was considerably worse. I had not ceded my rights to anyone for such publication, which would mean they were pirated editions. That really would be a problem. The Internet is awash with this type of abuse, and as far as I have heard, protection from it is just as difficult as protection from unwanted e-messages.

If my work did exist in the Virtual Library, the search would have to last some time. Regardless of increases in computer speed, the gigantic corpus involved could certainly not be searched in a moment. But that is just what happened. As soon as I clicked the mouse to begin the search, a new page appeared on the screen. This time it had a gray background, with black and white writing. A smaller picture also appeared in color, disturbing the uniformity.

At first I thought that the speed with which it had been found was a sure sign of something fishy. But when I found myself squinting at my own face on the screen, a shudder ran down my spine. That was me, no doubt about it, although I had no idea when and where the picture had been taken. I appeared to be somewhat younger, but it was hard to tell how much younger.

Under the picture, on the left-hand side of the screen, I found a brief biography. All the information was correct, except for the last bit. Unless something had happened without my noticing it, I was still very much alive. The facts about my death, though, were strangely undefined. The word "died" was followed by nine different years, separated by commas. Unlike the black letters before them, these numbers were white. The closest year was a decade and a half in the future, while the most distant was almost half a century away. Whoever had edited the entry obviously had a morbid sense of humor.

On the right-hand side of the screen I found a list of my books. It did not end, however, after the third book. It continued all the way to number twenty-one which, of course, was ridiculous. I'm not saying that such a voluminous bibliography didn't please me, but it simply was not mine. Two colors had been used here as well. The three books I had actually published appeared in black type, while the other eighteen works appeared in white. These other titles were presented in chronological order. The first dated from the following year, and there were forty-five years to go until the last date. So I was dealing not only with a twisted prankster, but someone who seemed to imagine himself a clairvoyant.

None of this mattered, however; I still had to find out the most important thing. Was this just the work of some idler who had nothing better to do than fool around with such nonsense? The Internet is full of people who think nothing of putting time and effort into pulling off stunts like this. Hackers are a good example. They invent and spread destructive viruses, even though they gain no benefit other than an insular satisfaction. I clicked the cursor on the first of my three books, certain that nothing would happen. But the arrow, unfortunately, turned into a hand again and the screen soon filled with text.

I had only to read the first sentence to confirm that this really was my first novel. A wave of anger rolled over me. My book was accessible to the whole world without any permission or payment! How dared they! Why, this was highway robbery! And then suddenly I was filled with the hope that perhaps it wasn't all there, that maybe only an excerpt had been posted, which might be somewhat bearable. But as soon as I scrolled down to the end of the page, I lost this faint hope. The whole book was there, from the first word to the last. I didn't even have to open the other two titles. I knew perfectly well what I would find.

Enraged, I reached for the mouse once more, clicked on the button, and returned to the previous page. I brought the cursor to the e-address at the bottom, then clicked again. My browser opened a blank email window with the site's email address in the "To" field. I stared at the empty page for a few moments, deliberating. Finally, I wrote "Piracy" in the "Subject" line, then started to write.

> *Dear Sir,*
>
> *A very unpleasant surprise awaited me when I visited the Virtual Library site. I found my three novels there freely accessible to anyone. Since I, as the copyright holder, never gave permission for such publication, it clearly represents an act of publishing piracy, punishable by law. I order you to withdraw my works from your site without delay. I would also like to inform you that my lawyer will soon be sending you a request for due compensation for damages, not only for the unauthorized placement of my books on your site but also for the inaccurate, and insulting, additions to my biography and bibliography.*

I signed my name at the end, without any closing salutation. It was impolite, but I couldn't think of anything that sounded appropriate. It would have been hard to put the formal "sincerely yours" or "yours truly." I also had trouble adopting a suitably severe tone for my missive; I had no experience of this sort of thing. The letter, I suppose, must have appeared harsh enough and a warning, although, to tell the truth, I did not count on it having much effect. The most that could be expected was for them to remove the page containing my works, while I hadn't the slightest hope of receiving any compensation.

I even doubted that I would receive a reply. But I was mistaken. Just after I sent the email, a message came back in response. The only explanation was that the editors of the Virtual Library, flooded with similar protest letters, had a ready-made reply to be sent automatically upon receipt of such a complaint. They probably didn't receive any other kind of letter. What did they have to say in their defense?

> *Highly esteemed sir,*
>
> *First, please allow us to express our deepest gratitude to you for having shown us the honor of visiting the Virtual Library.*
>
> *We hasten to dispel your fears. This is not an unauthorized publication of your works. Although the page devoted to you does contain the texts of your books, access to that page is not at all free, as you have assumed. It is allowed exclusively to you, and only once. Since you have just used this opportunity, you may rest assured that no one will ever again be able to access the page containing your bio-bibliography. You will see this for yourself should you try to return to it.*
>
> *Regarding the information that you have concluded is incorrect, please rest assured that it is accurate.*
>
> *Sincerely yours,*
> *Virtual Library*

So they had it all worked out. As soon as an author complained, they quickly removed the page. No page, no proof of piracy. I had nonetheless expected something more ingenious. That page still existed in the "cache" memory of my computer as irrefutable proof. All I had to do was hit the "Back" button and save it. Nothing easier. In addition, it seemed the Virtual Library considered writers to be so computer illiterate and naive that they would easily swallow the story about access to their page. Nonsense. As if something like that were even possible. Or that bit about the accuracy of the invented data. What a misjudgment.

I quickly clicked "Back" on the toolbar. But something unexpected happened. Instead of showing the previous page, the window with the letter from the Virtual Library closed, and the "Back" button became inactive, as though nothing had been stored in the "cache" file. I stared in bewilderment at the primarily black picture on the screen, uncomprehending. The page had to be there. I had been on it just a few minutes before and had done nothing in the meantime to delete it.

Obviously, something had gone wrong. I wasn't computer illiterate, but I also was not skilled enough to figure out everything that could go wrong with these strange machines. But it made no difference, I would enter my name once again in the search rectangle. Although I had been informed that access to my page would henceforth be blocked, it would be hard for them to do so instantaneously. Unfortunately, the search came up blank this time. The program informed me that no writer with my name could be found in the library that included all authors who had ever existed.

Confusion and anger started to get the upper hand. I looked like a fool who, thanks to his own rashness, had been taken in by a cheap trick. It even crossed my mind that a throng of happy people from some television station might burst into my study at any moment, revealing that all of this had been just a cleverly organized candid camera episode. But no one appeared and, after several long minutes, I did the only thing I could do. I clicked once again on the lower e-address and started to type a new email.

> *Dear Sir,*
> *I don't know how you did it, but that's not important. Your joke—I could use a stronger word—is tasteless to say the least. People like you are inflicting enormous damage on the noble idea of the Internet. You should be ashamed of yourselves. Don't forget that I still have the address of your web site. I will try to trace you through it. Your library might be virtual, but you certainly are not.*

Once again I used my signature, without any closing formality. Good manners were superfluous to the situation. I should have left out the "Dear Sir" too. The people behind this travesty did not deserve such a courtesy. When I sent the message I was again sure there would be no reply. How could they respond to my accusation? But I got one anyway, at the same instant, just like before. The speed of the reply should have aroused my suspicions, of course, since this letter could not have been prepared in advance like the previous one. All caught up in my anger, I did not give proper consideration to this impossibility which was, in any case, not the first one I had encountered at the Virtual Library. How strange it is, the way one so easily starts to accept things that have no explanation, particularly when computers are involved.

Highly esteemed sir,

We are sorry that you received the wrong impression. Making jokes is the farthest thing from our intent. All our efforts go towards the serious execution of our responsible work, which is the only fitting thing to do.

Sincerely yours,
Virtual Library

As I opened the window for a new letter to my unknown adversary, a sober voice inside tried to dissuade me. It was pointless taking any more part in such a farce. I had already achieved as much as I could, given the circumstances. The page with my works had been removed and further correspondence would lead nowhere. Unfortunately, one does not always listen to sober advice.

I suppose you expect me to take the list of books cited as mine seriously, even though they have not yet been written. I might have admired your ability to foretell the future if you had not been so indecisive regarding the year of my death. Nine possibilities! I would appreciate being informed when you decide on one of them. Timely knowledge in this regard would considerably facilitate the remainder of my life, however long it might be.

This time I even omitted my signature. That fact, and the conspicuously sarcastic tone of the letter, should have indicated what I thought of them, had they been previously unaware. Their pointed politeness, not at all appropriate to the circumstances, had started to get on my nerves. The answer arrived once again a moment after I sent my message, but this no longer amazed me. Sleights-of-hand cease to be interesting when they are repeated too often, even if you don't know how they are performed.

Highly esteemed sir,

We are unfortunately unable to inform you of when you will die. It is not easy to forecast the future. All nine possibilities have equal footing at this moment. Chance will decide which of them comes true. Your bibliography contains all the works from all these futures. However, you will not write and publish all eighteen of them on a single one of the branches of life that await you, to use a picturesque expression. Your later works will include at most eleven and at least six books. You were only able to see them all on our site. We therefore hope that we have justified our slogan.

Sincerely yours,
Virtual Library

Just as I finished reading the message, it vanished, the window in which it was located suddenly closing even though I had not touched any keys. A moment later, the same thing happened to the browser window. The only window left open was for email, but it did not contain the original message from the Virtual Library, although it should have been there, since I had not deleted it. Before I closed it, I checked to see if any new email messages had arrived in the meantime, but there were none.

I sat there for a long time, eyes unfocused, staring at the empty screen before me. I did not try to understand. The ways of the computer are often incomprehensible to me. I searched my memory, but hard as I tried the text written in white against a gray background to the right of my photograph did not become sharp enough to read. It seemed to be covered by a shimmering, impenetrable veil. Finally, even though frustration weighed me down, I abandoned my vain efforts and turned off the computer.

From then on, I continued to delete unwanted email

messages, but no longer right away. First I read them, even when it was immediately apparent that they did not deserve the slightest attention. I felt foolish as I skimmed through various incoherent offers, particularly since I hadn't the faintest hope of ever seeing among them one that was quite brief, on a black background. But such was the burden I had to bear.

2. Home Library

I UNLOCKED THE MAILBOX.

All I ever found in it were bills at the beginning of the month, but I still checked it regularly when I returned from work. I checked it on Saturday and Sunday, too, at the same time as on the other days, even though the postman didn't deliver on those days. Just in case. In addition, on Tuesday I always took a handkerchief and wiped out the dust that had collected inside, although you couldn't see the dust from the outside. We have to take care of such places, perhaps even more than those that are visible to the eye. People tend to neglect them, even though they are actually the best testimony to meticulousness.

There should not have been anything in my mailbox because it was only the middle of the month. But when I opened the wooden door, I saw a large book, hardcover bound in dark yellow. It almost filled the entire mailbox. In my place somebody else would probably have found many reasons to be surprised by this sudden apparition. First of all, who had sent it to me? No one had ever sent me a book before. Why would anyone, anyhow? Plus, it wasn't even wrapped, and nothing on it indicated it was intended for me. So why had the postman put it in my mailbox? And finally, how had he managed to fit it inside? The book was a lot thicker than the narrow slit through which he inserted bills. It certainly could not have got in through the slit.

I, however, wasn't surprised at all. I didn't let any

of these annoying questions upset me. Long ago, I realized that the world is full of inexplicable wonders. It's no use even trying to explain them. Those who try anyway just end up unhappy. And why should a person be unhappy when he doesn't have to be? Unusual things should be accepted for what they are, without explanation. That is the easiest way to live with them.

Before this became clear to me, various unaccountable phenomena had made my life miserable. For example, the number of steps between my second-floor apartment and the ground floor. I'm used to counting steps, half out loud, everywhere and on all occasions, even when I already know the number of steps. When I climb up to my apartment, there are always forty-four steps. Whenever I walk down to the ground floor, there are only forty-one. For a while after I moved here, I found myself in some discomfort because of this difference. I tried just about everything to figure out what was wrong.

I first attempted to outsmart the stairs. I counted them to myself while keeping my mouth firmly shut, so there was no way of knowing what I was up to. It didn't work. On the way up there were still persistently three more steps than on the way down. Then I counted them while walking backwards; although I walked carefully, this was not only difficult and dangerous, but for some reason also drew confused and suspicious looks from my neighbors. Despite my greeting them politely, raising my hat and nodding, they would just mumble in reply with their heads down. People can really act oddly sometimes.

Finally, it occurred to me to count the steps in the dark. I would leave the apartment after midnight wearing light, rubber-soled shoes so my footsteps wouldn't wake anyone. Without turning on the light in the stairwell, I walked down to the ground floor, then climbed back up to my apartment, down and up, up and down, until dawn. It wasn't hard, despite the murky darkness, because I knew the exact number of steps in either direction. I would have had a hard time—stairs can be dangerous even when you can see quite well, let alone in the pitch black of night like that—if I had stuck to what common sense told me: that the number of steps must be the same going up and coming down.

That's when I gave up trying to find an explanation for everything no matter what the cost. Common sense is all very well and good, but you can't always rely on it. Sometimes it is far more advisable and useful to accept a wonder. It might even save your neck, and that's no small thing. Not only did I survive the dark stairwell, I quickly regained my peace of mind. As soon as I stopped burdening myself with superfluous curiosity, I slept better, my appetite returned, and I wasn't chronically depressed, apathetic and anemic any longer. It's amazing how one simple decision can make a new man out of you in no time at all.

So now, instead of wasting time being amazed, I took the book out of my mailbox and examined it. The title was written in large, ornate black letters: *World Literature*. There were no other words on the cover, not even the author's name. I was not surprised, for how could anyone truly be the writer of such a work? I quickly leafed through the book and discovered there were even more pages than the size indicated because the paper was very thin, like onionskin. This suited the title: anything more limited in scope would hardly fit the bill. The edition seemed quite splendid in all respects. It even had a brown ribbon to mark your place when you had stopped reading.

I put *World Literature* under my arm and headed up to my apartment. I reached the twentieth step, then stopped short. Today was Tuesday! That fact had slipped my mind owing to the unexpected appearance of the book. I had no choice but to walk back down.

One should not let anything interfere with carrying out one's duties, not even an unforeseen event. Descending to the ground floor, I took from the inside pocket of my jacket the green silk handkerchief used exclusively to clean the mailbox.

When I opened it, another surprise awaited me: another thick, dark yellow book with the same title. Someone unaccustomed to wonders would probably have been flabbergasted. Such a person might have stepped back, heart racing, a shudder running down his spine. Once he had collected his wits, he would begin feverishly searching for an explanation, but it would be hard to come up with anything coherent. I hesitate to think of what he might do afterwards. Maybe even attempt suicide.

But I, of course, remained perfectly calm. There was no reason to get upset. I simply took out the second volume of *World Literature*, put it under my arm with the other one, and wiped out the mailbox. I only needed one hand for that, thank goodness. As usual, I concentrated on the lower corners, from which it was hardest to remove the dust and yet where it most collected, as if out of spite.

I locked the mailbox door once again and headed for the second floor. This time I did not get very far: I'd just raised my foot to the first step when a thought struck me and brought me back to the mailbox. As I opened it, a surge of excitement flowed through me. Everyone enjoys having premonitions come true, particularly if they are auspicious. Had one of my neighbors walked by at that moment, he would have seen my face light up when a third dark yellow book appeared behind the door.

I can't explain how I suspected it would be there. Intuition, I guess, but not only that. Such an idea would never occur to a person who was hostile to wonders. That's another advantage of not giving in to prejudice.

I took the new *World Literature*, but didn't put it under my arm. I couldn't hold three thick volumes. Instead, I placed the books in the crook of my left arm. Then I locked the door again, but this time I waited in front of the mailbox. I stood there for several moments, trying not to appear too impatient, then opened the mailbox a fourth time. Even though glad to see it filled once again, I found my previous excitement was somehow missing. Self-satisfaction is in bad taste. Or at least, showing it openly is.

After the thirteenth book I had to stop, mostly because of the weight. In my fervor, I'd forgotten that books, contrary to popular belief, are not light, particularly when gathered in a pile. They had to be carried up to the second floor. I certainly would have had an easier time taking them down the stairs rather than climbing up, because, *inter alia*, there were three fewer steps going down. In addition, the load turned out to be quite awkward. I had to stretch my arms almost to my knees in order to hold the books piled one on top of the other, while my chin on top secured this unstable arrangement, with my head forced back. I looked around uneasily. It wouldn't be good for one of my neighbors to see me carrying too many of the same kind of book. Who knew what they might think? People have a tendency to jump to conclusions.

When I finally got home, I was gasping for breath. I had a hard time unlocking the three locks, the armload of books briefly supported by just one hand. The bottom lock, next to the threshold, gave me particular difficulty. I had to squat, barely keeping my balance. If any other title had been involved, I might have had to put them down on the floor. Because I fastidiously clean the area around my front door, the books would not have gotten dirty, but the thought of *World Literature* against cold tile seemed somehow improper. Almost a sacrilege.

Once I entered the apartment, I was confronted by the problem of where to put the books. I hesitated and stood next to the door for a time, not knowing what to do with them. In the end, I put them on the table until I could give it some more thought. The best solution would have been a bookshelf. That's the right place for books. Unfortunately, I didn't have one. What did I need a bookshelf for when I didn't own any books?

Since moving to the apartment, I had not kept a home library. My apartment is small—just a studio. One little room, a vestibule, a kitchenette and a bathroom. You can't even turn around without banging your arms against the walls. And it is a well-known fact that books devour space. You can't reverse this law. However much space you give them, it's never enough. First they occupy the walls. Then they continue to spread wherever they can gain a foothold. Only ceilings are spared the invasion. New books keep arriving, and you can't bear to get rid of a single old one. And so, slowly and imperceptibly, the volumes crowd out everything before them. Like glaciers.

But now I had no choice. The books were already in my apartment and they had to be put somewhere. I couldn't just leave them in the mailbox. After all, I'm a mature, responsible man. How would it look if I pretended, ostrich-like, that they weren't there? If nothing else, inaction on my part would arouse the postman's suspicions the next time he tried to insert my bills and couldn't because the mailbox was full. He would wonder why I hadn't picked up my mail. He might even come up to ask me about it. And what could I tell him? No, ignoring the books was out of the question. I had to bring them into the apartment. Later I would figure out what to do with them.

Now the question became how to carry up the rest of them, assuming there were more. I couldn't do what I had done the first time. That was too inconvenient.

I had to find something suitable in which to carry the books. Looking around the room, I finally remembered something that would suit the purpose, although it was not within my field of vision. I took a large suitcase with brass reinforcements on the corners out of the double-fronted wardrobe. I could fit lots of books inside, which was all to the good. However, once filled, it would be extremely heavy. Sometimes you can't have your cake and eat it too.

Bringing up fifty-six volumes of *World Literature* all at once to the second floor was no easy matter. I had to hold the suitcase handle with both hands. On the twenty-eighth step, I realized I shouldn't have loaded myself down so much. However, if I'd taken fewer books, I would have had to make the climb several times, actually gaining nothing. Only an elevator would have made any difference, but unfortunately the building didn't have one. Not a single shortcut could be taken if I wanted to bring the books up to my apartment.

While I started to take out the books and put them next to the first thirteen, I realized I had another problem. One more full suitcase and the thin legs of the little table would give way under the weight. And then what? Before continuing, I had to devise a plan. Something like this couldn't be approached haphazardly. I had no idea how many more volumes would appear in my mailbox. Maybe just a few, maybe hundreds. Most likely the latter. This was world literature, after all, and had to be enormous, even when printed on onionskin. I had to prepare for the worst.

The furniture in my only room was sparse, which now turned out to be a blessing. Along with the table and wardrobe, I had four chairs, a bed, a dresser and a night table. I pushed them all into a corner, freeing up about two-thirds of the available space. Naturally, this had an equal and opposite effect: the area to the right of the door was now cramped and crowded. That didn't bother me. Exceptional circumstances require a man to make sacrifices without complaint. Besides, I had never cared much for comfort.

I spread newspapers across the floor in the empty part of the room. It was spotlessly clean, of course, but this way seemed more appropriate. Then I started to move the books. This required some planning. I began by arranging them in the corner farthest from the door—the same place I would have started if polishing the floor, for example. A stack of exactly forty volumes fitted from floor to ceiling. In order to place the last seven, I had to climb onto a chair. The tall yellow column would probably have toppled if it hadn't been leaning against two walls and secured firmly from above by the last book that I barely managed to wedge in. I got down from the chair, took a step back and admired the scene.

With my strategy established, all I had to do was get down to work. There could be no hesitation. Who knew how long the whole thing would last? I took the empty suitcase and headed downstairs. I had simplified the operation, so now I could act more quickly. After taking one volume out of the mailbox, I would just close the door briefly and then open it again. I didn't need to lock and unlock it. A new volume was already waiting inside. I became skilled at arranging the books in the suitcase, managing to fit in fifty-eight volumes.

My neighbors passed by several times, but no one paid any attention to me. All they did was look away and quicken their steps. It's hard to understand people sometimes. I don't mean to suggest that this lack of interest didn't suit me—I didn't want to explain my actions, even though in point of fact I didn't have to answer to anyone for them—but such indifference was nonetheless inexcusable. What if someone with suspicious intent, or even worse with questionable sanity, had been there in my place? These days, all kinds of disturbed people loiter around respectable apartment complexes.

As time passed, exhaustion inevitably crept over me. After the twenty-seventh suitcase, I could no longer reach the second floor without a short break. The most logical idea was to take a break in the middle, after the twenty-second step, particularly since it was on the first floor. But I ran into trouble after the forty-ninth suitcase, at which time I decided to take a second break. Forty-four steps cannot be evenly divided into three parts. I was forced to resort to an inelegant solution. The first time, I stopped briefly after the fifteenth step, the second time after the thirtieth, with only fourteen steps left in the third part of my journey. The dissonance of the solution bothered me until the sixty-third suitcase, when the need arose for one more rest. Forty-four is divisible by four, thank heavens, so I was able to stop after every eleventh step, i.e., on the landings and on the first floor.

When I brought up the ninety-second suitcase, its contents filled the area I had emptied. Before me rose an enormous dark yellow wall. To behold world literature in this way revealed its true majesty. Night had fallen long ago, but I was still surprised when I looked at the clock and realized it was 2:17 a.m.

I could work deep into the night without bothering my neighbors because I didn't have to turn on the light in the stairwell. I also took special pains to be as quiet as possible. I even took off my shoes. The entrance to the bathroom, where I kept my lightweight shoes, was blocked by piles, so I stayed in my socks, but thanks to the warm weather I was in no danger of catching cold. I probably should have changed into something more appropriate, but in my rush I failed to do so. All the hauling had completely wrinkled the suit I wore to work, my shirt was soaked in sweat and my tie was loose. At least I had taken off my hat.

An end to my torment, however, did not seem likely. Regardless of how many times I emptied the mailbox, it was full the next time I opened the door. I had no other choice but to find space for the new books. I hesitated several moments about which piece of furniture I could best do without. I finally decided on the bed because it almost certainly would not be needed that night. I would have trouble finding time to take even the shortest break. Although small, the bed was heavy. As I carried it down, I was consoled by the thought that it would have been much heavier carried in the opposite direction. I took it to my basement storage space. The space was small but empty because I had nothing to store inside it. I pulled the bed upright, anticipating that sooner or later I would have to put something else inside as well.

Shortly before 5:00 a.m., after the one hundred and nineteenth suitcase, my fears became reality. The space vacated by the bed was now filled to the ceiling with dark yellow volumes. I agonized over what to take to the basement next, and then realized that it didn't matter. There was no sense in fooling myself. Each piece of furniture would have to be removed in its turn, so the best thing was to take it all at once. Now was the right time, while everyone slept. It could be done inconspicuously and not under the inquisitive gaze of the neighbors.

I had no trouble moving the table, chairs, dresser and night table, but the wardrobe gave me a real headache. Not just because it was heavy, but because of its bulk. I staggered and swerved underneath it, struggling to keep my balance. On two occasions I almost fell. I carried it on my back most of the time, trying to make as little noise as possible, although I couldn't help some squeaking and cracking. With luck, I hadn't woken anyone up. In any case, no one came out to see what was going on.

Once I reached the basement, all my efforts almost went for naught. It took considerable ingenuity and maneuvering to get the wardrobe through the narrow door. Not only was my storage compartment crammed, but I didn't see how anything could be removed without breaking down the partition wall.

As dawn approached, the rest of the free space in the room filled up. Before blocking the bathroom entrance with books, I spent several minutes inside. It was either then or never. I came out a bit more refreshed and tidy. I hadn't been able to remove all the traces of the night's hard work, but I hoped I wouldn't look too shocking when I began to meet my neighbors in the stairwell. In order to improve the impression I made, I put on my hat and shoes.

When it came time to cover the door to the kitchenette with books, I thought I might take at least the refrigerator and little stove out of there, if not the dishes and cutlery. But I had to abandon that idea. I didn't know what to do with those bulky items. There wasn't any room left in the basement and I couldn't leave them by the front door. No, they could stay inside; even though inaccessible, they weren't in the way.

At 8:26 a.m., after the one hundred and forty-third suitcase, I had finally packed the room. Eight thousand three hundred and five books! It was truly an impressive sight; after wedging in the last volume, I stood in the solemn silence, looking on in admiration. Had anyone anywhere ever had a chance to see all of world literature crammed into such a small space? It left me breathless. The enormous effort had been worthwhile in the end.

I didn't have much time to admire the sight, however. I had to leave for work. In all my years on the job, I have never been late. I would be able to enjoy the books to my heart's content when I returned home in the afternoon. I would sit in the vestibule in front of the open door to the room and just stare at the dark yellow treasury before me. What else did a man need? A chair, perhaps? No, I didn't need a chair. My needs have always been modest. Since I'd already done away with all the other things, I would make do without a chair. In any case, I would not be sitting on the bare floor. I had a rug made of pure wool.

Descending to the ground floor, I unlocked the door to the mailbox once again. Even though it was only Wednesday, I took the green handkerchief and wiped the inside, although in my rush I was not as thorough as usual. Books are clean, particularly new ones, but after so many volumes passing through the mailbox, there must have been some dust left behind.

3. Night Library

I SHOULDN'T HAVE GONE to the movie first. If I'd known it would last almost two hours, I'd have gone to the library beforehand. I might have felt silly with several books on my lap during the movie, but I doubt anyone would have noticed. As it was, around 7:30 p.m. I began to squirm in my seat. I kept turning my left wrist towards the screen so I could see my watch. Although gripping, the plot seemed more drawn out than it should have been. I was tempted to leave before the end, but since I was sitting in the middle of the row, it would have been too awkward.

When the movie finally ended at ten to eight, I hurried out of the theater. I received several reproachful glances and heard muffled complaints as, apologizing, I cut my way through the movie-goers who were closer to the exit. If I quickened my pace, I might still make it. The library was not far from the movie theater. It closed at eight, but I was a frequent visitor. I could probably count on bit of forbearance from the staff.

Everything would have been different, of course, if it hadn't been Friday. Saturday and Sunday, the library would be closed, meaning that if I failed, I would have nothing to read over the weekend, a possibility that wasn't at all pleasing. Since I live alone, I am inevitably faced with an abundance of free time that has to be filled somehow. Long ago I discovered that reading was much more useful and pleasant than dulling my senses in front of the television.

The threat of spending the next two days in front of the television, filled with frustration and self-reproach, forced me into a run. Running wasn't easy, however, because it had started to snow while I was at the movie. Driven by the wind, the large, thick flakes fell at a slant, hitting me in the face as I rushed forward. I finally had to open my umbrella, holding it in front of me to ward off the snow. This slowed me down since I couldn't see where I was going. Luckily, I knew the way and in such weather there weren't many people in the street.

I reached the library at three minutes after eight. Looking through the glass door, I read the time on the large clock hanging from the ceiling in the foyer. The lights were still on, but if the door was locked not even my close relationship with the librarians would be of any help. I grabbed the cold doorknob apprehensively and pushed. I couldn't help but sigh with relief when the door opened. I entered quickly, turned to shake off the snow coating my umbrella, and then closed the door behind me.

I spent a few moments in the foyer cleaning the snow from my hair and stamping my feet on the doormat to remove bits of slush. I also took out a handkerchief and wiped off the water streaming down my glasses. I put my umbrella in the brass stand next to the door, then rushed up the narrow staircase to the main library area.

It was quite warm in the building, causing my cold glasses to fog up as I climbed the stairs. When I entered the large room illuminated by fluorescent lights, I had to take them off again and wipe them. Even though I am extremely near-sighted, I could move forward as I wiped my glasses since there were no obstacles on the wide, dark-red carpet before me. The tables and chairs were to the left, next to the tall windows. Holding my glasses and handkerchief, I advanced with long strides towards the counter at the opposite side of the room.

To the right rose shelves full of catalogues and various reference books which, owing to my blurred vision, looked like dark, overhanging masses.

I put on my glasses the moment I reached the counter. I had already thought of an apologetic excuse I could make for being late, one that, accompanied by a suitable smile, would put the librarian in a good mood. Unless ill-tempered by nature, people are usually obliging in such circumstances, even when they consider the request excessive—probably so they can take pride in their kindness afterwards. However, I had no one to give my excuses to. There was no one sitting behind the counter. Had my glasses been in place, I would have noticed this earlier.

I turned around in bewilderment. Perhaps, preoccupied with wiping my glasses, I had passed by the librarian without noticing him. But there was no one behind me; the long room was yawningly empty. There was actually little chance that we had passed each other. I might have missed him but he wouldn't have missed me, and the librarian would have been certain to address me. Hesitant, I turned towards the counter once again. Then I realized what had probably happened. Since no one was expected, the personnel had retired to some back room in anticipation of going home.

I coughed loudly, but no one appeared at the half-open side door that was the main entrance to the area behind the counter. The light was on in the room behind the door, but no sound came from that direction. "Good evening," I said, and waited a bit, then repeated it in a louder voice. Still no response. Silence reigned in the library.

As I stood there, not knowing what to do, the lights suddenly went out. All at once I was surrounded by darkness. The windows that had been dim rectangles a moment before were now the only source of light. Through them came the orange glow of the streetlights, muted by a coating of snow. As my eyes adjusted to the darkness, I looked around, trying to figure out what might have happened and having no easy time of it.

Then, from somewhere downstairs I heard a sharp metal sound, like a key turning in a lock. That same moment, I realized what was going on. The personnel did not have to go through the main room to reach the ground floor. As I had waited in front of the counter, they had reached the stairs some other way, or had taken the elevator. On their way out, they had turned off the building's power from the central switch. That was a reasonable precaution for an institution such as a library.

"Wait!" I shouted, running across the room. In the darkness the carpet became a straight, black strip, allowing me to move quickly even without light. But when I reached the stairs I had to slow down. It was considerably darker in the windowless foyer. The only bit of light came from the glass door at the entrance. I groped for the handrail on the right, grabbed hold of it and started downward, even though I was already too late. There was no one by the door.

Turning the doorknob and pushing brought anger this time, not relief. I was most angry at the librarians. How could they just lock up and leave, without checking whether anyone was still inside? True, I had entered after working hours, but even so. What if a thief had entered instead of me? The library security system clearly left much to be desired. But I was also to blame, quite honestly. I have never had a high opinion of people who leave everything to the last minute, and that is exactly what I had done in my haste. All because of a movie that I could have seen another time. In fact, nothing would have been lost if I'd never seen it at all.

Well, agonizing over it now wouldn't help. I had to devise a way to get out of the building. The thought of staying locked in the library until Monday morning made me shudder. That would not do at all, even though I certainly would not be bored surrounded by so many books. The heating might have been turned off with the power. The building might become colder and colder with each passing hour; they might find me frozen in two and a half days, in spite of my warm coat. There were other problems, too. I would not die of thirst—the restroom was probably in working order—but how could I survive sixty hours without food? And where would I sleep? I couldn't just sit and read the whole time. I shook my head, still holding onto the doorknob, as though expecting the door to budge. There had to be a solution.

What would I do if I really were a thief? A thief would not wait until Monday to be let out. What would someone like that do in my place? I thought about it for a moment, but everything that crossed my mind was either too violent, too dangerous, too hard to carry out, or required tools that I did not have at my disposal. All in all, it seemed I could not depend on any latent aptitude for thievery.

Then it dawned on me—a simple solution, but one a thief would never think of even in his dreams. All I had to do was return to the counter and use the phone there. Telephones work when the power is off. I would simply call the police and explain my predicament. They might think it was a crank call, but even if they didn't believe me right away, I would keep on calling until they checked on me. After that it would all be plain sailing. They would probably take me to the police station to make a statement. Even a run-in with the police was more acceptable than languishing in the library for two and a half days.

Stepping with care through the pitch black that engulfed me when I turned my back to the entrance, I mounted the stairs, my hand upon the rail. Even though I could see nothing, climbing was not difficult, particularly since I no longer had to hurry and everything would be better as soon as I reached the room. And it truly was better, but not just because of the meager light that poured in through the windows. Although weak and dimmed by the green plastic shade, the desk lamp at the counter seemed strong as a floodlight to me.

I stopped at the entrance to the main room and stared straight ahead. How could that lamp work if the power had been turned off in the whole building? Maybe I had jumped to the wrong conclusion. On their way out, the librarians had probably just turned off the ceiling lights. There could be no other explanation. But even so, someone had to turn on the lamp. When I'd left the room, it had not been on, and no one in the library but me could have turned it off. Or was I wrong about this as well?

As if in answer to my question, the door leading to the back room opened wide and someone entered the area behind the counter. I was rather far away, but I managed to make out a tall, thin, middle-aged man in a dark suit. He headed for the librarian's chair and sat down in it, turning his attention to something in front of him. He did not raise his head towards me. Even if he had looked in my direction, he would have had trouble seeing me since I blended into the darkness around me.

I remained hidden, trying to figure out the man's function. It did not take long: he was the night guard, of course. Why hadn't I thought of it before? I sighed with relief. My troubles were at an end. I wouldn't have to call the police. I would tell the man what had happened; he would have no reason not to believe me. Anyway, he could easily check the library's records and see that I had been a member in good standing for many years.

Even so, I had to adjust my approach to the circumstances. The night guard certainly did not expect someone to jump out of the darkness at him. Who knew how he would react? He might even aim his gun at me, and that was all I needed. I coughed and walked towards him slowly. After several steps I said in a mild, well-intentioned voice, "Good evening."

I had assumed he would stand up, perhaps even jump up from his chair. I would stop in that case and let him walk towards me, giving him a chance to collect his wits. Any sudden movement, even just walking toward him, would be inadvisable, since it could be interpreted as a threat. But, contrary to my expectations, the guard just raised his eyes towards me and returned my greeting, not the least bit surprised, as though my sudden appearance was quite natural: "Good evening. May I help you?"

I walked up to the counter. The man had a nicely trimmed, thick black mustache, but his hair was already turning gray. The suit he wore seemed of high quality. The handkerchief peeping out from his breast pocket was the same shade as his tie. I am unfamiliar with the dress code for library night guards, but I certainly hadn't expected this! The manager of the library might as well have stood in front of me, wearing his best suit.

"You see," I began, "I'm a little late. . . ."

"You're not late at all," said the man behind the counter, interrupting me. "We work at night. This is a night library."

I stared at him in bewilderment. "Night library? I didn't even know they existed."

"Yes, they do. And have for a very long time. Although very little is known about us. Were you interested in a book?"

"Yes, if possible. I really enjoy reading on the weekend. I was already afraid I would finish up empty handed this time. It's really nice that books are available at night, too."

"Of course they are. Although the selection is different than during the day. We only have books of life."

I thought I had misunderstood. "Excuse me?"

"Books of life. You haven't heard of them?"

I shook my head. "I'm afraid not."

"Too bad. I certainly recommend them. Quite interesting reading. Contrary to widespread belief, real lives are often considerably more exciting than those that are invented."

"Which real lives?"

"Everyone's."

"What do you mean—everyone's?"

"Literally. The lives of all the people who ever existed."

I silently studied the man on the other side of the counter for several moments. "There must be a lot of them."

"Yes, there are. One hundred nine billion, four hundred eighty-three million, two hundred fifty-six thousand, seven hundred and ten. As of the moment you entered the library."

I did not reply at once. I hoped that he interpreted my silence as an expression of amazement at the information he had just given me. What was going on here? Who was this man? He wasn't the night guard—that was quite certain. I also doubted his claim to be the night librarian. Whoever he was, I had to be careful. I was locked in a dark, deserted library with him. I had to avoid any conflicts, not deny anything, not contradict him, not enter into unnecessary discussion. Just wait for a chance to get out of there with the least difficulty. Suddenly, I wasn't interested in books anymore.

"You don't say!" I said finally, trying to appear properly amazed.

"Yes, but don't let this enormous number give you the wrong impression. Even though there are so many lives, each one of them is unique and unrepeatable. Precious. That is why they deserve to be recorded. Thus the books of life."

"So, more than one hundred billion of them. That is truly a gigantic library!" I figured a little flattery wouldn't hurt.

"Yes." A proud smile appeared on the stranger's face. "And constantly growing. A daily update is made of books on the people who are living now. And there are more than six billion of them! With new additions arriving all the time. Mankind is multiplying unchecked."

I nodded in admiration. "If I understand you correctly, the books of life are some kind of diary."

"You might call them that. But they are very objective diaries. That is their main attraction. Nothing is left out, nothing is hidden, nothing is shown in a different way. They are perfectly true. Which is only fitting. Like documentary films. You'll see for yourself when you read one of the books of life. Which one would you like?"

I thought it over. "I wouldn't know. It's not easy to decide when there are so many to choose from. Which would you recommend?"

"Almost everyone chooses the book about himself first. Which is a little strange since they have already read that book, in a way. But many still find it full of surprises and revelations. People are mostly inclined to forget things or suppress them."

"Do you mean to say there is a book about me, too?" My surprise was not exactly feigned.

"Of course. Why should you be an exception?"

I hesitated briefly. "All right. I'll take the book about myself."

"Fine," replied the man in the dark suit. "Wait here, please. I'll bring it to you at once."

He got up and headed for the back room, leaving the door ajar behind him. I stood in the small circle of light around the counter. I started to feel warm. I still had no idea what was going on, but asking for the book would let me end the whole thing calmly. I would take the book he offered, thank him, and leave. Everything would be much simpler once I left the library.

What the man brought me several minutes later was not exactly a book. It resembled a large binder. A thick sheaf of pages stuck out from between brown cardboard covers. Noticing my puzzled look, he hurried to explain. "This is the only way to add new pages during the update. The book will only be bound when there is nothing more to add." He smiled at me again. "Luckily, in your case that time has not yet arrived."

I returned the smile and took the binder. It was quite heavy. My name and date of birth had been printed in large, blue letters on the cover. The place for the other date was blank. I put the binder under my arm, reached into my jacket pocket, and took out my library card. "Is this valid for the night library, too," I said, handing it to him, "or does it require separate membership?"

"No need. We do not stick to formalities here. You are already a member by virtue of the fact that our stacks contain a book about you. In any case, we don't lend books, so there is no need to keep records."

"You don't lend them?" I asked, confused. "Does that mean I can't take this with me?"

"Unfortunately, that's impossible. It's the only copy we have. Something might happen to it outside the library, and that would be an irreparable loss. All traces of you would be lost, everything kept inside. It would be as though you'd never lived. We cannot take such a risk. But you can read it here at your leisure." He pointed to the tables on the right. "Make yourself comfortable and turn on the lamp. You can have as much time as you need."

I shouldn't have accepted it. I should have thanked him for the offer, told him it was late, I was tired, promised to return another time, and left at once. But I didn't. Vain curiosity won out. It isn't every day you get to read a book in which you are the main character. I wouldn't keep it for long, just leaf through it, I told myself. I sat down at the nearest table, pushed the button on the table lamp and placed the binder in front of me. The stranger at the counter bowed his head, engrossed in his own work.

If I hadn't been in a hurry, I would have started at the beginning, although I wouldn't have been able to testify to the accuracy of the account. Who still remembers their earliest days? I turned the binder face down and opened it from the back. I wanted to see how up-to-date it was. This all seemed like a lot of fun, of course, but a flicker of apprehension rose somewhere in the back of my mind. I felt like someone who doesn't believe in fortune telling, standing before a clairvoyant who is about to tell him his future.

The last page had been filled with tiny writing. A heading with today's date straddled the middle of the page. I started reading from that spot. Somewhere towards the bottom I reached into my coat pocket and took out my movie ticket. I compared the row and seat numbers with the ones cited in the book of life. A lump formed in my throat. The last sentence brought vividly to memory the clock in the library foyer whose hands showed three minutes after eight.

I glanced at the man sitting in the librarian's chair, his position unchanged, and then looked around uncomfortably. I suddenly got the impression of invisible eyes piercing the darkness, staring at me from all sides. This sensation made it hard to concentrate on my reading. But I had to continue despite an overpowering feeling that I would certainly not like what was to come next.

I began to turn the pages impatiently, leaving the end of the binder, heading towards the past. I searched for special dates in my life, dates when something had happened that no one else would know about except me. Or should know. Or had a right to know. And yet they still knew. Everything was written down there before me, all the dry facts, like a court indictment. Every secret that I had hidden not only from others, but often from myself. I felt hopelessly naked, like a hardened criminal whose crimes have suddenly been disclosed to the public.

I closed the binder. Beads of sweat streamed down my forehead, and not just because I was wearing a coat. I sat there a while longer, unmoving, my eyes blank. Then I turned off the lamp and went slowly up to the counter. I put my alleged book of life upon it. The stranger smiled at me again, but I remained serious and dejected.

"This isn't a night library, right?" I said in a hushed voice. "This isn't a book of life, either. It's my dossier. And you are some kind of secret police, spying service, or whatever you're called. I don't know much about such things. Congratulations. You've done a wonderful job. I had no idea that such surveillance was possible. Truly unbelievable. And terrifying. All right, now what? You know literally everything about me. There's nothing you can accuse me of, but you've collected more than enough to keep a hold over me. So you can blackmail me. That's what you're up to, right? The only thing I don't understand is why you had to invent that fantastic story about the billions of life stories since time immemorial, when you could have done perfectly well without it. Particularly since it's not the least bit convincing."

"Nothing has been invented, although I don't blame you for thinking so. Almost everyone who reads his own book of life reaches the same conclusion as you. It's quite understandable."

"But the story has its weak spots. You overlooked

some details. How, for example, did you know which binder to bring? I didn't introduce myself beforehand."

"We knew. Everyone goes to the night library sooner or later. It was your turn today. We were waiting for you."

"Really? Are you waiting for someone else after me, perhaps? If you are, I've got bad news for you. The entrance is locked. No one else can come in. And what kind of a night library is it that's locked at night, huh?" I hoped I sounded caustic enough.

"You're mistaken," replied the man behind the counter softly. "It's open. You'll see for yourself when you go downstairs."

We looked at each other for several moments in silence. The smile lingered on the stranger's face.

"Do you mean to say," I said finally, "that I am free to go?"

"Certainly. How could you be stopped? Libraries are free to enter and exit as you like. That's how it's always been. Night libraries are no exception. Unless there's something else you would like to read, nothing prevents you from leaving."

I didn't think twice. "I don't think I care to read anything else. Thank you."

"You're welcome. We are pleased that you visited us. Good night, sir." He took the binder, stood up, nodded to me, then walked into the back room.

"Good night," I replied, when he was already on the other side of the door.

I stayed in front of the counter a little while longer. The silence began to thicken around me. I could feel the ghostly eyes from the darkness stabbing me in the back. The man did not return. I turned and headed down the long, dark carpet at a faster pace than I had intended. I stopped at the end of the room and turned around briefly. The lamp had been turned off.

Holding onto the rail, I descended to the ground

floor. I grabbed the doorknob, but didn't twist it. For the third time, the outcome of this simple movement filled me with apprehension. The previous times had been easier. I would not have been in any serious trouble if the door hadn't opened. It would only have caused a minor inconvenience. I would have been without anything to read over the weekend, or I would have had to call the police to come and get me out.

Now, however, I didn't dare think about my fate if the door turned out to be locked. I would be trapped with no way out. But I couldn't hesitate forever. The doorknob slowly turned. When I pulled the door, it glided smoothly towards me and wrapped me in a whirlwind of large snowflakes. I quickly went out and took in a deep breath of cold winter air. The door closed automatically behind me.

I stood in front of the library, hands in my pockets, collar raised. I had no reason to stay there, but somehow I didn't want to leave. Before I finally left, I turned once more towards the entrance. Not much could be seen through the glass. Just beyond the door rose an opaque wall of darkness. The clock hung from its very edge; the rod that attached it to the ceiling could not be seen in the darkness, so it seemed to float. My gaze passed fleetingly over that round, white surface with its hands and numbers. At first, I didn't realize the problem.

The nature of my new disturbance only became clear after I had taken a few steps away from the library. I stopped in my tracks, then rushed back to the entrance. I pressed my face against the glass and sheltered my eyes with my hands. A shiver ran down my spine. I stood back from the door, took off my glasses and raised my left wrist. The conviction that I would see something different was fragile and unstable, but what else remained? The feeling disappeared instantly, as happens to futile hopes. Both clocks, the one inside and mine outside, showed the same time: three minutes after eight.

I shook my head in disbelief. This simply could not be. I had spent at least an hour in the library. Maybe even an hour and a half. That was quite certain. Every moment was still vivid to me. My experiences could not have been imaginary or an illusion. On the other hand, time cannot stand still. Regardless of their power, the secret police still cannot stop time. So what had happened? There had to be an explanation.

There was only one way to find the answer: by entering the library a second time. The thought did not appeal to me at all, but reliving an impossible mystery for the rest of my life would have been even harder. A shiver went through me when I reached for the doorknob. I pushed the door but it didn't move. I tried once again, harder, but it didn't budge. The library was locked, just as it should have been. Libraries don't stay open at night. There are no night libraries. Working hours were over and the personnel had gone home. I was too late.

I had to resign myself to the situation, particularly since I didn't know what to do. I couldn't break into the library, of course. Even if I'd wanted to, how could I have done it? I was no burglar, I hadn't the talent for it. I hushed the voices inside me that opposed my withdrawal. What else could I do? What was the point of standing there in the darkness and the snow? I would only catch cold needlessly or appear suspicious to some cop on his beat. I put my hands back into my pockets, hunched my shoulders, and headed down the street through the thick swarm of snowflakes.

I didn't get very far this time, either. I stopped in mid-step, next to the nearest lamppost, although I couldn't figure out why at first. The vague feeling came over me that I had missed something. I had overlooked some detail. I racked my brain, but it was just out of reach, like a word on the tip of your tongue that you can't remember. I looked toward the sky. The wide, orange beam of light from the street lamp was dotted with innumerable flakes, slowly floating downwards, carried by the wind. The moment they started to fall on my face, it dawned on me.

I turned and hurried back to the library entrance, almost slipping in the slush. I no longer needed to shield my eyes from the outside light. I no longer truly needed even to look inside because, even before I did, I knew what I would see, in spite of the darkness within the library. The handle of my umbrella was sticking out of the cylindrical brass stand.

4. Infernal Library

THE GUARD ESCORTING ME stopped before a door in the hallway and knocked. He waited for a few moments and then seemed to hear permission to enter, although nothing reached my ears. He opened the door, pushed me forward without a word, and stepped inside after me, grabbing hold of my shoulder to keep me there as he closed the door behind him. His grasp was unnecessarily firm since I had already stopped, not knowing what else to do. He probably didn't know how to be more gentle. We stood by the door, obviously awaiting new orders.

As with everything else I had seen so far, the ceiling was extremely high. This impression was accentuated here because the distance to the ceiling was considerably greater than the length and width of the room. I was suddenly overcome by the dizzying feeling that it would be more natural for the floor and one of the side walls to change places. But, of course, I could not expect the natural order of things to be maintained in this place. That time had passed for good. Who knew what unusual experiences were in store for me. I had to prepare myself for much worse.

The room was poorly lit and sparsely furnished. Hanging from the ceiling on a long wire, a weak bulb covered by a round metal shade shed most of its light on a backless wooden chair that stood by itself in the middle of the room. A man sat at a desk opposite the door, his back to the wall. Only visible above the shoulders, he concentrated on the computer screen in front of him. By the indistinct glow of the monitor, which created no shadow, his long face seemed almost ghostly pale. His short, thick beard appeared grizzled in the odd light and he wore semicircular reading glasses. I could not determine his age. He might have been anywhere from his early forties to his late fifties.

He didn't seem to notice us. The guard and I stood patiently by the door, as motionless as statues. Finally, without taking his eyes off the screen, the man raised his left hand and made a brief, vague gesture, which nonetheless had a clear meaning for the guard. He grabbed my shoulder roughly once again and led me towards the chair under the light. He released me only when I had sat down, then stood directly behind me.

While I waited, my gaze began to wander. The feeling of confinement caused by the height of the room was intensified by the uniformity of color around me. A sickly shade of olive-gray covered everything: the walls, the ceiling, the floor, the chair, the table. Even the monitor was olive-gray. The paint on the walls was cracked and peeling in places, showing patches of dry plaster the color of a stormy sky. It felt as if we were inside a faded and worn shoebox, once green, placed on end.

The room might have been less gloomy if there had been a window, even one with bars. But there were no windows. Working in a place like this could only be considered punishment. I looked at the person behind the monitor with a mixture of pity and dread. Even if I disregarded all the rest, there was certainly no reason to expect good of someone forced to work here for any period of time.

The deep silence in the room was suddenly broken by fingers tapping on a keyboard that I couldn't see. The rapid typing did not last long. When he was finished, the man raised his head, took off his glasses and laid them on the desk next to him. Then he squinted and pinched the bridge of his nose with his thumb and forefinger. He remained in this position for several moments before opening his eyes and nodding to the guard. The guard moved off at a brisk pace. The metal door opened with a squeak and then closed behind him.

We looked at each other without speaking for some time. I felt uncomfortable under his silent inspection, which expressed more aversion and bad temper than harshness or threat. I quickly realized that he wasn't the least bit happy about the upcoming conversation with me. He behaved like someone who has been doing the same job for too long to be able to find anything appealing in it. I had seen that expression on the faces of some older investigators and judges. Finally the man sighed, drew his fingers across his high forehead and broke the silence.

"You realize where you are, don't you?" He had a deep, drawling voice.

"In hell," I replied after hesitating a moment.

"That's right. Although we don't use that name anymore. Are you aware of why you have come to this place?"

I didn't answer right away. It was clear to me that there was no sense in hiding or denying anything, but I didn't exactly have to incriminate myself, either. "I can guess. . . ."

"You can guess?" He raised his voice. "Even here we rarely see a dossier like this." He knocked the crook of his middle finger against the screen.

"I might be able to explain. . . ."

"Don't!" he said, cutting me off. "Spare me, if you please! How inconsiderate you are, all of you who sit there. It isn't enough that I have to learn about the disgusting things you've done; you want me to listen to your phony, slime-ball explanations, too. They make me even sicker than the crimes themselves. In any case, there's nothing to explain. Everything is perfectly clear. We know all about you. Every detail. Would you be here if that weren't the case?"

"Mistakes do happen, . . ." I noted softly.

"There are no mistakes," replied the man. "And even if there were, it's too late to rectify them. There's no way out of here. Once you're in, you stay for good."

I knew that, of course. Everyone knows that. But I still had to try.

"What about repentance? Does that mean anything?" I asked in the humblest of voices.

This time he didn't have to say anything. His expression told me exactly what he thought about my remorse.

"Don't waste your breath. I have no time for such nonsense. I'm inundated with work. The world has never been like this before. Can you imagine the burden on my shoulders?"

I could imagine, but since the question was rhetorical, I just shrugged. For a moment I thought the man wanted to complain to me about his hardships, but then he changed his mind.

"Forget it. It's not important. Let's get to the point. We have to find out what would suit you best."

"As punishment?" I asked cautiously.

"We call it therapy."

"Burning in fire is therapy?"

"Who's talking about burning in fire?"

"Maybe being boiled in oil or drawn and quartered . . ."

"Don't be vulgar! This isn't the Middle Ages!"

"Sorry, I didn't know. . . ."

"It's simply unbelievable how many people come here with preconceived notions. Do you think we live outside the times? That nothing changes here? Would this go along with such barbaric brutality?" He tapped the side of the monitor.

"Of course not," I readily agreed.

"Every age has its own hell. Today it's a library."

I blinked in bewilderment. "A library?"

"Yes. A place where books are read. You have heard about libraries? Why is everyone so amazed when they find out?"

"It's a bit . . . unexpected."

"Only if you give it perfunctory consideration. Once you delve into the matter, you see that there's nothing unusual about it."

"It never would have crossed my mind."

"To tell you the truth, we were also a bit surprised at first. But what the computer told us was unequivocal. It is quite a useful machine."

He paused. Several moments passed before I understood what was expected of me. "Quite useful, indeed," I repeated.

"Particularly for statistical research. When we input data about everyone here, the trait that linked by far the greatest number of our inmates, 84.12 percent to be precise, was their aversion to reading. This was understandable for 26.38 percent, since they are completely illiterate. But what about the 47.71 percent who, although literate, had never picked up a single book, as though fearing the plague? The remaining ten or so percent read something here and there, but they'd wasted their time since it was totally worthless."

I nodded. "Who would have thought?"

He looked at me askance. "Why does that seem strange to you? Take yourself. How many books have you read?"

I thought it over briefly, trying to remember. "Well, er, not a whole lot, to tell the truth."

"Not a whole lot? I'll tell you exactly how many." The rapid sound of typing on the keyboard was heard once more. "In the past twenty-eight years of your life you started two books. You got halfway through the fourth page of the first, and in the second you didn't get beyond the introductory paragraph."

"It didn't catch my interest," I replied contritely.

"Really? And other things did?"

"I never suspected that not reading was a mortal sin."

"It isn't. Although the world would be a much better place if it were. No one's ever been sent to hell because they didn't read. That's why this trait was overlooked until we brought in the computer. But when, thanks to the computer, we noticed this connection, we were able to take advantage of it. In several ways. You might even say that it led to a true reform of hell."

"No one knows anything about that."

"Of course no one knows. How could anyone know? That's where all those prejudices come from. This place has never been the way most people imagine it: an eternal torture chamber run by merciless sadists. Tell me, do you smell that sulfur everyone talks about so much?"

I sniffed the air around me. It was dry and stale, a little musty. "No," I had to admit.

"We were simply a jail. With a few special features, that's true, but the system here differed very little from what you found in your jails. We treated our inmates here the same way you treated yours. Why should we be any different? If there was brutality and abuse here, that meant we were following your example. As conditions improved over time in your jails, the situation here became more bearable. Things went so far there was a danger of going against the basic idea of hell."

"What do you mean?"

"Recently your jails have almost been turned into recreation centers. You might even say they're modest hotels. You're the best judge of that; you spent a lot of time in jail, and it wasn't the least uncomfortable, right?"

I thought it over. "No, you're right, although the food wasn't always that good everywhere. Especially dessert."

A fleeting sigh escaped from the man behind the monitor. "There, you see. Well, now, we couldn't allow some of those privileges here. Weekend leaves, for instance. Or using cellular phones. How would that look?"

"But that would make it much easier to serve your time . . ."

"Perhaps. But it must never be forgotten that this is hell, after all. So we found ourselves in a bind. We couldn't follow the liberalization of conditions in your jails any longer. We were threatened with the one thing we have been accused of since time immemorial: being the incarnation of inhumanity and jeopardizing human rights. Luckily, that's when we found out about people not reading."

"Excuse me, but I don't see the connection."

"It was a simple matter. We made reading compulsory for everyone. This enabled us to combine the beautiful with the useful. First of all, our inmates could get rid of the main shortcoming that brought them here. If they had read more, they would have had less time and motive for misdeeds. Reading for them is truly healing. That is why we consider it therapy, not punishment, even though it might be a little late. But it is never really too late for something like that. And what do we call the place where everyone loves to read?"

"A library?"

The man spread his arms. "Of course. And a library is the last place to be accused of violating human rights, wouldn't you say? At the same time, this step removed the extremely embarrassing tarnish we had acquired. Furthermore, we turned out to be considerably more humane than your jails. They have libraries, of course, but what's the point, since they are almost never used?

It's as though they don't even exist. Take your own case once again. Did you ever go into a library in one of the many jails you were in?"

"I didn't even know they had them," I replied truthfully.

"What did I tell you? But don't worry, you'll soon have a chance to make up for what you've missed. And much more than that, in effect. Before you is literally a whole eternity of reading."

I stared at the man for several moments without speaking. "So that's my punishment? Reading?"

"Therapy."

"Therapy, yes. There won't be anything else?" I tried to suppress the sound of relief in my voice, but without success.

"Nothing else, of course. You will sit in your cell and read. That's all. You won't have any other obligation. I must, however, draw your attention to the fact that eternity is a very long time. You might get bored with reading at some point. That happens to many of our inmates and then they become very clever. My, what tricks they resort to, giving the impression that they're reading, even though they aren't. But we have ways to see through all those crafty ploys. In such cases we must, unfortunately, use forceful means to get them to return to reading. With the most resistant and stubborn they are sometimes rather painful, I'm afraid."

"What about human rights? Humanity?"

"We don't lay a hand on them. This is exclusively for their own good. We can't let them harm themselves out of spiritual indolence, can we?"

"I suppose not," I replied, not quite convinced.

"Those are the main things you should know. You will grow accustomed to conditions here. It will probably be a little difficult at first, until you get used to it, but you will finally realize that reading offers incomparable satisfaction. Everyone becomes aware of this during eternity, some sooner and some later. I hope in the meantime that you behave in a mature and sober manner and do not compel us to resort to force. That will make it nice and easy for everyone."

Since my unquestioning agreement was clearly understood, I nodded. For the first time, the corners of the man's mouth turned up a little, forming the shadow of a smile.

"Fine. Now let's see which therapy would suit you best. What kind of reading material would you prefer?"

It was a difficult question, so I took my time answering it. "Maybe detective stories," I said finally, in a half-questioning tone.

"Ah, certainly not!" replied the man, frowning again. "That would be like giving a sick man poison instead of medicine. No, you need something quite the opposite. Something mild, gentle, enriching. Pastoral works, for example. Yes, that is the right choice for your soul. Idylls. We often prescribe them. They have a truly wondrous effect."

He saw an expression on my face that might have been disgust. When he spoke again his voice had returned to its initial sharpness.

"If you think this unjust, you can take consolation in the fact that I would give anything to be in your shoes. Enjoying idylls. At least for a while. But I can't, unfortunately. They won't let me. Instead, I am forced to read exclusively the abominations and baseness that simply gush out of here. Like water from a broken dam." He tapped the monitor again, this time on top. "And eternity for me is no shorter than it is for you. That's not fair. Whenever you hit crisis-point, just think how much I envy you, and you'll feel better."

He stopped talking. The incongruous height and dreary color of the room suddenly seemed to collapse in on him, twisting his face into a mask of contempt and despair. He looked at me a moment longer, his eyes turning blank. Before he reached for his glasses and put them on again, he turned his head towards the door behind me. He didn't say a word, but it squeaked right away. The guard's firm hand found my shoulder. I got up off the chair under the light bulb and headed outside. On the way, I took another look at the man behind the desk. He had almost completely sunk behind the monitor, engrossed in a new dossier. A moment later the door hid him from my view, and I set off down the hall with the guard towards my cell, where an eternity of reading awaited me as well.

5. Smallest Library

I didn't realize I had one book too many until I got home. I should have had three in the plastic bag, but I took out four volumes. The old man had put the books into an old, crumpled bag, stained with something black on the outside. I had made no remark about the bag, not wanting to offend him. How could I tell him that it made no difference to me if the books he gave me got wet in the rain? Everything would have been different, of course, had I brought an umbrella, but it hadn't looked like rain when I'd left home.

The old man perfectly matched the bag he had given me. Greatly advanced in age, he had a wrinkled face and gray beard in which the rare streaks of dark hair resembled bits of leftover food. His clothes were no different from his face. His long, threadbare and dirty coat, which almost touched the ground, was patched here and there and, although the weather did not call for it, buttoned all the way to the top. It was early spring, but unusually warm and filled with sudden showers. Had I met this man anywhere else, I might easily think he was a beggar.

The old man's unsavory appearance, however, did not stand out among the used book sellers who displayed their wares all year long, even during the cold winter months, every Saturday at the same place, under the Great Bridge. They would bring folding tables, plastic crates for mineral water, or even large cardboard boxes that they would cover with newspapers, thus creating a makeshift stand. If it weren't for the books on these stands, the spot would resemble a flea market.

But looks can deceive. These were by no means simple peddlers with only the most basic information about their goods. Although one would never guess it from their unkempt, almost tramp-like appearance and the location of their stalls, a few words with them would quickly reveal that they were excellent book connoisseurs. Should you express an interest in one of the books on display, the seller would provide you with a mass of information about the author, publisher, reviews, reader reception, possible previous or later editions. Sometimes you might even hear a detailed history of a specific copy that was more exciting than all the rest.

The information was as trustworthy as if you had opened a literary encyclopaedia. Nothing was hidden or embellished, as might be expected of those who are only interested in selling their goods. Sometimes you would have the strange impression that what you were being told was intended to dissuade you from actually buying the book.

For more than a year I had been walking under the Great Bridge every Saturday, above all for these conversations with the booksellers. In the end I would buy one book or another, not because I wanted to have it so much as to compensate these people whose words provided the impetus for what I myself had been trying to write.

Over time, I became better acquainted with some of the booksellers I habitually saw there, and so enjoyed their additional esteem as a regular customer. Whenever I appeared, they would pull books out from under the counter that they'd kept for me, and the conversations we struck up would not be interrupted, I believe, even at the cost of losing another customer who might be ready to spend quite a bit of money. Several times I was tempted to propose that we continue our discussions elsewhere, but I held back. For some reason, I had the feeling that it would not be the same. Indeed, it was as if they could not exist anywhere else but here.

I had never met the old man before. Since all the places under the bridge were occupied, he had set up shop at the very end, where there was no longer any protection from above, as though he had been excommunicated by the others. He could only stay there until the first drops of rain forced him to seek cover. This would not have been difficult since he was the only one with a mobile stand. It was a cart that had once, long ago, been used to sell ice cream: a wooden box with two large wheels and two long handles for pushing it. I hadn't seen one since childhood. The bright paint that had once decorated this affair was completely faded or peeled, but I could still make out the shape of an ice cream cone with three large scoops painted on the front.

The other sellers would let me look at the books without offering their comments. They would only strike up a conversation with me when I asked a question or had selected a book. That was the generally accepted custom. The old man either did not know this or did not care. He addressed me as soon as I walked up to his stand.

"I have what you're looking for," he said in the hoarse voice typical of chain smokers.

"How do you know I'm even looking for something?" I replied a little abrasively, glancing over the old books that covered the top of the cart. The two conical metal lids that had covered the two openings for ice cream had been replaced by an unfinished bare board. A pile of old books, seemingly dumped out of a bag, lay on top of the board.

"It's not hard to tell. It shows on your face."

"Shows on my face?" I repeated, bewildered, examining the old man. That very instant I realized what I had missed when I first glanced at his face. His head was turned towards me but not his eyes. The eyes stared to the side, unfocused, blurred. The man was blind.

"Yes," he said. "If you know how to look."

"So that's it," I said, nodding. The awkward feeling that came over me only intensified when I realized the senselessness of this movement.

The old man was suddenly seized by a fit of coughing, hollow and hoarse, like the echo of distant thunder. It seemed to come from the very depths of his lungs. He put one bony hand over his mouth, the other on his chest, and bowed his head. He stayed in that position for a while.

"You are a writer, aren't you?" he said in a whisper, after catching his breath.

"Does that show on my face, too?" I asked, also in a low voice.

He didn't reply at once, wheezing for a bit. "No, but there's a smell about you. Writers have a smell. The harder the time they're having, the stronger the smell. You didn't know that?"

Inadvertently I sniffed the air around me. The prevailing smell came from the river: humid, sour, with traces of rotting debris brought by the spring floods. "No, I didn't," I had to admit.

"It makes no difference. What's important is that there is a remedy. We'll find it right away." He started to examine the pile in front of him with his fingers. He took book after book, felt it lightly, and then put it back with the others or set it aside, as though able to see with his hands. Finally, when he had made his choice, he held out three books. "Here, this is what you need. They will help you."

I hesitated briefly, then accepted the offered volumes. They were bedraggled-looking. One had no cover at all, its front and back pages dog-eared. Another had been destroyed by someone's merciless scribbling.

And the binding of the third was so broken it was in tatters. In addition, dust had accumulated in all three books. I had no reason to buy them, especially since I already had them in much better condition.

Nonetheless, I decided to take them. They would be of no use to me, but how could I refuse a blind old man? However, it wasn't just compassion. His cleverness deserved some reward. The bit about writers having a smell was pretty good. I might be able to use it somewhere. Although, of course, he had not recognized me by any smell.

As I was rushing home, I realized that there was only one way he could have known my profession. Several stands before his cart I had spoken briefly with one of the sellers of whom I was a regular customer. He asked how my new book was coming, and I had given a vague answer. The man could see that I didn't feel like talking about it and had changed the subject. We hadn't been that close to the old man and we were surrounded by a noisy crowd, so that under normal circumstances he would not have heard us. But people who have lost their sight have extremely sharp hearing.

"How much do I owe you?" I asked, reaching for my wallet.

The old man coughed again. This time the hacking lasted a bit longer. "You owe me a lot," he said at last. "But not for the books. They are free."

I looked in bewilderment at his empty eyes. "Why would you give them away?"

"Because that is the only way for you to get them. I don't sell books."

I expected him to say something else, but he clearly felt that this answer was sufficient.

"You have put me in an awkward position," I said after a short pause. "I don't know how to repay you."

"Forget it. Give me the books so I can put them in a

bag for you. It will rain soon and they might get wet, and that would be a real shame."

I looked towards the bit of sky not blocked by the bridge. Clouds had started to gather, but there were still patches of clear sky, so it didn't look like it was about to rain. I didn't say anything, however, since the old man appeared quite sure of himself. Maybe blind people can forecast the weather in addition to hearing quite well.

I put the three books into his outstretched hand and he bent down behind the cart, opening the door down there. He felt around inside and finally took out a crumpled, stained bag with the three books inside it. At least that's what I thought at the time. It was only upon returning home that I discovered that he had added a fourth. He must have done it then. There had been no other opportunity.

"Thank you very much," I said, taking the bag gingerly with two fingers. I was glad the man couldn't see my expression. "Goodbye. I hope we'll see each other again soon." As soon as I'd said it, I realized how inappropriate this greeting was, but it was too late to retract it.

"Farewell," replied the old man, politely overlooking my blunder.

On the way home, I thought it might be best if I got rid of the unwanted gift en route. But the sky dissuaded me from my intention. When I climbed up onto the Great Bridge, I saw that the old man had been right. Storm clouds were rushing in from the west, dragging a dense curtain of rain with them. I had to hurry if I didn't want to get caught in a downpour. I had no time now to look for a trashcan in which to dump the bag. Just as I stepped inside my front door, rain began to fall.

I could have put the bag in the garbage can in the kitchen, but I didn't. What I had been prepared to do outside without hesitation suddenly seemed inappropriate indoors. Sacrilegious, in fact. One doesn't throw books away, after all. Not even such worthless copies. I would put them out of sight somewhere. That would be the same as if I had thrown them away, but my conscience would be clear.

The fourth book that appeared when I emptied the bag stood out from the others. First of all, it was in excellent condition, although also an old edition. I turned it over in my hands, staring with bewildered curiosity. It took some time for me to realize there wasn't even a speck of dust on my fingers.

Nothing had been written on the chestnut-colored canvas cover, but that was not unusual. The book had probably had a paper cover that had been lost in the meantime. In the middle of the front cover was a shallow imprint, the stylized depiction of a pointed quill, an inkpot and an image resembling a sheet of parchment. The pages were edged in a shade of brown that matched the cover.

I opened the book. After a chestnut-colored blank flyleaf, the words *The Smallest Library* were written at the top of the first page in tiny, slanted letters. This didn't exactly fit the appearance and format of the volume. Someone had been too modest when naming the edition. Something more imposing would have been preferable.

I turned the page and the first surprise awaited me. The second page where information about the book should have been given was blank, while the third page contained only one word, which I assumed must have been the title of the work. But the author's name was missing. Filled with doubt, I looked for several moments at the inordinate whiteness before me. This was unusual to say the least.

Then I realized where I might find the copyright information. Some publishers put that page in the back. Although this would not explain the author's missing name, it was still worthwhile to check. I leafed through the book quickly, noting as I did so that it was a novel whose chapters had only numbers and not titles. When I reached the end, I discovered there was no information there, either. After the last printed page there was just one white one, then the chestnut-colored back flyleaf, and finally the cover.

I had therefore received from the old man an anonymous edition by an anonymous writer. I had yet to hear of such a combination, but it clearly did not follow that this was impossible. Although I am not uninformed about the world of books, my knowledge is by no means comprehensive. There was one place, however, where all information about absolutely all officially published works should be found: the National Library. I closed the book, laid it on my desk, and switched on the computer.

The National Library web site made it possible to execute rapid searches, even though it had an enormous stock of books. I typed the only information I had into the space marked "title." I was convinced that this would solve the mystery because any other outcome would be quite unimaginable. That would mean this was an unregistered edition, shedding new light on the whole matter. The old man's appearance may not have been exemplary, but I doubted he was ready to get involved in any nefarious dealings with books. In any case, the other booksellers under the Great Bridge, proud of their honesty, would not allow him to do that.

Nonetheless, about half a minute later the message on the screen told me that a work under that title did not exist in the catalogue of the National Library. I sighed deeply and drew my left hand through my hair. This was becoming awkward. Perhaps I had been wrong about the old man after all. I thought back to parts of our brief conversation that I'd skipped over lightly, although they should have aroused my suspicions.

Still, it was hard for me to believe that the blind man with the ice cream cart had been dishonest. My intuition, which rarely erred, protected him. Without taking my eyes off the screen where the message about the unsuccessful search quivered dully, I tried to find some way around the seemingly inexorable conclusion that something illegal was going on. The only extenuating circumstance I could think of was that the book had been a present and had not been sold, which excluded any self-interest. This, however, could not be used as an excuse for the fact that the title did not exist in the National Library catalogue.

Then, like a drowning man grasping at straws, I thought of something highly unlikely. Perhaps I had remembered the title incorrectly. I was certain I hadn't, for I'd just closed the book and the word had been simple and short, but sometimes such commonplace oversights can occur. Maybe only one letter had been different. After all, computers are very literal machines. I picked up the brown book from the desk in front of me and opened it again.

What I saw on the third page simply could not have been true. A lump formed in my throat. The difference was much more than one letter. A completely different title, consisting not of one word but three, greeted me. The book started to tremble and I stared at it in disbelief for several long moments, until I finally realized my hands were shaking. I had to place them in my lap to calm them. I squinted at the new writing, doing my utmost to find some explanation for this impossibility, but I couldn't think of anything. A book cannot change its title by itself. Everyone knows that. But it had just happened. What kind of trick present had the old man slipped me? And why?

I could not find the answer to this question just sitting there helplessly, staring at the third page. I had to do something. But what? Take a closer look at the book, perhaps? The first time I had just flipped through it. If there was some trick involved, that would be the best way to find out. But the chestnut-colored volume lay motionless in my suddenly sweaty hands a little while. It required considerable willpower to raise it again.

I turned another page—and stared wide-eyed at the beginning of the text on the fifth page. It was a novel, as I had expected, but no longer the one from a moment before. This time the chapter was denoted by a title rather than a number. And the letters were a different size: smaller, with less space between the lines. I was holding a completely new book.

This was too much. I reacted as though someone had tossed me a burning object: I threw it away from me and jumped off my desk chair. The book fell on the keyboard and pressed some keys. The National Library site suddenly disappeared from the screen and the speakers emitted a high, broken squeak.

If not for the noise I wouldn't have dared touch the book again. But I couldn't stand the sound; it grated against my overwrought nerves. Carefully, as though picking up something that might bite me, I took the book off the keyboard. The squeaking stopped at once, but the screen still had no picture.

I stood in the middle of my study beside the chair, now at some distance from the desk, and held the book out in front of me. I had the feeling something was about to happen, but I couldn't guess what, so I didn't know how to prepare myself. Several slow, tense minutes passed. When nothing happened, I realized it was foolish to stand there, waiting. I had to act.

Having returned somewhat to my senses, I concluded I had only two choices. I could put the book back in the dirty bag, add the three others, and throw them all away at once, not in the kitchen garbage can, but in a dumpster outside, as far away as possible, maybe even in the river, in spite of the rain that still poured down. I would thus be free of the cause of my troubles.

Or, I could open the book again. That didn't appeal to me at all. I shrank from what I might find there. Once I had been through an earthquake. The most unpleasant part of that experience had been losing the solid ground under my feet, something I had always counted on to be there. Here I risked shaking an even more important foothold: reality.

But it was too late. Reality had already been shaken to its foundations. I could remove the book physically, but not from my memory. I could not continue to live a tranquil life, pretending nothing had happened. That would be like burying my head in the sand. Sooner or later, I would start to buckle under the weight of unanswered questions. So I actually had no choice.

I opened the canvas cover slowly, as though something might jump out of the book. Somehow I already knew what I would see on the third page, but I still started a little when I saw the new title. This time it consisted of two words. I didn't have to leaf through the book to be convinced it was a new novel.

But I did so anyway in order to check something else that had occurred to me. Turning several pages at a time, I soon reached the end. The typeface was now large, double spaced, and the chapters had both a number and a title. I went back to the beginning in the same way. There was no change. It seemed that the change only happened when I closed the book. The work stayed the same as long as the book was kept open.

I closed the book, then opened it again. That was it! By some magic, I had a new novel. I repeated this simple operation and smiled with pleasure at the same outcome. I had not come a single step closer to solving the problem, but at least I knew what was in store for me, so the tension eased a bit. It's amazing how much easier it is to accept the impossible once you are no longer afraid of it.

To show myself I no longer feared the chestnut-colored book, I started to open and close it quickly. I watched in fascination as the titles on the third page changed each time. I was filled with something like the ingenuous excitement that overcomes a child who has been given an amusing toy that produces unusual effects. I thought for a moment that the title of the edition was quite fitting after all. This was truly the smallest library, but by number of volumes, not titles. Indeed, what can be smaller than one single volume?

Then, after I had opened and closed the book a dozen times, I suddenly froze in mid-motion. The question that dawned on me suddenly turned my delight into something close to horror. What happened to the work after I closed the book? My discoveries so far indicated that it disappeared without a trace. Each title appeared only once. That meant that I had just lost more than ten books irretrievably with my thoughtlessness!

I couldn't let this happen again. I held the book open firmly with both hands, so it wouldn't close by accident. I started to think feverishly what to do. How could I save something as short-lived as a work that only existed so long as the book was open? Nothing came to mind. I have never been good at coping under pressure. That's why I can never write to deadlines. Then, when I was ready to sink into despair, something so obvious occurred to me that I would surely have slapped myself on the forehead if my hands had been free. Photocopying, of course!

There was no need to hurry. I could wait for the rain to stop. Spring showers don't last long, and the work now between the covers was safe as long as I kept the book open. However, my patience ran out. I held the book in one hand, fully open though that wasn't necessary, and rushed to the vestibule. I grabbed my coat and umbrella and quickly went out into the hall. Since my hands were full, I had a bit of trouble putting on my coat. Once I got outside, I had to lower the umbrella all the way to my head, the brown volume under my chin, in order to protect it from the heavy downpour.

I splashed along the wet pavement quickly, taking no notice of the fact that my shoes were full of water after only a few steps and my pant legs were soaked almost to the knee. Luckily, the small stationery store that had a photocopier was not far. When I entered the store, shaking my umbrella after me, the owner looked at me in amazement. The woman clearly had not expected any customers in such a cloudburst. She must have wondered what urgent matter had forced me to come in just then, but she didn't say anything.

I said that I needed to photocopy something and waved the open book. I didn't give any explanation, although it would have been proper to do so. What, in any case, could I have said? She kindly offered to do it herself, but I declined the offer. I did so unnecessarily roughly because I was terrified at the possibility of someone else getting hold of the volume. The woman shrugged her shoulders and indicated the machine in the corner, then went back to her reading behind the counter.

I placed the book on the glass, lowered the heavy plastic cover and pressed the green button. The bright light went back and forth and a moment later a copy of the third page emerged from the side opening. At least that's what I hoped would happen. But there was nothing there. I turned the paper over, thinking the print was on the other side. Both sides were blank. I raised the lid and turned over the book. The title was still there, but it was invisible to the machine.

Noticing that I was turning over the book and the piece of paper, the storekeeper asked me if anything was wrong. Did I need help? I quickly replied no, everything was fine. In order to allay her doubts, I continued with the photocopying. I turned new pages, pressed the button on top, and completely empty pages continued to come out of the machine. From where the woman was standing, she couldn't see them, and she soon lowered her eyes to the newspaper in front of her, convinced that her strange customer had found his way.

The senseless photocopying was not so useless after all. It gave me a chance to steady my nerves after this new surprise. So I couldn't photocopy the book. I assumed that the same thing would happen if I photographed or scanned it. I shouldn't waste time on that. What was I going to do about the potentially short life of the individual works? I could not keep the book open all the time to save one book, because then all the others would become inaccessible. And if I wanted access to another work, this one would disappear forever. I couldn't see a way out of this conundrum.

Then a dark thought formed in my head, sending a shiver through me. Maybe that was the whole point. Maybe the whole thing was devised intentionally to be a Catch-22 situation. A very spiteful and malicious person stood behind *The Smallest Library*. Someone brazenly pretending to be a blind, benevolent old man with an ice cream cart, who generously handed out books. If I wanted to escape this trap, I would have to face him again.

I picked up the fifty-some empty pages, folded them lengthwise and put them under my arm. I hesitated briefly after raising the plastic lid, then quickly closed the book and put it in the large pocket of my raincoat. One title more or less—what was the difference? Approaching the counter, I put down a bill that was more than enough to cover what I owed her. I left without a word, feeling her inquisitive eyes on my back.

It was still raining, but now only small drops came sprinkling down. I opened my umbrella and headed briskly towards the Great Bridge, taking a shortcut. In an alley, I threw the bundle of blank papers into the first container without stopping. As I loped forward, the clouds first became lighter, then thinned out and finally, when I was already close to my destination, rays from the hidden sun poked through them here and there.

There were still a lot of people under the bridge. Many who didn't have an umbrella, as I hadn't at first, stood on the edge of the covered part waiting for the rain to stop so they could leave. They blocked my view of the far end, where the old man had set up his cart. But as I made my way to the middle, where the crowd thinned out, I realized I wouldn't find him there. He had been under the open sky before, so the downpour had certainly caused him to find shelter somewhere under the wide metal structure.

I started to turn around, searching, but there was no trace of the old ice cream cart. I certainly would not fail to see it. The space under the bridge was rather large, but it would be impossible to pass unnoticed there. Had the old man left during my absence? That seemed unlikely. Would a blind man pushing a bulky cart go out in such a thunderstorm? No, that would be reckless and dangerous. Unless, of course, the blindness and the rest had been a sham.

I wandered through the stands a while longer, not knowing what else to do, as my frustration mounted. Of the many questions besieging me, one slowly started to outweigh the others. Why me? Why had this happened to me, of all people? What set me apart from the others gathered in this place? The fact that I am a writer? A writer who hasn't been able to write anything worthwhile for quite some time? Wasn't that damnation enough? Why did I have to be given this book?

As I walked aimlessly, I found myself close to the seller I had talked to just before the fateful meeting. I thought for a moment to ask him about the old man. He could hardly have escaped his notice. But I didn't do so. Asking questions would only get me entangled in a web of explanations about something that had completely escaped my understanding. I might even be forced to take the volume out of my pocket and show it to him, which I wanted to avoid at all costs. But one other thing also discouraged me from conversation, something I dreaded most of all. What if the seller said he hadn't seen a blind man with an ice cream cart?

There was no reason to stay here any longer. The weather had cleared up considerably. Now there were far fewer visitors under the Great Bridge. This time I headed home slowly, no longer in a hurry. I hadn't gone very far when I became aware of the smells. First of ozone, then many others in dense clusters everywhere, brought out by the rain: the smell of new leaves in the tops of the linden trees, the damp young grass, the covering of humus in the little park, the washed flowers in the flowerpots. It seemed that even the water covering the sidewalk and pavement in large puddles had a smell of its own.

And at intervals, somewhere in the background of these strong smells, dampened by them, I detected a weaker smell that seemed vaguely familiar. It was omnipresent or else was following me. It was unpleasant, like the stink of sweat, but different, arousing thoughts of something strenuous and hard. Even painful. I tried to decipher it, but without success. The effort was not in vain, however. Quite unexpectedly, as I tried to figure out the mysterious smell, I thought of something which should have occurred to me a lot sooner. Before the photocopying, certainly. I quickened my pace almost to a run.

I took the monitor and keyboard off my desk since I didn't need them. I could have done the job faster by computer, but I never wrote using the computer. Instead, I took out a large notebook that had been empty for a long time. I didn't start to copy right away, however. When I picked up my pen, I was filled with the fear that this might lead nowhere. What if the pen left no mark, even though brand-new? I didn't know. Yet what could I lose by trying? Things certainly couldn't be worse than they already were.

I was unable to suppress a sigh of relief when the title of the novel appeared several moments later at the top of the first page. Clear and legible. I closed my notebook briefly and opened it again. No miracle took place. The writing was still there, as it ought to be. I turned the page in the book and sat back comfortably in my chair. Under the title I wrote "First Chapter" and then continued to the first paragraph.

Long and difficult work lay ahead of me. The novel was printed in tiny, single-spaced letters. But hardship is to be expected in the profession of writer. There is no respite. There are no shortcuts. Pain is part and parcel of the experience. That is why the pleasure is all the greater when things are brought to an end. When I copy the last page, I will simply close the book, and this work will exist solely in my manuscript. Who could reproach me then for adding my name above the title?

6. Noble Library

A NOBLE LIBRARY IS much like a stomach. Strict attention must be paid to what goes into it. Only proper and fitting items should be allowed to enter a noble library. Should a book that doesn't belong find its way into such a place, it would be just like recklessly swallowing something unfit for consumption. Nausea and disgust would result. Those were my exact feelings upon entering the study and finding a book in my library that I had not put there. I felt a revulsion so strong that it completely supplanted the natural question as to how the book had got there. In the same vein, the first thoughts of a man whose stomach contains something improper will not be how it got there, but rather how to be rid of it. Health is, after all, more important than sheer intellectual curiosity.

I took hold of the book with two fingers and pulled it out. It certainly did not belong there, above all else because of its size. That's how it had caught my eye on the crowded bookshelf that covers one whole wall of my study. I've always felt the greatest possible disdain for paperback books. They are the ultimate profanation of an ideal that must remain exalted and noble at any cost. Only the ignorant and uninformed claim that a book should not be judged by its cover. Ostensibly, a great work remains a great work regardless of its packaging. Nonsense! Packaging must mirror the contents. Would you wrap a luxury item in old newspapers, for example? And what is a great work of literature if not the most luxurious of all items!

I didn't let the title deceive me. The title would have suited a deluxe edition, leather-bound, with gold lettering; it seemed almost sacrilegious on the ordinary plasticized cardboard of a paperback. But, then, the people who make paperbacks are known to be unscrupulous. Nothing is sacred to them. They will not hold back from using the most sublime words if they believe it will make them a profit. All they care about is money. I truly don't know where we'll end up if we keep on misusing, trivializing and cheapening everything in this way.

Holding the object at arm's length, I walked briskly towards the kitchen. I stepped on the pedal of the garbage can under the sink and opened my thumb and index finger. The paperback fell with a thud among the garbage where it belonged. I brushed my palms together. There! One must not be thin-skinned in such situations, but resolute and harsh. The treatment should be the same as for vermin. Like bedbugs or cockroaches. One must brook no quarter.

I returned to my study with a feeling of relief, but an unpleasant surprise awaited me. Although I had just thrown it away, the paperback book stood right where I'd found it a moment before: in my library! Blood rushed to my face. What was the meaning of this? Straight from the garbage to the bookshelf? The book was not only where it didn't belong—it had messed up and contaminated everything else around it. How awful!

This time I threw caution to the wind. I grabbed hold of the intruder and plucked it out, disrupting as I did so the impeccable order of the bona fide books surrounding it. I am always irritable when my bookshelves are out of alignment, but that could wait. I had to take care of this interloper, once and for all. I didn't hesitate for a moment. I opened the book approximately in half and did something I have never done before: I tore it in two. This, however, failed to quell the anger inside me—on the contrary—so I continued to tear it with undiminished vehemence.

Soon torn up and discarded pages were strewn all over the rug. Under other circumstances, this would have horrified me, but now it only increased my fury. Completely out of control, I sat on the floor and started tearing up the pages into tiny pieces. Almost confetti. I didn't stop until the last page had met the same fate. When nothing was left upon which to vent my rage, I finally calmed down.

Looking around at the scattered bits of paper, I was ashamed of what I'd done. Such an outburst of anger was highly uncharacteristic of me. But, worse yet, as I'd vented my frustration I'd felt enormous pleasure, almost delight. I had to ask myself if I'd lost my mind. All right, I'd been offended and provoked; it might even be said that a great injustice had been done to me, but even so. A man must restrain himself, after all. What would we come to if we gave free rein to our darkest impulses?

In addition, I had made a terrible mess, I who was so proud, even inordinately so, of my own neatness. I sighed and got up off the floor. I went to the closet in the vestibule, took out the vacuum cleaner and returned to the study. I spent a long time cleaning it thoroughly, as if the machine could suck up the invisible traces of my bad behavior along with the tiny pieces of paper. The vacuum cleaner became quite overheated before I finally turned it off. I detached the hose, put it all back in the closet and then went into the bathroom to take a shower, since I'd broken into a sweat.

I emerged refreshed and calm. I'd been through an unpleasant experience, but at least it was over now. The best thing would have been simply to forget the whole matter. Why obsess over how the book had gotten there? I couldn't care less. The knowledge would only burden me unnecessarily—and I couldn't exclude the possibility that I would not find an answer. In any case, now that I had most certainly rid myself of the annoying book, it no longer mattered.

My hopes, however, were premature. One glance at the bookshelf from the door to my study was all it took to realize that my troubles had just begun. As though mocking me, there, between two precious old tomes, stood the paperback, wholly untouched. My face flushed once again. I closed my eyes and took a deep breath, nodding slowly.

At first it seemed I was losing control of myself again. But the thought of what I might do were I once more to be blinded by rage helped me keep the upper hand. Blindness would not be a good ally here. I had to keep cool. I'd tried force and it hadn't worked. Now I had to try something more sophisticated. I had to plan things out. If you can't beat your enemy, try to outsmart him.

I was, unfortunately, completely inexperienced in this regard. Never once had I faced the challenge of getting rid of any books. Until then I had only tried to acquire them, something I'd become skilled at over time, as evidenced by my library. How was I to get rid of a book? And no ordinary book; rather, one that persistently refused to disappear, one that defied me with its insolence. I sat in the armchair facing the bookshelf and stared at the thin, short spine of the intruder. I began to draw the fingers of my left hand across my brow, as I always do when in deep thought.

Before long, an unusual comparison crossed my mind. I would be having this same trouble if I'd decided to kill myself. I wouldn't know exactly what to do in such circumstances, either. Although it might not appear so, I don't believe it's an easy thing to take your own life. But at least I would have at my disposal the diverse and abundant experience of previous suicides. Particularly the successful ones. Maybe I could use one of their methods on the paperback book.

I liked this idea. It sounded promising. All that remained was to choose the method. Taking stock of the several possibilities that popped into my mind, I decided that drowning would be the most appropriate. If I had decided to commit suicide, I would have chosen drowning. Particularly because there's no blood. I have an absolute horror of blood. In addition, the act of dying itself takes place under the surface and not before eye-witnesses, so no one suffers any shock on your behalf. Finally, there's a certain element of romanticism in it. Many great loves in literature have ended by jumping into the water.

Of the two things I needed for the drowning, one I had at home. I went to the pantry, opened the large cardboard box where I keep tools and various supplies, and took out a large ball of twine. The twine was thin and thus could not be used on myself, but would be more than sufficient for the wretched little book. I cut off more than I needed, just in case.

I had to go outside to find the other item I needed, although I wasn't quite sure where to look for it. Indeed, where can a man find a large rock in the middle of a city? I certainly could not break off a piece of the pavement or the facade of some building. The only place I might find a rock was the park, so that's where I headed. Before that, I put the book and twine in a large travel bag. They could have fit in my pocket, but I would need the bag for the rock. Walking through the streets with a huge rock in my hands would have been ridiculous. I would undoubtedly arouse suspicion among the passersby.

Finding a rock in the park was no easy matter. There were far fewer candidates than expected, and I had to find the proper moment to take one without being noticed. In the middle of a stretch of lawn lay a round flowerbed surrounded by pieces of chipped stone, half buried in the ground. I had to wait until there was no one nearby, which took quite some time, and then expended considerable effort in pulling one out. I had no time to clean the dirt off the bottom half. I quickly put it in my bag and moved away, leaving a hole in the stone ring similar to the hole left by an extracted tooth.

I was out of breath by the time I reached the bridge. The rock was considerably heavier than it looked; I had to carry the bag under my arm, not by the handle. I headed for the middle of the bridge because the water under that part was the deepest and fastest. Whatever sank there had no chance of surfacing. It turned out, however, that fulfilling my intention was no easy matter. Passersby were scarce, but there were many cars, including occasional police cars. I had to appear as inconspicuous as possible.

Turning towards the railing, I squatted down and took the rock out of the bag. I hoped no one could make out what I was doing from the road. Seeing me in that position, they would probably think I was an oddball or a drunk, but not a suicide. In any case, people in cars rarely care about what's happening outside. I tied one end of the twine firmly around the rock and the other end around the book.

Then I stood up and put the rock on the top of the railing. I didn't drop it right away. I stood there motionless for some time, pretending to be a stroller who had stopped briefly to enjoy the view from the bridge. Finally, when there seemed to be fewer cars, I pushed the rock and the book. They took longer to fall than I had expected, and the sound when they hit the water was considerably louder than I would have liked. Dragging the book after it like some sort of tail, the rock hit the surface flatly, producing an enormous splash.

If anyone had been on the bank around the bridge, my actions would have been detected. I quickly moved away from the spot so that no one would connect me with what had fallen. Once I'd put some distance behind me, fear was replaced by the feeling of relief and good spirits that befits a job well done. My hands were dirty from the earth, my coat as well, but I paid no attention to that. I had gotten rid of the book—that was all that mattered. Let it rest in peace amidst the mud at the bottom of the river.

But instead of being wherever the rock had pulled it, the book was waiting for me in my library upon my return. Not the least bit wet and muddy. On the contrary: clean and dry. When I saw it this time, however, I was not filled with anger as before. I only thought dully that things had gone too far. Everything has its measure, rudeness and impertinence as well. No paperback book could string me along like that. This had already become a question of honor.

As I cleaned myself up in the bathroom, I tried with the greatest composure to go through the other possibilities at my disposal. Jumping from a great height was also a favorite among suicides, and in literature. No small number of protagonists had sealed their fate in this way. There would be blood, of course, and eye-witnesses shocked at the none-too-pleasant sight, but this was unavoidable. My conscience was clear. I might have cause to reproach myself if I hadn't tried drowning first. I wasn't to blame for the failure of that scheme.

I didn't need to make any elaborate preparations to set in motion this new idea. I took the book off the shelf again and put on my coat, paying no attention to the fact that it was still wet. I might have dried it a little with a hair dryer, but I had run out of patience. This situation had to be resolved as soon as possible. It had already gotten on my nerves, something not at all advisable considering my high blood pressure.

I decided to climb to the top of the tallest building in town, not because a smaller building would not have served the purpose, but because it was the most suitable for the task at hand. There was a viewing deck at the top. When there wasn't much wind, like today, they let visitors go out onto it. A high wire fence surrounded the deck so that no one could accidentally or intentionally plunge from the precipice to his death over thirty floors below. If I'd been the suicide, I would have had a very difficult time, but things should have been easier for a paperback book.

I had my share of trouble nonetheless. The only person on the top of the building was a uniformed guard. If there had been other visitors and if my coat had not had a large stain down the front, he most likely would not have paid much attention to me. As it was, however, he kept his eyes glued on me, which was a serious hindrance. I spent twenty minutes or so walking along the fence pretending to look at the city panorama before I had a chance to spring into action.

Someone called the guard on his walkie-talkie; while he turned this way and that, trying to find the best position for reception, I whisked the book out of my pocket and tossed it over the fence. The man didn't notice a thing. I waited for him to finish his conversation, nodded to him briefly, giving a broad smile, and headed for the elevator. I was filled with elation and pride. It's no small thing to outwit a professional.

As I approached the ground floor, I imagined I would find a crowd of people around the fallen book. But there was nothing of the sort. The street bustled with people going about their business. What terrible indifference, I thought. Who cared about the fate of a book, even if it was only a paperback? Then I realized that I had accused the passersby unfairly. How could they show any compassion when there was no call for it? There was nothing anywhere near the spot where a book thrown off the viewing deck should have landed.

I went home, crushed by an evil foreboding that came true as soon as I entered my study. As before, the paperback book waited for me in the same place in my library. This stubbornness was truly shameful! It left me with no other choice. The time for handling the situation with kid gloves was over. There was a much more gory suicide than the ones I had already attempted. If it had suited an extremely refined literary heroine, I didn't see why it was out of place for the book. I removed the unseemly copy and headed straight for the train station.

I couldn't gain access to the platforms without a ticket, so I bought a ticket to the closest destination, although I wasn't going anywhere. I checked the schedule, found out where the next train would arrive, and went to that platform. I moved away from the passengers waiting for the train so there would be no witnesses. Some ten minutes later, a locomotive pulling a long line of cars started to enter the station. I let the first two cars go past, then turned my head away as I threw the book under the wheels of the third.

After the train had passed, I was briefly tempted to look at the rails, but I held back. I wouldn't have been able to stand the terrible sight: the completely mangled remains of the little book. Although it certainly deserved to disappear, I felt a certain sympathy for it. There had been no need for this to happen, but the book itself was to blame. In any case, it was all over now. There was no reason for me to stay there any longer. I would only appear suspicious.

This time upon arriving home, I wasn't even surprised when I found the paperback book where it certainly had no right to be. And in perfect shape. Not a hair missing from its head. What else could I have expected? I would have been amazed, in fact, had it been otherwise. My previously kind thoughts were replaced by deepest loathing. I couldn't look at it anymore. It was not worthy of being in the same room with me.

Not knowing what else to do, I headed for the kitchen to fix something to eat. This dashing around because of the book had kept me from eating all day long. My stomach growled and hunger pains prevented me from thinking properly about what I should do next. I put the cloth on the table and laid down a plate, knife, fork, spoon and linen napkin, then opened the refrigerator. The choices were rather meager, however: a piece of dry cheese, a partially eaten sausage, half a jar of mustard and two lemons. It was clearly time to go to the store.

As I was closing the refrigerator, an idea came to me. I didn't take it seriously at first. Nonsense crosses my mind from time to time, as I suppose it does everyone's. I tried to drive it away, as I always do in such circumstances, but it refused to go. The longer it stayed with me, the less outlandish it seemed. Finally, I realized I had found the only real solution to my problem. I felt like slapping myself on the forehead. Of course! Why hadn't I thought of it before?

I went to my study, took the paperback book off the shelf and returned to the kitchen. I put it on a plate, sat down and tucked the napkin under my chin. First, I removed the cover with the knife and fork, as I would with a shell or wrapping. What was written on it promised true enjoyment, but one could certainly not rely on the honesty of whoever had produced it. Who knew what kind of a can of worms might be hiding behind the praiseworthy title *The Library*.

I could see by the table of contents that the book consisted of six parts. I assumed that each one had a different taste, so it was not advisable to eat them at the same time. I cut out each piece separately. Before commencing my meal, I wondered whether to add any spices. I looked at both sides of the cover, hoping to find some sort of instructions or advice in this regard, but since I found nothing, I decided not to try any experiments lest I spoil things. In the same vein, not knowing which drink would be most appropriate, I decided in favor of plain water. I couldn't go wrong there.

'Virtual Library' was quite reminiscent of a good Russian salad. It might have contained a bit more mayonnaise than suited my liking, though. 'Home Library' was like a thick, hearty beef soup with noodles. It seemed too hot, so I blew on the spoon. 'Night Library' corresponded to stuffed peppers. They contained the right proportion of meat and rice, which is very important for that dish. 'Infernal Library' was an excellent cherry pie. I don't really care for dessert, but this was an exception. 'Smallest Library' brought coffee with cream. I would have preferred something lighter, but one shouldn't be too picky.

I didn't know what could possibly follow this, but there was one more piece of the paperback on my plate: 'Noble Library.' Although already full, I didn't want to leave anything uneaten, and I was intrigued by it. I put a small bite cautiously into my mouth and started to chew. The taste seemed vaguely familiar, though I couldn't tell whether it was mostly savory, piquant, sweet or sour. It seemed to be all of these at the same time.

I continued eating, striving to figure it out. I was certain I'd tried it somewhere before. I liked it, perhaps more than all the rest. When I had swallowed the last piece, the pleasure that filled me was impaired somewhat by the fact that I could not recognize what I had eaten. But I didn't let this slight dissatisfaction spoil my good mood. I had accomplished my purpose. Not a crumb of *The Library* remained on my plate.

I got up from the table and headed towards my study. I felt not the slightest dread as to what I would find there. The paperback book might have been able to return from all the other places, but not from its current location. Its presence inside me was more than certain. I opened the door wide and smiled triumphantly at what my eyes beheld. The ugly intruder no longer sullied my noble library.

Steps Through the Mist

Contents

1. Disorder in the Head
2. Hole in the Wall
3. Geese in the Mist
4. Line on the Palm
5. Alarm Clock on the Night Table

1. Disorder in the Head

Miss Emily opened the door to the first-year classroom at the girls' boarding school. The quiet murmuring of twenty-six freshmen subsided and they all stood up as though by command. They were wearing identical navy-blue dresses that reached down to the mid-calf and buttoned up to the chin, completely plain, without the least embellishment. Even the buttons were covered with the same blue cloth. Only the white collars of their blouses interrupted this uniformity, varying slightly in shape. Not a single girl wore her hair loose; they all wore braids.

Miss Emily's brown dress was of the same plain cut as her students' uniforms. There was a small brooch pinned to its left-hand side that almost blended into the background. Her dark hair, streaked with grey despite its lingering thickness, was pulled back into a bun. Her tiny eyes gazed mouse-like through her round wire-framed glasses. The low heels of her high-topped shoes did not add much to Miss Emily's height. She was still shorter than most of the sixteen-year-old girls who were now waiting, motionless, for the signal to sit down.

She went up to the desk and set down a stack of papers and a leather glasses case. Her eyes passed over her students and she nodded briefly. The room was filled with the rustling of dresses and scraping of chairs, and then she too sat down. She set her spine firmly against the back of the chair, from where it would not move until the end of the class, as though glued in place. Only her head in lively movement would be at variance with this stiff body.

First she concentrated on arranging the objects in front of her. In addition to those she had brought, there was a small vase containing two purple wildflowers, a wooden pen holder, a long thin pointer, a large globe and a glass half-filled with water, covered by a linen napkin. She did not strive for any special pattern. The priority was that everything be lined up, to offset any impression of randomness. She abhorred disorder, both external and internal.

"Good morning, young ladies." Her feeble voice matched her stature.

"Good morning, Miss Emily," chimed twenty-six voices all together.

"I hope you slept well. From what you have written I can see that some of you are not getting the rest you need at night, particularly at your age."

She stopped talking and laid her hands on the pile of papers in front of her. It was a collection of dreams. Whenever she commenced teaching a new class, the first thing she did was have the freshmen write down their dreams of the previous night. This was the best way to get to know them. Nothing spoke more eloquently about the girls than what they dreamed. It was here that they showed their true nature. In addition, dreams are the first indication of the disorder that threatens to overwhelm young minds. And that could only be thwarted if discovered in time, before it seriously corrupted the personality. After that it was very difficult, perhaps even impossible, to remove.

Of course, there were always freshmen who would try to deceive her. They wrote inauthentic accounts of their dreams, resorting to invention for various reasons. Some simply had not dreamed anything or could not remember their dreams, but were reluctant to admit this. Others were ashamed of their dreams. The most dangerous, however, were those who made them up in order to outsmart her. Those were the girls in need of special attention. Such duplicity was a clear sign of a wayward disposition. What she found additionally offensive was the fact that they underestimated her. As though it were that easy to deceive her! With experience measured in decades, she was able to recognize without fail not only false dreams but those calculated to poke fun at her.

Among the twenty-six papers that had been given to her at the end of the last class, she was certain that three belonged to this latter type. They were all signed, but since she still didn't know the girls, their names meant nothing to her. All the same, she would soon see which of the young ladies considered themselves smarter than she. Nothing would teach them a better lesson than to experience a little public humiliation. They had to find out immediately that they would reap what they sowed. There could be no leniency in this regard. It was the only way to set them on the right path.

She took the first sheet from the pile and turned it over. At the bottom, next to the girl's signature, Miss Emily had written a great warning sign in red ink: three horizontal parallel lines cut by a vertical line. She used many similar symbols, with meanings known only to herself. Generations of freshmen had done their utmost to break these codes, but none had succeeded as yet. To make them even harder to decipher, Miss Emily periodically introduced confusing changes that made sense only to her: new signs appeared and old ones changed their meaning.

"Will Miss Alexandra please stand up."

At the penultimate desk of the row next to the window a willowy girl with large eyes and prominent cheekbones rose to her feet. Miss Emily examined her carefully. Not at all unexpected. These freshmen who got their height early were the first to have swollen egos. They thought they were special because they were taller than their classmates and nicer-looking. As if that could make them superior! But she had a remedy for such over-confidence.

"Ah, that's who you are. Fine." She put Miss Alexandra's paper to one side and then took another one from the pile. "Now would Miss Theodora please be so kind as to introduce herself."

A plump girl in the third desk of the middle row slowly stood up. She had red hair with curls that not even the tight braids could straighten completely. Her face was sprinkled with freckles. Miss Emily pulled up the collar of her dress slightly around her neck. She didn't like freckles at all. They were a mark. There was always a reason for them, as was evident this very instant. It was, of course, no accident that she had singled out this girl's dream.

"There you are. Very good." Miss Emily held up a third paper with a warning sign on it. "The last one to introduce herself is Miss Clara."

A short girl wearing thick glasses stood up in the first row, in the desk by the door. Her head was bowed and her right hand was clutching the three middle fingers of her left hand. Strange, thought Miss Emily. Of all the freshmen this is the last one I would have suspected. She could almost recognize herself some forty years ago. But experience had taught her how deceptive appearances can be. Even though Miss Clara seemed the epitome of modesty, what she had written clearly indicated that that was merely a superficial impression.

"All right. Now would the rest of you girls please take a good look at the three who are standing."

This caused a stir. The girls who were sitting started to look around in bewilderment, staring at the three standing girls, who were just as confused. Several neighboring heads drew together and whispered. Miss

Emily let the uncertainty gain momentum. She had put on this show many times and knew exactly when to speak again.

"You don't see anything unusual?" she asked at last. All the faces turned towards her. "I don't blame you. There's nothing that can be seen. One would say there is nothing special about Alexandra, Theodora and Clara. But this is not so. There are things that cannot be discerned by the eye because they are hidden. Terrible things that are not the least fitting in the honorable individuals that we all hope you will become after you leave this school. One such thing is a penchant for lying."

Miss Emily paused to allow her words full impact.

"This is a very bad characteristic. It is particularly dangerous when it appears in younger individuals. A girl who starts to lie early in life will most certainly not stop there. What inevitably awaits her is a wayward life of even worse sins. All lies, however, are not the same. Although no lie can be justified, some can be understood to a certain extent. Let's take, for example, your compositions on what you dreamed. Almost half are not true. You thought you could fool me, but that, of course, is impossible. I am quite capable of telling real dreams from false. I do not hold it very much against most of you, though, this resort to fabrication. You did not act out of ulterior motives. You found yourselves in an awkward position and lying seemed the only way out of it. You will learn in time that sincerity always serves you best in any difficulty you might encounter."

Miss Emily took the pointer and started to draw it back and forth through the closed fist of her left hand.

"But the motives of these three young ladies were not in the least naive. Their fabrications were fully intentional. They treated me condescendingly, wanting to show their superiority. Arrogance went along with the lies, and it is hard to find a worse combination.

They were convinced I would not see through them, but they have greatly underestimated me. Now the time has come to face the consequences. It is always unpleasant, but cannot be escaped. In any case, it is for their own good. Confession and repentance are the first steps towards redemption and healing."

The pointer stopped moving. A hush filled the room for several moments.

"So? Let's hear what you have to say."

It was not clear which of the girls was expected to speak first. Miss Alexandra glanced questioningly at Miss Theodora, who replied with a shrug of the shoulders. Miss Clara kept her head bowed. Her eyes had become glassy and wet. The tears had not yet started to flow, but it was certain that nothing could stop them. The tension in the classroom grew along with the look of impatience on Miss Emily's face.

"They didn't lie."

The voice was soft and came from somewhere in the back. A multitude of braids swung when the inquisitive heads quickly turned around to look. Miss Emily twisted her neck.

"Who said that?"

The girl who rose from behind the last desk in the middle row did not stand out in any way. She was thin, with dark hair and regular features, quite common among the uniformed girls. Only her eyes set her apart. Miss Emily knew about such eyes—and didn't like them. Behind their clarity, vivacity and penetrating power stood a character that was most difficult to handle. Willful and persistent, it resisted submission and molding, and served as a very bad example to the other girls. She had to be cautious from the very start.

"What is your name?"

"Miss Irena."

The name sounded familiar to Miss Emily. She had taken note of it while reading the girls' dream compositions, but forgot why. She put the pointer down, then took the pile of papers from the desk and started to leaf through it. She had gone through about one third of them when she suddenly remembered. The paper she was looking for was at the very bottom. She had left it there, intending to address that case at the end, after finishing with the ordinary ones. It was quite unusual. Over the years she had received a wide variety of compositions, but it had never happened that a girl would turn in a paper with only a signature and nothing else.

"Ah, you are the one. Very nice. And this was your dream?"

Miss Emily raised the empty sheet of paper so all the girls could have a good look.

"Yes."

"Should we conclude based on this that you didn't dream anything?"

"No, you shouldn't."

"So that's it. You did have a dream, but for some reason you did not consider it necessary to inform us about it. Would you perhaps tell us the reason?"

"I did tell you the dream."

"You told us? I don't see any report here. Does any of you freshmen see better than I do?"

She began turning the page over slowly from one side to the other, making an arc with it in front of her. The question was not directed at anyone in particular, but several girls nonetheless briefly shook their heads.

"It's mist."

Miss Emily's mouse-like eyes immediately squinted.

"I don't think I heard you too well."

"That's mist," repeated the girl from the end of the middle row. "I always dream about mist."

"You dream about mist?"

"Yes."

Miss Emily adjusted the pointer's position a little so it was parallel to the edge of the desk.

"Very interesting. You only dream about mist? You must be very bored when you sleep."

"I'm not. There's another dream."

"Oh, there is? So why didn't you write about that other one?"

"Because it isn't mine."

"It isn't yours? Then whose is it?"

"Someone else's."

"How can something in your dream belong to someone else?"

"It's no longer my dream. The mist suddenly disperses and I enter someone else's dream. I dream what others dream."

Miss Emily looked at Miss Irena for several moments without speaking.

"My dear, I have heard all manner of concoctions from freshmen during my many years of tenure at this school, but I must admit that you have outdone them all. Do you really expect us to believe what you just said?"

"Yes." The girl's voice was even, as though confirming something quite ordinary.

"And just why should we believe you, might I ask?"

"Because it is the truth."

"How can the truth be that you dream other people's dreams? Has anyone else ever heard of something like that?"

Her eyes swept over the class, but this time not a single head moved. Miss Emily felt awkward. The conversation had taken an unexpected turn and she was no longer in complete control. She had to put an end to this nonsense as soon as possible.

"I think that's enough for now," she continued. "I must warn you that you won't get very far with such stories. A rich imagination is not greatly appreciated here. Other virtues are fostered in this school."

"It's not my imagination. If it were, how would I know that these other girls aren't lying?"

"Of course they lied. I should think I'm the best one to know that. And you are no better than they are. You have not only concocted rubbish, but stubbornly insist it is true."

"I can tell you their dreams. I dreamed them along with them."

Miss Emily's first thought was to resort to her tested procedure. Miss Irena should leave the class at once and report to the principal. Such impudence had to be properly punished. As a lesson to the others. But if she did that, she would be admitting defeat. She had been offered a challenge and had to reply. In any case, why not? Let the girl say what she had to say. She would only embarrass herself. Of course she could not know what the three girls had dreamed. Particularly since these weren't their real dreams, but fabrications.

"All right then. Let's hear. It will give us a fine chance to see that lies are always short-lived."

"Miss Alexandra dreamed that she was in an asylum for the mentally disturbed after a traffic accident in which she hurt her head. She had terrible visions that frightened her. A doctor came to visit and she told him about her visions, but he didn't believe them. Miss Theodora dreamed that she was skiing. An unusually dressed man sat next to her on the ski lift. He explained that he was not there by accident. He had come to see which path she would take to ski down the slope. For some reason this was very important. Miss Clara dreamed that she was a clairvoyant. A young man came to her parlor with a strange request. He wanted her to confirm that he only had a short time left to live."

When Miss Irena finished, the girls kept their heads turned in her direction several moments longer, then all turned towards Miss Emily. Only Miss Alexandra and Miss Theodora continued to stare at the last desk in the middle row. All that broke the silence was the sniffles and sobs of Miss Clara, who had not moved since she first stood up.

Miss Emily's face flushed with anger. There had always been girls who considered themselves smarter than she, at least in the beginning, but something like this had never happened before. This was a true conspiracy! Four of the freshmen had plotted to make her look foolish. Fine! Now they would find out just what they were up against.

"Did you really think this would work? That I am gullible enough to fall for your ploy? That I would believe this nonsense about dreaming other people's dreams, when there is a far simpler and more natural explanation? You found out that I always assign a composition about dreams at the first class. That is no secret, in any case. Then you cleverly planned this whole thing. Three would write invented dreams and one would ostensibly know about them. Your plan, unfortunately, didn't succeed. If you wanted to outsmart me you should have devised something much more convincing. Now you will all go . . ."

"I was in your dream too."

Miss Emily quite disliked being interrupted in the middle of a sentence. In any other situation she would have severely reprimanded a freshman impertinent enough to do such a thing. This time, however, there was no reprimand. Staring into the clear eyes at the other end of the classroom, irritated above all by their composure, she picked up the pointer again. She held on to the middle of it tightly with both hands.

"Really? You did me the honor of visiting my dream too? And just what was that dream, if you please?"

"The one you dream all the time. Night after night. The dream about the old woman whose alarm clock is broken and she goes to the watchmaker's . . ."

The crack of the dry wood breaking in Miss Emily's

hands echoed so loudly that several of the girls flinched. Miss Clara raised her tear-streaked face in fear.

"Enough! We don't want to hear your drivel anymore. Leave at once and report to the principal. You others sit down. I'll take care of you later."

The three girls quickly took their seats, but Miss Irena did not head for the door.

"It wouldn't be a good idea for me to go."

This was insubordination. Miss Emily had given an order and it had to be carried out without question. But suddenly her destabilized authority did not seem so important.

"It wouldn't? You don't think, by any chance, that we will miss your company?"

"You will. In a way. If I leave the classroom, it will cease to exist."

Miss Emily stood up slowly. She had never done this before in the middle of a class. Without the chair back, she felt somehow without support, as though floating. She put the two parts of the broken pointer on the desk, briefly bemoaning their mismatched appearance, their slightly different lengths.

"We had no idea that someone so important was with us."

"I'm not at all important. Quite the contrary. I am very secondary. This is not my dream. I am only a guest in it, as usual. But when I leave it, the dream will cease to be. All of this will disappear. There is nothing on the other side of the door but mist. Do you still want me to go and report to the principal?"

The classroom sank into silence. Miss Emily could almost feel the girls' eyes on her: confused, questioning, expectant, frightened. Had she been alone with Miss Irena, she might have given another answer. This way, she had no choice.

"Yes. That is a risk that we must take."

Miss Irena walked along the aisle with slow steps.

She reached the door and put her hand on the knob. She stayed like that for several moments, as though pondering whether or not to say anything, but she didn't utter a word. She turned the knob and the door started to open.

Miss Emily did not see what was on the other side. She quickly turned her head the other way and stared out of the tall windows at the sunny summer morning. She kept her eyes turned in that direction as the door slowly closed behind the girl.

2. Hole in the Wall

The hospital attendant walking in front of me went up to door number seven on the left. It was made of white metal, like all the others in the hall. Against the dark-red wall they looked like widely spaced teeth in a giant jaw. He unbolted a small rectangular peephole, opened it, peered inside briefly, then bolted it again.

"You shouldn't have any trouble with her. We put her in a straitjacket, but not because she's aggressive towards others. She tried to commit suicide, as you know." He indicated the file I was holding. "Just in case, I'll stay close by. If you need me, all you have to do is call."

I nodded. The attendant took a magnetic card out of the breast pocket on his white coat, swiped it through the small terminal by the doorframe and opened the door. He let me go in, but didn't close the door after me. He stayed there, watching. I turned towards him and nodded once again. The heavy door closed on its hinges almost soundlessly and the attendant's large figure disappeared behind it.

I have never liked the white color of the padding that lines the walls and floors of these rooms, as though someone has taken great pains to increase the anxiety of the patients forced to spend time there. The same can be said of the bright fluorescent lighting that is never turned off, nor even turned down during the night. The only thing that disrupted the depressive uniformity of the room was a small window high up next to the ceiling on the wall facing the door. It was actually a ventilation shaft with two thick vertical bars instead of glass. This metal protection was quite superfluous; it was impossible to climb up there even if a person were unencumbered by a straitjacket, and nothing larger than a cat could squeeze through it.

The girl was sitting under that opening, her back leaning against the wall. Her legs were bent and her chin was resting on her knees. She looked at me, smiling. I recognized the person whose photo I'd seen in the hospital file: a round face, large, lively brown eyes, small ears, a short, slightly turned-up nose. Dark blond hair reached to her shoulders. Only a rough attempt had been made to comb it, but this did little to diminish the discreet beauty of her face. As it was, her uncombed hair actually made her look younger; if I hadn't known that she was twenty-six, I wouldn't have given her more than twenty-two or twenty-three years.

I dropped to the floor myself, leaning against the door. I always try to put myself at the same level as my patients. As a rule, this creates an impression of equality and helps establish contact with them. I stretched out both legs so the bottoms of my shoes touched the easily soiled padding as little as possible. I put the green file on the floor next to me.

"Hello, Miss Katarina," I said, returning her smile. "How are you?"

"Hello, Doctor. I'm fine now. I'm glad you came."

"Let me introduce myself. I'm Dr. Alexander. I'm replacing Dr. Sonja who has been in charge of you up to now. She had an accident and will be absent from work for two or three weeks. Luckily it wasn't anything serious. She fell down the stairs in her house and shattered her shin. Her leg is in a cast, but she's in fine spirits. She's slowly getting used to the crutches."

"Poor Dr. Sonja. Please tell her that I'm terribly sorry

about what happened. It must have been quite painful. But, as you say, she'll get well soon. There won't be any consequences. She'll forget both the pain and the crutches."

"I hope so."

"Believe me, that's what will happen."

We looked at each other for a few moments without talking. Finally, I tapped the file on the floor. "Yes, you would know that, wouldn't you? If I've understood correctly, you feel you are able to see the future?"

"I am," she replied in an even voice, as though saying something quite banal.

"Perhaps you could have warned Dr. Sonja of the trouble that awaited her." I said this cheerfully, in jest, certainly with no sound of reproach.

"Perhaps. But even if I had, it would have made no difference. Dr. Sonja didn't believe me."

"It's not easy to believe something like that."

"I know. That's why it's easy to put someone in a place like this just because they claim they can see the future, even if it poses no threat to anyone." There was no reproach in her voice either.

"You are a threat to your own self. That is primarily why people end up here, not because they feel they possess unusual abilities. Didn't you stop eating? And then try to commit suicide?"

"It was a clumsy, slapdash attempt. Mistaken, in any case."

Silence reigned once more. I glanced at my outstretched legs and then looked at her again. She was still smiling.

"There's something I don't understand," I said, shaking my head. "It's odd that your file makes no mention of it. I don't know why Dr. Sonja neglected to talk to you about something that seems to me pivotal to the whole matter: what it was that led you to attempt suicide. If what you claim is true, that you have the gift of seeing the future, then you are the last person in the world one would expect to kill herself. Many people would give their eye teeth to be in your place. It's hard even to imagine all the possibilities available to someone who knows what the future will bring."

"Of course Dr. Sonja wanted to know why I tried to kill myself. But I refused to talk about it."

"Why?"

"There was a reason."

"There was? Does it still exist?"

She didn't reply at once. A questioning look flickered across her face, conveying some hesitation.

"How do you picture the future?" She answered at last with a question.

She'd caught me off guard. I scratched the top of my head as I do automatically when something puzzles me, then I shrugged my shoulders.

"I don't know. I haven't thought about it very much. As a time that is to come, I suppose?" Even as I spoke I realized this was highly unoriginal. I feared I'd earned her derision, but there was none forthcoming.

"Until recently that was the same attitude I had towards the future," she said in a voice full of understanding. "What will be will be. A person has little influence, if any at all. We enter the mist, not knowing what awaits us there. Then, after the accident, everything changed."

She motioned her head toward the file. This released her from the obligation of having to explain. She had rightly assumed that I'd studied her file thoroughly before coming to see her. She'd been in a serious traffic accident some three and a half months before. She was the only one of four passengers to make it out of the smashed-up car. And just barely. At first the doctors gave her little chance. Although there hadn't been much bodily injury, she had hit her head, resulting in a deep coma. It had taken seventy-three days for her to come out of it. At first there seemed to be no harmful consequences, but soon afterward she started claiming she could see the future. Of course, no one took her seriously. Similar notions appear sometimes among those who have had severe head injuries. Faced with this skepticism, Katarina first withdrew in protest, almost autistically, and then refused to eat. The surgeons soon realized she was no longer within their domain so they sent her straight from the hospital to us.

Naturally, not a bit of real progress could be expected in the mere two weeks that Dr. Sonja had been working with her. As a rule, such patients require considerable time and patience. It was enough that the doctor had got her eating again. This good sign, however, was soon darkened by the unexpected suicide attempt four days previously. Fortunately, as Katarina said herself, it had been a rather clumsy attempt, easily thwarted. The rules had then required that she be transferred to this room for a while as a precautionary measure

"In what sense did things change?" I asked.

Katarina stretched out her legs like mine and shook her head a bit to loosen her hair. These were the only two parts of her body that she could freely move. The bottoms of her pajamas rose a bit above her socks, revealing part of her calves. I knew quite well how uncomfortable she must have been with her arms confined in the straitjacket, but I could not change that as yet.

"The mist lifted," she replied tersely.

I waited to see if she would say anything more, but when nothing was forthcoming I spoke again.

"And the future was revealed to you?" I tried to say this without the slightest skepticism, as though stating an obvious fact.

She shook her head. "There isn't just one future. That's what confused me the most at first."

"What do you mean?"

She hesitated briefly. "It's a beam . . . enormous . . . As soon as I close my eyes, in a waking state, it's there. I see it clearly, it fills my whole field of vision under my closed eyelids. There's nothing else but the beam. It consists of an infinite number of thin strands that seem to be made of frosted glass. Each of them is a future."

She stopped a moment, as though wanting to let me absorb this image.

"But they cannot all become . . . real. What I mean to say . . ." I thought I knew what I wanted to say, but somehow I couldn't find the right words. I don't have much experience in talking about the future.

"They can't, that's it. Only one will be real in the end. But until this happens, they are all equally possible. Each of these strands. Completely equal. Until one singles itself out."

"Singles itself out?" I repeated in amazement.

"Yes. It starts to shine with an internal glow, turning transparent and expanding at the same time, pushing the others into the background. In the end it fills up the beam's whole space. That's all there is, that one future that will become real. It stands before you crystal clear. Everything can be seen in that one strand that has detached itself and expanded. Everything that will happen."

I stared at her for a while in silence. "But I can't see it," I said at last. "That's what it's all about. It seems that only you are privileged to see it."

For the first time since we'd started talking, the smile disappeared from her face.

"You don't believe me, do you."

"It might be easier to believe you if I could understand why someone who has access to the future decided to kill herself. We're still coming up against this issue."

She bowed her head, resting her chin on her chest. Her hair was like a veil covering her face. From behind this came only the gentle sound of slow breathing.

When she spoke, her voice was muffled and somehow far away.

"What do you think, what decides which of the strands will start to glow? What decides which of the countless possible futures will become real?"

"You've got me there," was my reply after pondering briefly. "Chance, perhaps?"

She sighed deeply. "Chance, yes. That's what I thought at first. Then the ability I have acquired would still be bearable."

As she didn't continue, I asked cautiously, "If it isn't chance, then what is it?"

She raised her head again. Her hair fell back and parted, revealing the middle of her face. She reminded me of a picture I'd seen on a billboard somewhere. "Not what but who," she said, more softly than before.

I looked at her several moments, eyes blinking. "Someone chooses which future will become real? Who could that be?"

"Isn't it obvious?"

I made a rueful face. "I'm afraid not. At least not to me."

A shadow of a smile returned to her lips, as though wanting to forgive me for my lack of insight. "I don't hold it against you. I too needed some time to see what had been standing clearly before me from the beginning: I coexist with it. I, of course, am the one who makes the decision, the one who singles out the strand that will prevail over all the others. I choose the future."

"You?" This time I was unable to suppress the disbelief in my voice. "How?"

"It's actually very simple. That's what led me astray. As I look at the beam of all possible futures, my eyes under my eyelids are not quite focused. So the strands are slightly blurred. But as soon as I fix my eyes on one, it starts to detach itself. In the beginning I mistook the cause for the effect. I thought that my eyes focused on the strand that had singled itself out for some other reason, with my having nothing to do with it. But things, unfortunately, are just the opposite."

We spent about half a minute in silence. Katarina clearly felt that she had now explained everything quite satisfactorily, and at first I didn't know how to continue the conversation. Suddenly, all my experience working with patients like this no longer seemed to help. I finally found my cue in her last sentence.

"Why 'unfortunately'? Isn't being able to choose the future far more advantageous than only being able to see it? Now I understand even less why you wanted to take your own life."

Katarina's face took on the expression of a teacher with a dull-witted pupil in front of her. "What's so advantageous about it?"

"Why, you could choose a future without suffering, misery, hardship. There must be some like that among those countless strands you mentioned."

She shook her head slowly. "Utopia? Heaven on earth? Don't be naive. There is no such future. Not a single strand is without suffering, misery and hardship."

"I wasn't thinking idealistically. What I had in mind was a future in which there was very little of that. One in which most people lived happily."

"But there would still be unhappy people."

"That's inevitable, you said so yourself."

There was something reproachful, accusing in her eyes. "Would you consent to be the one to choose who should be sacrificed on the altar of the happy majority?"

She'd caught me by surprise again. My hand was already reaching mechanically for the top of my head, but I stopped it at the last moment. Scratching my head suddenly seemed out of place. "That's a very difficult question."

"Yes, it is. And just think about what a heavy burden it is for someone who, without the slightest desire, has to decide which future will become real, knowing in the process that this will inevitably bring suffering, misery and hardship to someone. No human shoulders can hold up under that. I doubt that even God's shoulders are strong enough. There is only one force capable of dealing with this chilling responsibility: the blind and impassive force of chance. I have to give back to chance what belongs to it, as soon as possible, since it has reached me by some mistake. I hope that now you understand why I have no choice."

"But suicide is certainly not the only solution."

"It isn't? What else do you suggest?" Her voice was filled with sarcasm.

"You told me that this . . . beam of strands of the future . . . only appears when you close your eyes in a waking state, isn't that right?"

"That's right."

"Well, then, don't close your eyes except when you go to bed."

She shook her head back and forth. The ends of her long blond hair swayed as though blown by a gentle breeze. "If only things were that simple. You give me way too much credit. Do you really think that any human being could resist such temptation, could have such self-control? In any case, I tried that already. It was the frustration I felt after it failed that led me to that clumsy suicide attempt."

"Which didn't succeed, thank heavens."

"It didn't. Because it was so clumsy. There was anger and despair behind what I did, and they are poor allies if you want to do a job properly. It was only later, after I'd calmed down a bit in here, that I started to think things over coolly and collectedly." Her smile widened. "As you can see, there's an upside to being put in a straitjacket."

"That's not the only one. In a straitjacket, which is indeed rather uncomfortable, you are effectively prevented from doing something reckless. No one has managed to kill themselves in one yet."

"Then I will be the first one to succeed." I detected a hint of pride in her voice.

"How?"

"You'll soon find out. Things are underway and nothing can stop them."

"Are you quite sure about that?"

"Of course I'm sure. Don't forget the powers at my disposal. That's what finally crossed my mind, sitting here on the floor, as the anger from my failed attempt slowly dissolved. Why embark on something uncertain and questionable when everything can be carried out without fail?"

"You mean. . . ?" I made a vague circular motion with my hand.

"Yes. All I had to do was choose the future in the beam where my suicide attempt succeeds. It didn't turn out to be quite that easy, however. I picked through the strands for three full days, searching for the right one. And I finally found it."

"Which means that we are already in that future?"

"We are. And it shows you how choosing what will happen is connected to inflicting pain on others. In this time strand Dr. Sonja falls down the stairs. I feel really bad about it. She was kind to me and full of understanding. Please ask her to forgive me. Try to explain that it simply couldn't be avoided. Your efforts will be in vain, however. You won't be able to convince her because you will never believe it yourself. Not even after you find me dead here tomorrow."

My eyes slowly looked around the inside of the padded room. I have never liked these mournful white isolation cells, but now it seemed the most appropriate sanctuary for this girl who clearly was still in the throes of sinister thoughts. Restrained by the straitjacket, this was the only place where she was completely safe from her own self. I've had patients with suicidal tendencies from time to time, but they were all much more typical, ordinary cases. Never before had I heard such an intricate and unbelievable story. And told so convincingly. Working with her would be difficult, but also challenging. I would try to talk my colleague Sonja into letting me handle Katarina's case or at least work together with her on it when she returned from sick leave.

"Of course I won't find you dead, Katarina," I said, in a voice I hoped was the epitome of conviction and self-confidence. "You will be alive and well when I come to visit you tomorrow. How could it be otherwise? We will continue our conversation then. It is extremely interesting."

She did not reply to this. A shadow of sorrow and compassion seemed to pass over her face, like a teacher who finally realizes that all her efforts have been in vain, that her pupil is too dull-witted to understand the simple things she has explained to him.

I took the file and got up from the floor. I gave two sharp knocks on the doorframe and the attendant's face appeared in the peep-hole almost the same moment. Evidently he had been standing in front of the door. I nodded my head. When the heavy door opened, I turned towards the girl.

"Good-bye Katarina," I said cheerfully.

"Farewell, Doctor," she replied, no less cheerfully. Two friends who were parting after a pleasant chat, smiling warmly at one another.

I didn't find her dead the next day. She hadn't meant it literally. When I arrived at the sanatorium her body had already been taken away. The initial doubts about the cause of death had been solved as well. When her breakfast had been taken in at eight o'clock they'd found her curled up on the floor in the position in which she always slept. With her back to the door. One look at her face was enough for them to realize that she was no longer alive—Katarina's pretty face was completely deformed, grotesquely bloated and distended. Whatever had caused this ugly death mask was no longer in isolation cell number seven, so it was not clear what had actually happened until the forensics report arrived.

Katarina was allergic to wasp venom. Sometime early in the morning, between six and half past six, an insect, which could only have flown in through the opening up by the ceiling, had stung her on the left cheek. She died some twenty minutes later. Certainly before seven. There was only one problem. The girl must have been wakened by the sting. Why hadn't she called for help, since she was perfectly aware of the risk she ran? She'd had enough time, but had done nothing.

I was the one they expected to answer this question. I did so in my first and last report on Katarina. The reason she hadn't reacted was most likely because the sting enabled the execution of her previously failed attempt. It was a very unusual suicide that had taken advantage of an unbelievable tangle of circumstances. Indeed, what are the chances that a wasp will find its way through such a small opening right into a room with an individual who is allergic to its sting? Completely infinitesimal, one would say. But it happened just the same. Perhaps such holes should be closed up for this reason. In any case they are almost useless. And you never know when and how such an inconceivable incident might occur again.

I said nothing about the motives that had led the girl to raise her hand against herself on two occasions. What could I have said, anyway? I'd had only one chance to talk with her, and that was certainly not enough to come to any reliable conclusion. Perhaps my colleague Sonja would be able to shed more light on the case, since she'd spent more time with Katarina. When I had finished my report, I got in my car and headed towards her house. I wanted to tell her the tragic news in person. And give her the message that had been sent the day before.

3. Geese in the Mist

THE SKI LIFT STOPPED about one third of the way up the slope. That was the last straw. If I'd been alone on the two-seater I would have cursed out loud. Instead I swore to myself, which wasn't the same. Only a coarse profanity would have let me vent my feelings. Some days nothing goes right. When that happens the best thing is to stay in bed, but we never know what awaits us, of course, so we dash headlong into the future like geese in the mist.

First there hadn't been any hot water in the bathroom. Irate, I'd called hotel reception only to learn that something was wrong with the boilers. I was kindly advised not to worry. The repairmen were at work and there should be hot water early in the afternoon. This information comforted me as my teeth chattered under the icy shower. As if this wasn't enough, the plastic shower cap slipped off my head for a moment, partially wetting my hair, so I had to wash it, although I hate doing it in cold water.

Then came the incident in the dining room. I shared the table with a family of three that had apparently never learned civilized behavior. During every meal the father would return from the buffet table with a great deal more food than he could possibly eat. He always left more than half of it on his plate. And was proud of the fact. Plus, he chomped on his food with his mouth half-open. In addition, he always had a newspaper spread out in front of him.

The mother was excessively talkative and inquisitive. She didn't hesitate to adopt an intimate, chummy manner towards me even though I maintained a persistently reserved, formal demeanor and was several years older. She inundated me with questions, one of which was repeated every time we met. She was determined to find out why I had gone skiing alone, even though I'd made it perfectly clear more than once that I did not intend to disclose that information to her. The fact that I wasn't with anyone aroused her suspicions.

The son, somewhere around five or five and a half, was a restless soul. He fidgeted in his chair, made a mess of the table, dropped his silverware on the floor, talked too loudly. His father paid not the slightest attention to this and his mother would mildly reproach him only when he had really gone too far. As soon as he started to play with the large tube of catsup, I had a feeling something unpleasant would happen. As I hesitated, wondering whether to ask the boy's mother to take the tube away from him, he pointed it at me and squeezed.

I don't think I was his intentional target, but nonetheless a thick stream suddenly gushed across the table and hit me in the middle of my chest. A large red spot blossomed on my white sweater, as though I'd been wounded. I jumped off my chair, not knowing what to do in the initial confusion. The little boy started to giggle and his mother finally did what she should have done before it was too late. Taking the tube and putting it on the table, she said to her son, in a not-so-angry voice, that in future he should be careful of the direction in which he pointed the catsup.

The father's reaction pushed me over the edge. As though doing something perfectly natural and expected, he got up, put down his newspaper, took a linen napkin, and without a word began wiping it over my breasts, removing the catsup! I looked at him in disbelief for several moments, as the desire to slap him rose sharply inside me. Nonetheless I held back, mumbled something angrily and left the dining room, feeling a large number of inquisitive eyes on me.

As I tried to wash the spot out of my sweater as best I could with cold water, the weather changed. This happens very quickly in the mountains. When I entered the bathroom, the window had been filled with completely blue sky. Less than ten minutes later, the sky had turned into a gray rectangle with no depth. This was all I needed. Of the five days I had been there, two had been spent in the hotel because bad weather had put skiing out of the question. I needed to head for the slopes as soon as possible if I didn't want this day to be ruined too.

As I hastily tightened my bootstraps in the ski room, I tore the nail on my right index finger. I bit my lower lip, as I always do when overcome by anger. If there's anything I can't stand it's a torn nail, but I would have wasted a good fifteen minutes if I'd taken off my boots, gone back to the room where I had some nail scissors, and then come back down to put my boots on again. I put on my mittens, hoping they would at least lessen the damage, but knew that the torn nail would keep bothering me until I took care of it. Everything was conspiring against me.

On emerging from the ski room, I found myself in a cloud. I could only see a few meters in front of me. From time to time the ghostly figures of other skiers materialized out of the dense wall of gray. I slowly made my way towards the foot of the ski lift, afraid that it might not be working. When the cloud cover is complete or a storm is blowing, they shut down the lifts. Fortunately there was no wind, and if I had any luck at all only the area around the hotel would be veiled in mist, while the slopes at a higher altitude remained bathed in sunlight. At least, that's what I hoped.

I let out a noisy sigh of relief when I saw the moving line of skiers waiting to get onto the ski lift. Finally something good was happening in a day filled with nothing but bad luck! My satisfaction, however, did not last long. It was lessened by the person who sat next to me on the two-seater. The man had been behind me in the line and I hadn't had any reason to turn around, so I didn't see him until he appeared next to me on the lift. He didn't do anything to annoy me; his appearance alone was enough.

I have always been irritated by non-skiers who take skiers' places on the lifts instead of hiking through the mountains, which would be much healthier and more beneficial for them. In addition, the man was by no means suited to this place. Even if one disregarded his age—he must have been in his sixties—he had dressed in clothes more suitable for an evening on the town than trekking about the mountains in this weather: hat, bow tie, white scarf, long fur-trimmed coat, thin leather gloves, umbrella, fancy shoes. He would have a great time when he got out at the top. I smiled with a certain suggestion of malice and, as much as the cramped two-seater allowed, turned my back on him.

We had already come out of the cloud when the ski lift shuddered to a halt. I knew the reason immediately: the power had failed yet again. This had happened every day since my arrival. The hotel reception had a ready explanation for this inconvenience, too. The worn-out grid was being renovated. Starting next season there would be no power outages. I felt like gnashing my teeth. Next season! A lot of good that would do me here and now. Here I was, hanging helplessly a good fifty meters up in the air, in the company of a man who was probably the last person I wanted next to me, without the slightest idea of how long it would take for the power to come back on.

As though reading my thoughts, the man suddenly

addressed me: "Don't worry. The lift will start working in seven and a half minutes."

I have never been one to talk to strangers, particularly when I don't find them likeable and am in an awful mood, as I was at that moment. My first thought was not to reply, but then I would appear immature and impolite. I would have been happier if he hadn't said a word, if we had spent that time in silence as we hung there, caught between heaven and earth, but now I had no choice. Social considerations, however, did not require me to be excessively polite.

"Really, seven and a half? You must be clairvoyant!" I made no effort whatsoever to hide the mockery in my voice. I turned my head briefly towards him, with an ironic smile, then turned away from him again.

"I'm not," was his simple reply.

The conversation might have ended there. If I had not said another word, no one could have reproached me for being rude. But the rage that had been gathering inside me all morning wouldn't let me stop.

"Then how do you know exactly what's going to happen?" This time I turned my head towards him for a bit longer and was thus able to get a better look at his face. He looked exactly like my idea of a retired civil servant: plump cheeks, thick well-groomed mustache that didn't go over his lip line, small watery eyes. His aftershave lotion had a pungent, piercing odor. I don't know where I got the impression, but I was convinced that he was either a widower or unmarried.

"It's not hard, if you know the cause. Then it's easy to predict the effect."

"So you know what caused the power failure, even though you were sitting here on the ski lift when it happened? Congratulations!" My voice was still sarcastic.

"It's my job, ma'am, to know," replied the man simply, as though this explained everything. My derision clearly had not gotten through to him. "The ski lift was stopped by the failure of a tiny part in the power sub-station. It's smaller than a matchbox. Such a tiny cause, and such a huge effect." He indicated the long line of seats in front of us filled with irate, impatient skiers.

"Isn't that utterly interesting!" I knew I had gone too far, but his equanimity was driving me mad.

"Yes," he replied, taking my words literally. "The future is most often shaped by small things, very rarely by incidents of large proportions. Take, for example, the fact that we had no hot water in the hotel this morning."

"You're staying at the hotel too? I haven't seen you."

"That's because I'm inconspicuous. People don't usually take any notice of me, which is useful." He stopped briefly, hesitating. It seemed as though he'd been about to add something to his last sentence, but then decided to leave it unsaid. "The hot water heater broke down because of simple carelessness on the part of the man who maintains it. He let sleep get the upper hand and didn't do what he should have. And just see how many people had to take cold showers this morning as a result."

I was suddenly filled with unease. It seemed as though I could see the frosted glass on the shower door in my suite gradually turning transparent, making me visible to inquisitive eyes.

"Yes," I said, for the first time in a normal voice, "very unpleasant. In addition my shower cap slipped off by accident and my hair got wet." I instinctively touched the ends of my hair under my woolen hat. It was unnecessary, of course, because I had dried my hair with the hair drier before going out.

"Accident, yes," repeated the stranger. "A vague concept used as a good excuse for ignorance. There are no accidents, ma'am, only our lack of information."

I was angered by the superior tone in his voice. I

have always felt an aversion towards men who show off their alleged intelligence.

"But how could I know in advance that my shower cap would slip off? You can't predict something like that!"

He looked at me several moments without speaking. "Perhaps," he said at last. "But even you could have foreseen what happened to you in the dining room."

The anger that had just subsided flared up inside me once more. Not so much for the condescending "even you," although that was part of it. I felt myself exposed to unwanted looks again, naked. "You know about that too?" I asked. He certainly must have heard the snarl behind my words.

"Of course, I was there. I eat breakfast too."

"I didn't see you."

"I told you I'm inconspicuous. My seat is in the corner, behind your back. In any case, the incident was such that no one could have missed it."

"It all happened so fast," I said, as though defending myself. "I didn't have time to get out of the way. But it wasn't the boy's fault. His parents are to blame, of course."

"You are partially, too. It must have been clear to you from the start that something bad might happen to you in such company. You should have asked them to move you to another table. Particularly since there was no special reason for them to put you there in the first place. The waiter did it indiscriminately, just as he did with the other guests. He could have given you another seat in the same way. Had he done that, your sweater wouldn't have a spot of catsup on it now."

"But how can the waiter be blamed? He certainly could not have guessed what would happen."

"I didn't say he was to blame, just that his arbitrary decision was the cause that led to adverse effects. Fortunately, they are harmless in this instance."

I shot him a piercing glance. "Have you ever tried to remove a catsup stain from wool?"

"No, I haven't. I don't suppose it is easy. What I wanted to say is that even the permanent loss of a sweater would be nothing dramatic. It is simply an unpleasant matter, basically nothing more serious than, let's say, tearing your fingernail."

I stared at him suspiciously, inadvertently wrapping my right index finger in the other fingers in my mitten. I didn't have a chance to say anything, however, because the ski lift started to move at that very instant. The seats stretching before us towards the mountaintop rose up briefly and then rushed forward like a team suddenly whipped by a coachman. The man pushed up his left coat sleeve a bit, looked at his watch and nodded in satisfaction. "Exactly seven and a half minutes, just like I told you."

He might have expected me to show a bit of admiration, but I didn't. I was haunted by completely different thoughts. "You say accidents don't exist?" I asked in a low voice.

"That's right, they don't," he agreed, also speaking more softly than before.

"So that means that you're not here by accident either. Who are you, anyway? What do you want from me?"

He didn't answer right away. We covered half the distance between two ski lift towers in tense silence, staring each other in the eye. I tightly grasped the handles of the ski poles in my lap, slightly raising the pointed ends towards the other side of the seat. We were almost at the halfway station in the middle of the slope. All I had to do was raise the safety bar and quickly slide off my seat. I doubted he could have prevented me from doing it.

"Rest assured," he said at last. "You are in no danger from me. I don't want anything from you. I am only an observer."

"Observer?" I repeated questioningly, not knowing what else to say.

"Yes. I am here to see what you do. Nothing else."

"What do you mean, what I do? Isn't it obvious? I'm going to ski down the mountain. What else could I do?"

"There are many ski runs down the mountain."

"So? What difference does it make?"

"If it made no difference, I wouldn't be here now."

"I don't understand you. Do you mean to say that I will be in danger if I take one run and not another?"

"You? No. You are completely out of danger."

"Then who isn't? Please stop playing guessing games with me. I'm not at all in the mood."

Silence followed once again. The halfway station was quite close. I raised the safety bar, ready to push off down the rise that reached up to the bottom of the seat. I expected him to say or do something, but he just looked at me wordlessly. We stayed like that without moving as we passed by the halfway station. The ski lift employee standing in front of the hut made of roughly hewn wood looked at us briefly, without interest. When he was behind our backs, I lowered the bar.

"I'm not playing guessing games with you," he said with a slight tone of relief in his voice, as though pleased I hadn't gotten off the lift. "The fact is I am allowed to tell you very little. You must make the decision all by yourself. Any involvement on my part would create enormous difficulties."

"But what decision? You've still got me confused."

"Which run you choose to ski down the mountain."

"Why is that important? This run or that. They all lead down, don't they?"

"That's right. But what happens afterwards is not the same. Each run has its own continuation in the future. It is the start of a chain of events and each has a very different outcome. Fortunately, most of these outcomes are pretty innocuous, but some are not. Sometimes, not often, such ordinary causes, such as which run you decide to take down the mountain, can result in truly catastrophic effects. You've heard the story of the butterfly harmlessly fluttering its wings and ultimately causing a hurricane on the other side of the world? Of course the butterfly is not to blame, but should one stand idly by and do nothing to interrupt the chain of events that leads to misfortune?"

At first I didn't know what to reply. The confusion that overcame me had muddled my thoughts. I stared dully at his round face, ruddy from the cold. His cheeks were dappled with a network of winding capillaries, like those of a drunkard. He looked back at me with steady eyes in which I thought I could detect impatience and expectation.

And then, as though the internal mist clouding my mind weren't enough, one started on the outside too. It all happened in a split second, as usual. One moment we were traveling up through the brilliant blue mountain morning sky, and the very next we were in the middle of a dense, gray, almost palpable mass. With my attention distracted, I hadn't noticed the direction from which the cloud had come. Probably from below, otherwise I would have seen it before then. Everything suddenly became unreal around us. We seemed to be floating in nothingness. If it weren't for the empty seats that appeared at regular intervals going in the opposite direction, only visible when they were quite close to us, we would not have felt that we were moving at all.

"What do you do to prevent a disaster? Kill the butterfly, I suppose, before it flutters its wings? Remove the cause before it happens?" My voice was trembling slightly, although I tried to say this as calmly as possible.

"That would be the simplest thing, yes. Unfortunately, that cannot be done. You have to let the cause happen, and only then react."

I let out a deep sigh, then inhaled a breath of air. It was filled with tiny, prickly drops that would be used as the raw material for some future snow. "But how is it possible to tell which butterfly will cause the disaster? There are countless numbers of them."

"It's possible," replied the man tersely. I waited several moments, hoping he would add something more, but he remained silent.

"What is it about me that singles me out from the other skiers? Why is it important which ski run I in particular take? What if you are mistaken, what if I am not at all the right person?"

"We are not mistaken." Once again his self-confident brevity didn't tell me a thing.

"And that's all the explanation you have to offer?" My voice was tinged with anger again. "You appear out of nowhere, tell me a twisted, fantastic story and expect me to believe you."

"It isn't necessary for you to believe me." It seemed that nothing could shake the man's composure. "I am aware of the fact that my words must seem confusing and unconvincing. But I can't tell you anything further without disturbing an order that must remain untouched. I have actually told you too much already. The best thing would be for you to act as though we had never met, as though this conversation never took place. We will soon reach the top of the mountain. Get off the ski lift and simply take one of the runs down the slope. Don't even think about which one. Do it spontaneously, like you always do."

"Simply forget this ride up the ski lift? As though I came up to the top all alone?" It was impossible for him not to hear the mixed hurt and disbelief in my voice.

"That would be best. In any case, you will never see me again. Nor will you find any trace of me at the hotel; it will be as if I never set foot on this mountain."

I chewed my lower lip and nodded. That instant the

cloud became drenched with brightness and started to thin. Soon we were above it, in perfectly clear air. The bright blue sky and sparkling white snow forced me to squint, and I lowered the sunglasses that had been pushed up onto my hat. We were almost at the top. The two skiers on the seat in front of us were just getting off.

I raised the safety bar slowly. I did not take my shielded eyes off the man on the seat next to me. I knew that he would not say anything else to me, and I had no desire to say anything to him, either. Maybe he was right, after all. Why not pretend that this meeting had never taken place? Isn't oblivion the best protection against the ugly occurrences that take place in life?

I slipped off the ski lift seat, made a short turn to the right, and stopped a bit to the side of the path that skiers were taking down the slope. I stuck my poles into the snow in front of me and leaned on them. The seat I had just been on moved forward to a covered area where a huge horizontal wheel slowly turned. The seat made a semicircle around the wheel and then headed in the opposite direction, downhill.

The man did not let me out of his sight. First he turned around in his seat to keep me in his field of vision, and then when he realized that wouldn't be enough he got up and kneeled on the seat, without taking care to lower the safety bar. The ski lift employee in front of the hut at the top shouted something at him in warning, but the stranger paid no attention. He stayed in the same position, holding onto the back of the seat as he rushed inexorably towards the edge of the cloud. He was too far away for me to make out the expression on his face, but it was easy to imagine.

I let the doughy gray matter swallow him up completely, then waited a few more moments. When it was certain there was no way he could see me, I did what was expected of me. Quite spontaneously, without thinking, I headed down one of the runs. Like I always do. It was highly irresponsible with regard to the future, I know, but that responsibility had been forced upon me. I hadn't accepted it voluntarily. In addition, even if such a future were devoid of disaster, I would only be a puppet, my strings pulled by someone else's invisible hands. And if there is one thing I simply cannot tolerate, it is someone manipulating my life. Regardless of the pretext.

Several moments later, when I too plunged into the gray lake, I thought with a smile that we actually don't understand geese. Dashing headlong into the mist doesn't have to be the least bit unpleasant.

4. Line on the Palm

I CAREFULLY EXAMINED THE client at my door. This is extremely important in my work. A person's outward appearance says a lot about his future. Or rather, about what he would like to hear about his future. People don't go to a clairvoyant to be told bad news and then have to pay for it. They don't need someone like me for that. What they expect from me is help, as they would from a doctor or clergyman. And I provide this help. The basic motto in my line of work is: the customer must leave my parlor satisfied. After that, things take their own course.

Actually, if I were to predict that something bad was going to happen, I'm certain almost no one would believe me. This seems to be part of human nature. If you tell people something that suits them, they all accept it eagerly, regardless of how implausible or even impossible it might appear. Sometimes it seems the more incredible the favorable prophecy, the easier it is for them to accept. They don't quibble. And of course, if you tell them something that doesn't suit them, they immediately become doubtful and suspicious. They launch into a debate on reliability, and then on the meaning of divination, endeavoring to show it's all pure quackery that only the gullible would swallow. If that's true, then why on earth did they come to see me?

The customer's age made him unusual from the start. Mostly middle-aged people visit me. Younger people are not overly bothered by the future because they think they have it in abundance. They have all the time in the world before them. Older folks know they don't have any future, so it doesn't interest them very much. Between the age of forty and fifty, however, people start to settle their accounts. And the realization of their own mortality is always part and parcel of this. Although almost no one would be willing to admit it, what brings a great many people to my parlor is the newly aroused fear of death. What they want most of all from me is a guarantee that judgment day is still a long way off. And of course I provide this guarantee. At a very moderate price, even though they would be willing to pay much more. One mustn't profit from the misfortunes of others.

The young man was no more than twenty-five years old. I don't remember a younger person ever coming into my parlor. His height was emphasized by a long, olive-drab raincoat with broad lapels. A light-weight white scarf was thrown casually around his neck, its ends reaching almost to his waist. He had a long face with regular features, more masculine than handsome. His thick black hair was combed straight back from his high forehead. He wore small round wire-rimmed glasses. Shortsightedness at his age probably resulted from years of intensive reading. His umbrella was in its sheath, hooked over his left arm.

He was wearing thin, black leather gloves that made his hands invisible. That's the first thing I examine in any customer. If you are skillful at noticing things, which I must be in this job, hands can reveal a vast amount of useful information about a visitor. Shoes as well. The young man's shoes were clean and polished in spite of the bad weather. Even overly clean. This indicated a finicky individual, inclined to nit-picking, someone who has difficulty changing an entrenched opinion. The way he'd tied his laces indicated someone who liked orderliness, regularity, symmetry. It was unlikely he could see nuances. Only extremes: either-or. This was not exactly a good sign. It was much easier to work with less orderly, more easy-going visitors. The ones I liked the best were actually those who paid no attention at all to their appearance.

He hovered at the door to my parlor, examining it with the same curiosity that I turned on him. This was clearly the first time he'd come to a place like this. His eyes skimmed through the semi-dark room, absorbing the details. I was certain that he was taking it all in, that nothing escaped his attention. His lips suddenly pursed into a grimace of disapproval, even disgust, when he saw the little glass boxes on the small shelf to the left of my worktable. They contained several specimens of what were erroneously believed to be traditional trappings of the fortune-telling trade: the wing of a bat, tail of a rat, eye of an owl, tooth of a wild boar, skin of a snake, claw of a hawk. . . .

I don't like these things either. That's why the shelf is positioned outside my field of vision when I sit at my worktable, where I spend most of my time. But these things have their purpose. They impress the customers. The great majority of my visitors come with a completely stereotyped notion of what a fortune-teller's parlor looks like, so I don't dare let them down. Everything here is set up and modeled after what you'd find in a popular film.

The finishing touch is a small cauldron of water—electric, but a fire seems to be underneath it—with wispy steam rising in a column, colored pink by the beam of a hidden red light. From time to time a strong, seemingly exotic fragrance emanates from the steam, although what I put in the water to get it is something quite ordinary. Whenever possible I try to avoid using that fragrance additive because after a while it gives me a headache and even makes me nauseous.

When I felt I had given the new customer enough

time to inspect the parlor, I bowed briefly and said, "Good evening, sir. Please sit down." My hand motioned towards the chair on the other side of the table.

"Good evening," replied the young man, staying by the door. If I'd heard his voice over the telephone, I would have said he was at least ten years older.

Periodically I have a visitor who, after entering the parlor, seems instantly to regret having done so, and would like to leave without delay. Two or three have almost run out of the room, horrified, after spending less than a minute inside. Those who make it through that first minute usually stay. I know from experience how best to act towards reluctant customers who can't seem to detach themselves from the door. I strike up a conversation about something innocuous, neutral. So they can relax. Afterwards everything is a lot easier.

"It's not raining," I said half-questioningly, nodding towards his umbrella in its sheath.

"No, it's not," he said in confirmation. "Mist has set in, although the weathermen forecast rain. That's why I brought it."

"Weathermen," I repeated with a proper dose of derision. "Don't count on weathermen when it comes to forecasting the future. They don't know a thing about it. They pretend what they're doing is some sort of science, but all they really know how to do is make an educated guess. And most often it turns out to be wrong."

"But it's not like that here, is it?" His voice took on a tinge of irony.

"Of course not," I replied, feigning offense. "Would you come here if you thought I had no more skill than a weatherman?"

"The fact that I came doesn't prove a thing. Maybe I shouldn't have. Just like I was wrong when I listened to the weather forecast and brought an umbrella."

"Perhaps. But there's no way to know until you've

tried it. Since you've already given the weatherman a chance to show what he can do, it wouldn't be fair not to give me the same chance." I inserted a brief, tactical pause. "In any case, just to show you how much I believe in my abilities, here's what I propose. Although the usual practice here is to pay in advance, you don't have to. I will only take my fee at the end of the séance. And only if you are satisfied." This always works. People feel safe if they don't have to pay in advance for what might be bad news. Since there never is any, of course, they willingly pay in the end. It's not unusual for them to add a big tip, so when they leave there is mutual satisfaction.

He looked at me without speaking for a few moments. "But you can't know in advance whether I'll be satisfied. What if you predict something I don't like?"

"I'm prepared to take that risk," I said self-confidently. "Please, sit down." As he continued to stand indecisively by the door, I added with a smile, "Don't worry, nothing will happen to you." This was another tried and tested method with my male visitors. The easiest way to break them is to touch on their vanity. What, me afraid of an ordinary little old fortune-teller? With the ladies the same results are achieved using a calculated touch of flattery.

He finally left the door and came up to the table. He stood in front of me for a moment, confused, not knowing what to do with his umbrella, and then he hooked the handle on the back of the chair and sat down. I could have suggested he leave the umbrella and raincoat on the coat rack by the door—the parlor was heated, of course—but I didn't because I was suddenly convinced that he would refuse. He seemed like someone who only feels safe in the armor he has put on, sword in hand. Without them he would be naked and vulnerable, like a knight in a bedroom.

I didn't get down to business right away. In keeping

with well-established protocol, I first looked him piercingly in the eyes a good fifteen seconds, not saying a word. Few visitors are able to withstand this meticulous inspection. The others lower their eyes quickly and start to fidget. This assures that authority has been achieved. The conversation that follows is similar to that between a doctor and his patient or between a priest and a member of the flock. But the young man didn't flinch; his dark brown eyes calmly returned my gaze through the thick lenses of his glasses. In the end I was the first to withdraw, aware of the fact that a difficult séance awaited me. It couldn't be helped, though. Unfortunately, I was not in a position to choose my customers. Fortunately, such visitors are quite uncommon.

"So, you'd like to know what the future holds for you?"

"That's why people come here, isn't it?"

"Yes, by and large. Which of the procedures would you like to use? All the classic methods are available." I started to show him the paraphernalia in front of me. "Gazing into a crystal ball, reading several types of cards or the grounds from a cup of coffee you have drunk. There is also throwing beans, pieces of wood or bones. And astrology, of course. For a supplementary payment the future can be foretold through the entrails of a freshly slaughtered animal, although this requires special preparations. Particularly if the customer chooses a larger species. Such as an ox."

At this point I always smile broadly in order to show the horrified visitor that I am only joking. Usually I get a smile in return, often accompanied by a sigh of relief, but the young man's face retained its serious expression.

"If none of these techniques suits you," I hurried to add, "even though they have proved successful for thousands of years, there are also new methods. We could use a computer, for example." I turned my head towards the monitor on the corner of my large worktable. The fact that it was under a plastic cover with a thick layer of dust on top indicated the interest my customers had in modern forms of predicting the future. "I have an excellent, professional divination program. Imported."

"I'd like you to read my palm. If you do that."

"Of course I read palms," I replied in a tone that was intended to express, more than the words, just how amazed I was at such a question. "I didn't mention it because no one has asked for it in quite some time. It seems like palm reading has gone out of fashion. You may have been unaware, but fashions change in fortune-telling just like in everything else. Although, with palm reading, this is somewhat peculiar, since the palm is part of your body and can thus be considered the most direct, reliable indicator of your fate. I think you have made a good choice."

The young man, who until then had kept his hands in his lap, hidden from my view, slowly raised his right hand and laid it palm up on the green felt that covered the middle of the table, illuminated by a narrow beam of bright light.

I waited several moments, but since he wasn't about to do anything, I said, "It might be helpful if you took off your glove."

The gloomy seriousness of his face softened for the first time. "Sorry," he said, with an expression of discomfiture. He wasn't quick about it, however. He took off the glove with slow movements, almost with reluctance. He suddenly reminded me of a striptease artist starting her act. When he was finished, he briefly held his hand clenched in a fist before opening it up—apparently against his better judgment.

I didn't look at his palm right away, as some shoddy diviner would do. If you want your customer to take you seriously in this work, you have to respect formality. And formality here required that I first take a bit of cotton, put some alcohol on it and briskly rub the surface of his palm with it. Although the reason for this should have been obvious, many visitors were bewildered and asked for an explanation. I gave them one, trying to make it sound as professional as possible, sprinkled with Latin words.

After having thoroughly cleaned his palm, I took a large magnifying glass with a handle and frame of imitation ivory, wiped it with a gray linen cloth, and finally looked at his palm.

Even under the magnifying glass the young man's lifeline appeared quite short. I had seen other lines that suddenly stopped or branched somewhere around halfway to the base of the hand, but never one like this. It barely reached one-third of the way. If there really was something to this, my young visitor should already have met his maker. Luckily for him, this was just plain superstition. Luckily for me, that was quite widespread. Neither of us had any reason to complain.

I raised my head and looked him in the eyes. It was only then that I realized this had not been tactically wise. I should have continued calmly examining his palm as though there was nothing special on it. This way, he received confirmation that something was wrong. I quickly returned my eyes to his palm, but it was too late.

"I'm going to die soon." He said it in a soft, flat voice, as though stating an incontrovertible fact.

"Excuse me?" I asked with exaggerated surprise, not taking my eyes off what was under the magnifying glass.

"I don't have much longer to live."

"Why do you think that?"

"My lifeline."

"What about it?"

"See how short it is."

"I see. And so?"

"That means my time is almost up."

I laid the magnifying glass on the table and looked at my customer again. The calculated harshness in my eyes expressed legitimate indignation.

"My dear young man, if you know how to interpret the lines on your palm, why waste your time and money with me?"

I don't resort to this sentence very often because the occasions to use it, thank heavens, have been rather rare, but whenever I've said it the effect has always been as expected. This time, however, the effect was missing. Judging by my visitor's face, the rebuke had made no impression at all. I would have to act even angrier.

"It's simply amazing how some people fail to realize that palm reading is a very serious and responsible craft, and not something that just anyone can do. Skill is only acquired after thorough training and long experience, and natural talent is absolutely necessary. In this respect, it is not very different from medical diagnostics. Would you interfere in a diagnostician's work?"

The young man did not reply immediately. Something seemed to be weighing on his mind. When he finally answered, he disregarded my rhetorical question. "Do you think I might live a long life?"

I sighed deeply and picked up the magnifying glass again. This seemed to have done the trick. I bent over his palm and started to examine it once more. I did it slowly and meticulously, taking lots of time. With ordinary customers I stated my verdict relatively fast in order to create the impression that everything was clearly and easily readable. With such smart alecks, however, I had to do the opposite. They are only convinced if the prediction is made after exhaustive and lengthy examination.

"You will live a relatively long life," I said at last. "I

guarantee at least 84.5 years, although there is a chance that you might live to 90."

Not a single customer, regardless of how distrustful they are in the beginning, has failed to light up when they hear they have decades of life before them. Sometimes there are even touching moments, with tears and sincere confessions about the dark forebodings and fears that have brought them to my parlor. Some of those who have been relieved of a particularly heavy burden have even fallen into my arms. In those moments, as I pat them on the back, I feel proud of my line of work. Gone is the guilty conscience that haunts me from time to time. What people get from me, at a modest price, is measured not by how true or honest it is, but by how useful.

There was not even a flicker of a smile on the young man's face. "Guarantee?"

Now he really had gone too far. I had yet to encounter such ingratitude. "Of course I guarantee!" I almost shouted. "I can give it to you in writing if you want!"

My agitation didn't sway him. "But your guarantee can be easily invalidated," he said in a steady voice.

"Is that so?" His composure only fed the flames of my anger. "And please, won't you tell me just how?"

"Easily. I could kill myself."

I thought I hadn't heard correctly. "You could do what?"

"Kill myself," he repeated, as though stating the obvious.

I stared at his wooden face. I had underestimated this customer. He wasn't just one of the ordinary skeptics who come in periodically. I know how to deal with them. This was quite a different case. I'd never had a visitor who mentioned suicide, nor had I heard of any such customer visiting my colleagues. The young man certainly wasn't serious, but I still had to be careful. If anything were to happen, they might close my shop.

"Of course you can't kill yourself," I said in a tone that restored my previous composure. "Even if you wanted to. What is clearly written on your palm would prevent you. You will die an old man, whether you like it or not. Indeed, I see no reason why that shouldn't please you."

"But I can," replied the young man. With a rapid movement he pulled his right hand from the lighted circle on the felt and stuck it between the lapels of his raincoat. A moment later he pulled it out, holding a gun. I don't understand a thing about weapons, but this one seemed serious and threatening enough in spite of its small size. He held it in front of him, the barrel turned between the two of us.

I knew I had to say something if I wanted to retain control of the situation, but try as I feverishly might, nothing coherent crossed my mind. I just stared dully at the shiny, chromium-plated metal in the visitor's hand, feeling a lump form in my throat. I had never been that close to a firearm before.

"What's stopping me?" said the young man, breaking the silence. "It's quite a simple matter." He cocked the gun with his thumb and put it next to his right temple. "All I have to do is pull the trigger."

"Wait!" finally burst out of me. I jumped halfway out of my chair.

There must have been something funny about that because the visitor's lips curved into a gentle smile. He didn't put the gun down, but his finger relaxed on the trigger.

"Why?"

"You'd kill yourself just to prove that my prophecy isn't true?" The fact that my voice was shaking certainly didn't help, but there was nothing to be done. I slowly sank back into my chair.

He hesitated a long moment and then lowered the gun into his lap, out of my sight. An audible click meant the gun was no longer cocked. A loud sigh of relief escaped me.

"I would kill myself to foil predestination. That's the only way I have to beat it. I've thought about it for a long while. When you're marked like I am, you don't have time for much else." He raised his hand without the gun, turned his palm towards me briefly, then put it back in his lap.

"But I told you . . ."

"I know what you told me," he said, cutting in. "But it's all the same, don't you see? Instead of one predetermination you offered me another. And one that is considerably longer. Isn't it enough that I've suffered for almost two decades because of what's written on my palm? Should this agony now continue into old age? You can't imagine how heavy a burden it is. I simply wouldn't be able to bear it that long. It's utterly impossible to live if you know when you will die."

Silence fell on us like a heavy shroud. Even if I hadn't been experienced at interpreting my visitors' expressions, it was easy to read what was in the young man's eyes: a suicide's firm resolve to follow through on his intention.

"But if you didn't want to find out when you will die, why did you come to my parlor?"

"I didn't come to your parlor to find out when I will die. I know that already. I came here because this is the most suitable place to kill myself. The temple of predestination. It is only here that my act will have true meaning."

"This is no temple of predestination," I said in a muffled voice, like a criminal admitting guilt when faced with incriminating evidence.

"What else is a fortune-teller's parlor?" asked the young man, knitting his brow.

"A temple of false hopes. Those who decide to visit me don't do it for the sake of truth. Somewhere deep inside them everyone is aware of that. What brings them here is the suddenly aroused awareness of their own mortality. The same that has started to haunt you much too early. Indeed, I don't offer them the eternity they would be promised if they went to church. What I sell doesn't last quite that long, and so has less value. But there are those who would buy longevity."

"False longevity."

"False, of course. How else could it be? There is no true prediction of the future for the very reason that there is no predetermination. You are ready to raise your hand against yourself in order to beat an opponent that doesn't even exist."

"But my lifeline . . ." He raised his hand again, this time with the gun in it.

"Your lifeline doesn't say a thing. And neither does mine. Or anyone else's. It's all pure superstition. What is written in your palm has nothing to do with how long you will live. Right now that depends entirely upon you. You can pull that trigger and follow through on an enormous misconception. Or you can forget the whole thing and embark on an uncertain future, enjoying the very uncertainty it holds."

As I spoke these words, I tried anxiously to guess what his reaction would be. My worst fear was that he would pay absolutely no attention, finding my words false or not convincing enough, and would simply end things the way he had clearly intended when he came in my parlor. Another possibility, certainly less ominous although still very troublesome, would be to embark with me on a metaphysical discussion about predestination, waving his weapon under my nose all the while as his trump card. Curiously enough, I was least repulsed by what in any other circumstances would have appeared the most horrendous threat: that he would sue me for openly admitting that I consciously deceived my customers, even with noble intentions. That would certainly have closed down my parlor.

The young man sat there for a long time in silence, staring at me fixedly. Or maybe the time seemed long to me. Time can pass very slowly when you are waiting for something stressful. When he finally spoke, I was speechless with surprise for several moments.

"How much do I owe you?" he asked.

"You don't owe me anything, of course."

"No, please. I have to pay." He stood up, still holding the gun. His other hand picked up the glove on the table, then his umbrella from the back of the chair.

There was no sense arguing. How can you refuse money from a man brandishing a gun in front of you? I stated the lowest price that I keep only for special customers. This one certainly belonged in that category, so my generosity was well founded.

My visitor was suddenly in a predicament. Since both hands were full, he couldn't reach his wallet. Finally, he tucked the gun back inside his raincoat, fumbled around inside a bit, then took out his wallet. The banknote he handed me was considerably larger than the sum I'd asked for.

"I'm afraid I don't have change," I said in an apologetic voice. "If you could wait a minute, I'll go change it. Just around the corner. I'll be right back."

"There's no need to give anything back. Keep the change."

I didn't have a chance to protest because the young man made a brisk about-face and headed for the door. I thought he would leave without a word, but he stopped at the door, turned and said, "Good night."

My answering "good night" echoed in the empty parlor.

I stayed in my chair, staring blankly at the large banknote, turning it over and over between my fingers. Like a mantra, this monotonous, rustling sound helped me pull myself together. Life has taught me one thing: always look on the bright side, whenever possible, even in the most difficult situations. Although the visit that just ended had certainly been unusual and in many ways unpleasant, there had been no adverse consequences.

The most important thing, of course, was that I had prevented the young man from committing suicide, something that would have been quite detrimental to us both. He would clearly have been in a far worse situation, but I would have had my share of trouble too. If only he'd found some other reason to raise a hand against himself than just outwitting predestination! As if predestination existed; or rather, if it existed, as if it were at all possible to outwit it. A bonus was the fee. It would have taken at least five customers for me to earn what this visitor had left me so gallantly. And the days when that many people enter my parlor can be counted on one hand.

Finally, the incident I had just gone through started me thinking about putting in special security measures. We live in uncertain times, and additional precautions certainly couldn't hurt. Besides, I am visited by strangers who are all, without exception, burdened with troubles. Carefree, satisfied people don't go to see a clairvoyant. I'd been lucky this time, but I certainly didn't want some future customer to pull a gun on me. Maybe I should put an inconspicuous metal detector by the entrance, similar to those at airports. Provided it wasn't too expensive, of course.

I was roused from my thoughts by a sharp ringing. Usually my customers barely touch the doorbell, dreading what awaits them inside, but whoever was at my door now clearly wasn't the slightest bit afraid. Judging by the insistent ringing, for some reason he must have been in a great hurry to find out his future.

"Coming, coming," I shouted, getting up from my chair.

As I shuffled towards the door on limbs that had gone numb from sitting so long, it suddenly occurred to me that it might be the young man. He'd changed his mind and decided to do what he'd originally intended after all. Panic-stricken at this possibility, I stood there without moving, my hand on the doorknob, not knowing what to do. But the ringing simply wouldn't stop, so I finally opened the door a crack and peered into the dense mist that filled the evening.

The face I saw was not the young man's. In front of the door was a rather short, middle-aged man with a bushy beard, wearing a winter coat. I had never seen him before. His appearance, however, did not bring relief. He seemed upset, as though he'd just been through an ordeal.

"Excuse me, ma'am," he said in a trembling voice, unconsciously taking off his hat, exposing his balding head. "Yours is the only light that's on. Would you mind . . . letting me use your telephone? It's urgent. There's been an . . . accident."

"Accident?" I repeated.

"Yes, here . . . quite close," he said, motioning vaguely towards the left. "A young man was . . . crossing the street. . . . I didn't see him in the mist. . . . I was driving slowly, of course. . . . Suddenly he popped out in front of me . . . out of nowhere . . . I didn't have time to hit the brakes. . . . It all happened so suddenly. . . ."

"Is he injured?" I asked, although it was unnecessary. As an experienced clairvoyant, I had to know the answer.

"I'm afraid he's dead, ma'am. He's lying there . . . on the pavement . . . covered with blood." He raised the bloody, white scarf in his hand. "I tried to stop the bleeding with this. . . . He died in my arms. . . . I have to call the police. . . ."

The police soon arrived and made an inspection of the scene. There was no investigation since there was no need. It was a clear-cut case. Inattentive pedestrians periodically meet their end like that in the mist. There was nothing the driver could have done.

No one asked me anything. Why should they, anyway? I wasn't a witness to the tragic event. I didn't offer to make a statement either. What for? Why would the police be interested in what some old fortune-teller thinks about a routine traffic accident?

5. Alarm Clock on the Night Table

Miss Margarita's eyes popped wide open. She realized instantly that something was wrong. Lying there in bed, staring at the ceiling, she tried to figure out what had given her this impression. Had it come from her dream? But she couldn't remember dreaming anything. That was odd because she always had dreams, and always remembered them. Then she realized what was wrong. She was surrounded by silence. Turning her head towards the night table on her left, she looked blearily at the round old alarm clock with its phosphorescent hands and two dome-shaped bells.

It had been sitting there for more than half a century. Its ticking had only bothered her briefly in the beginning. She'd soon become used to it and now could not fall asleep without its steady metal throbbing. Once a year, when she took it to the watchmaker to be cleaned and oiled, she would lie awake in bed for a long time, sometimes all night. Miss Margarita used the clock only to fall asleep, not to wake up. During all these years she had never once set the alarm. There was no need for that; she was one of those rare individuals with a reliable internal clock, able to wake up at a precisely set time. Not a minute early or late.

The night before she had set her internal clock for 7:30. There was no way she could have failed to do this, for it was an invariable part of her preparations for sleep. After coming out of the bathroom, she would bring a glass of water from the kitchen covered with a saucer, although she rarely woke up at night and even then was hardly ever thirsty. Then she would read in bed for about a quarter of an hour, always from the same book, a slim collection of love poems that had been with her as long as the clock. She had learned them all by heart ages ago, but read them nonetheless. Finally, after turning out the light, she would simply wish to wake up at the usual time. That was enough. All that was left was to close her eyes and surrender to the lulling ticking of the clock.

The clock hands were now standing in a position that could not be correct: 12:07. Even though Miss Margarita's eyesight had faded, she could still make out the long, black hands against the white surface with its Roman numerals. All the same, she reached for her glasses, which had been placed next to the water on the night table where she could find them easily in the dark. After putting them on she saw more clearly, but what she saw hadn't changed. The clock had evidently stopped right after midnight. This was the first time it had stopped working completely.

She would take it to the watchmaker's right after breakfast. This would disrupt her day somewhat, but what choice did she have? She led an orderly life consisting of a well-established round of obligations. She didn't like to deviate from it because postponing or neglecting her duties filled her with unease, and once that crept into her soul it was hard to get rid of. But this was an emergency. The alarm clock certainly had precedence. The thought of the clock standing broken on the night table, with her doing nothing to fix it, would upset her even more. In any case, the sooner she gave it to him, the greater were the chances that the watchmaker would fix it that very day, so perhaps she would not be without it the next night.

She had a quick breakfast. She knew her sensitive stomach might complain, but she couldn't eat any more slowly. Fortunately, the meal was light, as it was every morning. She crumbled one and a half slices of day-old bread into a cup half-filled with warm milk. The milk contained one teaspoon of chicory and half a teaspoon of sugar. Indeed, the sugar was always a bit more than half a teaspoon, but she considered it to be half nonetheless, scrupulously following her doctor's orders. If she hadn't been in such a hurry, she would have waited for the bits of bread to absorb the milk completely and become soggy. But now she didn't have the patience, so she had to chew them instead of letting them slide down her throat.

It didn't take her long to get dressed either. She had two dresses for outings during the summer. She wore the less formal one to do the shopping and take her afternoon walk in the park, while she kept the other one for rare special occasions such as this. She stood in front of the mirror for a moment, deep in thought, and then decided to put on a brooch. She didn't like jewelry and decorations, but she decided that without any accessory she would look somehow incomplete. The greatest amount of time was spent putting on her little black hat with its lace veil. Unfortunately, this could not be helped. Before, when her hair was still luxuriant, she had put her hat in place with ease, but her hair had thinned with the years, making it harder and harder. Finally, she dabbed on some perfume from a small bottle with the label half peeling off. Then, fearing that was not enough, she dabbed on a bit more.

Outside she was greeted by a bright summer morning. The air was preternaturally transparent, as though rain had just washed all the dust out of it, but there was no trace of recent precipitation. Everything was dry, announcing yet another hot day. Smiling, she headed for the watchmaker's shop, a twenty-minute walk away. She had gone about one third of the way when she was struck once again by the feeling that something was wrong.

She stopped and stared intently ahead. Then she turned her head around slowly and looked behind her. She might have stayed in that position longer, but the ossified vertebrae in her neck soon started to complain. There had been no need for such exertions, however. Just one glance was enough to confirm that not a living soul was anywhere to be seen. She was completely alone in the middle of an empty street. And not only that. She suddenly became aware of something that the intoxicatingly bright morning had obscured. She had not seen a single person since leaving the house.

Strange. She went to the grocery store every day at this time and always met someone along the way. Even in the worst weather. That was her entire social life. Since she had no friends to visit or to come and visit her, the only chance she had of talking to anybody was when she ran across acquaintances from the neighborhood each morning. There were only strangers in the distant park and her walks there were silent. Her morning conversations in the street were not particularly profound: health complaints, passing on local news, exchanging thoughts about the weather, occasionally reminiscing about some bygone event. But she always felt satisfied and fulfilled afterwards, and the solitude of the rest of the day was easier to bear.

Why wasn't there anyone about? She mulled it over briefly but could find no explanation. She finally shrugged her shoulders. She certainly couldn't stand there waiting for someone to appear. She had to hasten on her way. Maybe the watchmaker would be able to tell her what was going on. There must be a simple answer, but she just couldn't find it. He would probably think her a senile or even dim-witted old woman when she asked. The best thing, actually, would be not to mention it. Was it all that important whether there were people in the street or not? This way was even better, as though the beauty of the day belonged to her alone.

When she was almost there, she realized there was something missing in this beauty. The row of chestnut trees along the street was usually full of birds, particularly in the morning and evening, tirelessly chattering, competing with the rustling leaves in the treetops. Now only the breeze could be heard up there. Where had they all gone? There was no time to dwell on this matter, however, because another, more important one prevailed. What if the watchmaker wasn't there? What if he hadn't come to work and had gone somewhere like everyone else? That would be really hard to take. Who would repair her clock?

There was a sharp jangling of bells above the entrance when Miss Margarita opened the door. She glanced towards the counter facing her and let out a sigh of relief when she saw the hunched figure of the watchmaker, a tube-shaped magnifying glass placed on the socket of his eye. He was engrossed in a repair job. He removed the magnifying glass, raised his head, squinted towards the entrance, smiled and stood up.

"Hello, Miss Margarita."

"Hello," she replied cheerfully and headed towards the counter.

As she slowly made her way, she noticed a change on the side walls of the little shop. She remembered quite well from earlier visits that there had been two identical grandfather clocks in mahogany cases. They rang out the hour in deep, harmonious tones and seemed very formal, like soldiers in dress uniform guarding the entrance to a castle. She'd envied the watchmaker. She would have been very happy to have such a clock in her parlor, but her income did not allow this. She had not even dared ask how much they cost.

Now both walls were completely covered with alarm clocks. They came in all types, shapes, sizes and colors, from elegant to ugly, from ornate to plain. Their bells were what differed most. She seemed to be at a dolls' show of metal hats worn by inappropriately stocky models. Those with two or three hats were particularly grotesque, which probably meant they had two or three heads. Then she noticed something that hadn't immediately caught her eye. The clocks weren't working. If they had, a deafening cascade of ticking would have gushed from both sides of the shop. No one would have been able to stand such noise for very long. The watchmaker did not wind the clocks after he placed them on the wall.

When she reached the counter, Miss Margarita took the alarm clock wrapped in white flannel out of her brown shoulder bag.

"It's broken," she said dejectedly.

The watchmaker took the bundle and started to unwrap it. He was a small, thin man with long side-whiskers and a high forehead. He was wearing a dark three-piece suit of classic cut, with subtle gray stripes. The only accessory was the silver chain of a pocket watch hanging from the buttonhole on his vest, leading to a small pocket on the left-hand side. It was hard to determine his age. The best guess would be late middle age. Miss Margarita had concluded long ago that he was one of those people practically untouched by age. The long intervals between the times she saw him seemed to have had absolutely no effect on him.

"Is it slow again, like last time?"

"No, it's not. It's stopped."

"Completely?" he asked in surprise.

"Yes, completely. Last night, right after midnight. You can see for yourself. I haven't touched a thing." Miss Margarita paused, waiting for the clock to emerge finally from the cloth, and then added, "I hope it's nothing serious."

The watchmaker in silence made a cursory examination of the clock lying on the unwrapped cloth on the counter. She tried to figure out the diagnosis by the expression on his face, but it remained completely blank.

"I'll have to open it up," he said at last. "Please take a seat, it might take some time." He indicated two armchairs with a small table between them to the left of the entrance.

Miss Margarita nodded and went to sit down. She would have been just as obedient if she'd been asked to leave the operating theatre and wait in the waiting room while they operated on someone very close to her. She would have cast the same worried glance towards the place where the vitally important business was taking place. But she couldn't see very much. The watchmaker was hunched over, practically under the counter, working on a lower bench located in the back. All that appeared was the upper half of his head, with the watchmaker's magnifying glass once again in place, almost touching the green shade of the lamp brightly illuminating the workbench.

The silence of the multitude of clocks hanging over her, behind and in front, started to weigh her down. Although she detested noise, she now felt it would be easier to stand if they were working. It would be confirmation that time was flowing. This way, it seemed as though time had stopped and the operation on her clock could last an eternity. Nothing moved around her; the inside of the shop, together with herself and the watchmaker, seemed to belong to a pictured moment, frozen forever.

The picture nonetheless soon came to life. The watchmaker slowly took the magnifying glass off his left eye, got up, took the clock from the workbench and placed it on the flannel cloth on the counter. He then took it in both hands, went around the counter, approached Miss Margarita, and sat in the other armchair.

"I'm afraid there's nothing to be done," he said in the voice of a doctor whose patient has just had a sheet pulled over his head. "Here, see for yourself."

He put the cloth with the clock on the little round

table between them. Just then Miss Margarita noticed that the clock had not been put back together. The back cover was off, revealing a tangle of tiny gears, springs, levers, screws and pins. Her eyes remained only briefly on these mechanical entrails, for she quickly turned her head aside. She was overcome by nausea, as though looking at an open human body in an anatomy class. The watchmaker did not notice this movement, and had already started to explain.

"These two gears here are broken. They're worn out. Unfortunately, they are highly important. You might say they are the heart of the clock. And nothing can work without a heart, isn't that so? If this were a newer model it would be easy to replace them, but no one makes spare parts anymore for such old models. The manufacturers are better off selling you a new one." He sighed and turned to look at the wall covered with silent clocks. "Just like your clock, all of these could have kept time and woken people up, if only there had been parts for them."

"But I don't need a clock to keep time and wake me up." She'd thought she would never reveal her secret to the watchmaker, but now she had no choice.

The watchmaker looked at her, puzzled. "What else could an alarm clock be used for?"

She did not reply at once. She felt ill at ease, as though having to answer a doctor's questions regarding something deeply intimate. But how can you expect the doctor to help if you hide something from him?

"To fall asleep," she answered at last, softly and reluctantly. "I can't fall asleep without its ticking."

"Then maybe you should think about buying a new one? It could serve that purpose, while also carrying out all its basic functions. There's no harm in having them, even if you don't use them. I will be happy to buy your old alarm clock, so a new one won't cost very much. As you can see, I collect them." This time he gestured towards the multitude of clocks.

"No!" said Miss Margarita, almost screaming. "I won't sell it!" And then, ashamed of such a violent outburst, she hurried to add, "It's a memento, you know, a very dear one, from..."

The sentence was left unfinished, but the watchmaker nodded nonetheless. "I understand. Please let me take another look at it. Maybe something can be done if all you want is for it to tick."

He put his hands under the cloth again and took the clock behind the counter. This time the wait seemed different to Miss Margarita. Her previous apprehension was replaced by impatience. She felt naked before the watchmaker and wanted this to end as soon as possible. Whatever the result of his attempts, she would no longer have any reason to go to this shop. If the clock ticked, all the better. If it didn't, she would certainly not buy a new one. Where would she keep it? Next to the old one on the night table? That would be nothing less than sacrilege. She would simply have to get used to falling asleep without any help. It would certainly be difficult, at least in the beginning, but what other choice was there?

From the smile on the watchmaker's face as he returned carrying the alarm clock, this time with the back cover in place, she understood she had nothing to fear.

"You were in luck," he said after sitting in the armchair. "From now on your clock will tick if you wind it regularly, although it will always show the same time." He started to wrap it in the flannel cloth. "That part of the mechanism is still in working order. It shouldn't wear out for quite some time. Here you are." He handed her the large bundle across the table.

"Thank you," she said, taking the wrapped clock. As she put it in her bag she could hear the soft ticking, muffled by thick layers of cloth. "How much do I owe you?"

"Goodness, nothing. It was such a small thing."

"Please, I insist..."

"Miss Margarita, I doubt whether you will be needing my services anymore. Consider this a small farewell present. You have been a loyal customer for many years. This is the least I can do to repay your fidelity."

She had never liked people to give her services free of charge. If she were to insist on paying now, however, the watchmaker might take offense and this was certainly something she wanted to avoid. Particularly if this truly was, as he felt, their last meeting.

"Thank you once again. I still remain in your debt." She stood up and he did the same. They stood in silence for several moments, and then she said briefly, "Good-bye."

The watchmaker bowed. "Farewell, Miss Margarita."

She turned and headed for the door. This was the first time she'd left this shop sad and not pleased. Just a few minutes earlier she'd wanted never to come here again, and now she hoped he was wrong. The alarm clock was old, it might break down again. That would give her the chance to bring it back for repairs. Suddenly it became important for this not to be her last visit to the watchmaker. She didn't like the hint of finality that went with it.

When she went out in the street, her first thought was that her eyesight had blurred for some reason, just like in winter when her glasses suddenly fogged up as she entered a heated room out of the cold. But it wasn't winter now, it was the middle of summer, plus she wasn't wearing glasses. Indeed, she saw better with them on, but she felt they didn't look good on her, so she preferred to strain her eyes a bit instead. Now even the strongest glasses would not have helped her see through the curtain of mist that had descended while she'd been inside. This was the exact opposite of the air's previously ethereal quality. The world that had seemed perfectly clear before had now become completely opaque.

She leaned her back against the shop door to obtain firm support. Wrapped in grayness that made it impossible to see even the pavement on which she was standing, she seemed to be floating in midair. She stayed there without moving for a time, not knowing what to do. She thought about going back inside, but then she would be faced with having to explain and would only become hopelessly muddled. No, that was out of the question.

What else could she do? She certainly couldn't stand there for very long. Then a simple solution appeared that did, however, require considerable ingenuity and courage. She would head home. Just like that. Where else would she find refuge on such an unusual day but in her house? It wouldn't be easy to get there since she couldn't even see her fingers in front of her eyes, but luckily all she had to do was move straight ahead. There were no turns. She would go slowly and carefully, using the row of chestnuts as her guide. The trees were placed at regular intervals so once she counted the steps between two neighboring trees, she would know exactly when to expect the next one.

It took great strength of will to leave the shop entrance and walk into the mist. Somewhere from the edge of oblivion flashed a memory from her far-off childhood when she was learning how to swim. Then she had been forced to overcome tremendous internal resistance to leave the shelter of the shore and venture out into deep water. The buoy that she'd headed for was only several meters away but to her the distance had seemed immeasurably far. She'd hugged it feverishly when she finally reached it. Now she was tempted to grab the chestnut tree in the same way, its outline only starting to emerge when she was already quite close to it.

She went slowly down the street, holding one arm out in front like a blind person holding a white stick. Her eyes were wide open, although useless. All they saw was the fluffy dough in which she was immersed. She soon felt dizzy from staring into the unchanging whiteness. She thought of continuing with her eyes closed, but couldn't find the courage to close them and bowed her head instead. After the seventeenth step, when she almost crashed into the second chestnut, the relief she felt rivaled that of a castaway thrown fortuitously onto land by a storm.

She continued with somewhat greater confidence, concentrating on counting her steps. This feeble encouragement soon evaporated when she realized that she would not be able to tell when she'd reached home. The tree growing in front of her house had nothing unusual about it, and she didn't know how many chestnut trees there were between her home and the watchmaker's shop. She had never counted them, of course. Why would she? Who would ever have thought it might come in handy? She stopped, bewildered, and then continued her slow steps. She would ponder that problem along the way. A solution was bound to turn up. Right now it was important to advance in the right direction.

Her hampered eyesight sharpened her hearing. She was between the sixth and seventh chestnut when she heard soft voices coming from somewhere in the mist. How strange people were, she thought. She hadn't met anyone during the glorious weather on her way to the watchmaker's shop, and now there was someone talking outside, in this obscurity. She crossed the distance between the next three trees, but the voices were still subdued, no louder than before, as though she'd come neither closer to those who were talking nor moved any farther away from them. Now, however, they seemed to be coming from the treetops, as though the birds had returned and were now chirping in the leaves with human voices.

She pricked up her ears and finally started to make out the words coming from above. They were disconnected parts of different conversations. Sometimes two people were speaking, sometimes three, and there were even more here and there. There were men's, women's and children's voices, old and young. The fragments were not long: they started in the middle of a sentence and then suddenly ended, so it was hard to grasp their meaning. Sometimes laughter would resound in different timbres: giggling, droning, chuckling, roaring. Much less frequently the conversation was serious and gloomy, and one was even filled with quiet crying.

Most of the voices sounded familiar to her. She was sure she had already heard them somewhere, but hard as she tried she could not call to mind the faces of those who were talking. This filled her with frustration. Her memory had recently started to fail her like this; she would be on the verge of grasping something, and then it would be maliciously whisked away. And then she noticed a regularity, a common characteristic of the bits of conversation from the chestnut treetops. There was a female voice in every fragment. Old, coughing, sometimes defiant. This was the moment of truth. She might still not have recognized her own voice—we don't hear our voice the same way others hear it—were it not for the defiance that was her manner of confronting the world, most often to her own detriment.

As though someone had pulled the veil from her memory, suddenly there were no more secrets. Regardless of how brief the fragment, she knew unfailingly when it was, where and to whom she was talking in these magically resurrected conversations. Her interlocutors' empty faces took on contours, features, characteristics. She saw them clearly on the occasions when they were talking to her, just as she could now remember the parts that preceded each fragment and followed it. Her life stood before her as clear as an open book intermittently underlined.

Making her way through the endlessly thick mist, hand outstretched before her, silently counting the steps between the chestnuts, she wondered whether the lines she heard spoken above were highlighted merely at random or with some purpose in mind. They were certainly not important conversations, most were just bits of small talk. It seemed to her as if someone had noted down parts of her book of life without rhyme or reason. Or else she was unable to detect any. She was just about to stop searching, when she noted a new pattern. It had to do not with the content of the fragments but with their distribution in time. Each one was farther back in time than the one before it, as though the book were being leafed through back to front. The farther she got from the watchmaker's shop, the deeper she retreated into the past.

Her voice became gradually younger and softer. It wasn't hard for her to imagine the increasingly younger face that went along with it. Her wrinkles smoothed out, the loose skin hanging sadly under her chin disappeared, the spots on her cheeks vanished and so did the yellow bags under her eyes. The many aches that had started to plague her in old age also faded away. She'd lived a healthy and tranquil middle age that from this vantage point had been possibly the happiest period of her life. She'd been alone, indeed, but that was something she had already become quite used to.

Most of those she now heard herself briefly talking to were no longer among the living. She had considerably outlived them all. She ascribed this primarily to her orderly lifestyle. The others had been their own worst enemies, not paying enough attention to their health. She knew that the most dissolute among them secretly made fun of her self-discipline and moderation, mockingly calling her ascetic, but she had been the one in a position to laugh last. She had never done this, however. She had been defiant and stubborn, yes indeed, but not malicious. The loss of each one had been hard for her. Tears came to her eyes even now as she heard their long-silent voices return once again above her.

The closer she got to her younger years, going home through the mist, the greater became her apprehension. It had taken a lot of time and effort to block out the incident from that time that had shaped all the rest of her life. Perhaps everything would have been different had she been able to wipe it completely from her memory, but that, of course, had been impossible. Although suppressed, it was still with her, re-emerging from oblivion, often at the most inopportune moments. She had no way of knowing how these audible fragments from her past would treat the incident, but she felt certain they could not ignore it.

Her anxieties came true, but not as she had feared. Judging by the number of chestnut trees she'd counted, she must have already been close to home when the noise in the treetops suddenly ceased. She stopped in bewilderment and listened hard. Now she longed for the surreal voices that had frightened her at first. Without them she felt hopelessly abandoned in the hollow silence of the mist. Then she heard a soft sound somewhere behind her. It was repeated at regular intervals, becoming stronger, as though the source were moving closer to her. She didn't recognize it until it was almost upon her. Someone was walking down the street, heading in her direction.

Judging by the spryness of the steps, it must have been a younger man who did not seem the least bothered by the mist. Miss Margarita stood stock-still, fearing there might be a collision. He didn't know she was standing there and might easily run right into her. She had to find some way to let him know she was in front of him. She cleared her throat, but at the same moment realized this was unnecessary.

Like the beam of a reflector sliding through the darkness, dispelling it, a clear oval bubble was making its way through the mist, moving down the street. When it came close to her she had a good look inside. The young man was tall and slender. His face had firm, regular features that were handsome in their accentuated masculinity. The rather long, slanted scar above his left eyebrow did not spoil this harmony; on the contrary, it even seemed to add to it in some strange way. The officer's dress uniform fit him perfectly. He was wearing high, polished black leather boots, soft white gloves and a service cap pulled down low on his forehead, almost completely hiding his short hair. In his left hand were two small packages wrapped in brightly colored paper and tied with red ribbons. One was flat, the other square.

Miss Margarita's breath failed her. She opened her mouth and made every effort to breathe deeply, but she suddenly seemed to be in an airless space. In addition, she was unable to move. Her heart began to pound frantically. The stiffness did not last long, however. She snapped out of it when the grayness surrounded her once again, after the oval had passed. She took out after it almost at a run. The doctor had strictly forbidden such efforts, but that made no difference to her now. Once she had caught up with the oval she continued at a somewhat slower pace, panting as she kept to its rear edge.

It was the safest way to reach home. The young man would take her there without fail. The mist was no longer an obstacle. The path stretched before her as clearly as that which would inevitably come to pass. He soon turned off the pavement onto a narrow stone walkway leading across the grass to the front door. When he took off his cap and rang the bell, Miss Margarita was standing hesitantly about halfway up the walk. She knew who would open the door to him, but it seemed somehow inappropriate, almost unnatural, to look at that person. In addition, she was still very angry with her. After all these years she still could not forgive her for what she had done.

The door opened, but the young man's broad back almost completely blocked the entrance to the house. For just a moment, before the door closed, she caught sight of the hem of a light yellow dress fluttering in the draft. She still had it, but kept it out of sight so as not to awaken painful memories. Miss Margarita remained on the walk, not knowing what to do. She was still out of breath, but not just from having moved so fast. The fact that she could change nothing in that far-off past that was taking place before her once again weighed more heavily on her than any physical exertion. Since it served no purpose inside the house, the oval bubble stayed outside, resembling a tiny island in a vast downy ocean, waiting for the young man whose visit would be of short duration.

The closed door did not prevent her from seeing what was happening inside. She accepted the two little packages with delight. She had always loved presents. She untied the ribbon on the flat package first. Smiling broadly, she went up on her tiptoes, closed her eyes briefly and lightly touched the young man's lips with hers in thanks. It was just a hint, a suggestion of a kiss, but their intimacy had not yet gone any farther. The deluxe edition of the poems looked magnificent. She'd wanted it so much! And how much she had wanted to receive it from him!

She couldn't imagine what was in the other package. Her patience got the better of her, as usual, so she pulled the ribbon and tore the bright wrapping paper. She quickly raised the lid of the square, purple box and looked inside inquisitively. Her smile instantly disappeared. Her face flared up as though she'd just been slapped. She shot him a look in which insult, reproach and the accusation of betrayal vied for precedence. She felt her eyes fill with tears. She stood there for several moments, staring at him without a word, and then did what the sharp voice of her defiant, proud nature commanded. She roughly put everything she was holding into his hands—wrapping paper, ribbon, book, box and the item inside it—turned and quickly walked out of the parlor. She almost slammed the bedroom door behind her.

She leaned against the inside of the door to prevent him from coming after her. How could he have done such a thing! After everything that had happened, the alarm clock was not only an insult but an injury. Two days earlier, while they were walking along the quay, why had she mentioned her ability to wake up whenever she wanted, without any outside help? She'd exposed herself to someone who was unworthy of it. He'd just laughed, almost as though mocking her. He'd said he didn't believe her, that no one could do something like that. And then, as though this were not enough, he'd added in a playful voice that he might believe her if he had the chance to see for himself.

She hadn't immediately understood the full meaning of his words because she was unaccustomed to such allusions. When it finally dawned on her that seeing her ability for himself meant waking up in the same bed, she turned on her heel in anger and quickly walked away from him along the quay. How could he think something like that? Who did he think she was? Why, they weren't even engaged yet! And even if they were, it would still be highly improper. He ran after her and when he reached her started to apologize, but she turned him a completely deaf ear. It was not until they were near her house that she spoke to him, her voice cold and official. She told him that he had greatly offended her and she never wanted to see him again.

Never. She didn't give him a chance to say anything in reply. She had turned her back on him once again and gone into the house.

Her anger lasted all through the evening, but softened the next morning. That was also part of her nature. Remorse was the flip side of her defiance. By noon she had already shifted the blame to herself for being so hard on him. Maybe he hadn't thought anything bad; it had just been a clumsy joke; probably he'd been unaware that such a joke might hurt her. In the evening the pangs of guilt from such serious questions were almost physically painful. What if he took literally what she'd said to him at their parting? How else could "never" be understood except as "never?" She could have gone looking for him and explained that "never" was not quite as final as it might appear, but that, of course, was out of the question. Her pride would not let her regret go quite that far.

The next morning he'd come to the front door in the dress uniform he'd been wearing when she first set eyes on him four and a half months before and fell immediately in love. A flood of joy streamed through her. She could barely stop herself from falling into his arms right then and there, on the doorstep. Only a few minutes later, however, had come the terrible slap with the alarm clock. Leaning against the bedroom door, she did not even try to hold back her sobs. It made no difference to her that he would certainly hear her in the parlor. Nothing made any difference anymore. This time "never" would be absolute and irrevocable. The only thing she wanted was for him to leave. To disappear from her parlor. And her life.

And he had left. The parlor and her life. First he'd put the opened presents he brought on the table. They belonged to her and she could do what she wanted with them. He certainly couldn't take them where he would soon be heading. He hadn't had the chance to tell her the main reason for his visit. He thought briefly about knocking on the bedroom door and giving her the order that had reached his house late last night. In less than three hours he would board a train that would take him straight to the front. But he hadn't knocked. He already knew her quite well. She would never open the door for him. He turned slowly around the room as though wanting to fix it in his memory. Then he put his cap back on and went out.

The oval bubble was waiting in readiness to clear his path through the mist that he didn't see. Just as he didn't see the tiny, stooped old woman that he almost brushed against. If he had been able to hear through the chasm of time that separated them, her sobs would seem strangely familiar to him. But he couldn't hear. She, however, heard the sound of his departing footsteps long after the opaque grayness closed behind him. She stayed on the walk, her eyes turned towards the invisible street, until silence reigned around her once again. Then she walked the remaining bit of cobbled path to the front door of her house. The mist had once more enclosed her on all sides, but she no longer had to walk with her hand outstretched.

She went straight to the bedroom. That was where she kept a chest full of mementos. There were faded photographs, yellowed letters, items greatly damaged by the ravages of time: a past significant to her alone. Among these old things was a wilted piece of paper. She took it and slowly started to read the four lines typed on it, although just like the book of poems, she had learned them by heart long ago. This text was not the least bit lyrical, although whoever had drawn it up had taken pains to give it a lofty ring. Telegrams sent by the army to families of the dead always sound somehow wrong.

She had received it only three days after leaving him in the parlor and locking herself in this room. She was not related to him, but her name had nonetheless been on the list of those to be informed in case of his death. The officer who had brought the news added awkwardly that there had been no funeral. The general slaughter at the front offered little opportunity for that, and it was rare for very much of the deceased to be left to bury. After the war, of course, a great charnel house would be made for all the fallen heroes, and she would be invited to the consecration. She had never been invited, and she certainly wouldn't have gone if she had. Her connection to it certainly was not the same as that of the others.

She put the telegram back in place and closed the chest. She stood next to it for several minutes, not knowing what else to do. What time of day was it? The vast mist outside made it impossible to tell by looking out of the window. This reminded her of the clock in her bag. It, unfortunately, could not help her find out the time because it no longer worked. Too bad. She had no other clock in the house. She would have to buy a conventional one. She didn't care very much about knowing the exact time, but one could not live without a clock, after all. She would keep it somewhere in the or kitchen.

She took the alarm clock out of her bag and put it on the night table, then sat on the bed. The clock's hands were fixed on the time it had stopped, but it ticked steadily as though still measuring something. She stared at it blankly. She stayed like that until she felt the repetitive sound starting to have an effect on her. It was certainly not yet time for bed, but this unusual day had completely exhausted her. Maybe she would stretch out a bit, just to have a little rest. She didn't even have to get undressed. She would just lie on the bedspread. She never slept during the day, let alone fully dressed, but what difference did it make? There was no one to see her. In any case, she was not accountable to anyone for her behavior.

She closed her eyes. Before she sank into the deep darkness and silence, two thoughts briefly crossed her mind. She was somehow convinced that she wouldn't have any dreams. That was good. She would have the best rest that way. Who knew what dreams might visit her? In addition, this time there was no need to set her internal clock. She had no reason to wake up at any specific hour. No urgent work awaited her anymore.

Contributors

About the author

Zoran Živković was born in Belgrade, Serbia, on October 5, 1948. Until his recent retirement, he was a full professor at the Faculty of Philology, the University of Belgrade, teaching creative writing.

Živković is one of the most translated contemporary Serbian writers. By the end of 2017 there were 93 foreign editions of his books of fiction, published in 23 countries, in 20 languages.

Živković has won several literary awards for his fiction. In 1994 his novel *The Fourth Circle* won the Miloš Crnjanski award. In 2003, Živković's mosaic novel *The Library* won a World Fantasy Award for Best Novella. In 2007 his novel *The Bridge* won the Isidora Sekulić award. In 2007 Živković received the Stefan Mitrov Ljubiša award for his life achievement in literature. In 2014 and 2015 Živković received three awards for his contribution to the literature of fantastika: Art-Anima, Stanislav Lem and The Golden Dragon.

Zoran Živković has been recognized with his selection as European Grand Master for 2017 by the European Science Fiction Society at the 39th Eurocon in Dortmund, Germany.

Živković is the author of 22 books of fiction:

The Fourth Circle (1993)
Time Gifts (1997)
The Writer (1998)
The Book (1999)
Impossible Encounters (2000)
Seven Touches of Music (2001)
The Library (2002)
Steps through the Mist (2003)
Hidden Camera (2003)
Compartments (2004)
Four Stories till the End (2004)
Twelve Collections and the Teashop (2005)
The Bridge (2006)
Miss Tamara, The Reader (2006),
Amarcord (2007)
The Last Book (2007)
Escher's Loops (2008)
The Ghostwriter (2009)
The Five Wonders of the Danube (2011)
The Grand Manuscript (2012)
The Compendium of the Dead (2015)
The Image Interpreter (2016)

About the artist

Youchan Ito was born 1968 in Aichi prefecture, Japan. She launched her career as a graphic designer in 1988, becoming a freelancer illustrator in 1991 and founding Togoru Co., Ltd. with her husband in 2000. In 2017 the company was reborn as Togoru Art Works. She works with a wide range of genres including cover art and design for science fiction, mysteries and horror titles, as well as illustrations for children's books.

www.youchan.com